THE WEAKENING

GREGORY SPENCER

THE WELKENING

A THREE DIMENSIONAL TALE

HOWARD
Fiction

THE WELKENING © 2004 by Gregory H. Spencer
All rights reserved. Printed in the United States of America
Published by Howard Publishing Co., Inc.
3117 North 7th Street, West Monroe, Louisiana 71291-2227
www.howardpublishing.com

04 05 06 07 08 09 10 11 12 13   10 9 8 7 6 5 4 3 2 1

Edited by Ramona Richards and Grace Rachow
Interior design by John Mark Luke Designs
Illustrations by Gregory H. Spencer
Cover design by UDG | DesignWorks
All rights reserved

Library of Congress Cataloging-in-Publication Data
Spencer, Gregory H. (Gregory Horton), 1953–
    The welkening / Gregory Spencer.
        p. cm.
    Includes bibliographical references.
    ISBN 1–58229–355–4
        1. Friendship—Fiction. 2. Marginality, Social—Fiction. I. Title.

PS3619.P4644W45 2004
813'.6—dc22
                                                        2004052362

Bibliographic information for chapter epigraphs are available upon request.

For my daughters, Emily, Hannah, and Laura,
who have known for quite some time
that the secret words were "Percy and Bones."

I Love You.

AWAY THEY GO FULL CRY, MAKING
THE WELKIN RING WITH THE MUSIC
OF THEIR DEEP-TONED NOTES.

ROBERT SMITH SURTEES, *HANDLEY CROSS*

CONTENTS

CONTENTS

GRATITUDE

If I were wise, I would express universally effusive appreciation for all of my many readers and supporters. But, no, I'm going to grant particulars. With an abiding gratefulness that reaches back twenty years and down six feet (to my very toes), I gladly acknowledge (in somewhat chronological order):

Percy, for calling our names with those warm green eyes;

Laura Wilson, for typing without whining, and calling from Portland to ask for more;

Dominic LaRusso, for seeing more than I dreamed;

Liz Heighton, for using the word "literature";

Christine Nizibian, for loving that "little guy," Percy;

Karl and Kim Schafer, for asking for a second helping;

Carri Svoboda, for defending Len enthusiastically;

Ann Woodruff, for not putting it down when David asked;

Jim and Ben Taylor, for reading with skill and affection;

Marilyn McEntyre, for encouraging "faithfulness to the vision";

June Michealson, for blessing creativity;

Patrick Steele, for working past the pain to the joy;

Sealy and Curtis Yates, for keeping their chins up while sending around the manuscript;

Terry and Sally Glaspey, for leading me to a simpler complexity;

James Coffey, for noticing a love for language;

Grace Rachow, for editing as a "coach," and living up to your name;

Jay Jaeger, for negotiating movie rights;

Ben Patterson, for reacting joyously;

Bob Ludwick, for standing among the chips when they were down;

Ramona Richards, for saying what needed to be said and seeing it through;

Philis Boultinghouse, for connecting me—always pleasantly—to Howard Fiction;

And, most of all, Janet, my remarkably patient wife,
for reading every draft with integrity,
for advising with wisdom (even when I pouted), and
for keeping me steady when I got "wobblerated."

PART ONE
THE MIND OF THE MISFITS

CHAPTER ONE
TWO BEGINNINGS

*If man could be crossed with the cat
it would improve man,
but it would deteriorate the cat.*

MARK TWAIN

 *At first, I felt sure I did not want to go. To enter their world of shadows, to cross the veil, I would suffer losses to body and soul. But when the call comes, who can pretend not to hear? So, I begin this story on the morning I heard the voice. And I give my word, I will speak what I know—and I know more than most.*

On the fourth evening of summer vacation, Len stopped killing people just long enough to feel a cereal-shaped hole in the pit of his stomach. Without remorse, he shot four more times, watched his victims collapse, and then, calmly, he turned off the video game. He slammed his leaning chair from two legs to four on the floor. Rising slowly, he slouched his way into the kitchen, breaking form with a karate kick against a wingback chair along the way.

As Len opened the refrigerator door, he saw his sister, Angie, sitting at the table, looking out the window. Unnoticed by her, he took in her "perfect" hair, "perfect" clothes, and—at least if his buddies were to be believed—her "perfect" profile. These flawless qualities reminded him of her ridiculously high GPA and chummy relationship with their parents.

He looked inside the fridge at the orange juice, shriveled celery, and day-old mac and cheese. Then he saw a jug of milk. He grabbed it and plopped it on the counter so hard the top popped off. He flipped a plastic cup out of the cupboard, clanked it down next to the milk, and snagged a bag of Oreos from the pantry. He glanced over at Angie. Then he noisily ripped open the bag, crushed three Oreos into the glass, and poured in some milk. Angie didn't flinch.

Len took her lack of response as a personal challenge. "Angie, I don't know what I'm going to do with you. You're so embarrassing. I have friends, you know."

"What do you mean?" she asked, her left arm resting blithely on the table.

"I have friends. Friends are people who hang out together. Don't you know that?"

Angie squinched her eyes up and shook her head sarcastically.

"You've just got to quit acting like you're from Jupiter's third moon. People talk about what you say." He burped. "Look, I'm not spying on my baby sophomore sister or anything—but you know that Jim guy who's always staring at you 'cause he thinks you're so freakin' gorgeous? He overheard you talking to some girls in the quad the last week of school." He smiled to show off the chocolate bits dripping down his teeth. Angie turned away. "He said you said that you loved the ginger cat with the warm green eyes. What's with that? You said that the fabric of the world was stretching or tearing or some such nonsense." He drained the glass and slammed it on the table. "Do you realize how crazy you sound?" He got a new glass out of the cupboard and poured some Coke in it. "Do you want some?"

"Sure, half a glass." She turned back to face him. "Len, I don't see why I should stop talking about what I see." She hunched over as if some revelation were about to appear in the palm of her hand. "More and more, the world seems to be awakening deep longings, and I wouldn't be surprised if there's some good reason."

"I can't believe you actually defend yourself. And what's with this 'reason' garbage. That's never exactly been your specialty." Len handed her a glass of soda, then opened the pantry door and grabbed a bag of tortilla chips.

Angie pushed back her chair and stood up. "Maybe you're just jealous you don't see the things I do."

"Angie, you are so clueless." Her confidence irritated Len. "Why would I want to see what's not there? You don't even realize how hard this is on me."

Angie set her Coke down. "Just because you just graduated doesn't make you God or anything." She placed both hands on the table and leaned over, catching Len's eyes in what he took to be a stare-down. But it wasn't a competition. Angie seemed to be looking past Len's eyes into deeper places. Her intensity made him uneasy. He backed up, bumped into the open pantry door, and dropped the bag of chips. "What I realize," Angie said, "is that the fabric of things is changing. Maybe it's not stretching or tearing. Maybe it's something else. I don't know. What I *do* know is that I am glad the ginger cat with the warm green eyes came into our backyard."

"Why me? Why did I get born into this lame family?" Len kicked the bag of chips into the pantry, got out another glass, and poured orange juice to the top.

From the living room, Charlotte Bartholomew called out, "Would you guys come in here for a minute?"

Rolling his eyes, Len turned his head in the direction of his mom's voice. "'Guys' is sexist, Mom. We learned that in McEachen's English class. You teach English, don't you? You should know."

"Fine. I'm glad to hear 'y'all' are learning to become sensitive. Now, would you and Angie be sensitive to your dear old mother and come in here?"

As if he were resisting a gravitational pull to keep him in the kitchen, Len forced himself into the living room and leaned the back of his legs against one arm of the blue corduroy sofa. After his slow-motion free-fall onto the cushions—not spilling a drop—he pulled his backwards hat down so that it covered his eyebrows. Angie followed him into the room. She picked "the ginger cat" Percy off the seat of the maple rocker, rubbed his head, and sat down.

Charlotte sat up straight in the rose-colored wingback chair. "I want to read you the beginning of my story."

Len sighed. "So, why is this necessary right now? I'm getting hungry."
"Because I need a focus group, that's why." Charlotte counted the pages in her lap. "I tell my own students in writing class to do the same."

"You don't need to get testy, Mom." Len stretched his legs on the sofa.

"I'm not testy," Charlotte said testily. "I just thought you'd be more interested in listening to me read my manuscript. Maybe you think it's beneath you."

"Artists." Len took a breath for his next attack.

"OK, Mom, we're ready now." Angie glared bug-eyed at Len. "Percy and I will listen, won't we, Percy? We can't wait to hear it. Really."

Charlotte smiled at Angie and sneered at Len. Then, she began to read aloud.

THE NEW AND IMPROVED ADVENTURES OF PERCIVAL P. PERKINS III AND BONES MALONE

CHAPTER ONE: The Golden Brooch

A solitary figure strolled confidently down an apartment corridor. "Ho, ho. Hum, hum. Oh, I know, I shouldn't enjoy this so much. What would Mama say? Dear me, wouldn't the Old Noodle wiggle over this one . . . Hey, what's this? Could it be the door to Mrs. Markle's fabulous furnishings? And the lock looks so lonely. 'Won't you please pick me, Ollie, pretty please, with easy tumblers on top?'"

As Ollie Ollie Otterson's banter twittered on, he picked the lock and slipped into the apartment.

"Now, where would she keep that gorgeous golden beetle brooch?" Ollie examined items on the mantel. "What have we here? A vase from some ancient Chinese Dynasty? Well, ting-a-ling-a-Ming. What's this inside? 'Handmade by Arnold Fishbeck.' That's just toodly-too bad."

Ollie dropped the vase with a crash on the floor.

"Lenny." Charlotte slapped her manuscript loudly in her lap. "Len!"
"What?!" Len rose like Dracula from the couch.

"Wake up. It's not a lot to ask."

"C'mon, I heard every word." He rubbed his eyes and yawned.

Charlotte gave him her I-don't-think-so grimace. "Angie was atten-
tively listening. You were in snooze-ville."

Angie smiled and batted her eyelashes.

Len gulped some orange juice. "OK, you smarty-pants queens. There's
a goofy-named character doing goofy stuff. Ollie is stealing a golden
brooch, just like Bennu keeps talking about."

Charlotte said, "Bennu keeps talking about Ollie?"

"No, he's obsessed with some stupid ancient beetle. Something he
read about in his nerdy AP history class. Go on, OK?"

Charlotte resumed.

At the same time, outside of the Jewel of the Nile
Apartments, Captain Henley Hornbrook confided in Percy
Perkins. "We overheard some toughs talkin' about Mrs.
Markle's rather loaded jewelry box: 'Nobody can get at it,
no sir,' they said. Then one of 'em said 'Nobody 'cept the
Master.' We was certain they meant that schemin' bandit
himself, Otterson. So we sent for you and came over our-
selves."

"*Tsk, tsk,*" Percy said, bopping his round derby that
looked like a hamburger sitting on his head. "That Otterson is
such a scalawag. As the brown book says, 'You can't tell a
crook by his collar.' Hornbrook, you take a few men up to the
roof. While you set up, I'll get my supplies and grab my dear
friend Delilah Hob." After opening the trunk of his magnificent
brand-new 1927 Pierce-Arrow automobile, the renowned
detective threw some rope over his shoulder and then
picked up a six-pound turtle. He said, "Thanks for the offer to
help, Delilah," and put a rolled-up flag in her mouth.

With Hob and hemp in hand, Percy walked over to the
lawn just below Mrs. Markle's second story window, passing his friend and unWatsonian sidekick, Bones Malone, with
a wink.

While Percy tied one end of his rope to Delilah Hob, he asked Bones to hold the other end. Rhythmically, Percy swung the rope back and forth until the brave turtle sucked all appendages into battle-ready absence. Then he flung the rope, and Delilah crashed precisely into the center of Mrs. Markle's living room. Instantly, Delilah thrust out her legs and the flag, which read, "Surrender, Ollie!"

As Bones tugged on the rope and pulled the turtle back outside, a startled Ollie Ollie Otterson saw Percy out the window and sprinted out the door. He ran swiftly down to the locked stairwell door (Rattle. Bam! "Oh Mama!") and frantically up to the roof ("I made it, Mama. Ain't I brave?"). Wheezing heavily, Ollie ran right into the waiting arms of Hornbrook's men in blue.

ﾟﾟﾟﾟﾟ

A ll's well that the cooks don't spoil, eh Bones?" Percy said in triumph, adjusting his pince-nez.

"To tell the truth," answered Bones, "I am kinda hungry."

The two comrades-in-snooping hopped into the Pierce-Arrow and sped away. Before Percy's familiar green vest was out of sight, one policeman wondered aloud, "How does he do it? How does he know?"

Captain Henley Hornbrook tapped the tobacco tightly into his pipe. "As you might reckon, the question ain't easily answered. Percival P. Perkins III is unlike most mortals. He draws upon waterfalls of knowledge, rivers of ancient wisdom (though not always well channeled), his own splish-splashing intelligence, streams of experience, flowing athletic skill, and he has a knack for being dry when everyone else is all wet. Of course, it doesn't hurt that Percy is a cat."

"Well, what do you think?" Charlotte had a way of asking this question that, to Len, snapped her in an instant from her role as Mom to her position as Professor of English at Willamette Community College.

Angie cocked her head. "I love it that you named the main character Percy after lil' ol' Percy here. It makes me think we have a real celebrity living in our own house." She held a hand up to Len, as if to say, "Don't you start in." "I can't believe he was a stray just a few weeks ago." Angie rubbed the orange cat under his chin, and he lifted his head for more.

Inspired, Len scratched his own chin and pulled on the lonely whiskers growing there. "Thanks for sharing, Ang. That's so special. Anyway, Mom, it's not a bad start. I don't get why you're writing about talking animals. Is this just a comic book thingy or are you trying to 'bury pop-philosophical ideas behind a playful facade'? I learned how to say that in McEachen's class, too. I dunno. I think you need to work a bit on character development or something."

Angie said, "Oh, Len, you can be so negative."

"It's not that I don't like it," said Len. He sat up and congratulated himself on this show of support. "You wanted critique, right?"

"Don't worry about it. I get criticized by my students all the time. I'm fine." Len knew she wasn't. Charlotte straightened her pages and rose abruptly from her chair. "Just let me know when you like something, OK, Lenny?"

"Mom, *please* stop calling me Lenny. I keep telling you to call me Len. I'm not a kid anymore." He stood and went eye to eye with her.

"You're right. I keep forgetting. And you only remind me a hundred times a day."

Len looked away and saw Angie wince. At first he thought Angie was taking his side, feeling his pain—and then he realized that, of course, Angie was objecting to the bickering.

As Charlotte walked out, Len stuck his hands in his jeans and called after her. "If a hundred times isn't enough, Mom, you just let me know. I could make it a thousand."

He winced back at Angie and left the room.

CHAPTER TWO

THE COMMISERATION

*He called himself the Misfit because he couldn't match what he'd
done wrong with everything he'd gone through in punishment.*

FLANNERY O'CONNOR, "A GOOD MAN IS HARD TO FIND"

 Lizbeth Neferti pulled on the hood of her sweatshirt and tightened the tie. She looked in the mirror. Some cat burglar, she thought. I'm more like a cow burglar.

Remembering her Saturday morning mission, she hunkered down and tiptoed out her bedroom and down the hall. She tried to step as lightly as angel wings— but stealth did not become her. As she passed family photos on the wall, she studied them.

There's Grandma and Grandpa when they were still in Egypt. They say they can trace our ancestry back to the pharaohs. Yeah, right. Ooh, there's a creak in the floor. Here's Mom and Dad at their wedding. Dad looks so dumb in that shirt with all the lace. And here's my baby picture. I started out so cute. Who knew I'd grow into this? Look at that. Bennu graduated last week, and Mom's already got the picture up. Typical Mom. Ah, Bennu's door is open a smidge. This is my chance.

With the force of a charging fullback, Lizbeth broke into the room, shouting "Yeeeearrrrgh!" at the top of her lungs.

Bennu adjusted his glasses about a sixteenth of an inch. "Hello, Lizbeth. What do you think of this line? I'm working on a poem: 'The

9

weightless hours of summer float by like untethered balloons.' Do you like it?"

"I'd like to be able to scare you once in a while."

"Sorry. The creaking floorboards don't help, y'know."

"I knew it." Her shoulders fell. "I'll bet that's why you thought of the word *weightless*. To show me exactly what I'm not."

"You don't have to turn everything you hear into a comment about you. I wasn't even thinking about you. Honest. Listen, here's my next line: 'in warmth and bliss, there is no end to this dreamy flight.'"

"Yeah, cool." Lizbeth noticed a slight narrowing of Bennu's eyes, a wrinkle of disappointment. She'd seen this expression often enough, especially when he got teased about his hooking nose. "Really, Bennu, you've got a knack for poetry. I'm not much of a judge, but—"

"I'm not done: 'for now the ride is smooth, and the breeze a perfect speed for gliding.'"

Bennu sat up on his bed, wadded up his reject papers, and threw them one by one into his trash can.

Lizbeth picked up a small plastic baseball bat and slugged one right back into Bennu's face.

"OK, ya got me. Happy now?"

"Happier. So, you gonna enter some poetry contest?"

"Yeah, it's called P.O.E.T.S., the Poetry of Excellence Training Seminar. I was hoping for something less cheesy, like S.L.A.P., Stop Lame Archaic Poetry."

Lizbeth smiled. Her brother wasn't a nerd like her softball-friends called him. So he had thick glasses. So what? He's an artist—and I bet someday—

"Bennu! Lizbeth!" Their father's alarmist voice came from downstairs. "Bennu, take out the garbage! Lizbeth, get going on the lawn!"

"He's always yelling," said Bennu. Then he yelled back. "But, Dad, it's Lizbeth's turn. I know it is."

Lizbeth started down the stairs. Their cockapoo, Sniffles, met her and turned over for a tummy-rub.

"No way! The chart on the fridge says it's you, Bennu! You can't argue with what's in black and white."

"I could if you gave me a chance!"

Lizbeth pretended she didn't notice Sniffles peeing on the carpet. "Horace, get down here!"

Lizbeth walked past her father just as he said this. She knew how much Bennu hated his given name, Horace Imset Neferti—and how grateful he was that she had called him Bennu when she was two. It was the best she could do, and even though *Bennu* sounds no more like *Horace* than her choice of *booga* for *milk*, the name stuck.

Bennu tromped down. "It could be worse," he confided to Lizbeth. "Those idiot McKenzie Boys call me Hawkman. So I have a beak nose, sue me."

In the backyard, Lizbeth mowed the lawn, momentarily cursing equal rights and the drudgery of the labor. She keenly wished to finish. She and Bennu had arranged on this Saturday morning to meet Len and Angie on their shared Lewis River dock by 10:00. Presently, it was 9:30.

So Lizbeth mowed with abandon. As she took a turn, she saw her dad, Martin, standing on the patio, wagging his finger. He yelled something over and over, but Lizbeth couldn't hear him. Reluctantly, she turned off the machine and listened to him chastise her for "missed" grass and other violations of suburban ethics.

"OK, Dad, I'll take care of it." She took a Kleenex out of her overalls and blew her nose. "But you don't have to yell, you know."

"I don't? Really? I'd be quite happy not to yell. But *not* yelling doesn't seem to work!" He stormed back into the house.

Lizbeth pulled out her cell phone and called Len and Angie to tell them she and Bennu would be late. Then she grabbed half of her shiny black pony-tail in each hand and yanked hard to tighten it against the rubber band.

"Why me?" She pounded the lawnmower handle hard. "Nothing works out for me. Maybe if I'd gotten some of Cleopatra's genes, I could have been Miss Jewel of the Nile or something. Fat chance."

Lizbeth put her foot on the blade cover and yanked the starter cord as if she were pulling out her own demons. Her strength was sufficient. She almost wished it had taken two or three tries. Like it would have for Bennu, she thought, and she let herself smile at his expense. Then she grabbed the mower and plowed ahead.

When she came in for a drink, Lizbeth saw Bennu rushing around, returning each room's wastebasket to its color-coordinated, rightful place. Then he bounded into the kitchen.

"C'mon," said Lizbeth, "we need to get out of here before Dad gives us more to do." She threw a couple of juice boxes into a daypack.

Bennu rummaged through the pantry. "Cookies, chips, soda pop, candy bars," he said. "The four basic food groups."

It was nearly 11:00 before Lizbeth and Bennu rushed through the backyard and out through their gate into the Wilder, the public strip of land behind the house, on the banks of the Lewis River. Dodging the occasional blackberry cane, Lizbeth said, "Bennu, wait up! I can't help it if my legs are shorter!"

"Oh, don't make excuses. Hurry up."

Thanks for the sympathy, thought Lizbeth. What do you know, anyway? You practically fly over the ground.

After a while, a crow squawked obnoxiously, and Lizbeth looked past Bennu to see Len and Angie sitting cross-legged on the old boards of the dock. She loved it when the four of them, "The Commiseration of Misfits" as they called themselves, got together. They said the name ironically, but Lizbeth knew it made sense. They didn't fit in, they all had "issues," and they enjoyed whining.

♋

As the four talked about their trials of the last four days, Len noticed Percy stroll onto the dock. Immediately, the ginger cat started stalking a moth that eventually landed on Angie's jeans. Percy slunk down, wiggled his backside vigorously, and leaped mightily onto his prey. Caught by surprise, Angie yelped and then pulled her white sweater up to look where she thought Percy had snagged it.

"So," said Bennu, "I guess you got to keep the cat."

Len saw that Angie noticed that Bennu looked at her exposed midriff.

Angie scratched Percy's head. "Yeah. He wandered into our backyard and wouldn't leave. He does these amazing things. If you kneel to pick something up, he hops onto your back and just sits there. It's awesome."

Len, squatting on the dock, leaned forward to attempt a handstand. "Mom named a character in her new story after him: Percival P. Perkins III. Pretty cheesy, huh?" His shaky arms gave way, and he fell in a heap. Then he suggested they visit the twin firs on the Old Peterson Farm, one of the few abandoned homesteads not yet subdivided into plots for homes. "Rumor has it," he said, "that it has an awesome tree house erected by some homeless guy who'd been a total squatter on the property."

Bennu stiffened noticeably. "Rumor also has it that the McKenzie Boys like to hang out there."

"Ah, yes," said Len, "the infamous Brutes from McKenzie Butte, a.k.a. the McKenzie Butte Boys, those lousy Mink Brothers, the Missing-Link Minks." He made his best Neanderthal face. "I say we go anyway." Hands on hips, he struck a pose as disdainful of physical threat as his slight frame permitted.

Bennu stepped up to Len so that his additional five inches in height were obvious. "I don't want to meet them anywhere, I'll tell you that."

"Be reasonable, Len." Lizbeth pulled at a broken cattail. It broke in her hand, scattering fluff all over her legs. "The Minks are from McKenzie Butte. There're all kinds of gangs up there. The Boys are bigger, stronger, hateful, and fully have it in for us. The tree house will be there another day."

"True." Len held his gesture like a lawyer in a bad movie. "But I don't like the idea of them dictating what we can and can't do. If we don't stand up to them, they'll just keep pushing us around." He paused. "C'mon, Lizbeth, you're a varsity softball jock."

Lizbeth folded her arms to cover her exposed biceps. "Thanks for the compliment," she said sarcastically. Then, her whole countenance changed. She felt herself blush with embarrassment and anger.

Angie touched her on the arm. "Is anything the matter?"

Contrary to her nature, Lizbeth took center stage. She walked over to the end of the dock and turned toward the other Misfits. "Look, I haven't told any of you. I've been meaning to—but I just haven't been able to say it out loud." She closed her eyes and faced the sun, hoping for warm reassurance. It did not come.

Len said, "Lizbeth, I don't want to be a jerk, but we need to get going here. Are you going to tell us or what?"

She felt her eyelids burning. "OK." She took a deep breath and opened her eyes. "On the last day of school, I hung around late with Laura and Hannah. I walked part-way home with Laura, then we split off near the Mini-Mart. I took a short cut behind the store." She stopped and gathered herself again. "I didn't see them at first—but there they were, all three of the McKenzie Boys leaning against the dumpster. They were flicking matches and just being the slime balls that they are."

Lizbeth paced as she enacted the scene. "I just wanted to get past them, that's all. Then Tommy pushed off from the dumpster, and Josh stood there in that disgusting undershirt and mouthed, 'bring it on.' They were doing other stuff, too. I tried to ignore it. They're so perverted." She looked as if she might cry. Then she lifted her head with bleary-eyed resolve.

"I looked toward the end of the alley, toward the sidewalk." She pointed toward the other end of the dock. "Somebody would surely walk by, right? But no. I was alone. The grossest one, Odin, he yells 'Stump!' He's so awful. He flashed his idiot tattoos like I was supposed to be impressed. His shoulders are so freakin' huge." Her eyes grew large, as if Odin were there on the dock, threatening her all over again.

"Odin, you know how he talks, said that I had 'trespassed in their official space.' Then he said he needed a kiss, like it was payment or something. I looked around. No one was coming. I looked at his brothers. Tommy faked a punch at me, and Josh flexed his arms like he was doing curls."

She stopped to let it all sink in. "What was I supposed to do? Fight them all? Scream? I kept walking. That's what I do best, right? Just plod on step after step." She took two long steps away from the river. "Then Odin grabbed me from behind. He turned me around and said in that fake charm crap, 'C'mon, baby, I like a girl with a little muscle on her.' His voice felt like knives carving me up. He said, 'Stump, you're not much to look at, but you'll do in a pinch.'"

Angie covered her mouth.

"I hated it, him, them. I hated his sick words."

Angie went to console her, but Lizbeth stayed in the moment, pulling away from Angie's hand as if it were Odin's.

"Yeah, that's what happened next. Hands. Hands grabbing at me. They seemed to come from everywhere. My heart went crazy. I thought I had to get away or I'd never start breathing again. I could see sunshine on the sidewalk. Somehow I felt that if I could just get there, I'd be OK. They grabbed my arms, and we fought. I yanked and yanked, but they were so strong. Me, Lizbeth, they were too strong for me. Then they pushed me down." Lizbeth knelt, facing the sun. "I just knew the worst was coming. I started to scramble away, but Tommy and Josh held my shoulders, and—"

She stopped and gulped. "Then Odin spoke again. He said, 'Hey, boys, look at that one.' I looked, too. They were checking out some thin chick walking on the sidewalk. Suddenly, I was nothing. The girl was Allison Rippy, you know, that songleader type who barely wears anything? Odin left me, and the brothers followed. They ran over to her and were practically drooling. Odin slipped his hand around her waist. Allison grabbed the bottom of her mini-skirt like she suddenly got modest."

Lizbeth stood up, trembling. She gestured to the imaginary McKenzie Butte Boys and Allison. "Odin, that jerk, turned back to me and said, 'Why'd I want to kiss you anyway, Stump?' I could see Allison's hands shake. Then I heard people coming up the sidewalk. So I ran out there, too. With all of us watching, Odin pushed her away and, I swear, he sucked her in with his eyes." She looked at them all stark and pale, as if innocence were a tangible thing that had drained right out of her.

Then Lizbeth stopped resisting the flow of tears. She wept freely, first into her own hands, then on Angie's shoulder. Some time passed. Len nervously paced, sat down, stood up, and acted frustrated and useless. He strode over to the shore and tossed rocks into the river.

Finally, Bennu spoke. "Sorry, Lizbeth." He offered a consoling hug. Then he broke away and stormed around the dock. "I can't believe they did this to you. Well, yeah, I can believe it—they're like that—but I can't believe they attacked you." He curled his hands tight with rage. "Just once, I'd like to get the Brutes from the Butte in my element. They should know what it feels like to be humiliated."

Lizbeth had heard this kind of threat before: the courage of one whose enemy is nowhere in sight.

Len pinched the bridge of his nose like an exasperated father. "So, you're going to get the McKenzie Boys to enter a poetry competition with you? Are you nuts?!"

"I know," said Bennu. "It'll never happen. But what I'd give to slowly sink my talons into them."

"That's kind of a gross image," said Lizbeth.

Len snorted. "Yeah, way to cheer her up, big brother."

"Oh, shut up!" Bennu faced Len. "At least I'm not ten feet away throwing rocks like a little kid." He turned to Lizbeth. "Hey, you got away, Lizbeth. Nothing worse happened. It could have been worse, you know."

Lizbeth bolted away from Angie. "What? I get mugged and you say it could have been worse? Am I supposed to feel grateful they didn't kill me but just called me Stump?" She marched toward Bennu, who backed up off the dock and over toward Len. "Why don't we count the ways to bash me? There's Tank, The Planet, and my personal favorites, Bessie and Betsy. Stupid cow names!" She glared at them with her huge round eyes.

"Liz," said Len, "Lizbeth, back off a second." He took a few steps toward the dock. "Look, do you want us to call the cops? We will. We'll do whatever you want." Lizbeth thought he looked frightened, as if he thought that speaking with tenderness would take years off his life.

"No. I'm fine. I'm OK, now." She glanced back at Angie sitting on the dock petting Percy. "I feel better just talking about it." She picked up a rock, sent it skipping across the river and safe to the other side.

"They're such pig-headed dorks." Bennu pushed his glasses up and flung another rock. "Until now, all they'd ever done was make fun of us. They've yelled every short-stuff name there is to Len: Pipsqueak. Dwarf. Mickey Mouse."

"OK, that's enough." Len swelled his thirty-two inch chest.

"Midget. Shrimpo. Weenie."

"I said that's enough, Beakface!" He walked over and sat down on the dock.

"They make sci-fi noises when Angie walks by," continued Bennu.

Angie acted as if she hadn't been listening to their conversation. "Really, Lizbeth, I feel so badly for you. My own shoulder hurts just where you said they touched you, and I feel a deep churning inside."

Lizbeth didn't know how to respond, to say thank you or wonder about Angie's sanity. At the same time, Angie's beauty made her compassion less credible. What did she know about suffering? Lizbeth knew it wasn't fair to think like this, but she did.

Then Angie pointed to a plank on the dock. "We're just like the little helpless ants right here. We've all had our share of enemies."

Lizbeth waited for Len to pop off.

"What?!" exclaimed Len. "Ants?"

Angie let an ant crawl on her. "Look, you know it's true. We're together because people think we're weird. We don't fit in. How many brothers and sisters hang out in high school?" She turned her hand around to keep the ant on top. "So, we've got to help each other, y'know, like birdseed in winter. We're like thistle seeds to the golden finch."

Len stood up and turned his back. "I can't take this."

"Angie," said Bennu, "first you say we're like ants, then we're like birdseed. That's a kind of mixed metaphor, don't you think?" Bennu stood up and stepped on the line of ants in front of Angie.

"Bennu!" she cried out. "Look where you're going."

Len poked Bennu in the chest. "Yeah, way to go, Bennu. First you insult me 'cause I'm short, then you say something dumb to Angie."

Lizbeth watched Bennu sweep his black curly hair out of his eyes. She knew Bennu was now reviewing the top 150 dumb things he'd said around girls.

Then Len waved his hand in front of blank-eyed Bennu, "You hoo, Mr. Metaphor Man, are you with us? You ready to go to the Peterson Farm?"

Like a bird, Bennu snapped his head around to Len. "Maybe you're right, Len. We shouldn't curl up in a corner every time we hear about them." He jutted out his chin.

"Guys!" said Lizbeth. "They think they have to stand up to everything. No wonder the world's in such a mess. I vote no. What do you say, Angie?"

Angie did not look up. Facing the sun, her cheeks glistened and her sweater shone in crystalline sparkles. Lizbeth thought she saw Bennu's knees actually buckle. Angie said, "Yes, I would like to rise into a tree and gaze with sweet longing on the valley below." She bowed her head, then pulled some lip gloss out of her pocket and delicately swabbed her lips.

Bennu picked at the grooves in a tire attached to the dock. "Angie, you, um . . ."

Len clapped his hands once and walked toward the canoe. "That settles it. Three to one. Sorry, Liz. It will all work out. You'll see. Bennu, why don't you, like, untie the canoe? I'll put the daypacks in."

Lizbeth thought, OK, I lost again, but don't blame me when things go bad. Then she sat into the canoe, her overall straps rising to the level of her cheeks. She said softly, "I knew my vote wouldn't matter."

"C'mon, Lizbeth." Bennu stepped into the number three spot. "Enough of this woe-is-me attitude. You know Mom hates it."

"What's with all this brother-sister mush?" Len pretend-hugged himself. "Don't you realize the pressure this puts on the rest of us? You should hear my mom: 'Lenny, why can't you be more like that sweet Neferti boy?' It stinks."

They pushed off and paddled smoothly down the Lewis, Len steering them into the swifter elements in the center of the river, Lizbeth paddling from the second seat to the front. Lizbeth watched Angie in the front seat glide a finger over the water, then point to the blooming dogwoods. But Lizbeth couldn't get her mind off of Len's bossiness. She knew that no amount of beauty would take his breath away. Not much of anything could keep him from talking either.

"I tell you, Lizbeth, I think you shoulda kicked Odin where you'd do some real damage." Len took off his hat. "You shoulda shown 'em we can't like be pushed around, not by nobody, no how." He snarfed and snarled like the Cowardly Lion, shaking his hair like a mane. "Hey, is everybody paddling? Seems like I'm doing all the work."

For a short spell, in a calmer section of the river, they drifted and enjoyed the ferny banks and the cry of a hawk overhead. Then the Misfits sliced their paddles into the water again. Lizbeth reveled in the pull and release, the way her own strength powered the canoe lightly over the surging, melted snow. Then she felt something at her ankles. Frightened, she shifted back in her seat, causing the canoe to wobble.

"What's up?" shouted Bennu.

"I dunno," answered Lizbeth, half-looking, half-groping blindly under her seat. She felt something soft and warm. "Oh, no, look."

"What?" said Len. "What is it?"

Lizbeth held up the stowaway. "Look who's tagging along. It's our good luck charm, Percy."

"Ah, cripes," said Len, banging the side of the canoe. "What are we supposed to do with him?"

"It's too late to do anything about it now." Lizbeth grinned. "Unless you want to go back." Len lowered his eyebrows sternly. "Well, then, we'll just have to deal. Maybe he'll protect us. He has claws, you know."

"Yeah, right," said Len.

Lizbeth knew Len wouldn't go back. That would mean giving in, a direction of the will he rarely chose.

Len swerved the canoe around to miss a boulder. "OK, Liz, he stays."

CHAPTER THREE
OVER THE RIVER AND TO THE WOOD

Danger and delight grow on one stalk.

ENGLISH PROVERB

 With no further surprises, the Misfits reached a small pebbly wash near the homestead where they could beach the canoe. After everyone had stepped out, Percy tightrope-walked the gunnels, and Lizbeth carried him to shore.

Len pulled on the canoe. "Took about thirty minutes, eh, Bennu?"

"Yeah," said Bennu, "but it will take a lot longer to get back, against the current and all. We should probably leave no later than five."

"We'd be fine leaving at five-thirty."

"What a shock. You're disagreeing with me."

Lizbeth looked for a reason to get away from this bickering. She walked over to Angie. Squatting down, she saw Angie gently holding a lily of the valley, then inhaling deeply. Angie moved to a bleeding heart plant that had a single flower hanging out like a welcome sign. As Angie traced the perfect pink heart with her finger, she glanced at Lizbeth and pointed to the tiny petal sticking out at the bottom, the part that made it look like the heart is bleeding. It was not pale pink like the rest of the flower. Unlike any other bleeding heart Lizbeth had ever seen, the petal became bright red toward the tip. Angie poked the tip with her finger.

It cut her. She said, "Oh!" and watched one drop of blood fall into the palm of her hand. Lizbeth waited for Angie to wipe it off or offer some bizarre interpretation.

"Just shut it," was all she heard. It was Len's "last word" to Bennu. Worrying that they'd start shoving each other, Lizbeth ran back over to them, pushed them apart, and said, "Let's get going."

Daypacks secured, the four trekked up the small bluff that rose above the river. In true feline fashion, Percy acted as if he were ignoring them, though he was never more than twenty feet behind. Lizbeth kept him in view. She loved to watch his orange fur darting in and out of the waving green of spring.

As the hill started to level out, Lizbeth spotted a ramshackle house at the top of the hill. Its weathered siding testified to years of neglect or, as Bennu suggested, lousy choices. "I don't get it. Why would somebody pick this crummy plot of land?"

Lizbeth ran her finger over some chipped paint. "Yuck. Look at the dirt inside and the graffiti. Such charming sentiments. It makes you sick." Then she noticed things were missing: siding, an inside door, a window. "Why would somebody just randomly tear up the house?"

"They didn't." Angie pointed out to the yard. "The homeless guy did. Look over there."

They all turned to gaze upon a most remarkable structure. It wasn't any ordinary tree house, not merely floorboards in a tree. About forty feet up, nestled into towering fir trees, were two entirely separate rooms with walls and windows, joined by a suspension bridge. Lizbeth almost laughed. "I can't believe it. They're like guest cottages in the sky."

Bennu ran over to a platform suspended by a pulley hanging from the second room. "Maybe we should take turns getting yanked up."

Then Lizbeth jogged over to a spiral staircase. She ran her hand over the banister that coiled fairy-tale-like around two trunks growing close together. "This is just too cool to be true."

Len stood right by her. "This is like something out of Robinson Crusoe." He put one foot on the first step and smiled a Cheshire-cat grin.

"We really have a choice?" Lizbeth stood out of the way and gestured for him to go. "You'd run us over if we went first." She half-hoped Len would return the courtesy. When, instead, he turned to walk up, Lizbeth said sarcastically, "No, please, you go ahead."

Len did not turn around. He tested the first few stairs. "C'mon. This is totally secure. It can handle our weight."

So Lizbeth followed Len, with Bennu next, and then Angie. Lizbeth felt the trunk on her left and grasped the banister on the right as if it were made out of polished brass. She made one revolution and looked down at the base of the tree. There was Percy licking a paw. He meowed. She waved at him. "We'll be right back."

As they got to the top and entered the first room, Lizbeth immediately noticed its finished quality. The windows, nicely set into the walls, provided ample light. The splintered clapboard on the outside contrasted with the smooth paneling inside. There was even a shelf with knickknacks.

Len kicked a beer can out the door and looked over until it crashlanded below. He said, "Pretty darned impressive. This guy really knew what he was doing."

Bennu touched the window molding. "I can't believe this. There's not even a draft coming in." He moved his glasses up and down, as if without them he might see something new.

Then Len hopped up and down.

"What are you doing?" shouted Lizbeth. "Don't you think we have enough weight in here already?"

"Don't bulge an eyeball, Lizbeth." He put his hands on his hips. "I'm just trying to see if it's as strong as it looks. Let's go over to the other room and check it out."

Lizbeth, closest to the other door, poked her head past the threshold, then stepped back. "There's no way that bridge is safe. It's just a bunch of ropes and boards slapped together by a lunatic." Swaying in space, the bridge stirred in her every dust speck of vertigo she possessed. She told herself that without courage no adventure ever amounts to anything.

Len stepped up next to Lizbeth. He said that the rope side-rails looked solid. Bennu gave a thumbs-up sign. Then Angie reminded Lizbeth that the tree houses weren't all that old. Lizbeth looked down at the wooden planks, then at her thunderous thighs.

Len took his hat off, revealing his frayed mop of hair. To Lizbeth, it matched her anxiety.

Len put his hat back on and hoped that, as he scrunched it down tight, he would also scrunch down his fear. He put one foot down. "OK," he said. "It's OK. It's a little shaky, but all suspension bridges are, right?" He tried to walk weightlessly. The second foot followed. To make matters more difficult, he needed to look down to assess the strength of each plank. The slightest puff of wind felt like a hurricane. He clutched the side-supports so tightly his knuckles hurt. When the bridge swayed slightly, he reacted and made the bridge jerk. Stop moving! he shouted to himself. But aloud he said, "The ropes are, uh, in good shape." C'mon, he told himself. Keep going. Then he yelled back to the others. "And all but one board is fine. Just watch the one that's half-way out."

With a final bound to the opposite landing, Len grabbed a branch and looked out at the river and valley below. He felt exhilarated. From this height, the crest of the hill no longer obscured the curves of the Lewis coursing through the valley toward the coastal range and the sea, with cottonwoods and willows lining the riverbanks.

Len stretched a hand to the others. "Next!"

Lizbeth stood like stone. "Why do I have to go next? Why don't you two go so that the bridge won't break until you're safely over?"

Bennu frowned. "So then we'd all be stranded? Look, if we thought you wouldn't make it, none of us would go!"

"OK, fine." She tied on a scarf to keep her hair out of her eyes.

"It's not so bad," boomed Len. "I made it. So can you."

Yeah, she thought, you weigh all of forty-two pounds.

The hand he extended to Lizbeth looked to her like a small-boned, lightweight nothing.

She stepped out gingerly, then clumped across in awkward lurches, wincing as she stepped over the broken plank. A loose piece fell to the ground, but the bridge held. "Miracles happen," she said as she arrived next to Len.

Now she held her hand out to Bennu. He pulled his hood up and cinched the tie. "I won't make it if I have to look down."

"What are you afraid of?" said Len. "You're so blind you can't see the ground anyway. Just look straight ahead, and we'll guide you."

Bennu obeyed, one handhold, one step at a time. He never looked down. Once across, he grabbed Lizbeth's hand and closed his eyes in gratitude.

Len said, "Congrats, Mr. Daredevil, you made it."

Lizbeth wiped Bennu's sweat off her hand and onto her overalls. She looked over to Angie. She knew Angie was not the type to creep inch by inch from the steps into a swimming pool. Here, too, Angie took one deep breath and dove across, not coming up for air till she stood on the other side. As they congratulated each other, Lizbeth tried to put from her mind the fact that the only way down led them back across the same fragile, swaying bridge. She released her grip on the branch near the landing and led the way into the second of the makeshift, abandoned rooms.

Unlike the other room, this interior offered mostly darkness. Dimly, Lizbeth made out some kind of partition that closed off part of the room.

Toward that cavernous space she walked, side by side with Len, as if they were competing for the first look. Lizbeth couldn't wait to see the next clever design from the absentee architect. Would they find a hobbit's hutch or a clever tree house bed?

As it turned out, they were greeted all right, but by a nightmare.

"Hello, my trespassing friends."

CHAPTER FOUR

The Lesson

People talk sometimes of bestial cruelty, but that's
a great injustice and insult to the beasts; a beast can
never be so cruel as a man, so artistically cruel.

FYODOR DOSTOEVSKY, *THE BROTHERS KARAMAZOV*

 Lizbeth froze. She knew the voice too well. Dread filled her, and all she could think about was not going through the horror once more, not giving them a chance to finish what they started.

The voice from behind the wall spoke again. "I don't suggest you try to run."

Lizbeth choked on the courtesy of these words. She glanced back at the open doorway. On the bridge one light, loose rope floated in the breeze.

Again the doomsayer spoke. "It will be better for you if you do as I say." The hulking voice sounded closer. Then, a towering form of uncontrolled manhood emerged, his well-developed upper body only partly covered with a cut-off shirt, his tattoos tense with muscular threat. One of them spelled his nickname in barbed gothic letters, "ODIN." His knife reflected a shaft of sunlight from the open door.

That was all Lizbeth needed. She ran out to the platform and over the bridge so fast she was not sure she touched the planks at all. When she reached the other tree house, she looked back at the other Misfits nearly trampling each other on their way out.

OK, she thought, they're coming. I can lead the way.

After Lizbeth descended several spiral steps, she heard a scream. Angie was hurt. Lizbeth climbed up two steps, until her head was even with the floor of the room.

Then she paused. Gripping the top of the banister tightly, she wondered, should I go back to help Angie . . . or keep going to help Angie? Bennu and Len are already there. If I left, I could get help.

She turned and moved down three steps, her left hand finding sap on the tree trunk.

How? From the nearest neighbor? Where? What good would it do?

She turned and went up two steps.

But I saw the knife, the blade shining. And I know those hands.

She stepped down swiftly, then stopped.

But how can I leave my friends? It's Angie that's hurt, fragile Angie. How can I even think of leaving? What if they need just one more hand?

Up.

I'll call the police on my cell phone.

Down.

I'm going to get help. 9-1-1. I'm not running away . . .

The call would not go through. Then Lizbeth heard noises coming up the spiral stairs. As Tommy bragged about his switchblade, Josh banged something hard against the tree.

Lizbeth bolted back up to the room and stumbled over to a window that looked out to the bridge. She saw Angie's foot dangling through a hole in the planks, her ankle bleeding. Len and Bennu pulled her foot out.

"Hurry!" yelled Bennu.

Odin stood calmly on the landing behind them. "I told you not to run." Lizbeth hated his perverse compassion. "Let's go find your friend, the fullback. She owes me."

Lizbeth turned back to the stairs. Tommy grabbed one of her arms and Josh the other. They pushed her over to the door. Tommy laughed. "Hey, bro', you lookin' for this?"

Odin walked across the bridge till he hovered over Angie. "We should teach these trespassers a lesson."

Lizbeth wondered if the bridge would hold. She stared at the tattoo on Odin's right biceps, an animal with a snake's body and a tiger's head.

"Time to go down," Odin said too pleasantly.

Lizbeth's strength seemed to have left her. She knew better than to have hope. And now, Len and Bennu and Angie—all had to go through what happened to her, and maybe more.

Odin snickered. He held the knife to Len's neck and ushered him back into the room, then down the stairs. Then came Lizbeth, Tommy, Bennu, Angie, and Josh.

On the curling stairs, Lizbeth wanted to push Odin over the edge like the fullback he claimed she was. Of course, with the knife near Len, she knew she couldn't. Then she craned her neck back but could not see Angie. She feared for her, imagining how Josh was prodding her down. By the time they reached the bottom, a tear had slipped down Lizbeth's face. Like a prayer, the tear seemed to her to ask for sympathy and rescue, mercy or grace, any good thing. She shook it loose. Unheard and unanswered, it landed silently on the clasp of her overalls.

The Boys tied the Misfits' hands behind their backs, then pushed them all to the ground. The ropes hurt Lizbeth's wrists with a hot-flesh kind of pain. She wondered why they needed to be so cruelly tight.

Now what? she thought.

She looked over at Len. She could see the indignation in his eyes. She worried about Len. Would he keep his mouth shut? Sharp pebbles dug into her knees, so she leaned over to relieve the pressure. She saw Bennu's fear screaming in its silence.

"What are you going to do?" asked Len harshly. "We've done nothing to you. Just let us go."

Odin looked like a father shocked at his own child's obliviousness. "You've come uninvited to our place of amusement. We don't appreciate the intrusion." He rubbed the stubble on his chin. "Tommy, put the one with the big mouth on the platform over there."

To Lizbeth, Odin's mean eloquence seemed to come right out of his snake-beast tattoo. She looked to Angie for support. Her head was bowed.

Clumsily, Len shuffled himself up on his knees. His voice became a growl. "We didn't even know you came here."

A lie, Lizbeth thought, but a forgivable one, even sensible. Her wrists hurt—and the burning pain matched her conscience, which, irrationally, took this moment to make her feel bad for Len's lie. The thin veil of shame left her feeling more vulnerable. Then Josh sat beside her.

Odin gestured to the ropes. "OK, hoist him up." Tommy yanked on the pulley-rope, jerking Len off the ground. As Len flopped onto the platform, Lizbeth felt Josh's rough hand rubbing up and down from her exposed neck to her cheek.

Bennu pushed at Josh and yelled toward Tommy. "Stop it! Stop it right now! You can't get away with this!"

"What does it matter, Mr. Nose?" Josh shoved him, Bennu's glasses falling into the dirt. Lizbeth stared at them, knowing that Bennu's despair would now take a quantum leap. "You'll all live," said Josh, wiping his hands on his undershirt. "I think."

As Tommy laughed, Len called out to the others. "We'll be all right. They're just trying to scare us."

It's working, thought Lizbeth.

Odin paced back and forth as if preparing for a grand decision.

Tommy pressed on the bill of his red baseball cap, curling the sides in more. "What next, O mighty O-ton?"

Lizbeth struggled to get away, but Josh tightened his grip and went to kiss her neck. "I like the spunky ones," he said.

"That's Odin to you, you loser," the elder brother shot back to Tommy. "Keep pulling. I think these folks have underestimated us."

With the platform five feet up, Tommy tied off the rope and gave it a solid push, causing Len to swing around erratically, a sight almost unbearable for Lizbeth to watch. Len lurched around on the platform, trying to grasp without hands and hold on without arms. The shift from one side to the next looked torturous, one leg dangling over the side, his head exposed in defenseless humiliation.

Josh kissed Lizbeth's neck, then stood to watch the scene.

Back and forth Len swayed. Slipping. Nearly falling. Straining to stay on. Lizbeth felt certain he would plunge out and hit the ground without the use of his hands to break the fall. She imagined him with a broken leg or neck. Then, surprisingly, Josh stepped past her and slowed the platform down. Perhaps the worst was over.

Then the Mink brothers picked up stones. They held them in their palms, calculating weight and grip. Tommy looked into an imaginary catcher's sign and nodded in agreement.

Bennu propped himself up as best he could. "What was going on? I hate not being able to see."

Angie told him.

Bennu glared at the shapes before him. "You have no right!" He rocked his head back and forth. "Stop it! Stop it!" His high-pitched wail sounded alien to Lizbeth, coming from depths that frightened her.

Josh walked over and kicked dirt onto him. "Shut up. Your turn will come soon enough."

At first the McKenzie Boys only lobbed the pebbles, making Len twist to avoid the hit, teeter, and nearly fall.

Then Tommy went up and spun the wooden shelf around and pushed it. The platform whirled, a roller coaster and gun arcade in one.

Josh picked up larger stones.

The Boys aimed now. One rock, spinning, missed. Another zipped past Len's shoulder. He slipped toward the edge. A third stone clunked loudly against the platform. Lizbeth wished she could cover her eyes with her hands.

"Close but no cigar." Tommy went into another windup.

Then Odin threw and missed.

Maybe they aren't really trying to hit him, thought Lizbeth. Maybe they will let us all go soon, thankful for our lives, never to come here again. Maybe Len was right.

But Odin's next rock hit Len, glancing off his thigh. It didn't seem to hurt him much, and Lizbeth still hoped the worst was over. The Boys huddled for a minute—maybe negotiating about how to release us, thought Lizbeth—but then turned and all threw at once, Tommy's rock finding its mark, striking Len's head. Blood splurted out and down his forehead and face. He collapsed onto the platform, his head hanging over the side.

Lizbeth screamed.

Odin grinned. "Good shot! Struck him out! Let's see what I can do."

Tommy ambled over to Angie. "Hey, beautiful, Josh lost the bet, so I get you. Get ready for a good time."

Lizbeth looked over at Angie, who was slumped over, weeping. "Angie," whispered Lizbeth, "quick, get up, run."

Tommy looked back at Josh. "You couldn't hit him from two feet."

Awkwardly, Angie leaned against Lizbeth and stood. Lizbeth told her to go, but she just stood there crying, looking overwhelmed, looking as if she would completely snap at any minute. Lizbeth couldn't bear it. She got herself up and pushed Angie. "Let's go."

Bennu cried out, "Where are you going? Don't leave me!"

Odin and Josh high-fived and looked for new stones to throw.

Tommy turned again to Angie. "C'mon, Beautiful, don't play hard to get."

Lizbeth started down the hill. "Angie, follow me." She looked back and saw that Angie wasn't coming. Angie stumbled around haphazardly, not gaining any distance from the tree houses or Tommy. She shuffled her feet, kicking up dust.

Furious, Lizbeth ran back. She heard Angie call out deliriously, "Mom . . . Dad . . . holding on . . . the Boys . . . at the Tree . . . letting go."

"Angie!" yelled Lizbeth. "No one else is here! No one's going to help us!"

Tommy jogged over.

Angie spoke faster. "Ropes, ropes dangling." Lizbeth caught up to Tommy and plowed into his shoulder. His red cap flew off and landed near Angie. She shouted now. "Blood! . . . I see a drop on the palm of my hand!" Her eyes glazed over. "The blood is flowing. It's raining now. The blood is splashing." She fell to her knees.

Tommy shoved Lizbeth over and charged toward Angie.

From the ground, Lizbeth could see Angie looking back toward Len. She seemed to be looking somewhere above him. Lizbeth followed the direction of her gaze. All she could see on the bridge between the tree houses was Percy.

Odin laughed and wound up to throw another stone.

Angie pleaded again, "Mom . . . Dad . . . Can't anyone help us?"

Lizbeth closed her eyes and hung her head in weary submission, waiting for the thud of a rock against Len's body, or a hand to drive a scream out of Angie's. Then she heard a voice above her. "Come on now. It's time to go."

Something about the voice was strange. Her courage spent, all she had left was morbid curiosity. Slowly, she turned her head toward the sky and opened her eyes. To her amazement, all was dark.

She opened her eyes as wide as they would go. She slapped at herself to see if she were dreaming. Then, in one kinetic lurch, she pushed herself up and looked around. Someone stood near her. Was it Tommy or Odin? She turned toward it, her mouth open. She couldn't see the face.

How could it be dark? Oh, my heart, it's beating so loud, I can't hear anything. I can feel it leap off my chest. What's happening to me? Who is this person? Wait. I pushed with my hands, the ones that were tied. "Bennu, Angie, where are you?"

As her eyes adjusted to the dark, she rubbed her wrists. The body of the voice came closer. She cried out, "Hey! Watch it!"

"Come now. Make haste. I know you have suffered, and I share your grief." A hand touched her shoulder. It came from underneath a long cloak.

She jerked around to push his hand away.

His hand caught hers. "Please, if we hope to endure this night, we must find shelter." The voice felt reassuring, like a father's tender embrace.

That's when she noticed it was raining.

PART TWO
THE HEART OF FEAR

CHAPTER FIVE
A TERRIBLE GOOD

How can we contrive to be at once astonished
at the world and yet at home in it?

G. K. CHESTERTON, *ORTHODOXY*

 *Writers of history look down from any number of moun-*
taintops. Some say these views are limited and not to be
trusted. But I tell this story not from a distant overlook. I
explain events from the valley where I lived them. I know
what happened—the trees, the blood, the rain—even if it is
as hard to believe as heaven.

"Wait here," the cloak said. "I'll get the others ready."

Sure, Lizbeth said to herself. I'll just stand in the rain while a stranger
who won't show his face prepares his men for me. No, thanks.

Though some nearby lanterns gave dim light, Lizbeth could tell she
stood at the base of a fir tree of some sort, and that other trees joined
together to surround them in a ring. She couldn't immediately see the
other Misfits, so she stepped back behind a tree. It was cedar. She could
smell it.

Mentally, Lizbeth jump-cut between the images before her and the
ones at the Peterson homestead: dripping night/blazing sun, dense
trees/sweeping vista, confidence/helplessness . . . This last realization jolted
her. She took stock of her body. Unaccountably, she felt neither weak nor

hurt, not even dazed or disoriented. Instead, she felt strong. Not just typically robust either, but more potent than ever, rippling with power. As she flexed anywhere on her body, those muscles seemed to lock into place with a click. She'd felt strong before—but never this strong, and never had she felt so good about being so strong. Although embarrassed by the thought, she wanted to celebrate with a shout or even a beastly snort.

Just as joltingly, she asked herself, where are the ropes and the rocks and the McKenzie Boys? Where am I? Where are the others? Where is poor Len?

Someone with a lantern moved out from the center, and she could see a body on the ground nearby, curled up in the fetal position. She ran over. Just before she got right up to it, the body moved onto its back. It was Bennu. One eye ventured into the open, and the other eye followed suspiciously. He smiled, as if he were enjoying the raindrops splashing all over him.

Lizbeth knelt and nudged him. "Bennu. Hey, Bennu, it's Lizbeth. Are you OK? You've got to get going. Weird things are happening."

Slowly, Bennu sat up. "OK, I'm awake. What weird thing has happened? Hey, when did it start raining?"

"Good question. But the harder one is *where* is it raining?"

"Are the McKenzie Boys gone?"

"I don't see them."

"If they're gone, who cares where we are? I don't even mind the rain dribbling down my cheek or the clammy sensation of my pants getting soaked. These drops feel to me like mist in a desert wind or—"

"What's the matter with you?" Lizbeth grabbed her brother by the shoulders. "You sound like you're entering another poetry contest." She felt that he was light as a feather, that if she lifted him up, he would fly away.

"I suppose I'm just trying to express the joy that comes as a rope to save me, but you have pulled the slack out, and now I fear the very same rope may hang me. Here, help me up."

Lizbeth felt as if she were curling fifteen pounds. "Look, I don't care if you want to talk funny. What's stranger is that I prayed to get out—to anywhere but there with the McKenzie Butte Boys."

"And now it appears your prayers were answered. We are *anywhere*. Ah, the noose tightens."

"Are you sure you're not feeling a little light-headed?"

"I feel light-bodied."

"Well, settle down. I'm scared. It's dark and it's raining, and I don't know where Len is or who Angie's talking to over there." She pointed over to the lanterns.

Bennu ran his hands through his hair, skimming water off. "What's the guy wearing, a hooded cape? No wonder I can't tell what he's wearing. I don't have my glasses. They fell off when I got pushed. They've got to be here somewhere." He looked around, quickly, with birdlike snaps of the head. He and Lizbeth did their best to look in the dark. "I'm dead if I can't find them." Splashing recklessly, he felt around on the ground. "C'mon, where are they? They *have* to be here."

"Bennu, get a grip. We'll find them. You're acting like a lunatic."

He inspected his nose and ears several times as if his glasses might suddenly appear. He looked and felt and groped and relooked, and then he froze, his hands stuck in wide-fingered surprise. "Lizbeth, it's too bizarre."

"What?"

"I can see the ripples in the rain-made pools, the swirls of Angie's wet, red-blond hair, the lifelines on my own palms. And, wait, weren't my hands tied? What is going on?"

"I dunno. But we've got to find Len. Let's see what Angie's up to."

Quietly—though Lizbeth wondered why they should be afraid if Angie wasn't—they crept up behind some ten or so figures in cloaks. All were facing away from them, toward the flame-powered lanterns on the ground. Occasionally someone pointed into the distance. Lizbeth and Bennu stood behind Angie and eavesdropped. Two cloaks approached Angie, one on each side. When they spoke, they revealed their profiles in the light.

"We've only just returned from dangerous missions, young lady." A tall male's bony frame could be made out even under his cloak. "No doubt mine was the most dangerous, but that is as it should be."

"My name is Angie."

"Forgive my rudeness. My name is Prester John. The urgency is so great that I forgot to be polite. Most of the time Highlanders show the utmost courtesy and respect." He gestured to the stern-looking woman on the other side of Angie. "This is my aide, Ellen Basala."

"Good to meet you."

Lizbeth was not at all sure it was good or that Angie should be so forward.

"Thank you." Ellen Basala bowed. "I'm glad to meet anyone His Eminence finds interest in." Leaning in to Angie, she added, "Of course, anyone who will listen to him is someone he finds interest in."

Prester John brought his hand to his head in some kind of salute. "Angie, excuse us now, but we must go to help develop the extremely sensitive military strategy necessary to cope with the danger we are in."

As Prester John and Ellen walked away, Angie received a tap on the shoulder.

"Angie," whispered Lizbeth.

Angie jumped. "What?"

"Angie, it's Lizbeth. Bennu's here. We've got to find Len. C'mon."

After Angie hugged Lizbeth wholeheartedly and Bennu awkwardly, the threesome turned back to the darkness over by the trees.

"There's no time to talk right now," said Bennu. "Let's split up."

Lizbeth moved out to the left from where she had been looking before. The cold, light rain kept falling, a persistent reminder that she was no longer on a hillside above the familiar Lewis. Blinking into the mist, Lizbeth stared up at the awesome trees that disappeared into the dark above her. As her eyes followed the trunks back down to the ground, she saw Len, unconscious, right by her feet.

He moaned. Lizbeth enjoyed the sound because it meant he was alive. She shouted to the others that she found him and then leaned over him to examine his head wound. She had trouble doing so. She found a little matted blood, but his hair—was it possible—seemed thicker and longer than she remembered it. Maybe the light rain had frizzed it out. Maybe the thrown rock, the blood and the dirt, made it seem thicker. She could barely part it. In her anxious compassion, she pressed his scalp harder and more rapidly until her uninvited massage made Len twitch in pain. She found the sore. Like a mother probing a child's bruise, she learned she wasn't appreciated. Unlike most mothers, she gave up.

"Ouch!" Len pushed himself up on his elbows. "What's going on?"

"I wish I could tell you." Lizbeth cradled his head with her left arm.

Curiously, Len sniffed repeatedly like he was searching for a scent. "Oh, my achin' head. Where's Odin? Isn't he gonna get us if we just sit here? Yuck, I feel woozy. I think I'm gonna faint."

Then he did.

Lizbeth helped lay Len back down. As Bennu and Angie ran up, she dug into her overalls and found some old tissue. With it, she wiped crusty blood from his face. The rain had already removed some of it.

"OK," she said, "Len needs attention. He needs a doctor. Angie, do you think it's all right to ask these people for help? What's with them anyway? Are they part of one of those historical reenactment groups or something?"

"I don't think so," said Angie, who had leaned over and checked Len's forehead for a fever. "I don't know who they are or where we are or why we are here—but I feel as strongly as anything that we should trust them. They seem good and right and true."

Lizbeth gripped the tissue tighter. "And you've figured all of this out in a few minutes?"

"Yeah, what makes you be so sure?" said Bennu.

"Because of their leader, the one standing directly behind you."

Lizbeth felt her heart pound. Before she could turn around, the leader stepped over to Lizbeth's left and knelt next to her.

"We have learned," he said, tenderly touching Len's face, "that a good friend who pilgrims with you is hurt." It was not the person she'd heard speak to Angie. It was the same voice she had heard earlier, before she opened her eyes in this place. He said, "I will do what I can." His quiet assurance did not settle Lizbeth's racing fears.

As he put both hands on Len's head, another member of the band, considerably shorter than the leader, came around to the other side, next to Angie. His lips shone pale orange in the light of the lantern. "Hello, I'm Terz. Things may look bad, but things will get better. They always do. All you need to know right now is that you are being helped by the Great One himself."

At this description, the "Great One" issued a short groan. "Your friend appears not to have a mortal wound."

"The amazing thing is," said Lizbeth, "he did. He got hit so hard with a rock it could've killed him." With worry still held in her eyes, Lizbeth looked up at Angie, who smiled back at her as if nothing more had happened than a little spill while running through the Wilder behind their house. Lizbeth tried to smooth out the wrinkles in her brow.

After pulling a satchel around from his side to the front, the lead cloak rummaged through it and pulled out several pouches. From one he took a leaf of some sort, creased it and held it under Len's nose. He wiped the secreting oils around Len's mouth, then crushed the leaf and sprinkled the remains into Len's hair. There was no immediate response. He tied up the pouch and returned it and the others to the satchel.

Terz patted Len on the arm. "There's no question, something good will come of this."

The whole procedure made Lizbeth nervous and suspicious. What's this hokum, she thought. Where's the science in a crushed leaf on the head?

Then the healer stood and gave orders to the others who had by now gathered around Len. "Mook, you and Alabaster put together a stretcher. The rest of you, assist these other souls as they have need. We've tarried long enough here in Circle Stand. I fear we'll be discovered. We'll go up the trail to Chimney Cave by way of Joseph's Ledge. Let's walk."

He paused and then, to Lizbeth's ears, spoke the most curious thing: "In Welken." The group responded in unison, "Of Welken." Another pause. Then they all set to work.

Before long, the ones he called Mook and Alabaster returned with a primitive stretcher, two tree limbs with a skin strapped to it. As they set the stretcher beside Len, Mook turned his noble, placid face to Lizbeth. "I can tell you are grieved at your friend's injury. We will do what we can to help. I am Mook of the Nezzer clan, and with me is Alabaster Singing."

"I'm Lizbeth. Um, thank you."

Mook and Alabaster lifted Len onto the stretcher. Mook said, "I hope we don't seem too rough with your friend. We must hurry. We are in great danger, a threat that grows stronger every moment we are in the open." He and Alabaster left them.

"OK," said Lizbeth. She didn't know what to say or what to ask. She looked down at Len. In the light of the lanterns, his form cast a shadow deep and foreboding. It worried Lizbeth. She gasped quietly at the sight of him motionless on the stretcher, but before she could sink into weighty remorse, the outline of Len's upper body caught her eye. "What do you think?" she asked Bennu and Angie. "Am I seeing things or does his body look larger? And his hair looks longer too. Maybe it's just because of the shadows."

"Shadows," said Bennu, echoing her. "Maybe that's where we are, a shadow-world, a place earth-but-not-earth, a parallel dimension."

"You've played too many video games, Bennu."

Angie felt Len's shoulders. He moaned again. She said, "But maybe this 'Welken' world is not a place of shadows. What if it's a place of light?"

"Doesn't seem like it so far." Lizbeth stepped aside as Mook covered Len with a blanket. She waited for him to walk away. "Where are we going with these people? How do we know they are friends? Lots of people act nice at first, but they're just hooking you in."

"Lizbeth," said Angie. "What cruel purpose do you see? All they've done is help. Maybe you have seen too many movies. Do you think we are in some black dream brought on by the McKenzie Boys?"

"I dunno. Any explanation seems as likely as the next."

Except, she thought, except that I don't feel like a shadow at all. I feel like I should test my strength, like I should push against something, a wall, a tree, anything.

The hike soon proved test enough. In the rain, the lanterns flickered and the mud lent unwanted weight to their boots. Yet they walked without complaint on the path upward, each step a movement closer, Lizbeth hoped, to a larger explanation.

The leader went first, then a few others. The trail was wide enough for three or four, though most walked single file. In the middle were the Misfits, Angie first, then Bennu, Lizbeth, and Len carried by two tall, strong-armed men. They were quiet. A few others brought up the rear.

∽❦∽

His head throbbing, Len awoke to the sensation of a rollicking earthquake. He winced in pain and felt wobbly in his joints. The ground, fluctuating between tolerable thumps and jolting bumps, seemed to toss him

40

about with little consideration for his pounding brain. If he'd been his usual wit-worn self, he would have made some sarcastic comment about getting ripped off by the camel salesman, but he was not well enough for levities. He lifted his aching head and saw a hand tightly gripping a wooden support. This hand, he surmised, must be responsible for the pain. It must be a threat, a McKenzie Butte hand, maybe Odin himself, carrying him to greater undoing. On a wider section of path, two others approached him, one on each side. He turned his head as best he could and saw that both were under five feet tall and quite round. Len felt surrounded.

"Lad," said the one on Len's left, "good to see you awakifying right before our own peepers. My name is Vida Bering Well, and on your mud-bespotted right is Jacob Canny Sea. We're both from Deedy Swamp."

"So what?" said Len nervously. Then he thought he'd better play along. "Yeah. Well, I'm Len Bartholomew from Skinner."

"Is that so?" Jacob touched the shaft of his dagger at Len's eye-level. "I've skinnered many a jack-jumping rabbit in my time, but I've never columbused such a town. Is it in Welken or do you have to mayflower to get there?"

Len opened his mouth to speak—but he didn't have any idea where to go from here.

"Don't confusify the young lad, Jacob." Vida tapped Len on the hand. "In fact, we should take our tongues and stitch 'em into a quiver. Can't your elephant remember we're being chased? The enemy might pouncify at any moment. Let's shut the blathering!"

Len used the quiet to try to sort things out. All he knew for certain was that things weren't going well.

Patience, he reminded himself. Wait for the opportunity.

Moments later, the group stopped. Len heard something about "Joseph's Ledge," and he took that to be the large space under a stone overhang above him.

Out of the rain, Len's carriers set the stretcher down on the edge of the opening closest to the hillside.

Despite the shooting pain that blurred his consciousness, Len sat bolt upright, to the amazement of his carriers. He felt a throb in his skull, clasped the fear in his heart, and held the sidebars of the stretcher in readiness.

The carrier in front spoke over his head. "We've disturbed him, Sutton. We must learn to set a stretcher down with more kindness."

The one in back looked Len in the eye. "You have no need to worry, stranger. My name is Sutton Hoo. Those of Durrow Wood are right strong and able."

Dimly, Len could see that both of his carriers were massive men, broad-shouldered and muscular, with long beards. Were these guys friends of the Butte Boys? Were they as cruel?

"Aye," said the other carrier, "Sutton speaks well and truly, as he always does." He shuffled over the end of the stretcher so Len could more easily see him. "I'm Zennor Pict. We won't weary of carryin' you. And even if I do, Sutton alone could carry you from here to Justice Island and back. Between the two of us, you'll be fine."

Yeah, you and the other McKenzie thugs, thought Len, remembering the pitching practice for which his head was the catcher's mitt. Alternating between delirious clarity and waves of nausea, Len decided to act. He took up his pallet and walked. At least he tried. Actually, he barely managed to roll off. Unfortunately, he chose to escape on the side next to the steep drop-off. While Sutton and Zennor watched helplessly, Len slid down the slick hillside, enjoying his freedom only briefly. In his path, some fifty feet down, a leviathan-sized boulder loomed, the surface of which he struck violently. He bounced off his hip, cried, "Oh no!" and hit his head on a smaller rock, only inches from his other wound.

෴

From Joseph's Ledge, Lizbeth called down to reassure him that his three fellow Misfits were there, that the McKenzie Boys were not, and that, as far as she could tell, they were safe for now. But Len didn't acknowledge her. She then realized that whenever Len next awakened, he still would not know.

Lizbeth, Sutton, and Zennor jumped down the hill after Len, trying not to imitate his fate. The steep slope had good plants here and there to grasp for a handhold. Steadily they traversed down and, with greater difficulty, made their way up to the path, hand over hand on a rope held by Mook and others, until Len was on the stretcher once more, less recognizable than ever.

After feeling relieved to be away from the tree house pulleys, Lizbeth now wondered if it were possible to feel more miserable. Dampness soaked to her bones. She and Len were covered in mud. The interminable path led mercilessly up and up. In the dark, she could not see where to put her feet, so water sloshed inside shoes that adhered to the mud like suction cups. There was plenty to commiserate about. To top it off, the Misfits were stuck with ten strangers.

Toward what end? she thought. Away from whom? What circumstances meant that the best alternative was a cave? And now that I'm in the very back, I can't see Bennu. He's probably OK. Probably.

An anaconda named doubt slithered into her mind and squeezed hard, bearing down on the worry of her unconscious friend on the stretcher by her side. She gasped for breath.

CHAPTER SIX

THE VOICE IN THE WILDER-NESS

Nine-tenths of wisdom is being wise in time.

THEODORE ROOSEVELT

Meanwhile, in the Bartholomews' backyard, Charlotte attempted to get perfectly comfortable. She grabbed a glass of iced tea, tossed a cushion onto her favorite chair, and pointed it toward the gate that opened up to the strip of land her kids called the Wilder, on the banks of the Lewis River. Here she could forget about groceries and faculty meetings, doorbells and phone calls, even adolescent wise-cracks about the way her gray roots contrasted so nicely with her dyed blond hair. She could concentrate fully on the exploits of Percy and Bones.

With pen poised, she reminded herself of the Rumpelstiltskin method: "It's OK to write straw. Write and write all the straw you can. Later on you can turn it into gold." She looked through the frame of the open gate and listened for a voice calling from the Wilder-ness.

Yellow pad in hand, Charlotte began.

CHAPTER TWO: Pyramids and Paddy Wagons

A few days later, Percy raced into Bones's driveway, screeching the tires and blasting the horn. The Master Detective went to the backyard to find his basset hound friend Bones Malone, the Master Gardener, swaying side to side, his straw hat cockeyed and a telescope at full extension.

"Avast ye, aphids!" bellowed Captain Bones from the quarterdeck of the tomato row. "You scurvy knaves will have to walk the plank, so to speak."

Percy tiptoed up and whispered, "Dreadfully violent this afternoon, aren't we, dear lad?"

Soon Percy and Bones were sipping iced mint tea in the cluttered living room that had belonged to Bones and his family for generations. Old newspapers leaned against stacks of *Canine Quarterly*. A good bit of dust collected on the bookcase. All in all it was a relaxed if unrefined habitation, a bit like Bones himself.

"I've just come from the precinct, Bones. Our beloved Captain, Mr. Henley Hornbrook, says that Ollie escaped before they could get him in the paddy wagon.

"They heard Ollie say something like, 'Oh, Mama, you shouldn't have shown me how to free myself from fetters. Now I can't obey the law.'" Perkins paused and smoothed his whiskers.

"Humph." Bones pulled out the tip of one of his long ears that had fallen into his iced mint tea. He shook his head. "Ollie Ollie Otterson, when will he stop infestin' these parts? I suppose the boys from downtown have no idea where he's off to."

"That's why I've come so quickly, Bonesy. In his haste, Ollie dropped this newspaper clipping on the ground."

As Percival P. Perkins III muttered about what haste makes (spoiled soup? a stitch in time?), Bones studied the evidence.

THE WASHINGTON INQUIRER
June 6, 1927 Good Morning

PYRAMID MYSTERIES!

(AP) Ancient treasures from the Mediterranean have been discovered near Akhenaten's tomb, says

45

famed archaeologist Sir Flounder Peters. Worth
millions, the relics range from gold masks to ruby
rings. Of particular interest to scholars are reports
of mysterious religious pieces that represent
Akhenaten's attempt to show that there is only a —

"So we're supposed to follow this critter across the
seas?" Bones asked in amazement. "I'm a gardener, Perkins,
not a walrus."

"I knew you'd see the urgency of it," Percy said, patting
his derby. "Now, where was I? I made a mental list of what to
tell you. Number one was paddy wagon. Number two was
pyramids. That's right, number three was Pratt. Oh yes, I've
been reading Ida Pratt's *Ancient Egypt: The Glory Years*.

"As she tells it, the locals have believed for centuries that
one of the tombs had a secret entrance. From the time of the
pharaohs to the invasion by the Muslims around 700 AD, one
family knew about the passageway but managed to keep
things classified for generations, allowing for a healthy standard of living. No one had been able to find the entrance or
catch those 'in the know' in the act. When the place went
Muslim, the family seemed to vanish."

"So you think that Ollie is after Akhenaten's riches? What
could be more far-fetched?"

Percy just grinned, adjusted his pince-nez, and waited. "I
suggest we leave on the absolute immediate."

"That would mean, of course, you've already booked us
passage."

"Ah, good point, Mr. Malone. Actually, no, I haven't made
reservations, but not to worry. I know which side of the bread
I've toasted. Though Ollie is getting a head start, I think we can
more than make up for it with a visit to Wise Dominic first."

"Must we? He's *your* cousin, so it's right jolly for you, but
I'll end up turning around several times in my skin when we're
there."

"He's a puma, true enough. But he's softened with age. He can't spring on you like he used to, yet the good words flow down all the same."

∽∿∾

A few miles away, out from the oily shadows next to Twisselman's Pawn Shop, a nervous otter slithered, rubbing his wrists and panting heavily.

"I don't see those blue knuckleheads anymore," said Ollie. "They must have given up the chase, hee hee. Now I can think about what to get for Mama." Ollie waited to catch his breath. "You know, Mama, if you didn't have such expensive tastes, I wouldn't live the lonely life I lead. Oh, I've wanted to go straight, forsake the life of crime, and become a model citizen. In fact, I shall right now. What should stop me? I'll turn myself in, serve my time, and become the goodest do-gooder goodness ever saw. Oh, but look at this lovely jade sphinx Mama would love . . ."

Charlotte gulped down the last of her iced tea. Hmm. I guess having Egyptian neighbors is wearing off on me. I seem to remember that Lizbeth once said something about her family following its line back to the pharoahs. I'll have to check with her mother.

Forgetting that she'd already finished her iced tea, Charlotte tossed back the glass until the ice cubes clunked against her teeth.

I need to pay closer attention to details, she thought.

CHAPTER SEVEN
AND THOUGH THIS WORLD
WITH DEVILS FILLED

Of evils that are very remote, men are not afraid;
thus every one knows that he must die,
but since people think they will not die soon, they do not care.

ARISTOTLE, *THE RHETORIC*

 After trudging along for some time, Lizbeth looked at her watch. It said 2:10, but the digital second display wasn't flashing.

Great, she thought, my watch is stuck, just like we are.

From the back of the pack, led by monkish figures, Lizbeth had little choice but to plod on to who-knows-where. She was happy she could see far enough ahead to notice Angie faintly.

Odd, she thought, she does seem fainter than the others. Must be my eyes.

Thinking it would be drier if she moved to the mountain side of the trail, Lizbeth slogged over and from there was able to get a better angle on Angie. She saw her talking to the one who had applied the medicinal herbs to Len.

She can be so naive, she thought. She's acting like she's known this guy since junior high.

With this classroom reference, a stick of logic hit Lizbeth a glancing blow. Maybe these are old theater friends of hers, out for a masquerade. That's it, she thought, we're on our way to a surprise party of some sort.

For a moment, Lizbeth held the stick of logic as a way to stay afloat in this capsized world. But just for a moment. She knew that reason could play tricks on those desperate for an explanation. Soon enough, the hypothesis splintered into pieces when she remembered one small thing. The rain. That would be a rather difficult special effect. She treaded water again—and reflected on her own naivete.

After another half hour or so, they reached a huge hole in the face of the mountain. Lizbeth had heard some of the strangers talking about "Chimney Cave," so she guessed this must be it. But she didn't really care. Anything to get out of the rain.

When she crossed the threshold, she felt the darkness of the place swallow her up, like she was walking into the mouth of a whale. But the cloaks thrust their lanterns into it, and the shadowy beast fled. Once inside, the weary travelers scraped off their mud. The small entry opened up into a large room furnished with chairs, cupboards, stools and tables—a less primitive setup than she thought she would find. Soon, the smell of wet clothing and sweat chased away any staleness in the air. After the six lanterns were hung up and a fire was started, Lizbeth noticed that the gray walls had been chipped down and flattened. As she warmed her hands by the growing fire, she saw here at the back of the cave the reason for its name, a natural flue that allowed for an inside fire pit. After checking on Len, who seemed to be breathing normally, she sat on a stool and scraped mud off her shoes.

Clearly, the Welkeners were familiar with Chimney Cave. As the leader made his way to the north side of the room, he conferred quietly with each member of the band. To Lizbeth, the leader seemed especially tender with the other Welkeners, touching them, speaking in low, serious tones, as if they had just shared some tragedy. "Are you well, my friend?" Lizbeth heard him say to one. And to another, "Have you been thinking of your good wife, the fair Gildas?"

When she smiled at Bennu, who was sitting on the other side of Len, Bennu said, "I'm trying to think of how to describe the hope he leaves behind. It's like the wake from a smooth sailing ship."

"Yeah." Lizbeth flung mud onto the floor. "Just what I was gonna say."

"Look," said Bennu, "he's getting ready to speak. He seems to gather all of us up with his eyes."

"What, a rake isn't good enough? Settle down, Bennu."

"So," the leader said and paused, as if the word meant something specific and weighty. "Good travelers, in these difficult times we have journeyed farther from our homes than would be prudent." Another pause. "Of course, prudence is not what brings us here." Without his cloak, the leader stood with his hands on his waist, thumbs hooked into a wide belt. His long tunic, a heraldic green, covering him from shoulders to knees, had slits on the sides up to his hips. Black pants were stuffed into calf-high boots. His leather satchel lay on the floor.

"We take solace in having arrived safe thus far," he continued, "yet this goal was not met without sacrifice, without loss, certainly not without sorrow. We have all walked in trust, not knowing how we could provide sufficient aid. What else could we do? A great evil has visited our land." He paced from sconce to sconce, occasionally tapping a wall with his knuckle.

As he spoke, Lizbeth began to like him more and more and the sound of this Welken place less and less.

Who needs a great evil? she thought.

She also began to feel a little too warm by the fire. As she scooched her stool a few feet away, she glanced at Bennu, thinking she'd see his wistful eyes. But he looked worried. She had hoped to draw strength from him, yet for some reason he seemed to be hoping for the same from her.

"What's the matter?" she asked.

"I don't see Angie."

"Really."

"I saw her come into the cave, but now I can't find her."

Len shuddered all over and blew out short grunts like he was dreaming.

"I'll stay here with Len. You go look around."

As Bennu got up, the leader continued his speech.

"The Dreaded One is still loose in the lowlands." His calm voice rose intensely. "Though his terrible acts moved us out of our homes and to this uncertain road, we have already found a good reward for our service. As usual, we learn part of our purpose for walking only after taking the first step. Because we banded together, we have rescued these four troubled pilgrims."

Some of the Welkeners looked back at Lizbeth. She waved and smiled like she'd been introduced to her parents' friends. She felt dumb.

"But before we learn their story, more urgent matters confront us. We must hear from the search parties. You were sent out to discover what you could to assist our mission. As you report, introduce yourselves to our visitors."

Two by two, the travelers revealed the lessons of the day. First, a tall, regal, long-necked man stepped forth, followed by a short woman with a frankly flat face. The man had shining, sun-bright yellow hair slicked back. It seemed to pull on his face so that his dark sparkling eyes, and his bridgeless nose, dominated. Lizbeth remembered seeing Angie talking with these two.

"My name is Prester John. I am here at the command of the Great Anuba, the only mortal soul in the Prester Highlands to whom I bow, amen. Our people, as you know, humbly serve any whose need becomes known to us. No one more humbly serves than a noble Highlander. We take great pride in this. With me is Ellen Basala, our best guide through the mountain regions. She is sure-footed and trustworthy."

"Indeed." Ellen Basala's wiry white hair shimmered in the fire's light.

"And she says no more than needs be said."

Murmurs and wry smiles followed.

"She is sure-tongued as well," said Prester John.

When the group suppressed a snicker at this remark, Ellen shrank back a little but maintained an alert stance. The way her combs curled back to hold her hair in place reminded Lizbeth of horns. Then Lizbeth's eyes met Bennu's from across the cave. Lizbeth shot a "what gives?" gesture his way. Bennu shook his head.

Prester John leaned on the hilt of his sword. "We were commissioned to go southeast, directly toward the gathering of homes in the alpine region of Durrow Wood, to a little village called Craig. At first, our sleuthing only led us to detect the startling loveliness of the land. Crags overhead brought the eye to deep fissures out of which gushed delicious waterfalls, some powerful and majestic as a young buck, others svelte and supple as a nursing doe. Here and there, perched precariously on a small, velvety meadow, clung a rugged Durrow house, no doubt inhabited by a hardy but charming family of herders. In front of us, the wood parted magically out into a vast, breathtaking valley, with a crystal brook and a troupe of prancing antelope. Lupine and starflower flowed in ribbons across our path. We were stunned by the beauty of—"

Ellen Basala interrupted him bluntly. "What His Elegance, the Prester John himself, is taking forever to say is that we had nothing to report—nothing worth talking about—until we started knocking on the doors of the homes in the valley. The thing you need to know is this: at every stop we were met with fear."

At this word, Lizbeth decided to listen more intently. She looked down at the sleeping Len and then back up.

Prester John attempted to reassert his version's authority. "Yes. Our visual ecstasy led us to doubt that any tragedy could await us. Then we met her, the face at the first door. I mourned for her countenance. Even now I can see her sorrowful eyes deep set into wells familiar with the flow of tears." He grabbed a wall-hook for support as his knees buckled slightly. "She was so grieved and hidden, filled with suspicion and tragedy. Her furrowed brow spoke of her mind's trembling. I noticed at once the torn pocket of her housedress. What does this mean? I wondered. And then I became acutely aware of a strange and delicate aroma . . . rosemary, maybe, and—"

"Your Elegance, really!" Ellen stomped her foot with exasperation. "The point is that we didn't learn much at all. Most of the time, no one answered when we knocked. Curtains were closed. Streets were empty. Children could not be seen. There was no talk or work or play—"

"Only one word was spoken." Prester John solemnly stretched his long neck toward his audience. "Whether whispered from behind a shutter or choked out from beneath a tear, it was repeated with dread. And the word was 'Morphane'!"

While the locals reeled back from the power of this name, Lizbeth turned to the now groaning Len. Still on his back, he held up his hands as if they had claws, and then he moved his legs up so that he was in an upside-down crouch. Lizbeth wanted to push them back down so that they wouldn't draw attention.

The next speaker took over. "Curious, for we heard the same repulsion to this name, Morphane. My name is Mook, of the Nezzer Clan. We claim the Nez River as our home." Lizbeth liked his look and manner, athletic and direct.

In contrast to the comedic pair who preceded him, Mook's seriousness felt to Lizbeth like sheer granite walls. Though his face was unflinching and inscrutable, Mook evoked peace in her, not fear. His rust-colored hair with its white tips fell against his shoulders like foxtails.

"My companion," he continued, "is Alabaster Singing, as lovely as the stone for which she is named, but just as silent." Alabaster bowed with her head in profile, revealing her long black hair with a four-inch swath of gray in the middle. Mook ran his hands along the copper stripes that ran down the front of his woven poncho. He took up the story again: "Our route took us to the west of where Prester John and Ellen Basala walked. Deeper in the wood we searched to get closer to this Morphane's path. We saw, not just the reaction to his name, but a field of destruction three houses wide. We looked for clues, searched the road for witnesses, and found nothing, just broken pots and trampled hedges. Though I did not wish to see death, I thought it odd that no bodies could be found." With each description, Mook moved, methodically acting out the scene.

Dramatically, Len swatted in the air with his right hand, just missing Lizbeth.

"Then Alabaster tugged on my sleeve." Mook looked pained. "She pointed to a ragged figure, an old woman slumped against a tree, not twenty feet away. I ran to her, preparing myself for a slashed chest or a twisted neck." Mook dropped to his knees. "I knelt beside her, brushed aside her greasy, matted, gray hair, and with the heaviness of certain dread, I gently lifted her head.

"By the roar of Alta Falls itself, I was shocked by what I saw. She was only asleep! I was so relieved I laughed aloud one stout, resounding 'Ha!' In fact, she slept so deeply that it took some rousing to awaken her. Then we were met with our next surprise. She sucked up her spittle, rubbed her eyes, and raised the lids to reveal two cloudy white globes, as vacant of use as a dewclaw.

"Utterly unafraid, she greeted us. 'All right! All right!' she shrieked like a hawk. 'By Soliton's glow, no need to rattle ma' bones 'til they snap. Give Bebba a moment or two, and she'll be out among the living.' She chuckled at this, the first bit of joy we'd heard since we left home. But her face quickly fell when we told her why we'd come.

"'Morphane, is it? I fear for you, I do. Bebba don't know why the sight of him frightens people so, but I can hear the fear when he arrives. It's terrible sounds, all of anguish, shrieks and gasps, a sucking wind like a cold snake whipping through tall grass. Whisssst!' She wove her hands in the air when she made this sound. 'And then,' she said, 'comes the worst part, when Morphane leaves. There's no wounded left moanin' and screamin'. It's far worse, Bebba will tell you. There's only silence, like a graveyard at dawn, all death and nothingness.'"

Lizbeth could tell that these Welkeners weren't just "telling stories." Even though the fire warmed the cave, she felt cold and alone.

Len relaxed his crouch and went flat again.

"And then she went on. 'I'll tell you more. I've heard that hateful beast himself. I only wish I hadn't. I can't remember it without tremblin' so. It's like a well that goes down to nothin', all hollow and pitiful. I could smell his voice . . . a kind of rancid noise. It's a cry unspeakable, like a prison cell for six packed with thirty prisoners, pleadin' for release, gaspin' for breath. I can't forget it . . . But—' And here she paused and then began again. 'Answer me this, you two pilgrims searchin' for death, why am I sitting here without a scratch?'

"She rose, knowing we had no answer, leaned against her stick, and stared deep into our faces with her blind white eyes. I grew restless under her gaze, as if by not seeing she could see more truly, right inside of me. I looked away." Mook waited for the mystery to settle on his audience. Lizbeth crooked her head as if Bebba looked inside of her as well. Mook said, "When I raised my head, she was gone."

Speaking of gone, Lizbeth thought, I wonder if Bennu's found Angie yet. She scanned the cave and saw him. He was up near the front to the right of the speakers. When finally he looked at Lizbeth, he pointed down like he'd found Angie. Lizbeth stared hard but saw nothing.

Sutton Hoo, a great bear of a man, and Zennor Pict, with heaping shoulders like a bull elk, turned to address the others in Chimney Cave. Sutton had bounteous blond ringlets tied together here and there with golden beads. Zennor's black beads at the end of his long brown beard clacked together when he moved. Leather breastplates covered their chests, exposing their heaping shoulders to the sun. They said they had only just arrived from the southern meadows of Durrow Wood. It was their land the others had come to save, and so their gratitude was deep and abiding.

All at once, Len pulled his knees to his chest, swung himself up, and opened his eyes. Startled, Lizbeth put one hand on his knee and asked, "Len, are you OK?"

"Oh, that hurt. I shouldn't have gotten up so quickly." Len moved his hands from his shins to his head, which pushed Lizbeth's hand off his knee. "Yeah, I guess. Except that I feel like I got run over. It hurts to open my eyes."

"Then don't. Just rest and listen. I'll fill you in on what you miss."

To Lizbeth's amazement, Len obeyed.

"The good Mr. Zennor Pict and I," said Sutton Hoo, pointing to Len in the back, "we carried the young pilgrim on the stretcher. No doubt our clumsiness had somethin' to do with his slidin' down the hill in the mud. Anyways, earlier, Zennor and I walked toward our meeting at the Circle. My wife, the long-suffering Gildas, had just given birth to our firstborn—a handsome daughter I might add—and so we were delayed. In our haste to reach the rest of you, we nearly missed the most tellin' evidence of Morphane's wrath." He fingered a golden bead dangling on his right shoulder. "It happened like this: Zennor, gracious as usual, saw that I was tired from my long night and hearty walk, and beckoned me to rest."

Zennor Pict nodded his head. "As your noble Gildas would say, 'Aye, and who would do otherwise?'" He smiled generously. "Of course, my own dearest Jarrow would, no doubt, have made the suggestion sooner and without my normal awkwardness. Anyway, with our backs to the bark of a towerin' pine, I noticed a strange scrape on the trunk, as if someone had made a grab and gouged a handful of the brutally hard stuff clean off the tree. No hand that I know could have accomplished that feat, so I looked closer, calling Sutton to aid me with his gifted eyes."

"Before long," said Sutton, "we noticed somethin' too terrible to believe. Holdin' fast to the bark was . . . the softest . . . was a—"

Here, Sutton Hoo's voice broke. He held his hands to his mouth, attempting to force the sadness back down. It seemed to well up several times and dance mournfully on his lips, making them tremble. Though she had no real reason yet to cry, Lizbeth's own tears followed Sutton's lead and came to just below the surface. Finally, Sutton pressed the woefulness down and went on. "Attached to the bark was what seemed to be, well, it was like the thinnest glove. We laughed at first, brutes that we are, until we examined it more closely. It was not a glove," he paused and struck his breastplate, "but the stiffened skin from a real hand. And then"—he covered his mouth for a moment—"we looked deeper at our surroundings. How could we not have noticed? How could we not have seen?" Sutton's tears overtook him, and he could not go on. He sobbed slowly in an unashamed way, tears flowing freely down his beard. He did not wipe them away.

Zennor took over, pacing and gesturing wildly. "Strewn about here and there were what we could only think of as the husks of townspeople— parts of them anyway—emptied of life, gripped now with somethin' from the ground. An arm-skin hung limp on the handle of a rake. Bits of skin clung to a rabbit where it was missing its paw."

The warmth of the cave no longer comforted Lizbeth. The news from Zennor made her feel exposed, like she was on a cliff in a storm. The shocking news led to more tears from the others, weeping upon weeping.

Len grabbed her arm. "What are they talking about, Lizbeth? Who are these people anyway? Am I on drugs?"

Lizbeth glanced back at him but did not answer.

Mook broke into halting sobs. "Sutton, Zennor, how can this be?" he said. "You *must* be saying more than you saw."

"No, we do not!" Sutton pounded his great staff violently. "It is far worse—for the tellin' of it does not compare to the seein' . . . to the feelin'—to the foul taste of truly knowin'. I saw the shape of a foot where it lay stuck to a tree stump. Here was the husk of a livin' thing, a skin-shadow of a person's ankle or toes, with the soul torn out of the flesh and the remains affixed to the stump!"

No one spoke. Breath, it seemed, had vanished.

Sutton labored now. "Do you not believe? Do you need more proof? I'll tell you what you do not want to know." He leaned against the wall and held both fists against his chest. "Zennor and I stumbled from one wisp to another, delirious with grief, tryin' desperately to discern their various shapes yet hatin' ourselves for learning more and more of this tragedy. Exhausted, I leaned against the largest boulder in the clearing. I wept without thought for stoppin'. I could not begin to understand what I saw. Who could?" He weakened and fell to his knees. Zennor came to his side.

"Then I turned my head ever so slightly and noticed another wilted husk hangin' from the boulder. At another time I would have taken it for a huge butterfly's wings, so soft and delicate-like. I should have buried my curiosity, but to my regret I did not. Something in me needed to witness this tragedy too. Gently, I pulled the shadow back; it was holdin' on to the rock. I could not discern the outline, so I leaned closer, putting my face against the rock so I could see the skin more clearly in the sunlight. Then I saw it!" He held one hand out as if cradling the skin. "I will never forget the face of that young girl. I could make out the nose, the cheeks—and those awful eyes lookin' at me, and the mouth open wide in horror!"

CHAPTER EIGHT
SHOULD THREATEN TO UNDO US

*When you kill a man directly, . . . [y]ou merely hasten his life's close
and conclude it; you do not take it. . . . If, however, you make a
man believe that you will arrange for his dying at any moment,
then you can, in effect, possess his life.*

ANNIE DILLARD, *THE LIVING*

 After Sutton's sad tale, Len moaned, not out of sympa-
thy but because Lizbeth accidentally bumped his head.
"Can't you be the least bit careful?"

"Sorry."

Groggy—and perplexed by the descriptions of
Morphane—Len rubbed his face and tried to wake up
and settle down at the same time. He saw Lizbeth wipe tears away. Around
the cave, the Welkeners were also busy grieving. Prester John patted
Sutton on the shoulders, and the others quietly conversed. No one took
the floor again. "Lizbeth, don't be taken in by these losers. We've got to
get out of here."

"I don't know what to think." She seemed to be studying the ceiling.

"We need to get everyone together. Where's Bennu and Angie?"

"I don't know."

"Well, what *do* you know?"

"That maybe you should go back to sleep!" She glared at him. "Look,
I don't know because I can't see Angie."

"What's that supposed to mean?"

"I don't really know. Oops, sorry. I mean, I'm supposed to see her, but I don't see her."

"What? Why are you *supposed* to see her? Would you please make sense? She's either, like, there or she isn't, right?"

"That's just it, she's there *and* she isn't."

"I am so lost."

"It's just good to hear you say that. Anyway, over there, to the right of Sutton Hoo, Bennu acts like he found Angie and keeps pointing at something, but I can't see anything."

"Yeah, I see what you mean—I mean I don't see."

"If that's Angie, it's the Angie-not-Angie."

"This is making my head hurt. I'm closing my eyes." He lay back down and clasped his hands over his face. The smells in the cave seemed so intense: the candles burning, the wet clothes, even Lizbeth.

"Wait a minute. Don't get up, Len, but I see something, a faint outline, something glowing around the edges. It's coming this way."

"What's it doing?" Len walked his fingers through his hair, on the way to his wound. He picked out some leaf fragments and tossed them aside.

"You mean, what's *she* doing. There, by a lantern on the wall, I can see her. She, well, she looks like she's mad at us. Bennu's coming too."

In the next few moments of silence, Len tried to piece things together. Clearly, the McKenzie Boys drugged us and were playing tricks on us. Any minute, they would burst in and show their ugly faces. The best we can do at this point is to create a diversion and sneak out. Sooner or later, we'll recognize where we are.

"Len," said Angie, "it's so good to see you awake." She tried to hug him, but he stiffened.

"It doesn't feel so good to be awake. My head is killing me—then again, it feels better than I thought it would." When Bennu gripped Len's shoulder, Len nodded his head like the dying soldiers he'd seen in so many movies. Then he sat up.

Angie folded her arms. "What I want to know is why all of you were ignoring me?"

Len looked stunned. "When?"

"Are you kidding? Just a few minutes ago when I waved my arms in your direction." She sat down next to Lizbeth.

Before anyone could answer, a short, squatty woman attracted their attention. At the front where Sutton and Zennor had just spoken, the woman, joined by a man of the same height and build, addressed them. "Excuse me. I beg your christification—really I do—but I'm afraid we must, I feel compelled to, that is, we really should keep reportifying." All four feet of her rose to address the whole group. The Welkeners sat so that those in the back could see. "I'm Vida Bering Well of Deedy Swamp, the lowlands near Mercy Bay, lower down than the Nezzer Clan, where the lighthouse is, with its great watcher of the fog, Mr. Alton Thikker Grey, the one with the black stripe, called Dunaway. No, no, no, the lighthouse has the stripe, not Alton Thikker Grey. And the stripe's not called Dunaway; the lighthouse is. Sorry to confusify. I guess I just need to be windexed." At this small joke, she tugged her wide belt that was already too high on her ball of a belly.

Len said, "I already heard from these two. They can't put a sentence together to save their lives. Why are we listening to these idiots?"

Vida held on to two of the four daggers stuck in her belt. "We, I mean, Jacob Canny Sea and myself, were fixing to meet Bors, that is, Aelred Broonsees for the fullness of his name, and his friend the dearest Sarah Wace, the Lady of Primus Hook. Forgive me, I'm so sorry to be speechifying our visitors with so many hello-my-name-is phrases. You'll be einsteining it all straight away."

Len whispered to Bennu, "Einsteining it? Who? What?"

Bennu whispered back, "I rather like the word."

"Anyhoo," said Vida, "they—Bors and Sarah, remember?—were to be walking through the Maidenhair Moor, right on to Circle Stand, whilst me and Jacob Canny Sea, we was trekkifying up the Nez River to meet them. Jacob, you go right on with what befell us. I mean, Jacob Canny Sea—to say all three names, that is—it's your turn for what happened."

"Yes, of course, by your leave, Vida Bering Well." Jacob Canny Sea, also built like a teapot, grabbed his large stomach and heaved it up in a way that reminded Len of Long John Silver in a cartoon pirate movie.

"Don't get your hopes up," said Len, his arms draped over his knees. "This guy ain't gonna be any clearer."

"Right where the meadow meets the wood, by Skane Lodge, we were to be attempting a daring rescuer's brunch." Jacob leaned against the back wall for a moment and then lurched forward. "Trouble is, something, or someone, got there and wreckified our rendezvous." He took out a comb and ran it through his plastered-down twenty strands. "Our first telltale signal was the flag of the Skane torn asunder, like so many shreds, hanging by its last hook-and-eye. So Vida Bering Well and myself, we trenched down and binoculared the scene, visual like, that is. A ruin of catastrophe is what it appeared to be, really."

Vida Bering Well pulled out a dagger and waved it around like she had entered the room. "I was suspicious about the door lingering like it was, that is, the one hinge ripped out of the front door to the lodge. I yelled, 'Hello, inhabitant!' but the possessor would not answer. So I, with my voice beginning to quiver like pig fat, I pushed open the door with the force of high tide, and bam! the whole oak vestibule came crashing at my feet, blowing me satchmo into the length of Jacob Canny Sea."

As if his name were a cue, Jacob Canny Sea took up the verbal baton. "I macarthered in, boots aflailin'. What else could I do? No doubt, a fight of centrifugal proportions had gettysburged the room. A broken table was all cattle-crushed. Chairs were broke and bedraggled. Resistance was everywhere! Even the sight of blood skewered the walls." He held out his long slimy fingers and massaged the air as if it were a sore muscle. "At the back was part of the vitality we were looking for. That journal Bors is always scrabbling in—there it was, the cover pilferized but the insides were lifelined all the same. I told Vida that at least a few goodly tidings graced the wreckage. Y'see, Bors appears to a'been writing in it just as he was lindburghed. Could be a map is what it is.

"So Vida Bering Well and myself, we bullhorned for the dearest Sarah Wace and Bors 'til our voices went all slanty and sick. We know how prized Bors and Sarah are to you founders here, especially those of Primus Hook."

"Hey," said Len, "here's our chance. Let's slip out of here while everyone's listening to these bums."

"What are you saying?" asked Angie, "I've dreamed of a place like this all my life."

"You've dreamed of mud and caves and hanging skin? Angie, what's the matter with you? Don't you see, we've been slipped some hallucinogenic drug."

She did not recognize the remark. And neither did Bennu or Lizbeth acknowledge his plea. Len sat up on his knees as best he could. Surrounded by his friends, he felt thoroughly alone. He held his head erect and realized that he was the only one who was seeing things well.

Vida let out a croaking warrior sound. "Then we came back, hopifying to get this journalization into the hands of our commissioned leader. That was when we visualized on our way out, by the most miraculous of insights, our new friend, that is, Terz. We thought he would be forty depths away at least. So forthwith we pony-expressed to him the journal and sped on our swampy feet to the Stand."

Angie turned to Lizbeth. "Listening to that is a workout. Still, I love it."

Len turned to stare some sense into Angie, but he couldn't find her. Then he saw Lizbeth tentatively reach out in the direction of Angie's voice. She seemed to have found something, as if she touched Angie's shoulder.

"Hello, Lizbeth," said Angie.

"Angie?" asked Lizbeth.

"Yes, I'm here."

"That's just it, Angie. You're only partly here. I can see you—and then you slowly fade away. And I know my eyes are fine."

This reality, as well as the entire room, began to spin around in Len's mind.

Lizbeth had been concentrating hard on these two from Deedy Swamp, enough to make some sense of them, while at the same time trying to process the Misfits' situation, Angie's partial invisibility, Bennu's poetic wanderings, and Len's escape idea. She felt that the best course of action, whatever it was, would be difficult to pursue, because as a group the Misfits seemed more divided than ever. She had heard that adversity brought people together, but that just didn't seem to be the case for them. Misfits again.

"Oh, Vida Bering Well, truly you honor me with your trust." A slender, wiry man with unpartable, short brown hair and shiny skin took up the narrative. "For those of you who have yet to meet my small, hard-to-notice self, I am Terz, most recently of Primus Hook. I am only too happy to serve the larger purposes and persons to whom I am devoted." Here he bowed to the head cloak.

Lizbeth tried to look interested in Terz while focusing on her conversation with Angie. She got up onto her knees.

Angie looked stunned. "What do you mean you can't see me?"

"It's not that I can't at all," said Lizbeth softly. "You sort of *pulse*. When you fade, I can see a kind of outline. You're sort of there—but see-through. I don't know, it's weird."

"It's even weirder for me. But the thing is, I was just going to tell you that you looked different, like you've been lifting weights or something."

"I know. I feel that way, too."

Out of habit, Bennu pushed on the bridge of his nose. "And me, I feel different too. My imagination is, well, soaring more than usual—and I don't need my glasses."

Lizbeth felt that maybe the Misfits were pulling things together. Then Len scattered things around again. He fainted.

Bennu caught him. "Oh, great. Just what we need. I thought he was feeling better."

"I thought so too," said Lizbeth. "Now I'm worried all over again."

"The only thing good about it," said Bennu, "is that he's a lot easier to deal with when he's asleep."

Lizbeth smiled just a crack. "True enough—but what do we do until he wakes up, *if* he wakes up?"

"Something's happening. Shh."

"I was on my own when I received Bors's journal." Terz resumed his story in a steady, unruffled manner. "I knew I was not worthy of its contents, so I went searching for the Great One where we separated, south of the lodge about half a mile, at the edge of Skane's tilled acres."

A gentle but firm voice came from the back, to the left of the Misfits. "As I've said before, do not refer to me as 'Great One.' My heart knows better than to believe it, and so does yours. Only Soliton is great."

Terz continued calmly. "Bors, alias Aelred Broonsees, and Sarah Wace must have been kidnapped or something worse." He put both hands in his baggy pants. "When I realized this, I caught up to my Illustrious Partner and showed him the journal. We ran down to the house where we thought Bors and Sarah had stayed the night before, a seldom-used place called The Endel Inn. He had left something there, so it wouldn't get lost or stolen." Terz cleared his throat and stared at the ceiling like a preoccupied professor.

"We had a difficult time finding the place." He pulled out his pipe. "It was tucked away in the high grass of the moors. Since dusk was descending, I thought we should veer back into Durrow Wood. At least then we'd not be late to our meeting in Circle Stand. Happily, I was contradicted by my companion, the one who does not wish to be called great."

Lizbeth looked over at Bennu. He was staring at Angie—at least where Angie *should* be. Lizbeth wondered if, in this more poetic state, Bennu would act more romantic than usual. She poked him to break his trance. "Bennu," she whispered, "just because you can't see her doesn't mean she can't see you. Staring at her, that is." Bennu turned to face the front.

At long last, the lead cloak took the floor. "My partner Terz understates the tension of that moment at the crossroads. The wood looked so inviting, and yet here I was carrying all that was left of my lifelong friend, Bors, to say nothing of my deep sorrow at the loss of Sarah Wace, whose countenance graced all in her presence. These two would not have surrendered easily, and so I decided that neither should we. I told Terz we should go out into the moors once again, to search for The Endel Inn. He respectfully objected."

"It's true." Terz scratched his head. "I haven't the perseverance I should."

Lizbeth took note of Terz's humility. She looked at Bennu and Angie as if to say, "I'm impressed."

The leader folded his hands against his green tunic. "When darkness became complete, when I thought we would lose all hope of finding the inn, I began to feel a great hole in my heart—that dread of losing something precious. In desperation, Terz and I stood on the highest mound nearby and screamed, 'Endel Inn,' with our strongest voices. We waited, scanning the horizon in all directions, our hopes sinking as the shadows grew. Terz tugged on my sleeve to go into the wood. I looked out on the Maidenhair Moor one more time and I thought I saw a glint of light to the southwest. I asked Terz if he saw it, but he did not." He paused, squatted down and drew a map on the cave floor. "Then it came again, a clear light, like a mirror of the sun calling to us—from *here*." He pressed a finger on the spot. "In a short while, we were at the door of The Endel Inn.

"The innkeeper came." The leader's voice rose. "He remembered Bors and Sarah well. A royal pair, he said, if ever he'd set his eyes on any. Bors had told him to give a letter to any who came in search of them, since only honorable folk would learn where he was. I have it with me." He reached into his satchel and pulled out some paper. "I'll read it to you now."

Lizbeth whispered to Bennu, "I'm getting tired of all these speeches. Len needs a doctor."

"OK, calm down," said Bennu. "I have a hunch we won't be in this cave for long. I've got this picture in my head of pictographs or hieroglyphics or something. At any rate, there's no immediate fear in the image. We'll be safe there."

"What are you talking about?" Lizbeth gritted her teeth. "Have you gone nuts? There's no fear in pictographs? Who cares? What's going on? Len's conked out. Angie's invisible. And you want to visit a museum. I want out of here."

"Here is the letter." The lead cloak held up the note.

To our good friends,

There is not time to tell you all we have seen. The peril presses against us.

My word to you is this: reckon hard the risk. We are stalking beasts of prey. Their scent is a stale perfume, a rancid, unapproachable smell. And here is a warning. Do not get accustomed to it. When the rotting meat smells sweet, their ways have become yours. May it never be so!

You were chosen for your love of kindness and justice. But remember this—none of you were called out because you were incorruptible. No one is—no one save Soliton.

In Welken,
Bors

"So. There it is. So."

To Lizbeth, these solemn words felt like hammer blows, as if he were saying, "There is the hard truth. You are not going home. Take it as it is."

She looked around the room and thought that the weight of what had been said seemed to push down even the broadest shoulders. The burden was palpable.

Bennu seemed to feel what she was feeling. "Lizbeth, we have not yet seen the enemy, but the glories of war are already spoiled."

"In Welken," the lead cloak said with dark faith.

In unison, a subdued "Of Welken" came in return.

Meekly, for she was afraid to break the mood, Lizbeth raised her hand as if she were in a classroom. "Pardon me." All eyes turned to her. "Excuse me, sir, we have learned everyone's name but yours. What are we to call you?"

The lead cloak smiled. "Forgive me. I am the Lord of Primus Hook and High Ambassador for Welken. You may call me Piers."

CHAPTER NINE
THE FLAME LEAPS INTO DARKNESS

What god will be able to rescue you from my hand?

DANIEL 3:15

 "We, er, want to, um, thank you for helping us so far, Mr. Piers, sir." Lizbeth nervously flicked more dried mud from her shoes.

"We have only done what we must." Piers held out both hands. "And that for love's sake, not duty's."

"Yeah, that's really cool. I mean, we don't like duty stuff, either."

Lizbeth cringed at her own drivel. She wanted to hide behind someone—but, wouldn't you know it, she thought—Angie was in front of her. Why couldn't crude Len be awake enough to say something stupid?

As if her mouth were a foot-magnet, she spoke again: "While we're, like, talking like this, could I ask you something? Do you happen to know when we get to go home?"

Arrgh, she thought. Why do I keep treating him like a magic school teacher?

"You are wise to care for such things," Piers said. "But the story has not yet been fully told."

"Oh," Lizbeth said as if she understood how this statement answered her question. But in her heart she wondered if Piers really knew anything about them or what home meant. Perhaps he just dodged the question because it was unanswerable. That was not a consoling thought. Into her soup of embarrassment came two parts disappointment and one part creeping cynicism. She tried to resist drinking this brew by studying something else about the little band that had adopted them. One characteristic was subtle but undeniable. Each person there was strangely a bit nearer to the animal kingdom than most humans.

She explained it to Angie. "It's not that they're like Peter Cottontail or anything. But you know how you look at someone and say, 'He moves his head just like a bird' or, 'She looks like a collie, with that long hair and pointed nose'? It's like that, only these people seem one step closer."

"Yeah," said Angie. "Nothing real obvious. Ears a little longer. A look of a fox in the eye. A bear hug that seems more bearish."

Lizbeth's spirit improved even more when she thought about how the Misfits were not the same as the four who were ambushed at the Peterson Homestead. Eyes had grown sharper, hair bushier, muscles larger. They were all different. And yet, rather than feeling more out of place, less themselves, they all seemed to Lizbeth to feel more fully alive, more truly themselves than ever. At least three of them did. Len was now out cold. Lizbeth wondered what it could mean that they felt better here, not in Skinner, Oregon, at least not in the twenty-first century. Why should they fit in here and not at home?

As Piers turned to face everyone again, greater urgency marked his face. "On our way back to Circle Stand, we swept down toward Durrow Wood, hoping to meet up with a few of you. Instead we met up with the horrors Sutton and Zennor spoke of. Where the eastern border of Maidenhair Meadow becomes the forest, we heard grunting noises, and the sounds of the mashing of plants. Whatever it was took no care to be quiet. We hid behind some fallen trees, and we soon learned that this thing took no care to protect what stood in its path. No care was taken at all.

"The rain hadn't yet begun, and in the full moon we saw an anarchy in the forest, beasts of all imagination and experience, creatures part human, part animal—or thing. We couldn't see them well, but it seemed that on one, an arm had a paw instead of a hand, and the arm dangled uselessly from the beast's side. Ears and horns, skin and rocks, legs and branches blended together, as if mixed in a pot. One monster with long claws oozed blood from its own thighs where the claws had scraped."

Lizbeth covered her mouth and wished once again to be back home.

While Piers continued with the story, Terz stood up and walked behind him. Terz seemed emotionally overwhelmed. He looked shocked and then strangely enraptured. Shielding his eyes, he acted like he was experiencing all of it for the first time, right in front of him in the cave.

"And then, the beasts trampled on." Piers took two big steps toward the group. "With fear in our hearts, we decided to follow them. As we did, we noticed that though they ignored each other, they also appeared curiously bound together, as if a net had been thrown over them. They churned through branches and bushes until they came to an opening near the edge of the meadow. It unnerved them. They cowered and shook in the exposure. Then one of them picked up a scent. Compelled to follow it, the monster moved out, sometimes moaning, sometimes howling, pulling the others in the invisible net. To us it seemed that they sniffed the evidence hypnotically, seeking the life that seemed most worth killing. And, of course, we worried that the scent they followed was one of yours."

Terz acted possessed. He started to grab at the air like he was pulling something in. The other Welkeners didn't seem surprised by his actions, but Lizbeth thought Terz had flipped out.

"Yet," Piers cocked his head, "instead of marching in a line, or in some ordered way, the swarm rotated haphazardly, without an obvious leader. The swarm of drones droned on. The rain pelted down. One beast whose whole right side was rock and dirt intentionally hit a tree with her rocky portion. Chips and pebbles broke off and were stepped on by the others. At each loss of stone, she seemed a little weaker, more depleted.

"Suddenly, the entire army stiffened, seized by some collective fear. They held fast in motionless alert, their faces turned to the north. We crouched behind some trees and looked where they were looking. Ahead of them, poised on a granite shelf, a huge, powerful animal stood as a sentinel. The moon backlit the beast, casting an eerie silhouette of his massive form. In these shadows, he could be seen well enough, more vividly than any good thing would ever hope to imagine. Power and death glowed out from him like raging fire."

As Lizbeth leaned in to watch, Terz crouched low behind Piers. He looked over the heads in the crowd at some imaginary place behind them. His eyes grew large, and he screamed silently. Then he relaxed. Lizbeth was nearly certain she saw a small smile curl up on his face. She said to Angie, "What's with the little guy? Looks like he went to one of your theater classes. Overacting 101."

"Hey," Angie said, "I think he's cute. Besides, you're distracting me. This thing he's describing gives me the chills. Literally. Look at my skin."

"Yeah, you're right." Then Lizbeth wondered why, this time, she could see Angie.

"Double the size of a panther." Piers held his hand at chest height. "He sunk his extraordinary claws into the rock like steely talons. No wind or rain could move him. His enormous neck, its tendons and veins taut and visible, held aloft his even more mammoth and relentlessly furious head. Angrily, the beast thrust his snarling muzzle side to side, as if trying to rid himself of his own face. I did not know what that could mean, yet the face seemed to want to twist back on its own muzzle, to gouge its own eyes. When it couldn't, the beast leaped off the rock and punished everything in his path, his muscles rippling with thunder across the sky of his whole body. Then we were certain. Then we knew this awful thing must be Morphane. And we knew we must get back to warn all of you."

Looking exhausted, Piers stumbled, his long green tunic swaying behind him. Though much shorter, Terz steadied him and helped him sit on a stool nearby. Piers panted heavily, while Lizbeth realized she had been holding her breath.

Suddenly, Mook whisper-shouted, "Quiet! Listen to the outside."

At first, only the rain could be heard above the flickering of the lanterns and the fire in the pit.

A false alarm? thought Lizbeth. No.

Faintly, then more certainly, all could hear slinking and moaning, scraping and crashing. Something was looking for a way in, something, if Piers was to be believed, searching to devour.

Her nerves on edge, Lizbeth opened her eyes wide enough to take in the whole world. Instead she saw the shuffling drones of Morphane approach the mouth of Chimney Cave, and she heard, from somewhere behind them, the Great Beast himself roaring his disembodied groan. He growled louder and then louder, menacingly, ceaselessly, a howl that shook her soul bare.

She would have gasped had she found the air. She would have run had she a place to go. She did what she could. She screamed. She looked around and saw the Welkeners grabbing their things and backing up toward the fire. She screamed again, and then she felt Angie's hand on hers. Angie screamed too.

"Look!" Lizbeth yelled. "They're coming!"

The drones came closer, grunting out their own terrible sounds. They entered the cave, first one, then three, then a dozen crowding against each other. Without haste, they scraped the walls of the cave. They sniffed after a scent. They filled the entryway. Then Morphane roared again, and at the end of it his deep catlike hiss caught Lizbeth's strength and wrung it limp.

Bennu's shrieks joined the others, and he fumbled while grabbing Len's shoulders. "Lizbeth! Get Len's feet!"

The dissonant voices and dismembered bodies writhed closer and closer, moaning themselves into the cave. Quickly, Welkeners snuffed sconces, grabbed lanterns, and put themselves between the Misfits and the enemy.

Lizbeth's heart pounded dramatically. She knew Bennu had said something, but it was drowned out by the moaning and the roaring and her own heart knocking down her rib cage. She looked back at Bennu. He pointed and yelled again. Who could tell what he said? She picked up a stool, in one jerk snapped off a leg, and backed up toward the fire.

She guessed this was it. This was her end, in some stupid cave, at the hands or mouths of sickening monsters, for no good reason. She swung the stool leg at no one, warming up, she thought, gathering her courage.

"I will not go down easily," she whispered aloud.

Then she noticed that the Welkeners in front of her were thinning. She looked to her right. To her surprise, each person, with brave patience, stepped into the fire, slipping between the blaze and the back wall of the pit. With steely discipline, Sutton Hoo and Terz led the Welkeners into the fiery furnace. Sweat poured off each firewalker. A few yelped when they touched the hot wall.

If only they could *run* through it, thought Lizbeth. But she could see that the space between the wall and the fire was too small, and the sloping ceiling of the pit too low to permit that luxury. Then Lizbeth worried more. Surely Morphane is to be feared if walking into a fire is a better than meeting him.

One by one, they stepped on embers behind the fire, until they reached the center, and then—as Lizbeth strained her eyes after them—disappeared.

The siren called Morphane screeched nearer. Lizbeth turned back to see his obedient drones sweep into the room as if pushed by a wind behind them. The siren came closer, reverberating louder and louder in the confines of the cavern. Lizbeth thought she might burst at the sound. She swung her weapon in the air, and it splintered against the wall. Howling, Morphane warned of his deeds. The thunderous noise said, "I'm coming. I am coming for you!"

Lizbeth turned to the fire pit. She saw Mook and Prester John carrying Len. Where were all the others? She turned around. Only Alabaster Singing was left! How did she end up at the end? Impatiently, Lizbeth waited for Mook to get moving though the pit. She pushed Mook from behind and felt the searing heat to her left.

As soon as she stepped in, she thought her toes would explode. The metal clasps on her overalls instantly baked into her skin. She wanted more air and gasped for it. She held up her mouth and tried to suck oxygen in, and she felt faint. She thought her face would turn to paper. Any second it would burst into flames. Which way was she supposed to go? Had she turned around? It was so hot. Blazing hot. Too hot to think. Too hot to keep going.

Then, as she began to slip away, someone's hand pushed her head down, and she half fell, half crawled into a passageway behind the Chimney Cave embers. She tumbled on to the mercifully cooler floor. Exhausted, she waited for strength to return. As she panted heavily, she watched Alabaster Singing stoop into the tunnel and turn back to face the fire. Lizbeth could not believe what she saw. Why would Alabaster do this?

Unable to endure not knowing, Lizbeth crawled on hands and knees back to her. She saw Alabaster, without expression, grab a stick, lean in, and rake a burning log toward the hole. Lizbeth thought that was it. Surely, Alabaster completed her task and would leave. Lizbeth turned to go toward the lantern that the others had left for them, but against all reason, Alabaster Singing lingered by the stone barrier. She motioned for Lizbeth to go ahead. Lizbeth did not, could not. She tried to step on her fear as she crawled back up to Alabaster's side.

From there they watched.

Then Lizbeth saw him. Through the fire, she saw Morphane leap into the cave. Morphane—he was even more frightening to see than to hear. When he dug his claws into the cavern floor, crushed rock chipped up and out. Wasting no time, he brushed aside his troops and forced his way to the front. The size of two tigers, he pounced dramatically for the kill, but landed only on Len's makeshift stretcher, scattering the pieces. Lizbeth thought she'd never seen anything so set on destroying, so bent on deep evil. Somehow, she thought, anger possessed this beast; it heaped itself high on Morphane's plate. And he ate.

The horde searched in their own way too, tasting the walls, sniffing the stretcher, poking their fingers in the hot wax in the sconces. Morphane, his face, that face! A roiling agony, a torturous motion of pain and disappointment. He paced the floor of the cave, pounded the ground with his paws. He raced back and forth, climbing partway up the walls with each pass.

He must be deciding what to do, thought Lizbeth.

Enraged, he approached the fire. Lizbeth knew that the most recent scent was there—at the back wall of the cave—and it led into the blaze. Morphane put his paws on the edge of the fire pit. Lizbeth could not believe Alabaster just kept watching, stoically, silently.

She must know, Lizbeth thought, she must know that we're safe.

Morphane drew back. The path must have been too narrow, or perhaps the fire had grown larger. He ran around it briefly and roared at the beast nearest to him. The dazed woman, rocks crumbling down from where her right shoulder should have been, somehow knew what he ordered her to do. In a pitiful, nearly human way, she pleaded with him not to make her do it, her mouth emitting a low choking sound. Swiftly, Morphane clamped his jaws around her good arm and thrust her toward the back of the fire, where the Misfits and Welkeners had just escaped.

Lizbeth figured Morphane must have wanted her to pave the way toward them, but she was too slow, too clumsy to maneuver past the flames and over to the opening into the tunnel. She stumbled, her cloak caught fire, and she jumped out screaming. But she could not elude Morphane. He leaped, fully piercing her forearm this time, and flung her again at the back of the fire. Crying out, she lurched into a small part of the pit not aflame. She tried to get to the back, where Morphane wanted her. The heat and her bleeding arm undid her. She looked at Morphane's hideous face and back to the fire. While Lizbeth and Alabaster watched helplessly, the creature awkwardly shuffled in their direction. Tripping on a burning ember, she fell right in front of them. Lizbeth fell backwards.

Then Alabaster motioned for Lizbeth to help her. They scrambled to the right side of the opening and, with all their strength, pushed on a circular boulder, rolling it back over the opening. When they sat and rested for a minute, Alabaster Singing whistled the despairing moan of the loon. And Lizbeth wept, for she knew that sealing off the passageway on the other side was the funeral pyre of a suffering being.

For what seemed like a day but was only an hour, Lizbeth and the other thirteen refugees shuffled along in the tunnel. As Lizbeth crawled in front of Alabaster, she could see by the light of the lantern Alabaster held—but her own shadow blocked her view, so she often hit her knee on a rock. Despite these frequent sharp pains, she scrambled ahead to catch up to Len. Once, when she had gained ground on Alabaster and the passage curved sharply, she found herself in near total darkness, moving tenuously in faith through the granite tube.

Before long, a light ahead helped Lizbeth see Mook, hunched over, half carrying, half dragging Len. He had difficulty maneuvering Len through the passageway, and someone moved to help. As she got closer, she realized that, for some reason, they were all keeping quiet, maybe to remain undetected by whatever enemies might be nearby. Lizbeth did not know why. But she soon discovered that the "paramedic" on the other side of Len was the tongue-twaddling Prester John.

"Oof. Upsidaisy. Uhh. For such a short fellow, he's unmercifully heavy. This reminds me of a rescue we once made in the Great Alpine Reef. So many had given up, but those with true courage—"

Ellen could be heard from in front of him. "Prester John, shh."

"I was only going to tell Mook of the lives we saved. Ouch, this is hard on my knees. One needs hope to provide light in the darkness, and—"

Ellen came on stronger. "With all proper honor due your name, I don't truly think that—"

Hush, good friends, hush.

"Was that you, Mook?" asked Prester John.

"No," said Mook, "but I heard the words 'hush, good friends, hush' spoken not so much to ear as to heart."

Follow your silence as you wind your way onward.

Lizbeth jumped at the sound of these words and hit her head on the tunnel wall. While she rubbed the bump, she looked ahead and could see a few more of the others resting in a wider section of the tunnel. Alabaster came up from behind.

Prester John said, "The voice belongs to Piers. We should all be absolutely quiet."

Then Lizbeth heard Len's disobedience. "Ooh," he moaned. "Uhhhnn," he moaned louder.

"You must be trying your best," said Zennor Pict to Prester John, "but perhaps I can assist your valiant efforts?" He shuffled back to relieve the Highlander.

Terz coughed in the tunnel dust. "Maybe it's good that he's moaning. It could snap him awake. We must be far enough from Morphane not to need to worry about noise so much." Terz edged past Zennor and touched Len's forehead. Lizbeth tried to get past Mook.

THE WELKENING: A THREE-DIMENSIONAL TALE

Then Len let out with a yell. "Hey, get your hands off me! Where am I?"

In response to Len's sudden improvement, Terz removed his hand. Len sat partway up and rubbed his eyes.

Mook said, "Watch it. He's going to conk his head again." He reached over Len and put his hands on Len's head.

Len slapped away Mook's hands. "Get your hands offa me. I don't care how big you McKenzie Boys are!" Then he attempted to stand and banged his head against the ceiling. When he collapsed onto the tunnel floor, Lizbeth came to his side. Looking up, she saw Angie across from her. At least she thought she did. To say that Angie was a wisp of a girl was not a metaphor. Lizbeth didn't know which worried her more, Len or Angie. She wished Bennu had also come back from the front of the line.

Besides Len's outburst, nothing but crawling and sweating and scrunching occurred until they hit a dead end. From the back, Lizbeth couldn't tell what was going on. She heard Sutton Hoo say that the door would not budge. Some rustling noises came next, after which several voices said at once, "Oh, it opens *toward* us!"

Piers asked that all lanterns be extinguished. In the few black and silent moments that followed, Lizbeth's mind jumped to memories of frightening darkness: the time when no one discovered her in hide-and-seek and the sun set and she didn't know what to do, the time when the power went out on a moonless night and she stood frozen in the street waiting for a car to come by so she could move safely, the time when—

"Halt! Who goes there?"

Sutton Hoo answered. "A dozen or so fierce warriors! Why do you ask?"

"I dunno," the voice replied in a loopy way. "I've just always wanted to say that." Then the voice laughed—but Lizbeth thought it was really more of a honk.

"Good, then." Sutton responded in a more relaxed tone. "Maybe you'll help us."

The gruffness returned. "Maybe we will. Maybe we won't. What's in it for us?"

Sutton sounded hurt. "Seems to me you had invited kindness—"

76

"Of course we did," the loopy voice said happily. "Fooled ya. Fooled ya. Honk!"

Thoroughly confused, Lizbeth wondered what would happen next. Then she felt a hand on hers ("It's me," whispered Angie), and everyone shuffled forward out of the tunnel. Every moment or two, a small yellow light flickered from the direction of the voices. Lizbeth could tell they were in a large room of some kind. Some natural light entered the space from high above them.

Sutton turned to Vida. "You give it a try."

"Oh, dear me," she whispered. "We of the various clans of Welken bring you stalagmited greetings, that is—"

"Shut up, knave! Do you take me for a sniveling aristocrat?"

"Well, no, actually I was just thinkifying that—"

"Think? Don't think; it'll make you stink! Don't you think so, Gandric?"

"Honk! Thinking's only good for catching the joke."

Then a new voice in Gandric's group shouted, "A more degenerate response could not have been issued, you pathetic excuse for a leader!"

"Oh, the insults I endure!" said Gandric. "As the chief guardian, I say, go, wretch, nevermore to burn our ears with your flaming tongue."

"Of all the low-down, small-minded, shrimpy things to say," the chastised one said. "That was only about five inches high! Honk."

Lizbeth ambled over to Bennu. "Weird, huh?" she whispered. "I don't usually want to laugh when I'm being threatened—except, of course, when you come after me."

"Shut up!" Bennu yelled.

Suddenly, things got quiet. Lizbeth grabbed Bennu by the elbow and tried to pull him more into the crowd.

A variety of voices broke the silence.

"Shut up? Who said this? He will never speak again!"

"Shut up? What about shut down? Nothing feels ever so good on my day off."

The rise and fall of her worries made Lizbeth dizzy.

Piers walked to the front. "Perhaps you know of the tragedies above ground. Perhaps you have an inkling that we come in the name of Soliton, that we are in Welken and of Welken. Perhaps somehow you can find it in your hearts to trust us. We come to learn of Morphane so that we might destroy him."

From the hidden creatures, the epithets for Morphane flowed freely. "Vomit. Blackened bile. Cursed one. He who smothers. Killer. Crusher of life."

Lizbeth's dizziness turned to a sick feeling.

Piers tried again. "Tell me then, what makes you so carefree and joyous?"

"Mint. Mint leaves and strawberry sauce. Honk. With just a pinch of rum. Honk! Actually, in all delightful seriousness, we are the guardians of the door. At least we were until Dr. Gangees gave the key away while laughing at his own joke. Honk!"

Lizbeth felt so relieved she hugged Bennu, and then felt silly for doing so.

"Shame!" Chief Guardian Gandric shouted. "Gangees violated his sacred vow. His darkened heart listened to some simpering argument from the enemy, falling for deceit after deceit. Oh, we heard about it afterwards, all the so-called reasons: 'We've guarded so long, no one remembers what for.' 'What difference could it possibly make?' 'The old ways just don't matter anymore.' To be sure, this Gangees has suffered since his pitiful mistake."

The guardians lit lamps.

"They must be beginning to trust us," said Bennu to Lizbeth, stepping back to get an appropriate distance from his sister.

Gandric bowed. "Welcome to Ganderst Hall."

Lizbeth walked over to the side so she could see the guardians' uniforms, floor-length black vestments with gold bars on the shoulders and a band of red down the front. The guardians' pale bald heads contrasted strongly with the black gowns and with their curiously orange lips.

I'm freaking out, she thought. There's too much Emerald City going on here. These guys are like that dope at the door to the Wizard of Oz.

She looked around at the vast cavern. Ganderst Hall was elaborately furnished with elegant tapestries and dramatic paintings each twenty feet high, all so at odds with the guardians' goofiness. As Bennu knelt beside Len, he motioned to Lizbeth to go ahead. She saw Angie flicker into her solid self, and then Lizbeth followed the others into the hall. She was amazed. Every chair resembled a throne, with curved legs and gilded feet, as if prepared for the noblest princes in the realm. Each table was a masterpiece of design and craftsmanship, boasting intricate parquets or painted historical scenes. Delicate goblets awaited fine wine. Most impressive of all, Ganderst Hall drew her eyes to four sculpted marble doors, each in the center of the four main walls of the room.

Weird, thought Lizbeth, they called themselves the guardians of the door, not doors.

As if she were reading Lizbeth's mind, Angie asked Gandric, "If you are guardians, what do you guard?"

"Which door did we used to guard, you mean; we, the betrayers, the fallen ones?" answered Gandric, his alternations becoming subtler. "Our instructions were clear:

> DENY THE EAST DOOR,
> WHISPERING THE PEACE AND KEEP
>
> OPEN THE WEST DOOR,
> ASCENDING THE POWER SO THAT YOU
>
> RELEASE THE NORTH DOOR,
> BURNING BRIGHT FOR JUSTICE AND,
>
> PRESERVE THE SOUTH DOOR,
> FLOWING INTO TRUTH AND GRACE.

"The shameful truth is this: After centuries of faithfulness, we began to doubt our calling. We could not believe that Welken's peace depended on our choices. Gradually, the weight of our burden grew lighter and lighter until we finally threw it off. Now the load crushes us like an avalanche without end."

Piers nodded sympathetically. "I'm curious. How could Welken's peace depend on a closed door?"

"Too simple, perhaps, to hold a world's complexity!" Gandric stopped speaking in his farcical voice. "Yet we had been gifted for this task. And we failed. We did not protect the Tetragrammaton behind the east Door. Its tiles are defiled. Come, I'll show you. With nothing to protect, the Door need not be closed anymore."

As he walked over to the east door, Lizbeth cut in line near the front. Gandric's shoulders hung low, but he led the group to the eight-foot high stone door and pushed with one finger. The enormous marble plank, embellished with chiseled grapes and vines, moved easily at his touch. Behind this door stood another door artistically made with wrought-iron bars. Once Gandric pushed open the second door, Lizbeth half-expected to see a vast cavern filled with a mountain of gold. She was disappointed. The room was unfurnished, and only large enough to comfortably hold seven of them, Piers and Gandric, and the five closest by: Lizbeth, Jacob Canny Sea, Terz, Zennor, and Bennu.

Lizbeth waited for Bennu and then examined the four walls. Painted floor to ceiling with landscape murals, the walls appeared to tell a story of some key event that took place years ago. Sutton said he thought he recognized one of the scenes, but Gandric ignored his comments. He was more interested in the wall opposite the door. There, he pointed to a broken frame shaped like a shield. It looked like a medieval crest, divided into quarters, upheld by strange creatures. Perhaps, thought Lizbeth, these were Welken's versions of griffins. The violated shield contained empty quadrants, four holes that sunk deep into the wall. At the center, an oval touched all four quadrants.

Gandric pointed to the spaces in the shield. "The Tetragrammaton. Our duty to safeguard. Four tiles possessing four symbols, a language both mysterious and purposeful. It belonged here but now is gone, recently stolen in fact, and the center ring, a golden beetle—a scarab amulet—has been missing for longer than the tiles."

Lizbeth elbowed Bennu when she heard this reference. He elbowed back. Then she saw Terz run his finger along the borders of each quadrant. He seemed quite taken with it, as if he'd never seen it before.

Gandric paced in a professorial manner to the opposite side of the room, framing himself in the open door. "To you this may seem like mere stolen treasure. But we had been told that the very foundations of Welken's good life danced joyfully in the security of those tiles. Over the years we stopped believing, or maybe we just forgot. In fact, we can no longer fully interpret these murals or read all the words in the ancient languages. In our prosperity we neglected to maintain vigilance; we stopped learning, stopped guarding, stopped training.

"And you don't know the worst of it. I must tell you—though confession can crush the confessor—we are the ones responsible for Morphane. We allowed the powers to be loosed. We denied our birthright on a whim, for our leisure, so we could play games. Out of the power fired into these tiles, Morphane was created. We know about his destructive acts, his ruthlessness." Gandric sighed. As he gestured over to the shield, Terz moved away from it. "We took the Tetragrammaton for granted. Now all is askew. We cannot speak or think right. But worst of all, a devouring evil roams freely, sucking up life and spitting out the remains."

"So." Piers's eyes reflected the sorrow of Gandric's story. "So what can be done now?"

Gandric took his hands out of his vestment pockets and pleaded with them. "The only thing we know for certain is that the tiles must be returned. The Book of Quadrille is clear about that much. If you care about Welken, if you want to defeat Morphane, you must help us get the tiles. We should know more than this, but we have ignored our calling. We have treated it even more lightly than our games. What are we to do now? We are not soldiers. We are inept guardians, incompetent scholars. Before long, Morphane will come here and consume us. He has an unyielding hunger. He has already destroyed three guardians. So we do what we do well. We lose ourselves in absurdities. We play riddles, make puns, and distract each other with mind games. We have become the guardians of play."

"Fiddle with riddles!" came an affirmation from the doorway. "Fun with puns! Honk! Honk!"

"Maybe, Gandric, one of us can glean something from these walls," said Piers.

"Yes, perhaps you could learn something about what to do next. But don't miss what we already know. We must find the tiles and return them to their homes in the Tetragrammaton."

"I believe, Gandric, that all of us here could be committed to that task."

Lizbeth whispered to Bennu, "What's he talking about? If I'm not in a dream, I just want to go home."

Piers continued. "I've heard a few things about the Tetragrammaton in my studies and in my travels. I know the tiles are important. But let's see what we can learn from the walls for now. Each one try."

Almost immediately Bennu had a contribution. "It is interesting how similar these figures are to hieroglyphics. I feel sure that if we brought back a translation guide, I could make some sense of it, like a Rosetta Stone for Welken. Being Egyptian has to count for something."

"C'mon, Bennu, get serious," said Lizbeth. "This isn't even our world, let alone our century! We just need to figure out how to go home."

"Fine. But while you're looking for ruby slippers, I want to study this awhile."

Lizbeth wondered how Bennu knew that she had been thinking about the Wizard of Oz. She was about to pout her way out of the room when she saw Angie step in. As Bennu and Gandric consulted, Angie fell into an altered state, holding her hands above her head, flat against the wall. She pressed her face against the paintings, moving over to touch the Tetragrammaton as if it could say something to her.

Bennu got close to Gandric and out of Angie's earshot. "Don't mind her. She slips into these trances every once in a while. She's worth watching—and eventually she'll snap out of it. But listen. I have a few hunches about these walls. If you could tell me more about the tiles and the amulet—that beetle thing—I might be able to help."

Lizbeth stepped closer to them.

"We don't know much about the scarab amulet. It's been missing for years. Some say the guardians began their descent when the golden beetle was taken. It had various inscriptions on it, but the languages were old and long dead. The scarab fit here, over the tiles, locking them in. I always thought the amulet could not be removed except by someone who could read the language."

"And the tiles, what was on them?"

"Simple paintings, really. You can see their silhouettes etched into the stone behind the place for each tile, four different mythological creatures: an ox, a falcon, a lion, and an angel."

"Mythological? What do you mean by that?"

"These beasts aren't real. They come from our folk stories."

"No kidding. Where we come from, all four are real. Well, not exactly. Some people don't think angels really exist."

"What are these creatures like?" Gandric demonstrated as much interest as he'd shown all day.

Bennu started out like he was reading a textbook. "Well, an ox is a stocky, powerful beast of burden, used for plowing fields in the old days. It's often seen with a yoke, a harness, around its neck. Sometimes our very own Lizbeth here gets accused of looking a bit like one." He smiled at Lizbeth, but she put her hands on her hips to let him know she wasn't amused. Bennu continued, "And the falcon: It's a bird of prey, swift, daring, with a great hooked beak and tremendous vision."

"Like Bennu," said Lizbeth, "only his nose is bigger and his bite is sharper."

"This is serious, Lizbeth, really." Bennu lost his look of disdain and went on. "Then there's the lion, the king of beasts, majestic, courageous, fierce, with a flowing mane like Len's mop of hair, and huge paws."

"Bennu, stop it," said Lizbeth.

"Why? What's the matter? Gandric needs this information."

"Don't you see what you're doing? You're comparing each of us to these animals. It's insulting. I suppose you think Angie is like an angel?"

"Actually, I was just . . . going to . . . say . . ."

He acted stunned, like he just realized the gravity of his own words. Lizbeth blushed as the revelation shot through her. She looked at Bennu and then over to Angie's ethereal, hypnotic gestures.

Angie turned her profile to them and froze, as if posing. She faded slightly then became opaque and faded again. "We are messengers. We are messengers without a message. We are gift-bearers without gifts. We are tile makers without—"

Then a mountainous roar tore into Angie's dream. Lizbeth shuddered. She pictured Morphane's teeth, his rampage through Chimney Cave, and his cold-blooded piercing of the human-thing that burned at the base of the fire pit.

CHAPTER TEN
JELLYFISH AND WATER-FUNNELS

Let him wander securely without fear.

CHRETIEN DES TROYES, *PERCEVAL*

 "Quick!" shouted Gandric, "we must go out a different way. If we don't take one of the four main doors, maybe it will throw him off. I know of another passage, past our living quarters." Moving more swiftly than his gown suggested he could, Gandric raced past the painted walls, out the East Door, past the South Door to their left and then down the next opening, a plain stone corridor dimly lit. He and a few others grabbed lanterns as they scurried out of Ganderst Hall.

As she ran out of the room with the Tetragrammaton, Lizbeth made sure Len got snatched up by Zennor, and then she saw one more example of guardian loopiness that added sadness to her fear. In the hall, the remaining guardians split into two groups. Those in their fierce alternation gathered weapons for serious battle. The others laughed and joked, fiddling with riddles while their Rome was about to burn.

Though the stone corridor drew the runners straight on, Gandric opened the second door on the right and continued through a series of serpentine choices: the first door on the left in the first room, the third door on the right of the second room, and so on. With every twist and turn, Lizbeth grew in confidence that Morphane or his army would not be able to follow, and grew in anxiety that their journey back home would be impossible to retrace. At some point, she thought, Mom and Dad would start missing them. She wondered if they were already out searching. Len bounced along obliviously.

Finally, Gandric paused to rest in a large banquet room. As Zennor laid Len on an oak table, he stretched his sore neck, and Sutton volunteered to take up the Len-baton for the next lap. Some of the fugitives panted with hands resting on knees. Others strained their ears toward the silence behind them.

"I'm uneasy," said Ellen Basala.

Vida Bering Well plopped her round body into a wide dinner chair. "I know what you flutterate. The panic is deep and flashfloodified."

Lizbeth tried to calm herself by looking at the carved quotations on the walls. She listened to Angie tell Alabaster, "I sense that so much of what needs to be known is housed in these forgotten words. Such a pity."

Jacob Canny Sea dabbed sweat off his forehead. "Aye, maybe we could appointify a search party to repossess the lostlings. Woe to those who bo-peeped the sheepy speech!"

Lizbeth chuckled at Jacob's reference. "Now, Jacob Canny Sea, where did you hear about Bo-peep? She's in one of *our* nursery rhymes."

"Bo-peep? A she? Never heard o' that even a once-let. In Deedish, 'bo-peep' is just a verbasaurus, primitive and old, a right toothy word for 'lostify.'"

"Well," said Lizbeth, "I just hope we all get home."

"Yeah," added Angie, "even if we are wagging our tails behind us."

Nearby, next to a hutch filled with plates on display, Gandric, Piers, and Terz spoke of strategies and options. Solemnly, they reviewed the barriers before them: a maze of tunnels, little food or drinking water, the injured Len, a herd's worth of tracks and scents for Morphane to follow, and most of all, Morphane the hunter himself. Lizbeth tried to think of some positive spin to put on things. She couldn't.

"What about making a stand here?" suggested Terz. "There are fourteen of us, not counting Len. We have a lot going for us. I'm sure Gandric the guardian can scrounge up weapons."

"No!" Gandric pointed dramatically at Terz, almost hitting him in the nose. "You don't understand. You don't fight Morphane. You don't resist him. You don't make plans and dig trenches and wait. You can only run. I know it sounds cowardly, but we must gain some time, to recover something from the meanings of the Old Ones. And, yes—you don't need to remind me—I know I bear the most responsibility for these losses. I come from a long line of forgetters. I'm lecturing now. Sorry. I just wish you would stop looking at me as if I could help. You see a failure, one who has betrayed his calling. I am to blame."

"Oh, Angie," said Lizbeth, "I wish I could help him feel better."

Piers calmly put a hand on the guardian's shoulder. "Gandric, the blame—"

"Stop!" Gandric clenched his fists as if he were holding his guilt and felt its weight. He appeared unwilling to let consoling words steal that duty from him. "I must answer for my choices. But, even so, we must keep moving."

"As you wish. We follow your lead." Piers bowed submissively. "I know that the—"

"Gandric," Lizbeth called out, hoping to distract him from his tortured confession. "Can you translate any of this on the wall? Something feels important here, especially this one."

Impatiently, Gandric strode to the wall and gazed blankly at the phrase. "Iron . . . nothing, nothing . . . friends . . . nothing . . . look, it's useless."

Just then a dreaded shuffle sounded from the other side of the door behind them. For a time, Lizbeth's breath stopped and she froze.

Then Mook leaped up and quickly blocked the door, stacking obstacles handed him by Prester John and Ellen. "Hurry now," he whispered. "Chairs and tables. Anything."

Lizbeth and Bennu looked around for weapons.

"Everyone!" shouted Gandric. "This way!"

After his swift hands moved a hidden panel in the wall, they filed out nervously, most struggling through the small opening.

As shrieks and pounding continued at the door, Lizbeth imagined the teeth she'd seen before. And ghoulish faces. And torn flesh. And feet that rushed to destruction.

Finally, they were out—and Gandric secured the panel from outside the room. Lantern in hand, he turned to face his guests. Lizbeth thought he looked like a field marshal in a movie, right in the moment when he knew he was out-manned, under-supplied, and moving closer to a disastrous battle.

"Only one torch, now," he ordered. "We can't give them any assistance."

The sound of demolition behind them punished Lizbeth's ears.

Into a labyrinthine madness again, thought Lizbeth, where all paths were sure to lead down, down, deeper into the mountain, farther from the surface. Gandric charged forward with his light, stooping slightly, walking fast but no faster than Sutton could carry Len. The necessary lagging troubled Lizbeth, but she knew they had no choice.

On they went: first Gandric, then Piers, Terz, Bennu, Lizbeth, Vida Bering Well, Jacob Canny Sea, Angie, Sutton carrying Len, Alabaster, Prester John, Ellen, Mook, and Zennor. As Gandric turned a corner, so did his torch, leaving the escapees in the dark. Lizbeth grabbed Bennu and felt for the ceiling with the other hand. Along the straightaways, the light returned. Soon, her back ached from leaning over. She thought about the taller Welkeners, Prester John, Sutton Hoo, and Zennor Pict, and how they must be suffering. Behind her, squatty Vida Bering Well stood erect. At various junctions, Gandric and Piers consulted quietly, Terz listened intently, and then all stepped out in the chosen direction.

To Lizbeth, one path looked just like the next. If Gandric didn't know where he was going, she thought, they would surely be lost. The air, cold and still, left a sweet dampness everywhere. In the quiet, Morphane seemed far behind, yet Lizbeth wondered how and why the Misfits were shuffling through a dank cave, trusting their lives to odd strangers, compelled to flee the wrath of a pursuing enemy. She listened to Bennu ahead of her.

"What's going to happen to us, Terz?" Bennu asked.

Terz seemed cheerful. "Oh, we'll get out all right. Just look on the bright side of things. Silver lining and all that, don't y'know. This is Piers of Primus Hook who's leading us. There's no one more likely to come through without a scratch. Puts a smile on my face in the roughest of tumbles, it does."

"Oh, c'mon. I've got plenty of scratches already. And what about Len?" Bennu poked Terz in the back gently. "What's the point of smiling? I mean, where is the sunny side of life down here in this hole?"

"Say what you will. I prefer to tell you myself how strong I really am. Look at Piers. Do you see him moping around?"

Actually, thought Lizbeth, Piers doesn't seem as jovial as all that. Piers acts like he carries a burden, that inside of him there's some pain that needs to be healed.

Gandric and Piers must have gained some ground and turned a corner because their place in the tunnel once again became dark. In this blackness, Lizbeth reached ahead. Bennu wasn't there. She skipped a step, grabbed and found nothing, then jogged a bit and swiped some more at the darkness in front of her. Still nothing.

"Bennu!" she said.

From behind, Vida shouted back, "What's all the shutters-to-the-wind a'flappin'?"

"Vida, at least you're there. Bennu suddenly vanished, and he won't respond when I call him."

"We'll columbus him soon enough. Everyone, stop spelunkeratin' and put a listen for the Bennu lostling."

In the dark, Lizbeth's hand found Vida's head. She said, "Sorry," and then fell silent.

After a few moments, Bennu called out from off to the side, "No! Don't do it! No, no!"

About this time, Piers and Gandric returned with the lantern.

"What's the matter?" asked Gandric.

Bennu, who'd had his back to the others, turned around slowly. "I must have been dreaming or something." Lizbeth ran over to him.

"No more dreaming," said Gandric. "Let's go."

"I'm OK," Bennu said. "I don't know what came over me. We can go. Thanks, Lizbeth."

Once the line started moving again, Lizbeth asked, "What was that all about?"

"It was so real, Lizbeth, so real. One minute I was listening to Terz, and the next minute I saw Bob Bennett, you know, the game show host of *Your Stuff/Your Fortune*. He smiled and I heard applause. I saw contestants trade stupid junk from their own garages for whatever was behind these bright orange doors. That beautiful ditz, what's her name? Oh yeah, Samantha Kitten, she pointed toward a door. She acted like she wanted to seduce the contestants."

"Do I really want to know all this?"

"Hey, why not. If nothing else, it will help pass the time. So then, Bob Bennett speaks in that I-love-my-melodious-voice voice, and he says, 'What will you give me for a chance at the grand prize door, Ned and Julia Prosser?' Weird, I remember their names. Do we know any Prossers?"

"Not that I know of. Go on."

"So Julia turns to Ned and says, 'OK, honey, here's our big chance. Let's trade what we've won so far, the lifetime supply of packaged lunch-meats and a hundred lotto tickets that might have paid for our daughter's college tuition.' Then Bob says, 'Sounds like a deal made in heaven, Julia. We'll now give you a choice of four doors!' Then, well, I'm embarrassed to say this—but remember, I'm just reporting the dream—Samantha twirled from door to door, and her face changed to Angie's. This Angie-Samantha stopped at door number four and smiled. Then, she motioned for the Prossers to choose this door."

"You're kidding."

"No, she even blew them a kiss. Man, what I wouldn't give for—"

"Bennu!"

"OK. Anyway, Ned and Julia talk it over. Julia says, 'I think she's pulling our leg, Ned.' And Ned says, 'You're right, Julia. It's got to be a setup.' Then Bob says, 'Time's up, contestants. What'll it be?' Ned says, 'Bob, we'll take door number two!'"

"What happened?"

"Bob celebrates like they'd just found a cure for AIDS and says, 'Door number two it is! You won't miss those lotto tickets when you see what's waiting for you!' Then the Angie-Samantha goes to the door, and Bob says, 'Samantha, open that door and show the Prossers their prize! Yes, Ned and Julia, take a look at your very own—'"

Bennu froze and Lizbeth bumped into him.

"Very own what? Bennu, c'mon."

"Angie opens the door a crack, and Bob says, 'Your very own Morphane!' Then this huge animal plows into the room roaring. He pounces on the Prossers. The last thing I see is Bob, a close-up of his face—and he's smiling."

"Bennu, that's bizarre."

"I know." Bennu swallowed hard enough for Lizbeth to hear it.

"Are you OK?" asked Vida Bering Well from behind. "You sound ghostified and all wobblerated."

Lizbeth saw that Terz had also been listening.

"It was just a daydream," said Bennu. "Yeah, yeah, I'll be fine."

"Ol' Terz will keep a little closer too." The little man tapped Bennu with his unlit pipe. "Maybe I can keep your mind on more victorious images. Remember: Attitude gives you latitude."

"I suppose." Bennu turned to walk. "Really, let's go on."

As Lizbeth tried to come up with a theory to explain Bennu's behavior, the line came to a halt. She looked ahead and saw Piers and Gandric conferring at a crossroads. They waved the line up, chose the left fork, and moved swiftly into a straight corridor that had no observable ceiling.

Before Lizbeth followed the leaders, Sutton Hoo came up with Len draped over his shoulder. "Your friend has been making more sounds. I fear I have not been gentle enough."

Lizbeth offered a consoling pat on Sutton's massive forearm. "You are being an awesome help. Maybe Len's just beginning to wake up."

The new passage narrowed, but the opening above them allowed all, even Prester John, to stretch to full height and enjoy total range of motion. He called out to the whole line, "By the Great Anuba, it feels good to stretch! I would never have mentioned the sacrifice my long, regal body was enduring, but now that I can stand, I will announce my rejoicing."

Try as she might to stay focused on getting home, Lizbeth smiled at these remarks.

"Aye," shouted Sutton back to Prester John, "my hope's reborn now that I can stand full in my right Durrow height." Len moaned, which prompted Sutton's profuse apologies.

Then Gandric lifted the lantern high over his head. Lizbeth soon discovered what he was trying to see. The delicious emptiness above them began to be filled in, at least part of it did. Wispy, stringlike vines or roots appeared, and the deeper the group walked into the tunnel, the closer and closer the vines descended. Though the vines were still a ways from Lizbeth's head, she turned back to see how close they were to Prester John's. About then, they interfered with his progress, so he brushed them back, instantly letting out a yelp.

"Ouch. What's going on here? What are these things?" He touched another one on purpose. "Ow. Be careful, everyone, these vines bite. As you might expect, I'll do my best to protect all in my care. I've faced various stinging adversities in my time." He leaned forward and spoke more quietly to Alabaster.

Lizbeth thought he'd chosen his audience well, since she could not verbally refuse him. Before she could laugh at her own joke, she turned back around to the front just in time to dodge a vine that hung lower than most. Staring at the sea of stinging vines ahead of her, some longer and thicker than others, she thought they looked like jellyfish tentacles, and they felt like them too. Soon, she and most of the others reacted to the stings, wincing and stooping down to avoid their reach— but occasionally finding a longer stinger. The corridor continued to narrow as well. Just in front of her, Piers and Gandric became truly miserable. Gandric scooted along step by step, clearly struggling to hold the lantern up.

Then Lizbeth felt water.

A shallow stream replaced the path, and they splashed and ducked their way onward, uncertainly, into deeper water. Threatened from above and below, Lizbeth wondered what persecution would assail them next. Something's always there to make my life miserable, she thought.

Abruptly the line halted. Ahead of her, Gandric and Piers squatted beneath the tendrils but were up to their knees in water. Behind her, Sutton called out that he couldn't keep Len from the stingers. All complained save Alabaster, who bore her pain with the moan of the dove.

"Ouch!" Len pushed himself up on Sutton's shoulders. "Ow. Hey, what's going on? Ow. Is this a bee hive? Ow, ow."

Lizbeth turned around. "Len, we're in a tunnel. Stay as low as you can. The vines above you have stingers."

"Yeah, I figured that out." Len slipped off Sutton's shoulders and into the water. "Ow!" he exclaimed again, but Lizbeth knew it was because the water surprised him, not because it hurt. Though he clearly still believed he suffered at the hands of the McKenzie Boys, Len hung on to Sutton.

Lizbeth held out a hand. "Len, here, lean on me."

"Yow!" Gandric brushed a tentacle out of his face. "It got me over my eye. But that is only the beginning of the punishment I deserve." He hunched over and rubbed his eye.

"Gandric," Lizbeth said, "stop condemning yourself. You're only making things worse." Her boldness surprised her. She renewed her hold on Len.

"Who's Gandric?" asked Len.

"Shh."

Gandric, Piers, and Terz discussed the predicament. Just beyond them, Lizbeth could tell that the shrinking corridor sloped dramatically downward, and that the stream they were walking in appeared to swirl down into a funnel of rock. Above them the stinging jellyfish vines. Below was their freezing feet. Behind them Morphane in pursuit.

"Over here, Piers, look." Gandric pointed to the right. On the wall hung an iron ring, above which an inscription lay. Lizbeth could make no sense of it.

"I'm cold," said Len. "I can't stand up."

"I know," said Lizbeth. "I've got you. Don't worry."

"What does it say?" asked Piers.

"I wish I knew," answered Gandric. "I should know—"

"Remorse will do us little good right now, Gandric. We need what grace will supply, not grief. So. So. What can you tell us?" Piers asked.

Gandric stood as tall as the nettles permitted and stared at the centuries old engraving. "I can only guess at a few words. One of the words looks like 'down.' Not much help I'm afraid."

Terz rubbed his chin knowingly. "It could mean to keep the ring down—not to pull it—or the water would rise higher. What if the ring controls some gates?"

"Hey! What's sloshifying up there?" At her back, Lizbeth felt a shove. It was Jacob Canny Sea pushing impatiently, rudely. Lizbeth tried to pull Len out of the way. Jacob pressed a shoulder against her hip. "There's no point in waiting to get arked out of the floodering!"

Lizbeth did her best to become thin against the wall. Yeah, right, she thought. Then Len slipped, and when she grabbed him, she blocked Jacob's path.

Jacob barked, "Make way! Red Sea it! Let's go!" He got between Lizbeth and Len. "I can claustrophile it no longer!"

"What are you doing?" said Lizbeth. "Wait!"

Lizbeth felt Jacob strain against Len, and then she couldn't hold on. Len crashed into Gandric and Piers, who were still studying the sign and the ring. In the high water, in the tumbling and shouting, Piers instinctively grasped the wall for support, his fingers finding the iron ring instead—and he pulled on it hard.

A great screech added to the chaos. Piers lost his footing entirely, hung by the ring with one hand and trying to grab Len with the other. Then the whole floor utterly gave way, creating a water slide toward the funnel. Len and Gandric fell in. Lizbeth followed. Within seconds, all fifteen plunged into the gaping throat of rock and down the slide.

ᜡ

The fall was mercifully brief, washing them into each other, tumbling them over and over until they sprayed out here and there in the dark. The water, while gushing them into the room with power and fullness, vanished just as quickly, falling straight down through a hole in the floor.

THE WELKENING: A THREE-DIMENSIONAL TALE

Groans and moans could be heard above the sound of the rushing water. Lizbeth sat up and checked her sore spots, hoping not to find broken bones. While she whispered for her fellow Misfits, the Welkeners said how glad they were to be out of the stinging tentacles.

Lizbeth didn't exactly feel safe. The light had been doused, and they were certainly lost. And the Misfits were doubly lost. Exhausted, bewildered, in complete darkness, Lizbeth thought they were like shipwrecked fugitives resting on some shore, waiting for the next day's dawn.

CHAPTER ELEVEN
THE WINDOW UNDER THE MOUNTAIN

How can the great suck of self ever hope
to be a fat cat dozing in the sun?

WALKER PERCY, *THE SECOND COMING*

 Without the sun, the "next day" was difficult to discern. After some rest, they roused themselves into the black. Once everyone accounted for themselves, including Len, Lizbeth quietly stated the obvious. "Well, at least Morphane's troops can't follow us here."

Ellen boldly broke the norm of whispers. "And we know what the ring is for."

Lizbeth laughed hard at this joke—a nervous response that subsided quickly. She realized that though it temporarily saved them, the ring could not make them eternally secure. New worries followed old ones and kept them looking around for a messianic measure of resolution.

Most pressing, they needed to find the lantern. While the Welkeners searched blindly, Lizbeth called the other Misfits toward her and Len. "Bennu, Angie, we're all safe."

"I don't feel so safe," said Len.

"You'll feel better soon," said Angie.

"Maybe physically—though I'm not at all sure I'm not hallucinating—but that doesn't make us safe. Oh, my head. These guys are out to get us."

"I don't think so," said Bennu.

"Yeah, well, all of you are being your typical naive selves. Somebody's got to keep us from being taken in. As usual it's me, delirious or not."

Then, Jacob Canny Sea: "I detectived the beacon! Since it was I myself who belly-bowled us into this befunkery, I'm truly delighterated to say I holmsed it right over here! Trouble is, none of you are edisoned enough to see my inventorliness."

Ellen said, "Between Prester John and you Deedy-Swampers, it's a wonder we ever know what anyone means. What's wrong with 'I found the lamp'?"

"I'll take that suggestion to the bowels of my heart."

"So, the lantern is found," said Mook with some irritation. "Yet it does not give light. We must find things dry enough to create a flame. Some of you *sound* clever. Action is what we need."

With that rebuke, another search began. Welkeners and Misfits spread out to find old twigs or dry grass, occasionally bumping into one another. Lizbeth discovered soon enough that feeling around in the dark may not always yield light but it does kindle the imagination. She conjured up giant centipedes and black widows and tromped on these projections with every step, her shoes squeaking.

After many bumps and apologies, Zennor said he'd found a few sticks. Piers asked for them because he had found his satchel and taken out a striking stone. Soon, a small fire burned in the center of the room, and the stout candle in the lantern was relit.

Only Len still felt left in the dark. Though his eyes were fine, he could not bring himself to see that anything good had happened to the Misfits. He studied the circumstances, looking for a rational explanation and a sensible escape plan.

In the flickering light, most around him removed their shoes and wrung out their socks. As Piers plopped down to pull off his boots, Len looked around at the room. The waterfall from the corridor above dropped underground, cleanly out of sight, except for a small stream that trickled down the center of the cavern. Though Len feared the fire would burn up the room's oxygen, he was glad for the warmth and light. He felt better about the oxygen when he could not see the room's ceiling. For some reason, he found himself pawing at the ground.

He didn't feel like getting up. Dizzily, he watched Angie roam around in some kind of growing ecstasy. "Hey, Len, check this out," she said. "This room is a replica of Yosemite Valley. OK, there's the falls, the gentle Merced flowing down the center. Even the granite faces rise up majestically."

Len shook his head. "As usual, you're nuts."

"C'mon, if you squint just right, you can see El Capitan, The Sentinel, Royal Arches, and further down, Half Dome."

Len's eyebrows rose to full are-you-crazy? height. But, of course, thought Len, this did not deter Angie. She acted so sure of what she saw, so frighteningly sure.

"It's all here in miniature scale, Len, except that the granite faces are all just a little taller than I am." Angie looked exuberant. "I feel like Gulliver. I'm a giant strolling down the ancient riverbed. Hey, Lizbeth! Turn around and look! We tumbled over Yosemite Falls, right onto Sunnyside Beach! Bennu, the lodge should be right over here!" She ran toward Royal Arches, pointing to some rubble.

Lizbeth and Bennu looked over to Len with what-gives? gestures.

"And over here is where we camped once." Awestruck, she jumped from likeness to likeness, fading in and out of view.

Len stared at Angie's faint aura. "Angie, where'd you go? I must be passing out. C'mon, don't lose it. Bennu, what's going on?"

"You're not going to like this, Len, but sometimes your sister is invisible."

"Man, I've wished for that so many times, but now it comes true here, wherever we are. Why does it finally happen when I don't want it to happen?"

Lizbeth stood by Len's side. "Angie, don't flip out on us now. You've been less spacey here. We don't need you to lose control." Then Angie motioned her over to El Capitan. Len tried to get up, but his head rebelled. He managed to get to his knees.

"You'd be excited, too, Lizbeth, if you could just see it. I know you haven't been to Yosemite, but haven't you seen pictures? Can't you *see* Yosemite?"

Len glared hard at the monoliths in the cavern, comparing their outline to an Ansel Adams photograph. Maybe, he thought.

Soon, others noticed Angie's excitement.

Len thought that Angie enjoyed having an audience. She said, "Gandric, Piers, what do you make of this? This room is exactly like a place where we come from called Yosemite Valley, a glorious canyon. It's a gift of thousands of feet of sheer granite faces, with a beauteous river wrapping itself through the middle like a ribbon. And here's the canyon, only smaller, except, except for this little detail." She squatted down and pointed. "Some of these rock faces have an inscription below them. Ha! I'd like to see that in the valley next time I'm there!"

Len thought, That's it. I'm suggesting a psychiatrist the next time I see Mom.

Gandric and Piers brought the lantern to each of the stone slabs. "I can make out a few words," said Gandric, resuming a detached academic tone. "This one, the one you call Royal Arches, has a 'one' by it, some words I can't make out, and then, 'Go hard.'" As he rushed over to the next slice of wall, Half Dome, he seemed excited that he could apply some expertise. "This one has a 'two' and a slogan as well: 'Go fast.'" Then he shuffled to the next one and said, "Yes, here at—what did you call this one?"

Angie pulsed faintly in and out of view. "That's The Sentinel."

"It has a 'three' and the phrase 'Go easy.'" Finally, Gandric interpreted the last sheer face, El Capitan. He turned, hands on hips, for the first time addressing the group with a look of accomplishment. "A 'four' and 'Go slow.'"

"Any idea what it all means?" asked Angie.

The hands dropped quickly. "I'm afraid not. I thought I wouldn't need to know—and I know more than the other guardians. It all seemed so useless, play-acting for an audience who would never arrive. Besides, to become chief guardian, you only have to know more than others, not truly know." He kicked at some rocks like an embarrassed ten-year-old.

Ludicrous, thought Len. The whole thing is totally ludicrous.

Piers ran his hand through his hair and then around the outline of El Capitan. "Forget what you don't know, Gandric, and look more closely at what it is in front of you. Don't these rocks remind you of something else? They do me; they remind me of the Doors of Ganderst Hall. Look closely.

They're elaborate slabs of stone about the same height. And feel this, along the edge. The dirt falls away to reveal these wide cracks. I'm quite certain they go deep."

As Gandric seemed to strain his memory for old teachings, others dug frantically around the outline of the arched stones, using sticks to carve out the definite boundaries of what looked more and more like doors.

Len found a stout stick and pulled himself up. He tried to discount the parallels, find another explanation. He was also preoccupied with his unresponsive body.

Angie rushed over to him. "Len, you're standing! That's great. We'll talk about your head later."

Thanks for the sympathy, thought Len.

"Now, you've been to Yosemite. You know what I'm talking about. Don't you see the Valley? Look over here. There's even a crack where a climbing route is. Admit it."

It does look a lot like Yosemite, but I'm not admitting anything.

"Len, this is your sister here."

Prester John moved over to Half Dome, the top of his head equal to the peak of the door. "The obvious question, which I am not too proud to ask, is, which one should we enter—or should we try all four? The Great Anuba taught me to seek wise counsel patiently. When the Highlanders called on me to respond to the deadly drought a decade ago (Oh, how I remember those thirsty children holding out their dry cups to me), I donned the monk's habit and sought holy advice. Along the way I met the dearest—"

"Your Eminence, your Importance," said Ellen, her tone full of reprimand, "will this story help us choose?"

Vida Bering Well stepped onto a rock. "I'm heart-pumped to pick the second door because it bespokens, 'Go fast.' Aren't we rabbiting to get untortoised?"

While Len steadied himself with his stick, he listened to the Welkeners debate, then reach a consensus to "Go Fast" through Half Dome. Terz stepped up to the door to try to open it. With remarkably little resistance, Half Dome submitted to the first significant push by Terz. Then the granite face stopped about an inch open.

Len stood as amazed as anyone. He thought the whole thing seemed like some dumb fairy tale.

Using the door as a backdrop, Piers faced the group. "At each cross-roads, Gandric and Terz and I have admitted to each other our inadequacy. So. So we do now to you. With our lives as fragile as rose petals, and the future of Welken carried by our choices, we admit we proceed without full knowledge, yet under the many eyes of Soliton."

Zennor put a foot on the same stone that supported Vida. "We admire your humility, Piers. You act on the wisdom you understand and do so with love and courage. What more can we ask? If you choose wrongly, we have all chosen wrongly, for we have chosen you. And we'll suffer together without regret."

"You are a hulking kindness, Zennor Pict. It is my fortune to travel with you by my side." Piers walked over to him, reached up and put his hands on Zennor's massive shoulders. "In Welken!"

Zennor and all the others shouted back, "Of Welken!"

But Len kept his tongue.

❧

Lizbeth thought that to say "Of Welken" felt good and right and true. She looked to Angie for confirmation, and Angie smiled, if such you could call the wispy line on Angie's now translucent face. Then she looked at Len's folded arms and stern eyes. She wanted to make the vote three against one, so she looked around for Bennu. She found him—but he did not look back. He seemed disoriented and certainly not caught up in the camaraderie.

Will anything ever be simple for you? she thought. As she stamped her foot in mild frustration, water issued forth from her shoe.

Piers edged the door open inch by inch until it was wide enough for passage. He held the lantern high, and one foot crossed the threshold.

"Wait!"

Lizbeth knew the voice.

"Wait! We can't go that way!"

It was Bennu.

"We shouldn't do this."

"Get a grip, Bennu." Lizbeth ran over and faced her brother. "These people are our friends, and they all said to go through the Half Dome Door. You're being disrespectful. Get your feet on the ground!"

"No! We can't pick the Second Door. Remember, I saw Samantha—no, she became Angie—and she told me plainly to pick door number four."

"You're not going to hung-jury us, are you?" said Vida.

Mook glared at him as if to burn a hole. "He isn't one of us."

"Bennu," said Terz, "please be reasonable. Surely our choices deserve your trust. You can't expect us to believe you."

As Bennu began his defense, he literally levitated a few inches off the valley floor. Lizbeth couldn't believe what she saw. "OK, I know it sounds crazy. But, Terz, you remember I had a daydream, and I told the whole thing to Lizbeth. Well, it wasn't just a dream. I saw this choice before me: four doors. The people there—it was a stupid quiz show—picked door number two, and it was a mistake." He floated closer to Piers.

"He did have the dream," said Lizbeth.

"We're supposed to pick door four. It's a message; I know it! In my dream, Angie said so. And I'll tell you what's behind door number two: Morphane!"

With these words, chaos erupted:

"Why believe him?"

"If we could just ask the Great Anuba—"

"Who asked them along anyway?"

"I appreciate his sincerity, but—"

"Ha! He thinks he's einsteined a better route!"

In the shouting, Lizbeth noticed that one figure did not join the fray. One person did not say, "Ignore him!" or "Give him a chance," or "Piers said to take number two." One person stood as solid as the granite doors themselves, a living signpost pointing to door four, El Capitan. It was Alabaster Singing.

"Quiet!" said Piers. Obedience followed. "Alabaster has made her decision. When she speaks, we do well to attend. Bennu's waking dream persuades me as well. And if Gandric is right, no amount of planning will stop Morphane. I say we cast our lot with Bennu."

101

Ellen Basala stomped a foot. "But why trust Bennu? He doesn't know our ways. He bears not our allegiances. What if these Misfits, as I've heard them call themselves, truly do not fit? What if they were sent by the enemy to confuse us?" Though she withdrew into the crowd, the murmuring suggested to Lizbeth that others were glad to have the opinion voiced and not to have had to express it themselves.

"I know this," said Piers, with a pause that respected Ellen Basala's complaint. "We have met these four for a reason. Did you not see the Tetragrammaton? What is myth to us is real to them. Think upon this for a moment. I believe they are here to aid us, to help us recover the tiles. They have trusted us. Now it is our turn to trust them." He held the lantern with one hand and opened his other hand humbly. Bennu alighted onto the ground.

The objections ceased. To Lizbeth's surprise, she heard no more grumbling. Then Piers walked from the open door of Half Dome over to El Capitan.

As he opened the door, their faith was instantly rewarded. The room filled with light.

Gandric smiled for the first time. "Ah," he whispered, "this must be what the stories call 'The Window under the Mountain.' Like so many things, I thought it was only a tale created to calm down children when they felt trapped. Now I know better. Cursed be my complacency, my high-minded second guessing!" He placed one hand on each side of the door frame and leaned into the light, his shoulder bars gleaming brightly. Then he pulled back with a look of revelation. "But wait. There's the phrase 'Go slow.' This statement is a command, not an invitation. I remember reading once in the Book of Quadrille that the Window has a certain magic of time and space. The light from the outside reaches through the shaft, much farther down than is natural, because the space from here to the surface has somehow been shortened. I don't understand it. I remember something else too. Some dire calamity awaits those who travel faster than they should."

"How will we know how fast we 'should' travel?" asked Piers.

"I read the Quadrille as a storybook, not as a guidebook. I didn't study it for recommendations."

Soon after they entered the Window, the meaning became clear, for the flow of light could easily be seen floating around, like dust in a shaft of light.

Piers led the way, then Terz, Zennor, and Len. If he were stronger, Lizbeth felt sure he would have resisted more. Zennor and Angie helped him along, but he kept talking about drugs they must have taken or special effects devices or elaborately concocted schemes of the McKenzie Boys. Ellen followed their trio, then Prester John, Sutton Hoo, Vida Bering Well, Jacob Canny Sea, Alabaster Singing, Bennu, Lizbeth, and Mook.

When Bennu stepped in, Lizbeth whispered, "Bennu, how did you do that?"

"Do what? I just reported my dream."

"No, the flying thing, the levitating thing."

"What are you talking about?"

"Didn't you feel a little airborne back there?"

"Now that you mention it, I was so into my speech that I felt like I was floating."

"Well, it wasn't just a feeling."

Bennu took his quizzical expression with him into the Window. Lizbeth waited for him to turn back and explain himself, but he didn't. Mook nudged her, and she stepped in. She turned full-faced into the light and felt it compress against her, carrying her when she walked its pace, resisting her if she pushed against it. Then she heard Mook call back to the one remaining, the guardian who was putting out the fire. "Please, Gandric, come. If we must 'Go slow,' then we must get started." Lizbeth looked back.

"We guardians have our tasks," he replied, pushing small logs away from each other. "We guardians have our duties. It is time for me to be faithful to them. I will not fail *ever* again. I will now do all that's expected of me, and more, and more upon more."

"Who can do *all*, Gandric?" Mook's voice sounded urgent. "You must come. We forgive you. No one expects you to right the wrongs. Do not take on more than you can carry."

Lizbeth thought she might be persuasive. "Please, Gandric, step into the Window. We will help you. The others are already moving on."

Gandric turned to address Mook and Lizbeth. Centuries of failure seemed to Lizbeth to rise volcanically through his veins, bubbling up into molten words, hot and flowing: "I will come when I have finished! For once in my life I will finish my duty! If I burn in this fire for doing my duty, then so be it. Now go! I will catch up."

Now Lizbeth felt torn about her own duty. To what section of the line should she be loyal? To Bennu, her brother, above her or to Gandric, the needy one, below? She wanted to wait, but the fear on Mook's face told her not to wait.

Gandric kicked at the fire angrily, sending sparks up into the guilt-laden air. To Lizbeth, Gandric's foot lingered too long in the fire, as if he wanted it to burn.

Then Lizbeth's choice—to her horror—was made for her. Before she could shout "Gandric, look out!" her anxiety took shape, appearing in the full-frenzied wrath of Morphane. The great beast rushed through the open door two and leaped onto the valley floor, just as Bennu had seen. His deafening roar pierced them all, a sound beyond all reckoning. Lizbeth knew she should run, that she had already seen what Morphane could do, that she should grab Mook and try to catch up to Bennu. But she and Mook stood transfixed and watched, terrified, as Morphane's tumultuous face turned toward Gandric. He bared his teeth and roared again, freezing Gandric in fear. He was no mere lion-beast. Morphane's head, as broad as a lion's shoulders, raged back and forth, his face in constant roiling motion.

As surely as Lizbeth avoided Morphane's gaze, Gandric, inexplicably, stared deeply into Morphane's eyes—if you could say that Morphane's writhing sea of faces had eyes to fix upon. Wave after wave of horrified faces rose out of his muzzle, Morphane's nostrils slowly lifting, rolling upward until they became eyes, the eyes stretching monstrously, transmogrifying until they rippled back to his ears, and then beyond, blending into his fur. A face in motion. A beast of a thousand faces and therefore of none.

Morphane growled again, fiercely, as if something he possessed had been taken from him. Gandric stared, his body stiff and his mind perversely captivated by the gaze of the beast. His eyes then locked onto Morphane's, and he said aloud, "I must pay."

Lizbeth grabbed Mook's arm. Then the unspeakable happened. The image of Gandric's face appeared on Morphane's moving visage. It couldn't be, but Lizbeth saw the mirrored Gandric reflected on the beast's face. No, it wasn't just a reflection. In some bizarre way, Gandric's face had leaped onto Morphane's face! If that were not impossible enough, Gandric's image then rolled over Morphane's features like a cloud over a hillside, adapting to the beast's facial landscape. At the start, Gandric's eyes aligned themselves perfectly with Morphane's nostrils, while his mouth was hidden in Morphane's chin.

Simultaneous with the transferred image came such a voiced agony as Lizbeth had ever heard. Morphane had not laid a claw on Gandric, but Gandric howled all the same. He grabbed his head in torment and writhed uncontrollably. Lizbeth lurched to go help him, but Mook held her firmly in the Window.

Then Gandric's face moved up Morphane's face, gradually, his eyes traveling along the sides of his muzzle until they were actually looking out of Morphane's sockets, a hideous, macabre sight, terror etched in the bugged-out globes. Gandric's nose stretched out in exaggeration over Morphane's snout. As Gandric looked out from inside Morphane, Lizbeth saw him looking at his own body convulsing in fear and helplessness. As Gandric roiled, so did his soul, his self. All that he counted as himself conformed to Morphane. To Lizbeth it seemed that a kind of insanity swept over him and that his psyche plunged deeper and deeper within. Gandric had no more choices to make. The buttresses collapsed around the walls of his mind and then these caved in. His eyes moved again upward on Morphane's face, peered desperately out of Morphane's ears, perhaps even seeing Lizbeth, and then his face vanished altogether, sucked into the beast himself. There had been no time for tears or physical resistance or even breath. All Lizbeth could think was that Gandric's person, his essence—the life he knew and called his own—had been swallowed up.

In seconds, it was over. All was quiet. Morphane struck Gandric's body once and then licked his chops. The body-that-was-Gandric got up, stooping in deference to the monstrous animal. Lizbeth thought that Gandric looked like part of the shuffling horde now, but she couldn't see any other drones there. When Gandric's body stood, Lizbeth could see that it took on part of the cave, this place of his last true experience. Attached to his soulless shell were an ember from the fire, a living mouse, and a few stray sticks. Gandric's vacuous gaze had no look of consciousness behind the eyes. It, for surely it was a thing now, slumped near Morphane and waited for orders.

Lizbeth bent over in disbelief. She was shocked, stupefied, crushed by the transformation and loss. She wanted to heave. Then something fluttering in the Window's light caught her eye. Though a witness to Gandric's defeat, she did not want to believe what floated toward her like ashes caught in a draft. It rode the air till it landed on her arm. She grabbed it, stretched it out, and then she knew what Sutton and Zennor had been talking about. Here was a husk, a skinlike memory of Gandric's hand. Down Lizbeth's face fell full-sorrowed tears. Before she began to sob, Mook yanked on her arm and pushed El Capitan shut. Silent and nauseated, yet too worried about protecting the others to give herself to her grief, Lizbeth realized that now she knew more than all the others about Morphane's power.

In that moment, she realized that sometimes ignorance is enviable.

CHAPTER TWELVE
SOMETHING ABOUT FOURS

Nothing is more common than for men to think that because they are familiar with words they understand the ideas they stand for.

JOHN HENRY NEWMAN

 Charlotte thought that the short chapter on Ollie's escape went rather well. She "rewarded" herself by taking a break and walking back into the house. On the kitchen counter, she saw a string of fruity candy in a straight line alternating between light and dark colors. Knowing that the artistic mastermind had to be her compulsively neat husband, she put a few candies in her mouth and then moved the pieces around into as random a pattern as possible. After saying "toodly-too bad" out loud, she refilled her iced tea and headed back outside.

There's just something irresistible about Ollie, she thought. Now where was I?

CHAPTER THREE: Wise Dominic's Ford

Now, Bonesy," announced Percy, as they approached a large door, "Wise Dominic is as friendly as a ladybug. You'll have him eating out of the back of your hand in no time."

Unconsoled, Bones trudged up the last step and stood directly behind Percy, about as hidden as a beanstalk in Jack's yard.

"Dear me, Boneseroosel, how are we to present our-selves as card-carrying criminologists capable of cracking codes like a bat out of the frying pan—unless—unless, old boy, you're able to keep your basset knees from knocking?"

With tornado force, the door swung dramatically open, taking Bones and Percy quite off guard. To their greater surprise, no one was there.

"Do come in," came a deep voice from another room. "I'm in the bay window, sunning myself. Come straight past the phonograph and the tapestry."

Cautiously, the decidedly undynamic duo walked past the gilded entry mirror, observing their own falsely brave faces, then past the family crest (with its motto "By the Mews") mounted above a medieval tapestry featuring cats of all kinds in full armor. Then, a trophy case. A medal from President Roosevelt for bravery during the Panama crisis. Volcanic rock personally collected from Mount Krakatoa. A Celtic cross from Queen Victoria for rescuing English treasures from looters in Asia. Percy admired the flower weave in the center of the cross.

Surrounded by Dominic's mementos, Bones felt rather foolish and small, a puttering gardener in the presence of greatness. "I'm not worthy," he whispered to Percy.

"Please, Bones, you've got him figured all wrong. I'm a chip off the ol' butter dish, and you're worthier than I. What have I got that you ain't got? Actually that's a good question. Let's see, a little style, perhaps. A fabulous car and superb taste. An irrepressible spirit. I could go on, but really, Bonesy, it's nothing compared to being a true-blue basset from Virginia. Besides, his bark is worse than all the tea in China."

"Mr. Malone!" Dominic's voice bellowed like a street preacher naming a sinner. Bones came forward. "My dear cousin Percy tells me you are the Patrick Henry of bassets:

'Give me celery or give me death!' Good on you. Now, please, sit down."

Deftly, Dominic dropped the monocle from his good eye into his cashmere shirt pocket. He sat up and adjusted his paisley silk bow-tie. "Anyone who can make sense of this muddle-mouthed cousin of mine has my full admiration. So, of what help can I be?"

"By the mews," said Percy, remembering the family crest, "may I remind you of our sworn foe, Ollie Ollie Otterson."

"Yes," yawned Dominic, revealing his glistening meat-shredding teeth. Bones winced.

"Ollie seems to be on to something big—and we feel like two peas in a haystack, if you catch my drift." Percy showed him the newspaper clipping about Akhenaten's jewels.

"I see," Dominic said. "Perhaps your Ollie is connected to a more powerful criminal or a worldwide conspiracy. Something deeper is afoul here."

"I've been doing a little ponderin' myself, sir," interjected Bones—surprising even himself by speaking. "If this pyramid loot's got Ollie's eye, maybe you have a map or know a guide who could help?"

"Yes, of course, Mr. Malone," answered Dominic. "Abu P. Cockles. He's a first-class snoop. I'll send him a telegram. But I have one more tip."

He leaned forward and whispered in Percy's ear.

"Fords?" responded Percy. "Really, sir, I'm rather partial to the Pierce-Arrow—although the latest Dusenburg's are—"

"Not Fords!" roared Dominic, raising every hair on Bones's spine. "Fours! Pay attention to fours! The pattern is clear. First, there was the barbershop quartet last weekend. The tenor looked right at me when he sang: 'Four to four in Baltimore; Has anybody seen my door?' Second, I called for a carpenter to fix the back porch—and four carpenters came. I said, 'What will you be putting in?' They said, "'Four new four by fours.' Third, my financial advisor, Forest Viers, called for the first time in four months and said, 'Dom, for four fortunate years, I've formulated a force to fortify your fortune.' And now, fourth, you've come."

"But there's only two of us," contradicted Percy, "even if it is fortuitous for any lovely ladies who might meet us."

"Please," rebuked Dominic, "be serious. You are the fourth *sign* of the importance of fours. And there's the pyramid."

"A pyramid? Isn't that a symbol of threes?"

"Could be, Percy, but my vision has been an aerial view which reveals the base of the four walls of the pyramid. Don't you see?"

"I see this," said Percy carefully. "You are the sagiest sage I know. If you say to search for 'fours,' then 'four-ward march' we will."

After their good-byes, Percy and Bones descended the great stone steps.

"All in all," mused Bones, "I reckon I didn't do half badly."

"You were spectacular, Mr. Bonesy Maloney," affirmed Percy. "By the way, you can stop twiddling with your overalls now."

As Bones approached the passenger side of Percy's Pierce-Arrow, he noticed he'd so twisted the straps of his overalls that the pant legs had been cinched up about five full inches, making Bones the finest high-water farmer in all of Virginia.

Charlotte took a sip of tea and realized that all the ice had melted. Bleh, she motioned with her tongue.

Hmm, she thought, I just noticed that Lizbeth likes to wear overalls just like Bones. Well, they are both a little on the lumbering side. That's OK. She's such a dear. Come to think of it, so is Bones. And what's this business about "fours"? I don't really know, but somehow I feel it's important.

Just then she imagined Ollie strolling on board a ship with some portly passengers. She scribbled down the idea on the next page.

CHAPTER THIRTEEN

RATIONALIZATIONS, RESISTANCE, AND THE RIVER OF LIGHT

It's not in your daddy's nature to travel in any
fashion except against the current, and the stronger
it tries to push him back, the better he likes it.

FRED CHAPPELL, *FAREWELL, I'M BOUND TO LEAVE YOU*

 Walking between Zennor and Angie, Len felt his strength returning. As he moved up the fluid air in the Window under the Mountain, he sometimes let go of Zennor's belt and made his way on his own. The sights around him took his mind off his pain. Like huge, electric snowflakes, sparkles of light rolled by him in slow motion down the thick air. Sometimes they clumped together into an illuminated snowball and then suddenly burst apart, the explosions shooting arcs of light spectacularly in all directions.

Len caught a few of the shimmering light-pieces and examined them. He felt like he was inside a kaleidoscope, sliding with the colors, feeling each refraction drift into dazzling symmetry. Then he saw sticks and bits of color spontaneously merging into mosaics of identifiable objects: trees, houses, even faces. After seconds together, they'd break apart—only to reassemble into a different picture downstream. Terz applauded and Zennor said, "Oh my!" at least a dozen times.

Only once did Len remember that danger might be catching up to them. That thought was quickly overcome by a growing desire to walk faster, even to run around in the river of light.

"I'm still not 100 percent," Len said, loud enough for Terz and Zennor to hear, "but I feel so much better. I'd like to jog around in this stuff. Actually, I wish I could swim in it."

Terz turned to Zennor. "Maybe Gandric overstated the risks."

"Perhaps so." Zennor pointed with joy at two sparklers that seemed to be talking with each other.

There's too much to see, thought Len, and to touch. How amazing to be able to actually feel pieces of light. I'd like to know why we can't just run around out here. Why should we not touch a rainbow if it only takes a short trot to get to it? On the other hand, it is weird that whenever I press harder into a shaft of light, I feel like I'm pushing upstream. Maybe there's something to the warning.

At the same time, he discovered that, in the Window's pull, any increased speed felt exhilarating because the colors streamed by faster, enveloping his senses. While reminding himself to resist, he saw slats of color stacking themselves onto one another, constructing an elaborate storefront with open doors. Light-tubes merged to become animated figures who welcomed the walkers inside with a sweep of the arm.

"C'mon, Angie," said Len, "we've just got to go say hello."

"More than anything, I would love to do that. Can we visit that blue one there, with the silver roof, and the trees in front with fruit pulsating in the branches?"

"Sure."

A sharp voice came from behind. "Len, Angie." It was Ellen Basala. "Don't go. I feel the pull, too. But Gandric knows some things about the Book of Quadrille. I will say this, it's too bad other temptations don't work against themselves like this one does."

***

At the rear, Lizbeth struggled with other temptations. Although the visual delights of the Window did not yet pull at her, she did get drawn into something. Images of Morphane and Gandric replayed themselves, and Lizbeth dove into the senselessness, the loss, the sense of abandonment. For all her newfound strength, where was its usefulness? Why did she have to see these awful events? All her life, she felt easily used and abused. What was different here? Nothing.

This downward spiral sucked her in and might have pulled her into her darkest self, if Mook had not pulled too, at her arm. "Look back," he said. "Something's there. Something's following us."

Lizbeth stopped and turned. There was something coming up the path. It was getting closer. What was it? She wanted to pick up her pace. She worried that Morphane had found their door. She studied the figure coming. It wasn't Morphane. It was too slight, too tall, too bent.

Lizbeth and Mook went forward some more, as quickly as they dared. Then Lizbeth looked around again. The person, the creature, walked faster, gaining ground. She could now make out details: a monkish robe, a glow by the feet.

Gandric is gaining on us, she thought—or what was left of Gandric. Lizbeth called ahead to Bennu, but he did not answer. The thickness of condensed light deadened her speech.

But Gandric was gaining.

Len said to Angie, "There's no harm in *wishing* to run, is there? What's your favorite so far? Mine is that orange castle."

"I'd like to sit in the turquoise palace over there." Light sparkles that lodged in her hair held strands afloat in the current. "The throne is fabulous. And look, four magenta manservants to wait on my every need."

"Yeah, I always thought you wanted to be a queen."

Would a side trip really make that much difference? Len wondered. Would it really matter if I ran over and then came back to my place in line? I wouldn't be trying to race ahead—only sideways.

"These are lovely, aren't they, Len? Stained glass glories. Neon wonders. It is enough to look at them, don't you think?"

Lizbeth's worries multiplied. She could see Gandric throwing his arms like oars into the river of light, pulling against it mightily, his robe billowing behind him. He was gaining, Gandric was, a sailor on the Window's tide.

Neither Mook nor Lizbeth paid much attention to the glittering sights around them. No light-stick house could displace their fears about the body-that-was-Gandric. With sadness, Lizbeth noticed the small flame that slowly burned his robe. He paid no attention as he swept his oar-arms powerfully against the golden light.

And he came closer.

Mook tugged on her arm—and she realized that she had been looking back so much she might not be walking as fast as she could. But then, she thought, do I really want to catch up to the others, to bring this beast closer to them?

Lizbeth trudged ahead at just the pace of the river of light. She began to lose hope. They were stuck between a slow and a bad place, and surely Gandric would catch them soon. Lizbeth turned again to see Gandric not fifty feet away, gaining, gaining, always gaining. Can't we go any faster? she thought. She looked back again. Forty feet. Another few minutes: thirty feet.

She grabbed Mook's rock-strong arm. "What are we going to do? He'll be here any minute."

Mook said nothing. He looked at Lizbeth distractedly, as if he were embroiled in an agonizing internal debate. He brushed her away, said, "Keep going," then, inexplicably, he slipped off the path and ran. Waving his hands to attract Gandric's attention, Mook darted toward a candy-striped cottage. Horrified, Lizbeth reached after him. She shouted, "Mook, no!" But Mook held his hand up, telling her to stay. Then she looked back. Gandric's body looked confused. He hesitated. He looked toward Mook with the vacant gaze of Morphane's drones.

As Mook reached the entrance to the cottage, a brilliantly blue figure placed a glowing hand on his shoulders. Mook turned back to Lizbeth and smiled.

When Gandric reached the place where Mook left the trail, he walked off also. Step by step, he moved on toward Mook.

What am I to do now? Lizbeth thought. Am I to watch Mook sacrifice himself? Oh, Mook, must you be *this* brave? Must you leave me here to watch and tell the others? And what if you don't succeed in taking Gandric down with you? Won't he come after us anyway?

Then Gandric stopped. Though he lost ground on the Window-walkers, though he wavered in his purpose, though he looked intently toward Mook, he did not reach the candy-striped cottage. Without any sign of reason or emotion, he resumed his voyage up the Window's currents. The oar-arms flailed away, the sail-robe filled, and Gandric came at them once again.

⚬⚬⚬

At the front, Len saw the path get wider and taller. Weary from walking, he asked Zennor to stop so he could see these new sights. Two golden columns rose from the floor. From the tops of these pedestals, gleaming streamers of royal blue and lime green twirled in the flow. At the ends of these ribbons, pieces broke off, turning into animated light-beings who floated softly to the ground. They landed lightly on their toes, pirouetted, and danced down the current. Linking the great columns was a brilliant rainbow arch, raining down colors that became stars, ornaments, rings, every playful shape imaginable.

Piers had stopped too. "It's too beautiful to be a trick, but I'm not sure what to do next."

In awe, many in line stood open-mouthed, and Len smiled at Angie so broadly that his cheeks ached. Vida said she felt thoroughly pearly gated. Through tears of joy, Prester John put his arm around Zennor and said, "Forgive me for what I am about to admit. I feel more truly alive here than in my own Highlands. What does it mean, Zennor?"

As Zennor gathered his thoughts, Piers and Terz conferred, and then waved everyone through the arch.

Looking up at the arch, Len thought it was like a laser light show, a video game beyond all experience. Solid beams shot everywhere, bouncing off the ceiling in an ever-exploding fireworks display. Len dodged the light beams as best he could—but then a lavender piece crashed against his chest. He braced for the pain, but instead of piercing him, it splashed against him. He laughed. Without speech, they all walked toward the falling light, putting themselves intentionally in the path of the cascading pieces. The more the light hit him, the more rejuvenated Len felt.

Then, as he looked beyond the arch, he felt his joy fade. He could see

115

almost nothing, no tangible colors, no light sticks, no lasers, no flowing anything—only gold, blinding in its shimmering brightness.

৩৶৩

Gandric retraced his steps back to the path. Lizbeth watched him go, glad that he was now farther behind. But she worried about Mook. While marching steadily on, she looked over at the cottage. There was Mook, shaking his head. Then, one of the blue men reached around from behind him and pushed. He nearly flew toward Lizbeth across the prismed space, and soon he was back by her side.

Gandric came on, steady in his threat. Lizbeth could now see the mouse affixed to Gandric's foot. It squirmed as Lizbeth took stock of its bizarre state, fighting gamely to stay alive.

So are we, she thought, so are we.

Dread descended on Lizbeth like a gladiator's net. Wrapped in its webbing, she found each step laborious and futile. Gandric would reach them soon. So preoccupied with what was behind them, Lizbeth had not paid attention to Bennu ahead of her. She turned forward again, and she could not see anyone. She screamed to those she couldn't see, "He's coming!" but the words bounced off the spinning wheels flowing off the rainbow arch and down the current.

Five steps behind.

Two steps behind.

Gandric caught them. His arms stopped rowing and started reaching. As Mook pushed Lizbeth aside, Gandric's fist hit Mook on his chest, sending him backwards. Without skill but without pause, Gandric delivered blow after blow. Mook fended them off defensively, as if he did not want to hurt Gandric. Lizbeth, too, found it hard to strike this body that they'd known as their friend. With one hand up as a shield, she kicked at Gandric's legs. Mook got up, dodged a few swings, and knocked Gandric's flailing arms to the side. Gandric lost his balance. As he tottered, Mook moved in. Making a surprising recovery, Gandric straightened up and hit Mook squarely in the face. Lizbeth looked for a weapon. She found a light stick on the ground and swung it hard on Gandric's back—but it instantly shattered uselessly into sparkles and glitter.

116

Up the trail they battled, Gandric burning Mook with his enflamed leg and Mook striking back at Gandric's vacuous face. Feeling helpless, Lizbeth watched. She picked up a rock, but Mook was too entangled with Gandric for her to get in a good shot. Then, when Gandric raised his arm to strike Mook, Lizbeth swung at it with the rock in her hand. Gandric's arm broke. It snapped with a loud crack and hung limply from his forearm. Lizbeth stepped back, shocked at the destruction she caused. Then something worse happened. Gandric did not seem to notice the injury. He did not cry out. He did not take stock of what happened. He hesitated—for one second—and then attacked with renewed abandon, throwing his dangling, broken arm at Mook, not seeming to care if it sheared clean off. Lizbeth kicked Gandric's legs, pounding his shins from the side. Up, up the trail they fought, entering the area of dazzling ribbons and lasers shooting off the columned arch. Then Mook drew his knife out of the sheath strapped to his leg.

Deftly, Mook swiped his blade at Gandric. He slashed Gandric's forearm and jabbed the knife into his thigh. Neither wound drew much blood. Gandric winced slightly but kept coming on. Gandric the relentless. Gandric the predator.

The knife that should have turned the tide had startlingly little effect. Nothing did. Snapped bones, sliced flesh, pounded ribs, nothing stopped Gandric. Mook was clearly tiring. With the knife being slashed around, Lizbeth kept her distance and, instead, looked for a way of escape. She thought she saw the others through the cascading lights. But they were moving away, beyond the waterfall, toward a golden glow. They did not notice the scuffle. Now ten yards ahead of the fight, she looked back.

The battered Gandric swung his good arm over and over. Lizbeth could scarcely bear to watch—to see Mook get hit, to see Gandric so disfigured. Mook tried to get away. Skin flapping from a knife wound, Gandric lurched at Mook's feet, tripping him. The knife flew out of Mook's hand and fell among rocks near the trail. As Mook dove for it, Gandric grabbed his ankle. Mook rolled toward Gandric, wrestling, panting, bloodying his knuckles as he bashed at the sticks of wood attached to Gandric's body. He hit and punched and gouged, but Gandric would not release his grip. He worked to get away. They kept moving up the

Window, crawling and scrambling together in a desperate union. Lizbeth did not run to get the knife, nor did she run back to Mook. With panicked patience, she waited for them to reach her.

Through the dazzling waterfall, they came, Mook shuffling on his backside through the columns, crab-crawling, stopping at times to hack at Gandric's grip. Lizbeth kicked at Gandric's ribs.

Lizbeth turned toward the blinding gold. She could see no one. Not Jacob or Vida or Bennu or Piers. All she could see was golden light.

Gandric pulled up to bite Mook's leg.

Lizbeth grabbed one of Mook's arms and yanked hard, jerking Gandric's head back. She dragged them both, and Gandric held fast to Mook's ankle. Gandric raised his head again, teeth poised. Mook could not reach down to fight off Gandric. Lizbeth pulled and Gandric bit. As Mook howled in otherworldly pain, Lizbeth summoned all her strength for one last yank away from the steely grip. She stumbled backwards.

The next thing she knew, two hands grabbed her and she felt lifted through the tawny curtain, out of the Window and into the real midday sun. Though blinded by the light, she saw Piers and Prester John.

"Keep pulling," she said. It was all the breath she felt she had left.

Soon, she was entirely out and the others grasped after Mook's arm. Then, just as Mook's head poked through the Window's opening, Gandric tugged him back down.

"Get him!" yelled Lizbeth.

One more good yank and the tug of war was over. The three Welkeners overwhelmed Gandric's strength and pulled Mook through the Window's threshold, the golden veil. When Mook's legs and feet finally came through, Gandric's persistent hand held the ankle still.

As the fresh air hit Mook and the body-that-was-Gandric, Lizbeth's worries over Gandric's threat left her, and all present observed what happened to those who strove too hard against the flow of the Window's current. Mook's red hair with the white tips turned partly silver. The crow's feet at the corners of his black eyes deepened, and a few new wrinkles appeared on his inscrutable forehead. He looked ten years older. Then Gandric's hand attached to Mook's ankle came out of the Window. Instantly, it aged to shriveled skin. Once his whole body was out of the

Window under the Mountain, Gandric lurched up for one more strike at Mook's body. As his broken arm rose, its age climbed with it, racing through the decades until it looked a hundred years old at its zenith. As it descended, the skin decomposed into dry leather, then turned to powder, falling off to reveal a bleached skeleton that looked baked in the sun for years. His whole body became bones, with no flesh or life on them.

The rescuers placed Mook on the ground and sat in shock next to Lizbeth and the whitened remains. Mook panted wearily. The bony fingers of Gandric's bony hand lifelessly held Mook's ankle still. A pained Piers broke them off.

Even in death, Lizbeth thought, Gandric would not let go.

As soon as she had breath, Lizbeth told everyone the full tale of pursuit and battle, and all grieved for the tormented guardian. Piers wondered aloud if some measure of serenity now belonged to Gandric, that perhaps the guardian's soul had been released. They buried him there at the entrance, leaving a few exposed bones as a warning to others of what no longer could be read and passed down from the Book of Quadrille.

❦

On the sober stroll down to a grassy knoll below the gravesite, Len motioned for the other Misfits to come to him. He pulled them away from the Welkeners. "Lizbeth, we're all glad you're OK. We had no idea what was going on behind us. But now, we've got to plan our escape."

Bennu leaned down toward a lupine. As he plucked it, he hovered for a moment in the air. "Len, your insensitivity knows no bounds. A breathing Welkener dies and all you can think of is getting away. Don't you feel any grief?"

Len did a double take when Bennu was in the air, but on the second pass, Bennu no longer hovered. "I do, really. I'm sorry Gandric's gone— but I didn't talk to him like you guys did. I was conked out most of the time. What's a guardian anyway? What's a Welken?" He pulled on his shoulder length hair. "Don't you see? Whatever happens here, we just need to get back to Skinner. I have to admit, though, that light show was awesome. I can't wait to tell my friends about it."

"Len, *we're* your friends, maybe your only friends." Lizbeth snapped a

119

few good-sized twigs in half. "Maybe you shouldn't just order us around."

"Look, you're right." Len looked down and then up. He put on his most sincere expression. "I just thought that, well, what I wanted, all of you wanted too." Len realized that this line didn't come out quite right. He sat on a large rock, and the others lay down on the grass. "It's not that I think you should all do what I think—OK maybe I do act that way sometimes—but I'm guessing you do have an itsy-bitsy desire to, like, go home, right?"

"I sure do," said Lizbeth.

"Well, then, what next?" He pulled his cap out of his back pocket, but he couldn't get it over his hair.

Angie ran her hands back and forth like she was making a snow angel in the grass. She faded from view as she spoke. "I accept with gratitude the goodness that speaks out here in the open. The fresh, crisp air, the smells of lilac and honeysuckle, the hillsides filled with lupines and poppies. I think a mockingbird is getting ready to sing hello."

"To me," said Bennu, "even the scrub jay—"

"Shut it," said Len, not about to get sucked into poetry. "Like I said, what's next? Where are we anyway?"

Ellen cleared her throat from behind them. "Durrow Wood fans out below us east and west. We're too far from Circle Stand to see it—that's where we picked you up. Just over to our right is the path that eventually leads to the Nezzer River. We've come out of the foothills of the Great Alpine Reef a few miles to the west of Chimney Cave. Come, I think Piers is ready to move."

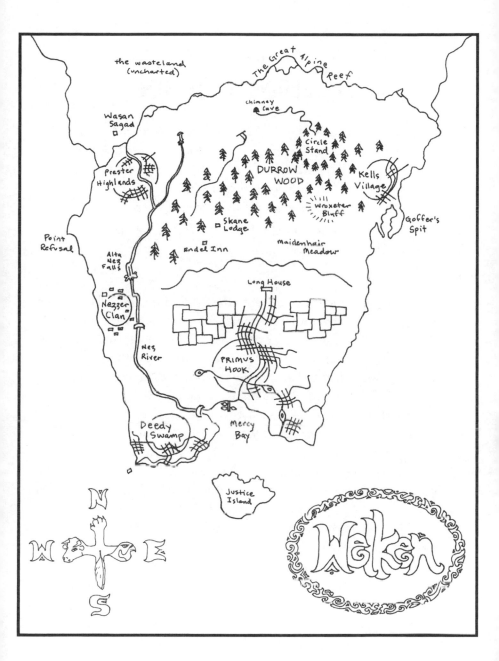

the wasteland
(uncharted)

The Great Alpine Reef

chimney
Cave

Wasan
Sagad

Circle
Stand

DURROW
WOOD

Kells
Village

Prester
Highlands

Wroxeter
Bluff

Goffer's
Spit

Point
Refusal

Skane
Lodge

Maidenhair
Meadow

Alta
Neg
Falls

Endel Inn

Long House

Nezzer
Clan

Neg
River

PRIMUS
HOOK

Deedy
Swamp

Mercy
Bay

Justice
Island

N
W   E
S

Welken

121

CHAPTER FOURTEEN
CATCHING A GLIMPSE

Laura hesitated, and said, "Pa, could it really be a fairy ring? It
is perfectly round . . . [and] covered solidly thick with violets. A
place like that couldn't just happen, Pa. Something made it."
"You are too old to be believing in fairies, Laura," Ma said gently.
"Charles, you must not encourage such fancies."

LAURA INGALLS WILDER, *BY THE SHORES OF SILVER LAKE*

 On the way over to the others, Lizbeth tried to tell Len about what he'd missed in Welken. "Well, you should know that we arrived in Circle Stand, and after Piers put some healing stuff on you, we walked to Joseph's Ledge. That's where you decided to go mud sliding."

"Yeah, smooth move on my part."

"So what are you thinking about all this?"

"I dunno. I still don't get it. When I wake up, I'm guessing, like, the whole thing will fade."

Lizbeth guessed that Len knew this answer wasn't adequate—but he had to supply some sort of order, some way of holding the unholdable in his mind.

"I just remembered," said Bennu. "When we arrived, it was raining. Now look at the sunshine. For the first time since coming to Welken, I don't feel like something bad is about to happen."

Despite all the suffering she'd observed, Lizbeth felt encouraged too. The bright spring day shone reassuringly on columbine and starflower. As they neared the others, an oriole alighted on the ground and announced his presence. Alabaster Singing whistled back the song.

Lizbeth considered Len's typical cynicism but decided to risk a senti-ment. "Have you ever seen anything so beautiful, Len?"

"OK, fine," said Len, suddenly curt. "It's a beautiful day. Take a pic-ture. Who cares? I'm sore all over and I want some answers. Bennu, where are your glasses and why do you prance around like some dopey gazelle? Lizbeth, you can forget Thunder Thighs. You look like Thunder Woman! Angie, why are you half ghost, half hologram?" He tore at some tall grass as he walked. "And me—why me? Why did I get conked in the head? Why is my hair so long and bushy? Why do my hands feel like kneading the ground like some stupid cat? What gives?"

Piers broke in. "I'm afraid we don't have time to stay here and talk." He straightened his tunic in his broad belt. "We can pause, yes, but not for long. Remember, we are only a few steps ahead of Morphane. He will keep com-ing, I'm sure, and there's something else we must do right away. It's—"

"And who's this Piers guy?" asked Len. "I don't like the fact that we're all like changlings in a sci-fi movie and here's some alien commander telling us what to do. Somebody needs to take charge here, and as usual, it looks like—"

"Len! Will you just shut up!" Lizbeth stood between Len and Piers. She couldn't understand why he reverted to such idiotic crankiness. "Why are you acting like this? It's like you flipped a switch back to your old self. Haven't you been watching Piers lead us?"

"It's kind of hard to do that when you're unconscious."

Lizbeth pulled on her straps so he could see her flexed muscles.

"Look," said Bennu, "you aren't God's gift to leadership, you know. For once in your life, you can't take charge. We won't let you." Lizbeth knew he'd wanted to say these words for some time.

Angie brought a calmer tone. "Len, you know we all love you." She paused. "Look around. It's not just the four of us. We're following Piers right now. He's not an alien commander. I should know, right?" She smiled. "He's clear and sound and wise. No matter how hard it is, we hope you can trust—trust us, trust Piers."

"If you'd just stop resisting everything," said Lizbeth. As soon as she said it, she realized she spoiled whatever shift to the positive Angie's words might have wrought.

Len folded his arms across his chest and leveled a steely glance at the other Misfits and Piers. Then his eyes started to roll back.

"Sit down," said Lizbeth. She and Bennu caught him. "Put your head between your legs. You'll be fine."

Len did as he was told. Staring at the ground, he said, "I am fine. I am not weak."

∿ ⸎ ∿

After a minute of recovery, Len lifted his head to show he was ready to go. With suspicion, he watched Piers open his satchel and address him. "The work we have to do is deeper than you can yet see, Len—and that's no fault of your own. Our world, Welken, suffers under a weighty transgression. The sorrow to be unsorrowed is wild and powerful and determined. You do not fully know this yet."

Fabulous. Insult my experience, thought Len.

Piers took some food out of the bag and motioned for a few others to do the same, to distribute what they had. "I will tell you this. You cannot be in Welken for long without becoming of Welken. Your friends have been awake longer. Listen to them. More knowledge than this will have to wait because the healing has not yet been completed."

"Yeah, whatever." Len nibbled on the edge of some hard tack. Then he thought, What healing? If you're sick, take an aspirin. This guy is a smooth talker if ever there was one. Welken, schmelken. And what's with this stupid biscuit. It's terrible.

"I couldn't help overhearing," said Terz, munching on some jerky. "Maybe the boy has a point. As I always say, 'Give the young freedom to express their feelings and be themselves.' If they make a few wrong turns, so be it. Soon they will find their way, and be rewarded with the pride that comes from doing things on one's own."

Now you're talkin', thought Len. He spat out a gritty piece.

"Terz," said Piers, "you have a generous spirit. And over the course of this journey, your words may stand as a prophecy. But for now, we must be going." He walked over to a bramble and pulled off some ripe berries, raising his eyebrows twice to give permission for others to come over and disregard his own command. Terz shuttled berries back to Len. "You four," Piers said, loud enough for Len to hear, "you Commiseration of Misfits, as you call yourselves, must return to your world. You will be of more help to us there."

Len stood and shook off his dizziness. "That's good news, Piers. I'm ready to go back."

Lizbeth ran over to Piers. "You can't mean that. We want to stay here and do what we can."

Len walked over to her and grabbed her arm. "Hey, Lizbeth, what happened to the ruby slippers girl? You've talked about going home more than anyone."

"Well, unlike some people I know, maybe I want to help others once in a while." Lizbeth threw Len's hand off—and Len guessed that her new-found enthusiasm was not entirely altruistic. She likes being needed, that's all, thought Len.

"Lizbeth," Piers said, "clarity will come as you keep looking. I don't know how all will unfold. But I believe that our worlds have not *collided* as much as they have *been woven* together."

Woven worlds? thought Len. Yeah, right. Like we're all getting stitched up by some great sewing machine in the sky.

Bennu came alongside Piers. "OK, I'm with you. We're with you, I think. So how do we get home and what do we do when we get there?"

"The answer to the first question is simple enough. We have to catch a glimpse."

"What?"

"Catch a glimpse. They carry a special way of traveling with them, in their bodies. You catch a glimpse, no easy task mind you, hook into its glowing parts and stretch the light."

Len could not even bring himself to protest.

"Perhaps the only way is to show you. Let's go to that grove of alder trees over there. Vida and Prester John, why don't you come along? Terz, tell the others to wait for our return." After Terz left, Piers continued. "Glimpses sleep during the day underneath alder leaves. They especially like the ones that curl over at the end."

Len thought he'd never heard of anything nuttier, as if Tinkerbell were real or light sabers weren't plastic toys for sale at the store for $10.95. Then he remembered the river of light. That was pretty nutty, too.

"Here we are," whispered Piers as he stepped under the trees' canopy. Delicately, he peered underneath a few leaves. "Now, glimpses are a bit shifty. It's not enough to shake a leaf and wait for them to drop into your hand. They are too quick and suspicious for that. They must be outwitted." After examining several trees (all the leaves looked the same to Len), Piers seemed to find what he was looking for and lightly tapped a few leaves with his finger.

Like bees disturbed from a nest, buzzing blurs of light zoomed out from the alders, flying around them so fast that Len thought he was in the center of a cartoon cyclone. Then, one by one, little beings came right up to him and the others, so close to their faces that they had to step back to see them. The glimpses hovered for a second or two, examined the Misfits up and down, muttered repeatedly, and buzzed off into a frenzied flight once again. They reminded Len of the migrating monarch butterflies he'd seen in eucalyptus groves in California, how they fluttered magically when disturbed. Only these little buggers were fast.

Piers put his hands on his hips. "Finding glimpses is the easy part. Catching one is another matter entirely."

At this invitation, the Misfits lurched toward the glimpses, slapping at them, cupping their hands to catch them, and running after them. Even Len. All of these attempts proved equally, utterly, embarrassingly futile. It reminded Len of playing touch football after school with Jeff Shima. Darting away from his opponents with ease, this guy laughed at the sport of it, at the sheer pleasure of his supremacy. Then, as now, Len thought, this is hopeless.

Len tired before the others and sat on a log. About the same time, Angie stopped chasing the glimpses and, inexplicably, jumped up into the cylinder of colored jet trails. To his amazement, Angie didn't come back down. She floated around with them, not exactly flying, more suspended in air. She seemed to be held up by these Lilliputians of light. Bennu was next. He joined the throng by prancing and then leaping into them. Instead of falling on his face, he joined Angie in the swirling flight.

Len guessed that the moving air churned up by the glimpses held them, like the way a current is created when a bunch of people walk around in a pool in the same direction. The only other explanation was that they were actually flying. No way. Yet, Bennu's nose did seem more beaklike than ever. Len leaned forward and watched Bennu and Angie spin around and around, until he became so dizzy that he fell off the log. Then he saw Piers do something the Misfits had not yet seen. Piers laughed. He laughed so hard a few tears slipped down his cheek. Len wondered how he could laugh so soon after Gandric's end. In fact, Piers seemed happier than before, as if he knew something the others didn't.

After a sigh, Piers shouted. "Not a glimpse here could match my wits today!"

Instantly the cylinder broke up. Angie glided to the ground and Bennu tumbled head over heels onto the blanket of oxalis that covered the forest floor.

One by one, glimpses flew into Piers's face.

"So no one can match your wits, eh?" said one. "That's because we'll outmatch it. We're all smarter."

"Barter?" twittered another. "What could he trade to increase his luck?"

"Stuck, you say? Piers will be as stuck as a hare in a trap."

"A map? Don't need one. I know right where I am. Piers is the bumbler."

"Plumber, indeed! Why, he couldn't unclog a stuck riddle with an ax and a hammer."

Piers bowed. "You honor me with your attention." At this, the glimpses stopped their parade of wisecracks and flew into a glimmery huddle ten yards away. "What shall it be?" Piers called over to them. "Insults or puzzles?"

"Oh, let's do insults," buzzed one. "They come so readily to the brain."

"Rain, you say? Not since yesterday. I say puzzles because ol' Piers hasn't got a chance."

"Dance? No, thank you, my ankles hurt."

The word games twaddled on, giving Len an opportunity to see the hovering glimpses more closely. They looked a bit like human wasps, but with the upper body clothed, possessing four arms, four wings, and two legs. Below copper brown heads, large abdomens glowed brightly, leaving a momentary swath of fairy light in the air, like a jet's trail of smoke. Len wondered if they had stingers.

Vida turned to Len and shielded her mouth so the glimpses couldn't hear her. "I've never friendified a group with such gobbledy-garbled verbifications!"

A glimpse in a yellow and black striped top flew up to Piers. "We've chosen puzzles, because we think you'll be all the more frustrated."

"You're so kind to take me into consideration," said Piers. "Who shall start?"

"Cart? Cart? No, sir, not before the horse, you know! We'll go."

Len put both hands on his head and smiled.

"An absentminded wizard named Nagflad lived in an airy spiraling tower with his loyal assistant, a dwarf named Droof. Nagflad was so forgetful that once, when standing at the tower's front door, he could not figure out if he was leaving or if he'd just arrived. So, over time, he'd developed a habit of pinching himself to jog his memory.

"The dragon Magus, Nagflad's feared nemesis, surprised the wizard as often as he could, hoping Nagflad would forget some incantation or potion. The servant Droof labored to overcome the wizard's absentmindedness so that Nagflad wouldn't make a mistake and stupidly counterattack with rose petals or goose feathers. If Droof could only get his master to take a teaspoon from the vial of dried owl's brains before he went into battle! Finally, Droof added his own special twisting pinch to Nagflad's posterior, thus reminding the wizard of the owl's brains and thereby immortalizing the saying . . ."

As Piers turned to the Misfits for help, the glimpse flew back to the swarm, which rested on neon green vine maple leaves, and all the glimpses whooped and twittered in triumph.

Prester John shook his finger at the winged riddlers. "Come to the Highlands some day, you buzzing bugs, and we'll show you how to play a game bravely."

Piers paced back and forth. "What do you think? Anyone want to guess?"

Bennu put a finger to his lips. "What about 'Save it for a brainy day'? No. 'Hitch a dragon to a jar'? No."

"Bennu," said Len, "you're good at this. All those word contests you've entered are paying off."

Bennu clapped his hands. "I've got it! The saying is 'Give them a pinch, they'll take a vial.'"

While the other Misfits and Welkeners groaned, the glimpses laughed on and on at their own "punny" humor.

Len shook his head. He wondered how many of these bad jokes they would have to endure to get back to Skinner. He picked up a leaf and tore bits of it off.

Piers took center stage. "Years ago, when my friends Sutton Hoo and Zennor Pict were young men, they came upon a herd of wild horses grazing near Maidenhair Meadow. A middle-aged shepherdess, Marion Phadrig, approached them. 'I spied you lads casin' me horses up and down as if they-in were sprightly lasses. Tell you what, if you kin git a horse o'mine to speak, I'll plain-out give it to yer.' The challenge made, Sutton and Zennor set out to teach the young stallion a word or two. They gave hour upon hour to the language trade, after chores, of course, but they never got more than a whinny or a neigh.

"One day, they were struck dumbfounded by a garbled sentence from the wild horse, 'Neighbors, -er-cud me-ah-hvv sum-rrhh-hay?' Delighted, the two lads demonstrated their student's skills to Marion, who promptly gave them the horse. While taking the stallion back to their homes, Sutton and Zennor heard the horse mumble the line over and over until they came to a partially washed-out bridge. Instead of turning around, the horse bolted from the boys, ran across the broken bridge, leapt as high as he could, fell, and was instantly swept down the river to his death.

"Sutton turned to Zennor and said . . ."

The glimpses flew into acrobatic contortions now, buzzing like a band of chain saws, first above Piers's head, then in a driving circle, then back to the alder leaves.

Vida and Prester John looked at each other as if to say "I don't remember anything about this horse."

After considerable buzzing commotion, a glimpse zipped up to Piers's face, panting. "We are happy to announce that we are deeply sorry to have unriddled the Lord of Primus Hook so effortlessly. Without a doubt, Sutton said, 'Wild horses couldn't steer us apart.'" Loud cheering burst forth from the swarm.

"We beat Piers! We beat Piers!"

"Beers? Much too early in the day."

"Pay? That's right! Make 'em pay, I say!"

"No, no, no," tut-tutted Piers. "You celebrate too hastily. Sutton turned to Zennor and said, 'You can lead a horse to mutter, but you can't make him think.'"

At this, the Misfits groaned, the glimpses moaned, and then pandemonium erupted. Len, who had been feeling so relaxed, worried about what the glimpses might do—what if they did have stingers? But, instead of cursing their loss, the glimpses were thrilled by Piers's story. They spun around, scattering sparkles in the air. Glimpsy laughter filled the wood, joined by Piers's own hearty slaps on the knee. The infectious joy swept over the Misfits. They looked at each other, laughed at the joke, at the buzzing good fun, and the release of all the pressure they'd felt as witnesses to Welken's troubles.

Len caught himself and tried to force the laughter back into a wry smile. He turned to Angie. "Don't you think it's weird that these word puzzles are about phrases from our world?" Before Angie could respond, the glimpses spoke up again.

"Muttering horses who can't think!"

"Did you say drink? Course I can, but I'm not thirsty!"

"You're right. It's not Thursday, but Friday, silly."

Finally, one glimpse flew over to Piers and said, "As usual, Lord of Primus Hook, we are at your service." His two right hands swept downward as he bowed.

"I don't get it," whispered Len to Angie.

"I think," she whispered back, "that the puzzles are social niceties, games to play on their turf as a way of showing respect. I'm guessing they would have helped us no matter what."

"We thank you, dear glimpses," said Piers solemnly, "for your gifts of laughter and joy. We have enjoyed this diversion from our weightier calling. So. So it is time to continue the journey. As all glimpses know, Welken is in danger. Part of our hope rests in these four friends. We need a volunteer to let us stretch the light back to their world."

The glimpses conferred briefly, then a dazzlingly bright one flew out. "I am Miss Zizzonte," she said. "In Welken, of Welken." In mid-air, she held her breath and pushed inwardly against her abdomen until the light that emanated from her hung as a golden drop. Several other glimpses swirled round, grabbed the orb, and pulled on its sides until it resembled a tiny trampoline.

Panting now, Miss Zizzonte said, "It's ready for you, Piers. Pull."

Piers plucked the sides delicately and pulled. Soon the circle was as large as a hand, and he could fit his fingers inside to pull it apart. He tugged at it until, finally, it hung in the air—a three-foot frame of luminescence. He motioned for Len to come up and look.

Len couldn't believe what he saw. Within the circle, as if on a video screen, there were the tree houses and the McKenzie Butte Boys, unmoving. A rock from Odin hung in mid-air, on its way to the platform where he once lay. Time was on freeze frame.

"Now what?" Len gasped. "Is this just a trick to send us back to the worst day of our lives?"

"The glimpse cannot hold this for long," said Piers. "Choose where you will enter and go."

"We have a choice?" asked Angie.

"Bennu," said Piers, ignoring Angie, "see if you can find a better place to enter."

"How? What can I do?"

"Get up higher and look through the ring from a different angle."

As Len watched in wonder, Bennu leaped, flapped his arms, and managed to stay stationary long enough to look in. "I see the bottom of the hill below the Peterson homestead. Can you pull the ring just a little larger? OK, good. Now, tilt it down and to the right." Then he swooped down and tumbled to the ground.

"Hurry!" pleaded Miss Zizzonte.

"I'm ready," said Lizbeth, stepping forward.

131

So, Len thought, she's the ruby slippers girl after all.

Piers led her up to the ring. "Step up and over. Go well."

She slipped in and then poked her head back. "Hurry up, the rest of you. I don't want to be alone."

With eyes that beseeched Piers, Angie stood at the cusp of two worlds.

"Piers," said Angie, "you showed us how we get back home—but what are we to do there?"

"I don't know exactly," said Piers. "Somehow you need to help find what the guardians lost. I wish I knew more. All I can say is to listen. Look well. Pay attention. There are glimpses in your world too."

"How do we get back to Welken?"

"Your vision is keener now. You know more than you think you know. What you used to mistake for a fanciful thought or a trick of the imagination might now appear as a meeting of our worlds. When the eye and heart are one, you'll know truly what it is you see."

With this blessing, Angie stepped through the portal, offering her hand to help Bennu over the lip of the ring. He took it, though Len knew he had no need.

Before Len stepped through, Piers put a hand on the Misfit's shoulder. "Len, you have a special burden to bear, the weight of not knowing. Though we must all suffer this heaviness at times, now it is your turn. I cannot help but think it will serve some good purpose. Your task is to discover that purpose."

"I will try to find my way, Piers," said Len, surprising himself with his gentleness. "I will try to be less flippant too." Haltingly, he stepped through the ring.

Just before the ring closed, he turned and saw Piers's face.

"In Welken," Piers said.

"Of Welken," Len said, "I guess."

༐༈ཉ

At the bottom of the steep grassy hill, the disoriented Misfits found themselves sitting in a bed of violets. For a few moments, they looked around and at each other without speaking. Lizbeth mentally pinched herself to see if the memories of Welken vanished with a twitch. She closed her eyes and saw the wrought-iron designs inside the south door in Ganderst Hall. She imagined herself talking to Ellen Basala and trying to understand Vida Bering Well.

Yet she also knew that the hard evidence of Welken was gone. Here they were at the bottom of a hill, smelling violets, listening to a piercing hawk overhead, watching the butterflies flit from flower to flower.

Everything seemed fuzzy to Lizbeth. She didn't quite know what to say, and she feared that by speaking she would force them back into real time. She didn't want to break the sense of being in Welken—or to cast doubt on the whole experience. At the bottom of this hill, there was no river of light or Deedy-speech or reassuring voice from Piers.

And yet, no Morphane either.

The first to speak was not any of the bewildered four sitting in the grass but a disgruntled McKenzie Butte Boy yelling about missing victims and having too much to drink that morning. His voice snapped the Misfits out of their daze.

"Hey!" said Lizbeth, "the McKenzie thugs are still up there. All the time we spent in Welken was like nothing here. Let's get out of here."

As Lizbeth jumped up, into their midst walked their favorite domestic pet, Percy, who had in his mouth Bennu's glasses. When she looked at Bennu, he gave her a yeah-I-need-them look. And then she noticed Len fitting his hat over his hair and that Angie was thoroughly visible. She flexed her muscles. Though no weakling, she wasn't rippling with strength.

Something about that felt like a loss, but it also felt very much like home, ruby slippers or no.

Without saying much, the four hurried back to the canoe they had stashed in the reeds. What would normally have seemed an arduous task, punting and rowing against the current of the Lewis River, felt to Lizbeth easy to bear. Sticking to the shallow banks, they paddled along, occasionally needing to get out and carry the canoe for a few yards. No one could get quite enough of petting Percy.

PART THREE
THE STRENGTH OF HISTORY

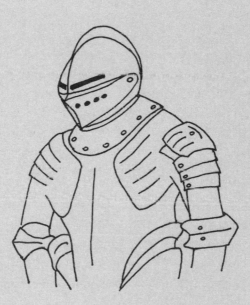

CHAPTER FIFTEEN

CHOOSING TO BE CHOSEN

I feel again a spark of that ancient flame.

VIRGIL, *AENEID*

 *Often I have said that Welken's mysteries have a way of getting inside those who live them. And the truth is, the place also touches those who only hear the tale. Who can resist it and who would want to? Surely not Bennu or Lizbeth or Angie. And Len? His story is just beginning. As the other Misfits have learned, there's something here of home.*

In the canoe, watching ferns and branches bob in the water, Len listened to explanations.

Bennu compared it to the tingling sensation of having his scalp massaged. Lizbeth spoke of the joyful anticipation of Christmas Day. Angie's version could be discerned from her contented smile. Len said nothing in response.

After pushing the canoe away from a large boulder, Len's head throbbed, a sensation he hadn't felt since before the river of light. "I guess you could say this day turned out differently than we planned. The breeze across the Lewis sure feels good."

"To me," said Bennu, "each description is like a fleeting introductory paragraph. Welken's story must be so much larger."

136

Lizbeth used some river water to wash mud off her shoes. "Don't forget Morphane. I saw him. Twice."

"OK," said Angie, "but you don't forget Ganderst Hall and silly Vida Bering Well, and of course, Piers."

For some reason Len couldn't put his finger on, his head wound irritated him more with every sentence about Welken. He stroked the water harder to try to take his mind off his head.

Lizbeth brushed aside some hanging willow branches. "Funny. We've only been back a half an hour and already Welken feels like a long time ago. It's like when you come back from vacation and it seems like you never left. This tree here makes me think that *it's* more real than my memory."

Len struggled to pull the paddle through the water. "No kidding, Lizbeth. You *want* to believe there's a saber-toothed tiger that sucks your face off? I don't think so. Did you sniff some happy powder or something?"

Bennu pulled his paddle out and let the canoe drift for a few yards. "Len, you can't deny the magic. You entered the Window under the Mountain. You stepped through the circle of light." The river's current started to turn the canoe around.

"I suppose. But maybe it was just some trick. Maybe we were hypnotized. Maybe we were all knocked out and rolled down the hill by those McKenzie idiots and we just woke up."

Bennu flicked some water at Len. "And we all had the same dream?"

"OK, my theory has some flaws, but let me think about it some more. In the meantime, let's paddle or we'll never get home."

***

The clunk of "Toy Boat Times Three" against the dock provided the final jolt of reentry. Exhausted and exhilarated at the same time, Lizbeth was grateful to get out of the canoe without knocking anyone into the water. She looked at her watch. It was 4:30.

This was it, Lizbeth thought, Skinnerian reality. Back to the ordinary. Back to parents and chores and the same ol' days.

"Come over as soon as you can," Bennu said to Len and Angie. "Maybe we can find a glimpse before dinner."

Lizbeth watched Percy lead the Bartholomews back toward their house. He swatted at butterflies as if nothing monumental had happened.

With each step, Lizbeth grew increasingly conscious of her sense of place—or lack of place—in her own world. She tried to remember what it was like to feel so powerful in Welken. She held out both arms like a bodybuilder, then thought about how dumb it looked.

I'm just not cool, she thought, period. I can't get any boys to notice me, except the wrong ones. She looked across the river to the home of Weyerhauser High's "chosen one," the cheerleader, the goddess, the all-everything.

And what am I? she thought. Just a stocky pedestal for her to stand on.

She looked back and saw her mom, Darlene Neferti, standing by the back gate, waving to the two of them. "Hello, children! Welcome to hearth and home!"

"Mom," said Bennu, shaking his head. "She has a singular ability to snap me out of whatever I'm thinking. She's not just 'over the top.' She's cappuccino foam gone amuck."

"Oh, here come my two little cuties!" She hugged Bennu and Lizbeth and led them through the yard to her treat on the deck, lemonade made with genuine lemon crystals. Then she wagged a finger at their cockapoo's wagging tail. "Now, Sniffles, why don't you come here and greet our great adventurers? That's right, Sniffle-piffle, go get 'em."

Sniffles ran up to them and squatted.

Bennu stopped and glared at the dog. "Mom! Sniffles pees every time she sees us. Argh. Get a cork!"

"I know. She's just excited to see you." Darlene snatched some paper towels and patted up the mess. "By the way, what did you two do in the Wilder today? Did you catch any tadpoles?"

Lizbeth wondered if she could feel any farther from Welken than she did in this moment. "Mom, we're just a little beyond tadpoles."

"I know!" said Darlene with a wink. "Can't you take a joke? You miss most of mine because you think I'm a dumb blonde. I'm not. I'm a dumb brunette."

Lizbeth wondered how this should make them feel better.

"Martin, our humorless wonders are here. Why don't you leave your little workaholic station and say hello?"

Martin leaned out of the window that faced the deck. "Bennu, Lizbeth, how are you doing?" He left the window and came outside. "I'm working on some ad copy for wine labels. You know me, I like to check them out with you guys. What do you think of these:

> The cabernet from Pleasant Valley Vineyards is at once cunning and rich. The large buttery smoothness delights the tenderest of palates and sparks visions of romantic white sands and warm Caribbean nights.

"Or this:

> Pleasant Valley Vineyards is pleased to announce its award-winning cabernet, crisp, oak-laden, with delicate hints of cinnamon and caramel, reminiscent of a cool stroll through a textured English garden.

"Which one do you like best?" Martin's smile said he thought both were outstanding.

"Dad, I don't know anything about wine," said Lizbeth.

"That doesn't matter. How do they *feel* to you?"

Bennu sighed. "Dad, they *feel* ridiculous. You just said opposite things about the same wine. How can something be cunning *and* delicate, warm *and* cool?"

Martin's veins popped out at them like stripes on his Hawaiian shirt. "Why do I ask? You just don't get it. This is art, not scientific reporting. Besides, I've heard you say 'Lizbeth, this is really hot!' And she'll reply, 'Really, that's cool.'"

"That's different, Dad."

"It always is." He stopped and then his eyes brightened. "Wait a minute. What a great slogan: Tide detergent—'it always is'—or 'Heinz ketchup—it always is.'"

Dumbfounded, Lizbeth said, "It always is *what*, Dad?"

"It *is*! That's what matters. Have you forgotten the Greek philosopher Parmenides: 'Whatever is, is'? Never mind."

Lizbeth longed for the sensible speech of Vida Bering Well.

When Len and Angie arrived at their own back gate, it was open wide.

Len saw their mother in the Adirondack chair. "Hi, Mom. How's it goin'?"

"I've had such a productive day," said Charlotte, glowing. "I've written *three* chapters while you've been roaming around."

"Really?" said Angie. "I'm impressed. What are the titles?"

"Well, there's 'Pyramids and Paddywagons,' 'Wise Dominic's Ford,' and 'Those Marvelous Muddingtons.' Want to hear them?"

"Love to, Mom," said Len, glancing at Angie, "but we're tired from, like, paddling. Maybe later."

"So you rowed then? That's 'like' paddling."

Len cocked his head and rolled his eyes.

Charlotte went on. "OK. I guess I can wait. You were so anxious for me to write more, I thought you'd want to listen to the story right away."

Angie patted her mom on the knee. "We do, Mom, just later, that's all. I'm kind of wobblerated right now."

"What?"

"Nothing."

An hour later, after Len ate a bowl of cereal and two fun-size candy bars ("Whoopee!" he said to Angie), and Angie taunted Percy with a catnip mouse, Len swung open the front door screen and Angie followed behind him. Len noticed that it didn't slam, so he looked back. His mother stood in the doorway. "Your story isn't going to rot or anything, Mom. We'll listen later. We have something important to do right now."

⌇⌇⌇

After saying "No, thank you" to Darlene's offerings of angel food cake and iced mango tea and "Yes" to chocolate-covered Rice Krispies squares, the Misfits finally left the house to find whatever it was they were supposed to get without knowing wherever it was they were supposed to look. Once out the door, they walked toward LaRusso Park at the end of the street, ten acres of rolling green that invited carefree thinking.

Lizbeth kicked a rock. "Something awesome is going to happen, I bet."

"So," said Len, "do we look for glimpsy fireflies or go straight to the Welken wagon?" He jumped on and off the curb as if on his skateboard.

"Very funny, Lenny dear," said Lizbeth, baiting him. "Maybe it will take more than five minutes, though I know that is four minutes and fifty-nine seconds past your quota of patience." Lizbeth could not believe that Len was as flippant as ever.

When they reached the wood chips around the play equipment, Angie held up a hand. "Wait! I think I feel a light Welken breeze."

"Yeah, right," said Len. "What you feel is the same late afternoon wind we get all the time."

"Over here," she added, ignoring Len. "Look in these birch trees, under the leaves." Len looked under one leaf and then sat on a stump.

"Hey! I found something!" shouted Lizbeth. "No, wait, just some aphids."

Len waved a fist in mock triumph. "Hey, Ang, I don't think there's a message here."

"Yes, there is," she said. "All good things remind me of Welken. All these beauties—the shining leaves, the soft rays of the sun—all these glowing things take me back to Piers and Terz, Prester John and the rest, don't you see? Wouldn't you love to be lifted by Sutton Hoo, weightless in his massive arms?"

"It's not so great, Ang, really." Len walked away. "My back still hurts, and my head is worse. At least my hat fits again." He took it off and rearranged it as his dad might straighten his tie, being sure to get it just right before going out in public. "I'm going to the corner store to get some chocolate. Anyone coming?"

One by one, the Misfits fell in line. Lizbeth watched Angie pluck jasmine flowers and inhale their scent. She also saw Bennu's glassy-eyed rapture. Along the path, they searched in bushes and looked inside trash cans. All they found was an empty can of Bud Light.

Once they got to the store, Len launched into his best Humphrey Bogart: "Spread out and case the joint. These glimpses could be hiding anywhere."

As Lizbeth obeyed, Len plopped down by the magazine rack and picked up the local newspaper. She cruised past the candy, trying not to dawdle since she knew what people thought of overweight girls lusting after calories. ("How can they just sit there and eat," she imagined them saying. "Don't they know they look fat?") She ended up in the wine section and started reading labels: "Wistfully robust," "A hearty, passionate burgundy," "A chardonnay soft as heather on the moors." Unbelievable, she thought, Dad's right in step.

She walked to another aisle just in time to see Bennu "accidentally" bump into Angie. Together they lifted loaves of bread to see if any fairies slept behind them. Lizbeth guessed he was about to say something stupid, like "Angie, you're the yeast in my sourdough."

Instead, the crusty cashier, Captain Mini-Mart as Len liked to call him, yelled, "Hey! There's one loaf you haven't squished yet! Let's make them all equal!"

Well, thought Lizbeth, I don't think *he* is going to remind anyone of a glimpse.

Eventually, empty-handed, Bennu, Angie, and Lizbeth wandered over to Len, who read the headlines to them: "'Sex Scandal in Washington.' 'Toxic Waste Spoils Four Midwest Rivers.' 'Shooting Spree in Texas Kills Nineteen Children.'" He paused. "Truly charming. I think I'll buy a new dead bolt. Oh, look! Something on the front page that's not a disaster! 'Museum Exhibit on National Tour.' Just gives you something to live for, eh?"

A voice bellowed from the counter. "You gonna buy the paper or just trash it and leave? You think this is a library?"

In no time, they were out the door and back at the Bartholomews.

While on the front porch, Lizbeth looked in and noticed Percy on the corduroy couch. She threw open the screen. "Percy, baby, how are you?" Len rolled his eyes. As Lizbeth picked up Percy, the top sheet of Charlotte's manuscript fell from the couch to the floor. "Hey, this is the book your mom is writing, right? Why don't we ask her to read us the chapters now? It's bound to cheer us up." Len took the hint.

Len found his mother on the back porch, in the chaise lounge with her eyes closed. He snuck up and shouted, "Hey, Mom!"

Charlotte bolted up. "That's not funny, young man."

"We're ready for those chapters now."

"You scare me to death, and I'm supposed to do what you want?"

"Mom, c'mon, we're all here, and there's enough time before dinner."

"I'm not opening my eyes."

"Too late. Mom, you're the one who was so bent out of shape when we wouldn't listen earlier."

"Amazing. *You* disturb my nap, and *I'm* at fault. Oh, well, focus-group beggars can't be choosers."

"I knew you'd see I had your best interest at heart."

Charlotte rubbed her eyes, followed Len into the living room, and straightened out the pages that Percy had made into his own crinkly bed. Soon, she recounted Ollie's escape and Wise Dominic's vision of the pyramid. She paused after these two chapters, drank a sip of diet caffeine-free supermarket brand cola, and readied the next page.

"What was that again, Charlotte?" asked Bennu.

"What was what?"

"That part about the fours."

"Wise Dominic said he'd been impressed with fours, that's all."

"Why?"

"How am I supposed to know? I'm only the messenger." She cleared her throat once again.

CHAPTER FOUR: Those Marvelous Muddingtons

On the gray deck of the ocean liner *Elephantisimo*, Ollie Ollie Otterson grew increasingly nervous. "I can't stand it, dear Mama," fumed Ollie. "Delicious happiness all around me, and no skull duggery going on. It's enough to break one's itty bitty black heart."

Ollie surveyed the passengers, his view darting from neck to finger to wrist, from pearl strand to ruby ring to jade bracelet. Zipping through the forest of passengers like a monkey late for a Year of the Banana celebration, Ollie snatched two watches and three wallets by the time he reached his own cabin.

"Proud of me, proud of me," he sang. "Oh, Mama, you'd be proud of me. I showed I could be good for two whole long days. Ain't I a disciplined boy? And then, oh, the thrill and the glory, the hot flush of success. This reminds me of home cookin', Mama. You doin' what you do best, with a smile on your face. And here I am, doin' what I do best, givin' my friends freedom from their valuables. I love to help others, Mama. It's my best personality."

❦

Just above Ollie's room, in cabin 228, a boundless ocean view appealed to Hammy and Porticia Muddington's love for things enormous. At a collective 750 pounds, the Muddingtons liked to say they were always "livin' large." To serve their needs, a butler named Cecil Von Sapp sniveled obediently. Moments after Porticia rang for him, she heard the doorbell and opened the door.

"So pleased to be of service, Mrs. Muddington," said a different butler. "What shall it be for brunch today? A fresh cucumber salad or my own recipe of mango blintzes with spearmint sauce?"

"Oh, hello," responded Porticia. "What happened to poor Cecil?"

"He's simply taking a lunch break. I'll be filling in for him in the meanwhile. My name is Maxwell Quicksilver. At your service, madam."

"Yes, thank you, Maxwell. I like you better already. I'm getting hungry waiting for Hammy to return, so be a dear and fetch me five blintzes, an espresso with cream, new potatoes with basil, a tray of fresh fruit, and oh, you surprise me!"

Faster than a cat jumping out of a bathtub, Maxwell was back with the culinary treats.

Porticia grinned widely at Maxwell and said, "My, my, my. I must try just a little of each one first." Having finished her taste test, she set her fork down, patted her lips with a cloth napkin, and asked Maxwell if he would be a darling and get her silk bib from the top dresser drawer. Thus protected from "accidents," Porticia threw herself into the task of eating with an abandon that shocked Maxwell's sensibilities.

Five blintzes. Gone. New potatoes. Poof! Apples and bananas. Kiss 'em good-bye. Then a full two dozen oysters in lorenzo dressing.

Maxwell realized that here was an appetite that fulfilled its every craving.

Porticia burped and then burped again. "What a daring surprise!" She raised her shucking knife, smiled broadly at Maxwell, whispered, "Thank you," in a saucy showgirl way, and promptly collapsed head first into the remaining oyster sauce.

"Pity," said Maxwell. "Mama gave me that lorenzo dressing recipe herself, after years of tongue-tiring taste-testing. Toodly-too bad!" Then as fast as you can say "Hammy's in the staff's quarters showing off his army medals, and Porticia's in the oyster bowl snoozing blissfully," Ollie opened every drawer, cracked every safe, and rifled through every suitcase.

"Oh, Mama," he yapped, "it's just too easy sometimes. A little druggy-poo in the foody-poo and, voilà, a little sleepy-poo. When I'm reformed, I'm going to teach seminars on 'How Not to Be Duped by Brilliant Robbers.' Of course, all the profit will go to you, Mama. Whoa! Look at all this! Emeralds and opals and gold and silver. There's enough here to fill a pyramid! There's enough treasure here to send it out on a museum tour. And I know I'll do that just after I show all of it to you, Mama. I'm becoming a better and betterer citizen by the minute."

His knapsack nearly full, the deliriously burdened burglar closed the door to cabin 228 and made his way downstairs. Unfortunately for him, he passed by the staff's quarters just as Hammy Muddington walked out. With his knapsack loaded, Ollie could not easily pass Hammy's fatness in the narrow hallway. Belly to buckle, Hammy and Ollie shuffled in opposite directions, smashing up against the walls until Ollie pressed too tightly against Hammy's medal-filled chest.

"Ow!" Hammy yelled as the point from the Purple Heart stabbed him. (He injured his wrist serving grub to the dough-boys in the trenches of the Great War.) Frozen there for a minute, Hammy glanced behind Ollie and noticed a hilt of a military knife sticking out of the knapsack. The inscription, "To Hammy Muddington, for valor and excellent dinner rolls," stared back at him.

"Hey! Where'd you get this stuff? Help! Thief! Help!"

The most pathetic chase in Ollie's entire career ensued, with five ship's mates rushing out of the staff's quarters and pulling Ollie away from Hammy and then away from his knap-sack. On the way to the brig, Ollie pleaded with his captors. "You shouldn't be disappointing my dear Mama like this, offi-cers. What am I supposed to do for her birthday?"

※

With a start, Porticia awakened, finding her face covered in oyster goo. "How positively lovely!" she said as she lapped up every drop. "And that dear boy, so humble he left before I could properly thank him."

Lizbeth laughed. "Cute, cute, cute. Ollie in disguise is a nice touch."

"They're a lot of fun," Bennu said. "Your characters, I mean. Where do you get your ideas?"

"That's hard to say, Bennu. I was talking with your mom about some CD she wanted, and she said she couldn't remember the name of the group exactly, the Rippingtons or Muddingtons or something. The origin of that idea I can locate. But most of the time, I feel like I'm just passing along what comes to me, not that I think it's some sacred text or anything. Much of it feels like a gift. Why?"

"I find it curious that we just read about a museum exhibit of Egyptian stuff, and here Ollie brings up the same thing. What are the chances of that?"

"Who knows?"

CHAPTER SIXTEEN
OVERLAPPING SEAMS

Awake, my St. John! Leave all meaner things
to low ambition, and the pride of kings.
Let us, since life can little more supply
Than just to look about us, and to die,
Expatiate free o'er all this scene of man;
A mighty maze! But not without a plan.

ALEXANDER POPE, *AN ESSAY ON MAN*

 From behind her head, Lizbeth grabbed Percy and put him in her lap. "I like it, Charlotte. Porticia Muddington is funny."

Len chomped on potato chips. "Yeah, the food is cool."

"Thanks. I hope you're not just being nice. I'm worried the reference to the pyramids doesn't quite fit. Any comments?"

"I think you need to hint more about what's ahead," said Len, wiping his hands on his T-shirt. "In the Wise Dominic chapter, he makes such a big idea about fours. Why?"

"We should all find out soon enough," said Charlotte with a smile. "All good things come to those who—"

"Wait!" shouted Bennu.

Charlotte flinched. "That's what I was going to say."

"No—*wait*—a minute." Bennu got up and paced around. "Something else is really wrong here—or odd—or maybe something is really right here. I don't know. I'm so confused. The whole thing is too weird to be believed."

"What are you saying?" asked Lizbeth.

"I think I've seen a glimpse."

"A glimpse?" asked Charlotte. "A glimpse of what? What do you mean?"

Bennu's eyes flitted side to side as he fumbled for an answer. "Oh, nothing, Charlotte. The story made me think of something . . . um . . . that I finished at the end of the semester . . . for . . . er . . . Mr. Giuliano, in History. Lizbeth, don't we have to be back for dinner?" Bennu opened the front door. "Thanks so much, Charlotte. Keep writing. I'm sure *this* one will get published."

Lizbeth imagined Charlotte opening a stack of rejection letters. "Bennu has a real knack for encouragement. See you later."

As Bennu and Lizbeth headed for home, Lizbeth repeatedly nudged her brother with one finger. "OK, you can tell me now. Where was the glimpse? You saw Miss Zizzonte? Someone new? A different kind of glimpse? C'mon, out with it!"

"I can't say just yet," he answered, stepping up on the curb to get away.

"What do you mean you 'can't say'?" She pushed him off onto the street. "I'm your sister, for crying out loud!"

"Let's see, how would Percy put it? 'For crying out loud and clear.'"

"Don't change the subject. What did you see?" She stuck her finger in his back.

"I'll tell you soon enough. I want to be more sure first. And knock it off with the poking."

"Arrgh, brothers! Why can't you tell me? Don't you trust me?"

"It has nothing to do with you. Not everything does, you know."

That quieted Lizbeth. She kicked at a fast food cup in the gutter.

He didn't have to say that, she thought. You'd think I'd get used to being hammered. What's that expression? Like water off a duck's back? My back is more like a sponge.

ᔕᑎᔐ

On Sunday, Bennu still didn't want to talk about his "glimpse." For some reason that didn't make sense to Lizbeth, he said it needed to simmer awhile. Besides, the family was busy. Loyal Copts, the Nefertis met on Sunday with a small group of other Coptic Christians. They followed the service with a leisurely Sunday lunch, then rest, during which everyone was supposed to spend some time praying. Lizbeth usually asked God for slimmer hips, but this Sunday she found her intercession turning to Welken's woes. Then, questions came. Was her God also the God of Welken? If not, what was she to do about the lines she'd learned: "God of the *universe*" and "In Him *all* things were made"? If so, then who was this God of both worlds?

Despite these worries, Lizbeth felt good to be praying about something besides her rear end.

A few blocks away, the Bartholomews kept their Sunday commitments also. At Jack's Gourmet Bagels—Jack's "Bagel Baptist," as Len called it— special communion could be observed between Jeff and the sports page, Charlotte with "Arts and Leisure," Len and the comics, and Angie and *Parade* magazine. With the front page largely ignored, they could all pontificate about politics without fear of contradiction by the facts. Special Muzak filled the air, and lattes were consumed with reverence and awe.

When Len asked Angie to switch newspaper sections, she held her hands over two photographs on one page of the magazine.

Len tugged at a corner. "C'mon, Angie, don't be stubborn. Let me see *Parade*. You can look at the comics."

"Just a minute, Len. Something is happening around the edges. The borders are moving away. And not just here. Don't you feel it too? Look, the two people in the photos can talk to each other now."

Len sipped his caramel mocha. "If you aren't done with the *Parade*, Angie, all you have to do is say so."

When they returned home, Jeff and Charlotte went off to nap, but Len and Angie gravitated to the kitchen.

Len grabbed a bowl and some cereal. "I'll tell you one thing that bothers me about this whole Welken business." He poured milk into the bowl. "You feel even more justified in your stupid hallucinations."

"I'm not listening." Angie put her fingers in her ears. "La la la la la—hey, didn't we just eat?"

"What's that got to do with anything?" He pulled her fingers out. "I mean it, Ang. Like I said a few days ago, it's embarrassing. You act like whatever you think of is perfectly acceptable. No filters. No screens. What if I did that?" Len lurched around the kitchen like a blind Frankenstein, speaking in a haunted voice. "I feel like I'm walking in jelly, grape I think, and above me are the gardens of Tripoli, vines of all kinds with pomegranates and berries getting in my hair—but the jelly on the ground is moving. I'm being swept away. Oh noooo—"

"I can see you aren't exactly ready to be called Leonard the Lion-Hearted."

"Oh, Ang, you hurt my feelings." Len stuck out an insincere lower lip, then heaped huge, dripping spoonfuls of cereal into his mouth. As the milk ran down his chin, he smiled with a mouth full of Cinnamon Donut Crunchies.

"Len, you can be so dumb. Don't you get it? You just imitated what we did in the tunnel when you woke up. The cave tentacles hit you, and you bumped Piers, and we ended up in baby Yosemite Valley. Why are you being such a brat?"

Rats, thought Len, I hate it when she's right about alternate universes.

❧

On Monday Bennu was ready to talk, so he assembled the Misfits in Len's room. Len sat on his bed under the Portland Trailblazers poster. Bennu brushed clothes off the never-used desk chair and sat down. As the girls plopped onto huge pillows on the floor, Bennu pushed his glasses up and ran his hand through his shiny black hair. "I've put a couple of things together. OK, I know this sounds ridiculous—but when your mom was reading about Percy and Bones, I felt like Wise Dominic was speaking right to me, like he was a messenger or something."

"Sure," said Len, tossing a pair of socks in the air, "and the *Cat in the Hat* means we should go back to Welken and look for Thing One and Thing Two."

Angie threw a shirt from the floor at Len. "I don't get it, Len. You walked through the river of light. You saw the glimpses in the alder grove,

150

didn't you? Why are you such a pain?"

Len threw the shirt back. "To tell you the truth, I don't know why. It's just who I am, I guess." He waited, trying to decide what to tell them. "Sometimes I'm not so sure what I saw. Other times, I just feel that, like, somebody's got to try to keep our feet on the ground before we all get sent to the funny farm. And another thing, why should we care about their problems?"

"Because," said Angie and Lizbeth simultaneously.

"Look, I liked the light show and the glimpses, too, but 'because' doesn't cut it."

"OK," said Bennu, "maybe this will help. Here's what I noticed: First, Wise Dominic's reference to the fours. Second, Ollie's newspaper clipping about the loot in the Egyptian tomb. Third, the reference to the museum exhibit. Remember the four missing tiles in the Tetragrammaton? Then this." He thrust out the newspaper they'd examined at the corner store. The lower right part of the front page, reserved for "good news," said "Museum Exhibit on National Tour."

> (AP) *NEW YORK*—The most astounding Egyptian artifacts since the tour of King Tut's treasures go on display this week in the Willamette Museum.
>
> Discovered recently in the abandoned attic of turn-of-the-century amateur archeologist Kieran Barth, from Robertsbridge, England, these riches are both visually stunning and mysterious.
>
> "Most vexing of all," says curator Leslie Green, "is a sacred Egyptian amulet with four rings inscribed in different languages. The foremost Egyptian scholars in the world have no current explanation, especially for the Coptic cross at the center." The exhibit is on display Mon.–Fri. 9 a.m.–5 p.m.

Bennu stood proudly, his arms folded like a general in a briefing room. "What do you think?"

"That's your glimpsy insight?" said Len. "It's about as likely to help us as the odds of us winning the lottery. Y'know, we have a better chance of being struck by lightning twice in one year. I read that recently."

Lizbeth got off the floor. "I think Len needs to drive us to the museum."

"Len," said Angie, "what about it?"

Even though he was intrigued, Len tried to look disappointed. "Fine. What else am I going to do with my time? Trouble is, my car's dead and Dad has already left for his office, no doubt informing previously happy people of their root canals and cavities. So we can't take the new car. Mom said she wanted to file exams and stuff at her office, but that can probably wait."

He left the room and found his mother in the kitchen finishing off her last swig of coffee. "Mom!"

"Hmm?" Charlotte looked up and choked on a bite of biscotti.

"Mom, could I have your attention for a second? You're always saying how you want no distractions so you can write. I have an offer for you! If we take the car, we'll be out of your hair *and* you won't be tempted to drive anywhere."

Charlotte put her cup down. "It's amazing how letting you have the car is actually helping me."

"Glad you see the logic of it, Mom."

"Fine. Just bring it home with gas in it."

"No problem—as always."

"That's what I'm afraid of."

⌇⌇⌇

Once into the shabby, unwaxed, four-door, baby blue Buick Skylark, the Misfits were anything but "ready to cruise." After several wisecracks about the boxy shape, torn vinyl seats, and perfectly preserved gutless engine, Len started it up and pulled into the reputation-threatening streets of Skinner.

What if some hot cheerleader saw me in this? thought Len. She'd probably . . . well . . . give me the same attention they all give me: zip, zippo, zilch.

At the corner of Broadway and University, the Buick loudly announced

152

its stop at the red light, courtesy of squeaky brakes. A low-riding, rust-bombed, gas-hogging, moldy green Ford LTD pulled up to the right lane limit line next to the four-cylinder Skylark. Familiar tattoos on the upper arm announced the driver's identity.

"Hello, my trespassing friends." Odin's deep gravelly voice sent shudders through the Skylark's interior.

C'mon, light, turn green, thought Len.

"You were rude to leave us so suddenly the other day. We'd like to have a little chat about how you disappeared like that. Smooth trick, eh, guys?"

Let's go. Green! Now!

"Perhaps we can meet again and pick up where we left off."

In the backseat, Tommy held up a tire iron. He started to open the door. From the front passenger seat, Josh reached out and grabbed his brother's right shoulder. "C'mon, Tommy, not here."

This must be the longest light in town!

Odin reached across the front seat and grabbed the daypack Bennu had left at the Peterson homestead. "Thanks for the snacks." He tossed it onto the Skylark's hood. "We always try to return what doesn't belong to us. Keep us in mind, won't you?"

Just before the light changed, Lizbeth hopped out and picked up the daypack off the hood, empty candy wrappers flying everywhere. Then the LTD stormed off at full throttle, leaving the Misfits in a plume of oil-drenched exhaust and the fading laughter of the McKenzie Boys. Len's face seethed red with anger, but his legs shook in contradiction. He slammed on the gas. The car lurched forward and died in the middle of the intersection. There, in the street, Len's mind was as stuck as the car, churning over and over the fearful images of pulleys, knives, rocks, and blood—but going nowhere. He looked over at Bennu's white face and hoped his friend wouldn't throw up in front of Angie. The horn of a pickup truck from behind added more pressure. Len got the Buick started.

Once on their way, Bennu looked in the daypack. "Well, they took everything. No surprise. But they did leave this." He held up a water bottle with yellow liquid in it. "I don't think this is Mountain Dew."

When the Misfits finally made their way inside the Willamette Museum's special exhibit room, no one was happier to be out of danger than Len. To compete with the LTD from behind the Buick's wheel felt like jousting a knight with a piece of string. Perhaps the image came to him because mixed in with the pharaoh's treasures were medieval armaments. As he and the others studied these paradoxes, they eavesdropped on the museum director's lecture.

"Of particular interest is the archeologist himself, Dr. Kieran Barth. He brought truckloads of ancient Egyptian and medieval English artifacts to his cottage in Robertsbridge, England, and then he arranged his attic precisely as you see this room now. The questions for us are: Why did Dr. Barth collect these pieces? Why did he display them in his attic this way? And what is the meaning of the scarab amulet featured in the center of the room? We leave you with these mysteries. Enjoy."

Enjoy? thought Len. Yeah, this will be an Ancient Artifact Extravaganza.

Once the other visitors moved on to another exhibit, Len could see that each wall of the attic had a number of artifacts centered around a figure that faced its reflection on the opposite side. Two sarcophagi looked at each other east to west, and two English knights in armor faced each other north to south, leaving the unmistakable impression that they were all staring at the amulet in the center.

Lizbeth examined some ancient writing. "Looks occultish to me, like the Golden Knights of the Dawn or something. It feels spooky."

While Angie dream-walked around the room, Bennu and Len stepped up to study the amulet. About six inches in diameter, the amulet was a golden heart-shaped scarab, a dung beetle that, the sign said, ancient Egyptians used to symbolize rebirth.

"Well," said Len, "there's nothing like a poop-loving bug to get my attention."

Bennu pointed to the description. "It says here that the heart shape was thought to help the wearer be found 'true of voice' at the final judgment. That's cool. And on the bottom of the amulet, there's a Coptic ankh, and scholars think there are parts of words in Latin, Gaelic, and hieroglyphics."

Len puffed on a pretend pipe and spoke in professorial tones. "According to Dr. Deadwood at the University of Boredom, the dung beetle represents the ancient pop invasion of the Rolling Stones—"

"Humor can hurt, you know."

"What?" Len turned to face his doubter. He looked down at a woman under five feet tall standing right next to the scarab amulet.

She smiled broadly at Len, revealing her nicotine-stained teeth. "I'm not surprised you don't understand. Why should you know about Egypt and England, mummies and armor? I, on the other hand, have traveled the trade routes, have retraced the steps. I can see into the heart of the scarab."

"Right," said Len. "I bet you've met Napoleon, too." He turned away. To Bennu, he whispered, "Why do we attract all the mental cases?"

"I do have credentials." She pulled him back by his sleeve. "I am Miriam Rashid, and I come from El Amarnd in Egypt."

"That's just fabulous, Maryann." Len put on a phony smile. "But I think we need to be moving on. We're just looking; we don't need any help."

"The name is Miriam. And you should stay. I have such a long story to tell—"

Len looked around. "Bennu, Lizbeth, can you deal with this lady? She says she's Egyptian."

"Fine," said Lizbeth, "and you can deal with all the stupid white people we meet."

Ouch, thought Len. You got me on that one.

The woman held up a badge. "You see, I am a museum docent. In fact, I am a special consultant, traveling with this exhibit. What are your names?"

"Lizbeth."

"Bennu."

Len said nothing till Bennu elbowed him. "Fine, I'm Len."

"Pleased to meet you. You might like to know that I'm quite an expert on this amulet. My great-grandfather was the guide for Dr. Kieran Barth as he toured the tombs."

Len leaned on the Plexiglas cover. "OK, Ms. Rashneesh, if you know so many secrets, why are you telling us?"

Miriam pulled Len's hand away from the clear plastic. "That's *Rashid*, Miriam Rashid." She adjusted her museum vest. "I am telling you because I come from a long line of *griots*, the storytellers of our tribe. But more than this, my family line has been concerned about this amulet for generations. Tradition tells us it has special powers if put in the right hands. You might say we are waiting for a fulfillment of prophecy, for the right wayfarers to come searching after the amulet."

"And you think it's us?" asked Lizbeth.

"I just met you—but we try to take everyone seriously. We griots have a gift for seeing the truth in a person. The eyes are windows to the soul, you know."

When Miriam squared around to study Lizbeth's face, Lizbeth looked away nervously.

"Keep looking at me, Lizbeth." Miriam gently pulled up on Lizbeth's jaw. "This may surprise you, but I see in you the power of the Nile Valley. You are fertile and strong. You are humble, yet as beautiful as luscious soil ready to provide all for a hungry nation."

Lizbeth turned her head. "I'm beginning to like this woman very much."

"Yeah," said Len, "it's like Pyramid Psychic Hotline just for us. How much do you think this is going to cost?"

Miriam looked at Len, passed him by, and then reached up and put her hands on Bennu's shoulders. "And you—you are Bennu, no? I will look far within you, too, and hmm, oh yes, I see much. I see that you are the turbulent wind of the desert. You are the eye of the hurricane, a calm center when the world about you has flown to bits."

Bennu bowed his head, as if receiving a benediction.

"OK," Len said with subtle defiance, "it's my turn, right?"

Miriam studied Len briefly, sincerely, then she broke her gaze. "I cannot see you through the eyes yet, only with them. In time, young lad, in time."

Len looked down and took two steps away from her. "Fine. Great. I guess I don't pass the test." He wanted the others to stop staring at him. "So what do you know about the amulet?"

"Dr. Barth came to Egypt in 1878, and he met my great-grandfather, Fa'uls Rashid. That's why I'm the consultant for this exhibit. Anyway, Fa'uls and his ancestors, my ancestors, had been waiting for generations to fulfill their promise to protect and deliver the sacred scarab. The amulet dates back to the pharaoh Akhenaten. Like most amulets, the hieroglyphics on the underside speak of good luck to the bearer. My family has passed down the meaning, so we know the glyphs say, 'In the east, peace.'"

Bennu held up his hand to interrupt. "Lizbeth and I . . . well . . . our parents say our line goes back to the pharaohs."

"I'm not surprised. And you might be especially interested to know that the beautiful pharaoh Arsinoc II sent the scarab to Julius Caesar as a peace offering before he left to conquer Britain. When he defeated a Celtic lord, local Druids convinced Caesar to let them inscribe the underside. They carved in obscure symbols, but my family knows they say, 'In the west, power.'"

"C'mon," said Len, "we're supposed to believe that dozens of scholars could not decipher simple words like *east* and *west?*"

"Bah! The scholars of antiquity, so sure of themselves and their theories, as long as they can take credit for them. The truth is they cannot read the words and they don't trust our oral history."

Len grunted and looked over at Angie. She walked to the scarab in the center, on the other side of the display from where they were standing. She sighed occasionally, as if the reception of knowledge affected her body as well as her mind.

Miriam stood on a step next to the amulet. "When Caesar returned to Rome, he wrote in Latin, 'In the north, justice.' The scarab was passed down to the emperor Octavian, who gave it to Cleopatra, the last of the pharaohs. When she learned that her lover, Marc Antony, had committed suicide, she passed the amulet to her daughter just before deciding to take her own life as well. It has been in our family ever since."

"You are a direct descendent of Cleopatra?" asked Lizbeth. "How fantastic!"

"Yes," Miriam replied, "can't you tell?" She offered the Misfits her pointy-nose, sunken-eye profile. She laughed at her own expense.

"So, what has happened during the last two thousand years?" asked Len, adding under his breath to Bennu, "and I'm not talking about your appearance."

"Later, my ancestors chose the Coptic way of life, and the Copts made the last alteration of the amulet. One level deeper into the scarab is a blend of the Egyptian ankh and

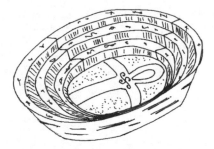

the Christian cross. On the cross, it says in Arabic, 'In the South, grace.' So, the whole inscription reads:

IN THE EAST, PEACE

IN THE WEST, POWER

IN THE NORTH, JUSTICE

IN THE SOUTH, GRACE

"It remains, I think, for the next true owners to explain the center of the cross, a flower weave of four petals. The—"

"There's that reference to 'four' again," said Bennu impatiently. "Even if all of this is true, Miriam, what does it mean?"

Before Miriam could answer, Angie broke into their circle, cupping her hands like she was holding the water of life. "The beetle rolled its ball like the sun. After the sun spent its night underground, then the journey would begin again."

"She's right," said Miriam. "The beetle rolls a ball out of the dung. My ancestors saw it as symbolic."

"The ball is rolled again and again," said Angie, her voice growing louder. "Its eggs are laid in the ball and, in time, rise from the earth. The scarab speaks of rebirth, regeneration, resurrection."

Len pointed to the dung beetle display. "C'mon, Ang, we know all this from the exhibit descriptions—"

"This scarab," continued Angie as if she heard nothing, "rolls many suns into the ground, waiting for its children." She turned and pressed both hands against the glass. "They will come."

"I like this one called Angie," said Miriam.

Angie moved her hands over the glass. "They will come. The children will come. And remember this, to the Egyptians *beetle* means 'to be transformed.'"

CHAPTER SEVENTEEN
FAITH TO MOVE MOLEHILLS

To believe with certainty we must begin with doubting.

STANISLAUS I OF POLAND

 Satisfied that the Misfits now knew something of what needed to be known, Lizbeth suggested they ought to try to find a way back to Welken. Soon, she was climbing into the backseat of the Skylark, congratulating all of them on their detective brilliance.

Bennu called shotgun. "See, and you all doubted my glimpse."

"Yeah," said Angie. "And if you hadn't made us go to the museum, I wouldn't have learned about the sacred beetle, how it rolls and gets reborn. It has to be key."

Lizbeth noticed Len's lack of participation in the happy conversation. "What do you think, Len?"

"The whole thing is ridiculous." Len draped his hand over the steering wheel. "Exhibit-shmibit. This Kieran guy is an old crackpot."

Bennu shook his head. "Don't you see? It all fits! You and Angie are English. We're Egyptian. And the docent. She was just waiting for us to arrive. When she described me, it was like having the best therapist in the world unlock my personality . . . OK, she couldn't see much in *you*, but . . . do you have a better explanation for all we've been through?"

"Of course I do. We really *are* misfits. We're just making stuff up so we can say that we amount to something. It's all a big joke!"

Bennu adjusted the right outside mirror to look at his teeth. "Negative, negative, negative. That's all we ever hear from you."

"It's better than cheesy positive, positive, positive.

Lizbeth hit the back of the front seat. "You guys are such losers. Why must every disagreement become a fight? Y'know, if more women were elected as presidents and prime ministers, there'd be fewer wars!"

Len stared her down in the rearview mirror. "Lizbeth, if your logic weren't so pathetic, you might find someone actually listening to you once in a while."

Lizbeth immediately shrank deeper into the backseat, her jaw tightening.

Len continued. "Bennu and I have a disagreement, and you totally condemn all men. Giving estrogen to males won't bring about world peace."

"That's enough, Len." Bennu pushed Len on his shoulder. "Lizbeth takes enough abuse without getting attacked from one of her so-called friends."

Though outward silence reigned for the rest of the trip home, inside Lizbeth the noise was furious. *When I was in Welken, I just wanted to come home. But why? Len hates me. Len hates everything. I have to have my brother stick up for me. My best friend is a girl so beautiful I can barely stand to sit in the backseat with her. Just look at that face. Oh. Wait a minute. There's a tear running down her cheek. Angie, I'm sorry. I'm a misfit, plain and simple. I'm a misfit in two worlds now.*

When Len pulled into the Nefertis' driveway, Bennu opened his wallet. "I can give you a buck or two for gas."

"Nah," said Len, "there's plenty of gas in this junk heap to get Dad to the office."

Lizbeth walked toward the house. *Stupid Len,* she thought. *He thinks free trips to the museum will cover for being a jerk. Think again, short stuff.*

161

Later in the evening, after dinner, Len and Angie sat in the kitchen. Len tried to think of small talk that might improve his reputation a little, but all he could think to say was that the Trailblazers won a play-off game last night. Angie wasn't interested.

Finally, Bennu and Lizbeth appeared at the front door. Lizbeth looked exuberant. "Look, let's forget about this afternoon. I was having a pity party, but now I've got this great idea."

Lizbeth flapped a tablecloth onto the carpet and used a compass to line up one corner in the north. She set a clock in there, a paperweight pyramid in the south because Egypt was below the equator, a Bible in the east since it was written in the Middle East, and the candles in the west because the sun sets there.

"Now what?" asked Len, feeling about as open as the post office on Christmas.

Lizbeth sat cross-legged on the tablecloth. "Everyone sit down, and put this fabric on your head. I thought we could call out to Welken." Percy strolled in and flopped in the center. "Percy, not now." She hurried him off the tablecloth.

Bennu and Angie rolled their eyes as they started to sit down.

Len leaned against a living room wall. "You've got to be kidding. Bennu, Angie, you're not falling for this, are you? Lizbeth, this is a joke. I'm just glad we're not outside where someone might see this."

Lizbeth crossed her arms in a pout. "Len, you can be such a dope."

"*I* can be a dope?" he said in disbelief. "I'm not the one with a napkin on my head, waiting for some virtual Piers to pop out of a phony pyramid."

Lizbeth put the Bible and clock back in the daypack. "Fine. I used to think you were one of us, that you understood why we needed to stay together, why we needed to trust each other. Maybe you don't even fit in the Misfits."

That one stung. He knew his "innocent" jokes sometimes led to a thin-eyed glare that turned and looked away. "OK, maybe I went too far." Len sat on the tablecloth. "But, think about it, you should see yourself: candles, pyramids, a shroud over your head? Do you really think a séance will work?"

"Well," said Lizbeth. "I don't know. But at least I'm trying. I'm taking what we know and doing something about it. We just learned about some

Egyptian connection. Weren't you paying attention?"

"It's amazing to me," said Len, "that you have an explanation for everything. Well, not everything has a purpose. Is there a purpose for me to raise two fingers right now? There. I did it. So what? Why won't you listen to reason? Why are you so hooked into this 'blind' faith?"

"Because it isn't blind!" Lizbeth packed up more things. "You are the one who can't see. We *know* what we saw, Len. I'm sure it's harder to believe for you, but it's not a trick. We talked longer to Piers."

"It made a difference, Len." Bennu helped Lizbeth with the candles. "Piers. His voice smoothes over the hollow places. It's not a matter of answering objections or sorting out arguments. When Piers speaks, the sound welcomes you home. You lay down your arms and walk, not blindly, not trampling reason, but walk with him into whatever Welken is or was or should be. Isn't it reasonable to trust what is good?"

What could Len say? What sarcastic remark would put them in their place? He said, "Don't you have *any* doubts?"

"Doubts?" said Lizbeth. "That's my middle name. I'd doubt I existed if it weren't for the huge footprints I make every time I step. I doubt my ability to get anything right. I doubt Piers would really want me to return to Welken. Yes, the whole thing seems dreamier, less real with each passing minute. But I do not doubt that for once in my life I felt I knew who I was and why I was made."

Len looked down. "Lizbeth, you're amazing." He paused. "You're honest and you have the courage to say what you think. And most of the time you do this without hurting anyone. Actually, I could learn a thing or two from you. But look, the truth is you have no idea how to get back—and I, well, even I know enough about Welken to see that *this* is not how we'd get there. We can't force it. Think about how we got there and got back." He touched Lizbeth's hand briefly. "You have good intentions, Lizbeth. But there's something about Welken that makes me think we have to be invited or maybe really needy or something." He stopped and blushed, embarrassed at his own words.

"Len," said Angie, "listen to you. We so need to hear what you have to say. Without you, we'd turn into dandelion seeds and get blown all over."

Len got up and flopped into a couch. "Well, my life is fulfilled now.

I'm a dandelion seed stopper."

Bennu put the pack on his back. "Maybe it isn't the right time for our return. Maybe we need to keep searching."

Percy rubbed against Angie's leg. She got up and looked out the window. "Look at the sunset. It's so beautiful—but it's just one tenth as beautiful as the river of light. I wish I could see just one more fuchsia star twirling against a shiny gold curtain."

～❦～

Each took a new "assignment." Bennu and Lizbeth went home to look into the Egyptian connection. Angie said she would try to find out about the knights in Barth's attic, but Len knew she would do whatever her inner voice led her to do. Although Len didn't take a specific task, he said that if Angie's muses struck him, he might push pieces of molding around the fireplace to see if they opened any secret passageways.

Alone downstairs, Len vacillated. As much as he wanted to be an integral part of the Misfits, he couldn't figure out how to lose his irascibility— or if he wanted to. It's part of my humor, he thought. It's part of who I am.

Trying to look busy, he wandered from room to room fiddling restlessly with knickknacks, as if he were Ollie Ollie Otterson measuring their value. Percy strolled in and rubbed against his leg. "Well, Percy, whaddaya think? Seems bizarre to me. When everything you see could be a message from some other world, where do you stop?" He picked up a ceramic Mickey Mouse. "Is Mickey telling us to get a telescope and look at Pluto? Ha! Is Dad's golf trophy a sign that we should look in the rough for lost glimpses? Hey, Percy, what's this?"

Len picked up a note from the mantel. In Angie's handwriting, it read:

Dear Piers,

>*We think we have discovered a clue to the Tetragrammaton.*
>*We want to return to Welken, but we don't know how. What are we to do?*

>>*In Welken, of Welken,*
>>*Angie.*

"She's certifiably bonkers, Percy, really she is. Now she's leaving notes for this Piers guy. What is he, Santa Claus? What's next, milk and light sticks?"

Then he found other notes around the house:

Dear Piers,

> *We'll be waiting for you on the dock at 7:00 p.m. on Wednesday.*

> > > *Angie*

Dear Piers,

> *Since you know more, much more than we, send a glimpse and set us free!*

> > > *Angie*

"Great! Now we're going for the secret rhyme approach. Maybe we should say it backwards while throwing popcorn over the left shoulder. I can't believe it, Percy. I'm trying to have a better attitude, but now I've got to figure out how to keep my sister from being committed to a mental institution." He paused. "Then again, I'm talking to a cat." Percy rubbed harder against his legs, meowing. "OK, I know it's my turn to feed you. I'll get to it. I've got to calm down first."

Len sat on the couch to review the situation. She can't *really* be crazy, he thought. After all, she's my sister. I grew up with her.

Percy jumped on Len, pushed against his stomach, and started to knead his lap. Len grabbed Percy. "You are a first-rate pest." He threw the cat casually to the floor, but Percy jumped right back up and kneaded some pillows, snagging a few threads.

Len got up and plopped next to the family-room bookcase to look through some old photo albums, hoping to find photographic evidence of Angie's sanity. She seemed fine. He saw pictures of her on the first day of sixth grade, at a birthday party, and on vacation at Yosemite. She looked a little unfocused at times, but she'd always been the artistic type, drawing, dancing, acting, and singing her way through life. Didn't

THE WELKENING: A THREE-DIMENSIONAL TALE

Mom and Dad always say that to Angie everything in life was created for her enjoyment? And *everybody* always said she was beautiful. I guess she is.

Percy rubbed against Len's elbows and meowed a little louder. "I'll feed you when I'm good and ready. Now scat!" He pushed Percy toward the coffee table. The cat leaped onto the glass top and licked his paws. You can't hurt my feelings, he seemed to say.

Len thumbed back through the volumes on the shelf, past his own toddler years and baby book, past his parents' wedding pictures. "Charming hairstyles, guys." Finally, he pulled from the shelf the family genealogy that the Bartholomew clan had researched and assembled after the *Roots* miniseries inspired them in 1977.

On the cover was an embossed Bartholomew crest, a common helmet-and-shield combination. The knight's helmet adorned the top of the shield, with flamelike waves of fabric flowing behind it. A red chevron cut through the middle of the shield, offset by two lions-in-profile on top and one below the inverted V. As a boy, Len often imagined himself slaying dragons, the flame cloth flowing behind him like Superman's cape.

Percy nudged him again. Len shouted, "Get away, stupid!" Then Percy leaped up and bit Len on the vulnerable underside of the arm, below the biceps.

"Yeow-you're-gonna-get-it-you-brat-of-a-cat!" Len grabbed his arm, tried to backhand Percy, hit the book instead, jammed his finger, let loose with a few expletives he hoped were not heard by his mom, and flopped onto the floor in mock death groans, his face landing on page eighty-three of the Bartholomews' genealogy.

Despite his aching finger and arm, Len could not help but notice a subheading that appeared about four inches from his nose. He pulled back to read it.

Kieran Bartholomew (1859-1933)
Changes Name to Kieran Barth

"OK, where's the fairy dust?" he said aloud. Then he read on:

Brother of Clive Gilbert Bartholomew
(1856–1945), Kieran gained a boyhood reputation
for brilliance. By eighteen, he knew seven languages and was on his way to an international
reputation as a scholar of antiquity. Never mar-
ried, Kieran formally changed his name to
"Barth" in 1906, severing himself from the
Bartholomew family. Shortly before his death, he
sent a letter to Clive, stating that he distanced
himself from the family "to protect them from any
embarrassment his research might cause them."
In Egypt he was assisted by the famous guide,
Fa'uls Rashid. Kieran's will stipulated that all
funds were to be used to maintain his room of
artifacts exactly as he had left it.

Len's rationalism shuddered deep within him. Too much craziness.
Too much evidence. Too much. He had to tell Angie.

Tearing upstairs, he found the door open from her bedroom into the
sloping attic space she often played in. A bizarre scene greeted him. There
was Angie, sitting on the floor. She had two Barbies and two Kens sitting
in doll chairs, and the Oxford *Book of Heraldry* on her lap. "Angie, you're
not going to believe what I found out."

"Look here." Angie pointed at the book. "Do you see what they call
the 'lion rampant regardent'?"

"Yeah." Len knew he would be hearing her story before he could tell his.

"And next to it, the coat of arms supported by the griffins?"

"That beast there, part eagle and part lion. Angie, what's going on?"

"I decided to set up a model of the exhibit. I put a brunette Barbie in
a chair. I thought of her as Lizbeth, and I said, 'Let's see . . . in the west,
power,' y'know, like the amulet said."

"Why would you do that?"

"And then I put a dark-haired Ken opposite her, where the other sarcophagus was. And I said, 'That's Bennu,' like he was a pharaoh. Don't
you think Bennu looks a little like a pharaoh? So then I said, 'In the east,
peace.' Too bad the knees don't bend, huh?"

"What's your point?"

"'In the north, justice.' That's where I put you, Len, a blond Ken, because, well, you think you're right all the time. Sorry. So that left one chair for me, 'in the south . . . with grace,' though I often feel like a klutz."

"That's it?"

"Yeah, and then, just as you came in, I looked at this book. I looked at what I had set up and then at the griffin and then at the scene and then at the griffin. And then the front legs of the griffin, y'know, the lion's paws, kept switching, like a hologram, to ox hoofs."

"And?"

"Well, I guess that's the point."

CHAPTER EIGHTEEN

NOT EVERYONE ON THE OTHER SIDE OF THE TRACKS HAS A HEART OF GOLD

We are as sick as our secrets.
ANN LAMOTT, *TRAVELING MERCIES*

 The next morning, Lizbeth sat on her bed, leaning against the headboard of her four-poster bed with the lacy canopy, an ultrafeminine statement she hoped would compensate for her indelicate calves. Beanie Babies made a pyramid of cute, happy animals at the foot of the bed. Though softball trophies stood neatly on two shelves, "stuff" (clothes, books, papers, softballs, CDs, and dolls) haphazardly covered every inch of the floor. "Dad!"

"What?" Martin's voice had that attempted-control-of-irritation quality.

"Can you come up here?"

He yelled up the stairs. "Why didn't you call me in when I was up there?"

"'Cause I didn't have a question then." Parents can be so clueless, Lizbeth thought. And I swear, no one walks up the stairs slower than Dad. "What's taking so long? Are you working on some new ad copy?" Argh, she thought, why'd I ask that?

"Actually," Martin said as he stepped into her bedroom, "I was just thinking about Bennu going to college next year and you being here alone."

"Don't remind me."

"Lizbeth, do you honestly know the color of the carpet? Not an inch is uncovered. Where am I supposed to walk?"

"Sorry, but hey, I like it this way. Why can't you just accept me the way I am? Mister Rogers did when I was growing up, and he lived in a Beautiful Neighborhood. Besides, I didn't ask you here for a lecture on neatness."

"You're right. What's up?" He dodged the breakables and sat next to her on the bed.

"I'm trying to learn some stuff about our Egyptian heritage."

"Well, you know that we're part of the Coptic church, that we trace our line back to some of the earliest converts to Christianity. As you've heard me say, Coptic Christianity flourished in Egypt until the Islamic revolution around 800 AD. Since then, Copts have been in the minority in Egypt and are nearly unheard of in the United States. That's why we need to keep meeting with the few other Copts in Skinner."

Lizbeth wondered if she'd ever be more than the oddball. "Yeah, well, I get tired of being called Hispanic—and then I feel bad, like I'm trying to get away from them or something, and I'm not."

"We've all been misunderstood, Lizbeth. But part of being an American is toughing it out. Something like 'When it gets rough, get tough.'"

"You don't have to turn everything into a slogan, Dad."

"I know, I know. In fact, 'Slogans or no, the world's on the go.' Just kidding."

"Bye, Dad." As Martin went back downstairs, Lizbeth realized that, as usual, her father had answered a question before he really knew what hers was.

Then Sniffles ran into the room.

"Out, out, you mangy dog! If you pee, I'll scream."

Sniffles wagged her tail and, with no apparent twinge of conscience, squatted on top of Lizbeth's lone English essay all last year that received an A.

"No, Sniffles, no!"

Lizbeth grabbed the paper and rushed it into the bathroom. "I can't stand it." As she washed it off, she decided she just couldn't get anything done there. She draped the wet essay over a towel bar and tromped down the stairs, running into Bennu, who was just coming upstairs. She pulled him down.

"We've got to get out of the house," said Lizbeth sternly.

"What's the big deal?"

Just then, Martin met them at the bottom of the stairs. "OK, what about this for a specialty coffee slogan: 'Dark and handsome: Aunt Polly's Chippendale Roast' or 'Bringing you a rapid tribal pulse from the foothills of Mount Kilimanjaro: Aunt Polly's Kenyan Caffeine Plus.'"

Bennu held his jaw like he was really thinking. "Lose Aunt Polly, Dad. Nobody wants crackers in their java. Could we borrow a car?"

"Mine's in the shop—and you know how your mother feels about you driving the Lexus. You can ask her if you want."

"Not much of an option," Lizbeth said as she passed Bennu on the way to the garage. "Let's ride bikes."

Soon they pedaled out, clacked a few gears, and sped into the Amazon Parkway bike lane. Lizbeth felt grateful that her churning legs sent a few endorphins marching to do battle with frustration. After some bathroom humor about how she should have written the essay on yellow fever, she sprinted ahead of Bennu and pulled into the front of the Jackson County Library–Willamette Museum Complex. Bennu followed close behind. When they locked their bikes and turned to walk up the steps to the library, they found their way blocked by a homeless woman and her shopping cart full of crumpled newspaper and plastic grocery bags.

She whispered to them, her voice a shadow of speech. "Spare some change?"

"No, thanks." Lizbeth wondered why she always said "thanks" to beggars. "We're just going inside."

"Please help . . . hoarse." The woman held her throat and coughed.

"We don't have any change," said Bennu. Lizbeth knew they did.

The woman's foamy spittle stretched as she opened her mouth. "Hoarse, so hoarse."

Bennu turned to walk away, but Lizbeth held a firm posture. "We can't help your throat, ma'am."

To Lizbeth's surprise, the old woman reached out and grabbed Bennu's arm. "I . . . hoarse, I . . . hoarse." Each word was louder than the one before. She pulled him closer. Then she whispered in his face, her onion-breath wafting over to Lizbeth. "Hear . . . hoarse crying? Hear . . . hoarse sighing?"

Worried that a brain-scrambled sociopath held Bennu, Lizbeth yanked on his arm. Though free, Bennu kept staring at her. "I'm sorry, we can't help you. I'm not a doctor. There's a drinking fountain by the front door." The woman lowered her head, hunched over her shopping cart, and shuffled off on the sidewalk toward the museum.

When Lizbeth turned to grab the railing on the stairs, she looked up toward the entrances to the library and museum. What she saw made her heart sink so fast she thought she could feel it touch bottom. "That's got to be, like, the weirdest thing I've ever seen."

"Yeah. The McKenzie Dolts coming out of a museum."

Since the library and museum shared the same stairs, the two Misfits could see the three Butte Boys on the museum side of the metal railing that separated the entrances.

"Here they come." Lizbeth moved away from the banister. "What do we do?"

"I dunno. Fly away?"

"Easy for you to say."

Tommy pushed Josh and laughed at him as he stumbled down the first step. Josh recovered and slugged Tommy on the shoulder, sending him into the railing. Just when Lizbeth hoped Odin would call his brothers "knuckleheads" and all three of these stooges might not see them, Odin stepped between Tommy and Josh. "My, my, my. Look who's comin' up to greet us. Don't be shy, boys. Say hello."

Lizbeth and Bennu froze.

"Hello, dorks," said Josh.

Lizbeth and Bennu backed down a step.

"Hey," said Tommy, "it's Stump and Hawkman."

Lizbeth and Bennu backed down some more. With frenzied calm, they walked over to their bikes.

Odin grinned like a stock swindler at a new widows club. "Oh, look, guys, Mommy and Daddy let the little ones ride all the way to the library. They must be big boys and girls."

Tommy and Josh caught up to them and pushed the Misfits away from the locks. Lizbeth tried to act unfazed. "So, what brings the three of you to the museum?" She couldn't believe no one was nearby. Where were all the book lovers when you needed them?

Odin grabbed her arm while Tommy and Josh held Bennu. "Let's just say we were doin' a little research. Yeah, a little freakin' research. Just like we're about to do right now—with you."

As Lizbeth struggled to get away, Odin motioned for Tommy to run and get the car. With Bennu in a half-nelson, Josh had little trouble moving him from the bike rack to the curb. Tommy came from their right and pulled part way to the curb, on the wrong side of the street. The LTD sputtered out smoke, which drifted up over the car as Tommy hit the brakes.

Josh and Bennu both coughed. "Sorry about that," said Josh. "As soon as we get some cash, we're going to dump this pile of rusted bolts."

"At least you have a car," said Bennu.

Lizbeth could not believe this guy-talk camaraderie. "What car do you want?"

"Shut it," said Tommy. "Get in the car." He opened the back door. The dent at the hinges made it pop. "I hate this piece of crap."

Josh pushed Bennu in, holding his head down just like in cop shows. When Odin did the same to Lizbeth in the front seat, she slid over quickly and opened the passengers' door, planning on climbing right out.

"Why thank you, sweetheart," said Tommy as he grabbed the door and hopped in, "my brothers don't usually show me much courtesy." She turned around to look at Bennu. His body seemed to have collapsed in on itself, his shoulders hunched in, legs together, and head down. "Bennu," she said, "think about Piers."

Odin put the car in gear. "What are you talkin' about? There's no pier in Skinner. Talkin' in code won't help, y'know." Just then he hit the gas, yelled, "What the—" at a car coming at him, slammed on the brakes so hard they all jerked forward, and he pounded on the horn. He gestured out the window to the other car. "Get out of the way!" Then he swerved the Ford to the right into his proper lane, but the other car did, too, and wouldn't let him pass. Bumper to bumper, both cars came to a stop. Odin turned to his brothers. "It's trouble." Then he threw open the door. "Hi, Mama."

A bony woman with bottle-blonde hair got out of the tinny Toyota pickup. In a tank top and jeans, her weathered arms looked ready to strike. "Oliver!" Lizbeth couldn't believe her ears—Odin's real name. "Oliver Stanley Mink, where do you think you're going?" Since she couldn't get through the thin space between the bumpers, she put both of her hands on the hood and leaned over the LTD.

Odin had made his way to his side of the LTD's hood. "Mama, we were just gettin' a little culture."

"Your Daddy is about ready to whip all a'you. He sent you to the store two hours ago. You don't come back—disappointin' him as usual. Then he made *me* go out, as if I got nothin' better to do, and I run into you blockin' traffic." Though slight, she had a fierceness in her jaw that looked to ram through whatever got in the way. Right now Lizbeth liked her, the cigarette and scowling face and sense of mean justice.

"C'mon, Mama." Odin's body went slack. He put his hands in his pants pockets. "The first store was out of the beer Daddy likes, so we were tryin' to get over to Ralph's when these two hoodlums threw rocks at our car."

Lizbeth didn't like the way the Boys' mother pulled herself off the hood, like she believed him. She put her cigarette out on the fender then walked behind the LTD and around the car till she stood next to Odin. "Out of the car, all a'you." Josh and Tommy got out on the driver's side; Lizbeth and Bennu on the other. "You're up to somethin'. All I got to say is this: don't mess up." Lizbeth and Bennu backed up between two parked cars on the side of the street opposite the museum. Lizbeth wondered if she meant, whatever you're doing, "Obey the law" or if she meant, "Don't get caught."

A car came up behind the LTD and honked.

The three brothers stood tall yet meek before their mother. She gestured rudely toward the car that honked, then grabbed each son's face around the mouth and squeezed their cheeks till each son drew back. Lizbeth had never seen such self-controlled mutual hatred. Then Mama slapped Odin hard. "Go get the beer."

Odin just took it. He rubbed his chin like it didn't bother him, like it focused his resolve, or at least, like it was better than the alternative. Mama got back in the truck and backed it up. The McKenzie Boys slammed doors, and then Odin laid rubber for thirty feet.

Bennu and Lizbeth rose from behind the car, crossed the street, and slowly climbed up the steps of the library. "Do we go home or just keep at it?" asked Lizbeth.

"No point going home."

"I suppose. But I'm all shook up."

"It does dampen one's enthusiasm, don't you think?"

"I dunno. Maybe some people kinda like getting mugged."

"I'm talking about the homeless woman."

"Bennu, you can be so strange. We're almost raped and pillaged or whatever they were going to do to us, and you're back on the stinky lady?"

He opened the front door. "She had some nerve, grabbing me like that and saying such nonsense. How do you end up like that?" They walked in toward the stacks. "I suppose she has some tragic past, but why doesn't the city do something about it? We should have more laws."

The librarian at the desk put a finger to her lips. Bennu and Lizbeth tiptoed past her in exaggerated fashion and found an open table.

"I'm tired," said Lizbeth. "The whole thing's wiped me out."

"Don't make excuses. You always fall asleep whenever we get in a library."

Bennu opened a history of Egypt that Lizbeth had brought, while Lizbeth put her nose in the family's genealogy.

"I didn't need glasses in Welken." Bennu raced through page after page of historical text, to Lizbeth's sleepy amazement.

"One ancestral name seems like any other, Bennu," she said. "How can you read this stuff? It's so dry, like deserts of Egyptian sand. Hey, I'm a poet, too. I'll just close my eyes for a minute, OK?" She tucked her head into the crook of her arm. "Bennu, wake me up in five minutes. That last ordeal with Odin totally took it out of me."

"OK." Bennu put his finger on a paragraph. "Before you nap, listen to this." He shook Lizbeth. She propped her head on her fists. "*Bartholome*, the Italian version of Bartholomew, means 'son of Ptolome,' and remember, Cleopatra was in the Ptolomeic line of pharaohs. Maybe we're distantly related to Len and Angie. That is awesome."

"Yeah, cool," said Lizbeth, a response she would have uttered no matter what Bennu had said. "Now let me conk out, OK?"

She put her head on the table and quickly drifted off. In what seemed like seconds, Lizbeth was dreaming. In cartoon-calendar style, the years flipped back like an unfurling notepad. A cartoon Minotaur led the way, smiling a toothy ox-head grin. The Minotaur beckoned her to come along as it happily hoofed through the years. It stopped first at 1907 and pointed to the Cairo museum. Once inside, the Minotaur put its arm around Akhenaten's mummy, just rescued out of storage by a famous British Egyptologist. With a fanfare, Akhenaten came out of the sarcophagus and staggered around in Hollywood-mummy style, then waved to the Minotaur and Lizbeth. Another threesome appeared: the Egyptologist, Kieran Barth, and Bones Malone.

Before Lizbeth could think "What!?" the years flipped backwards furiously. The Minotaur, Akhenaten, and Lizbeth, hair blowing by the force of the flapping calendar pages, held hands as they flew, Lizbeth in the middle. Occasionally, Lizbeth could make out some famous event from her aerial vantage point: Napoleon at Waterloo or Columbus setting sail. Finally, at 1350 BC, the three came to a screeching halt, heels digging into the ground until they were knee-high in the sand. How fun, Lizbeth thought. Akhenaten was so happy to be back in his own time period, he somersaulted on their way to the palace, the City of the Horizon.

There the pharaoh introduced the Minotaur and Lizbeth to his wife, Queen Nefertiti, who said, "Pleased to meet you, Lizbeth."

"The pleasure's all mine, your highness. Do you know that my last name is Neferti, which is almost like yours?"

"I'm very happy to be related to you, Lizbeth. You must be an excellent and noble queen in your own kingdom."

"Hardly. I didn't even make the volleyball team."

"I want you to meet my second daughter, Maketaton."

"This is too much." Lizbeth curtseyed. "My middle name is Maketa. And I'm also second born."

"You must have been sent by Aton. Please take this sacred amulet as a gift, Lizbeth, and remember."

"Oh, thank you, Queen Nefertiti." Lizbeth looked down at the golden scarab. It was the same as the one in the museum, only without the later inscriptions. "I'll treasure this amulet. But what am I supposed to remember?"

Before the queen could answer, the Minotaur grabbed Lizbeth's hand so hard that the scarab fell, and the next thing Lizbeth knew they were flying forward through the years. Lizbeth looked back at Akhenaten and Nefertiti waving good-bye. Princess Maketaton picked up the amulet.

From high in the clouds, the Minotaur swooped down into the flipping calendar so that Lizbeth could view a flurry of key events several centuries later. While Cleopatra reclined seductively on her throne, Caesar and Marc Antony arm wrestled on the floor of a pyramid. Events and people swirled together in a Wizard of Oz tornado. Whole pyramids spun around, Roman soldiers hung onto palm trees, and hieroglyphic images looked worried. Cleopatra and Marc Antony tried to embrace but could not. As they drifted apart, Cleopatra passed something to Antony, a rock of some kind. He dropped it, and it zipped out of the whirlwind, flashing speedily in the theater of Lizbeth's mind until the wind stopped and the stone thwacked into a hillside of clay.

The Minotaur motioned for Lizbeth to sit. Holding her knees, Lizbeth watched part of the clay change into the form of a hand, its palm displaying the stone. Then the rest of the body appeared in the hillside. With eye-popping speed, the body that held the stone transformed dozens, hundreds, thousands of times, the bodies sculpted into the hillside in Claymation. Figures were sometimes male, sometimes female, old and then young, at times content or in great pain. One figure leaned over the amulet as a clay arrow shot above him. Another rubbed the amulet as if for good luck. Gradually, their clothes and tools became more modern.

Finally, the clay made its last permutation. When in her dream Lizbeth rose to look more closely, the Minotaur held a hand toward the clay as if to say, "Ta-da, there it is." The profile was clear. It was Miriam Rashid holding the amulet. In the center of the amulet was the Coptic cross, complete with the flower weave just like the one in the museum.

Lizbeth awoke with a start. She panted heavily, nearly hyperventilating. Sweat trickled down her forehead. The room felt cold, and nothing seemed to move. She saw the research librarian reading the newspaper at her desk. One of the fluorescent lights buzzed. From the computers, keyboards clicked faintly. Then Lizbeth caught sight of Bennu. He appeared mesmerized by the history book before him. Over and over he said to himself, "I . . . hoarse, I . . . hoarse, I . . . hoarse."

Worrying that she was still stuck in her dream or that Bennu had gone mad, she interrupted him. "Bennu. Hey, Bennu. What's up? Why are you back on that homeless lady?"

"Look!" Bennu stared at a photograph. Shaking off her wooziness, Lizbeth came over behind him. He said, "Here, in *The Life and Times of Ikhnaton the King*, it says, 'Eye of Horus.'" He pointed to a paragraph. "See it? I'll read:

> Horus, the son of Isis, avenged the death of Osiris, but in doing so lost an eye. The eye was healed by the god Thoth. . . . The Eye of Horus became a sacred symbol of healing among Egyptians.

"And here is a poem that begins 'Hear Horus crying; Hear Horus sighing.'"

Lizbeth gave him a so-what look, holding up the palms of her hands.

"Don't you get it? The homeless lady's 'I . . . hoarse' equals 'Eye of Horus.'"

"Do you really think so?"

"Yes, it has to be. This one I know in my gut. I can't believe I've never thought of it before, but Horus is the Egyptian falcon god. And my name is Horace. And in Welken, I was turning into something lighter than air, something that flew, some bird, maybe a falcon." Bennu panted now.

"Bennu, that's not all. You've got to hear about my dream."

After Lizbeth described her claymated vision, Bennu said, "And you think my connections are out there? Yours suggest that Disney and Welken are in cahoots."

"What does it really mean? Are we supposed to believe that parallel universes exist and they're somehow related on purpose? Whose purpose?"

"I don't know. And we don't have time to philosophize. We need to get going. We've got to call Len and Angie and get them down here."

"OK, I'll call on my cell. I'll tell them to meet at the Barth exhibit next door."

At the museum while waiting for Len and Angie, Lizbeth told Bennu to study the west side of the exhibit and that she would study the east side. Lizbeth guessed that Barth paid homage to Akhenaten somewhere, maybe on the artifacts next to the two sarcophagi. They discovered that Thutmose IV, grandfather to Akhenaten, was told in a dream by a sphinx: "I am like one who is ill; my limbs are being ruined. The desert sands press against me." Bennu wondered aloud if this was a reference to the wounded horde of Morphane. There was also an image of the Sacred Cat of Baslet, and various kinds of scarabs. They found the description again that said a scarab provided a deceased wearer with assurance that he would be reckoned "true of voice" at the last judgment.

An impressive claim, Lizbeth thought, but you couldn't test it until you were dead.

Bennu found lions associated with Amenhotep III and his wife Tiye, the parents of Akhenaten. Certain "scaraboids"—beetles with human or godlike heads—surrounded this couple's images. And he saw hippo, cow, and bee scaraboids. He asked Lizbeth if she thought they should visit the zoo.

On the east wall by the male sarcophagus, Lizbeth read about direct connections to Akhenaten: "In contrast to his predecessors, Akhenaten attempted to change Egyptian religious practice into what modern scholars called the world's first established monotheism, the worship of one God, Aton, represented by the disc of the sun." She called Bennu over to read Akhenaten's "Hymn to Aton," written in 1375 BC:

WHEN THOU SHINEST AS ATON BY DAY

THOU DRIVEST AWAY THE DARKNESS.

WHEN THOU SENDEST FORTH THY RAYS,

THE TWO LANDS ARE IN DAILY FESTIVITY.

MEN WAKEN AND STAND UPON THEIR FEET

WHEN THOU HAST RAISED THEM UP.

"I see what you mean," said Bennu. "The links are obvious."

"They are?"

"Actually, I have no idea." He grinned widely. "We need Angie. Where are they anyway? I'm getting antsy. Say, what about this line in the hymn: 'The Two Lands are in daily festivity.' Do you think the two lands could be Egypt and the United States?"

"I don't know. How could something written over three thousand years ago matter to us?"

"Maybe time is not what we imagine." Angie walked up from behind, startling Bennu and Lizbeth. Then she answered their unasked question. "We crept up on you when you were staring at that poem. I don't think you'd have noticed a diesel truck."

"Besides," said Len, "these museum signs say, 'No shouting at friends who've been to Welken.'"

"What have you discovered?" Angie walked over to the hymn and touched the foreign words. "I remember liking the feel of the smooth stone and the finely cut words. The museum light across the deep letters made me think of the sun shining through a canyon, the way the walls are illumined by the rays gradually and—"

Suddenly, the museum alarm went off.

"This always happens when I forget to put money in the parking meter," said Len. "Anybody got a quarter?"

"Shush!" Lizbeth went over and shook Len. "Can't you take anything seriously? What if something's really wrong. What if something's being stolen?"

"I guess you could be right," said Len. "I couldn't help thinking of all the phony fire alarms at school."

Then they heard a series of clunking noises.

Instinctively, Bennu ducked. "Oh, wait. Must be dead bolts somewhere. That's spooky."

Lizbeth backed away from the doors. "What if someone has a gun?"

"All right, I admit it. I don't like this either," said Len, "especially the fact that we haven't seen any guards yet. But, hey, this isn't a bank. Nobody's gonna come in here and, like, start shooting."

Bennu motioned for everyone to get down. "Shut up. I hear something."

From a crouch, Len surveyed the room. When he saw they were alone in Kieran's attic exhibit, he stood back up.

Bennu joined him. "Maybe we should defend Barth's stuff."

"I'm not going to sacrifice my life for these old rocks," said Len. Then he thought, Even if we are related to Great Uncle Kieran.

"What are we going to do?" Bennu paced in abbreviated fashion.

Angie looked at the entrance to the exhibit. "Maybe we should see if we can lock—"

Before she finished, they heard footsteps. The Misfits ducked behind the scarab pedestal. Len could see two men dart around nervously, as if they were uncertain of what to do. Then another calmly went about his business, breaking open a case here, snatching something off a wall there. All three wore hooded sweatshirts and masks.

The calm one told the other two, "Tommy, Josh, take anything gold, no matter how small."

Lizbeth squeezed Bennu's arm.

"But what about the alarm?" Josh scratched his nose under his mask.

"C'mon, have some courage, Josh." Odin used a small crowbar to open a glass case. "This museum is so lax in security, it's pathetic. There's never been a robbery here, ever. The idiot security guards will take at least five more minutes to come bumbling in here. Anyway, I only want one more thing."

"Hurry up and get it." Tommy stuffed a handful of medieval bracelets into his baggy pants. "I'm outta here in two minutes whether I'm with you or not."

"Shut up, Tommy." Odin's irritation did not make him raise his voice. "What're you gonna do? I've got the keys to the car. Now help me push this cover off that gold bug. It's got to be worth thousands."

With the Misfits cowering behind the cabinet housing the golden scarab, the McKenzie Butte Boys pushed on the plexiglas top until it gave way, narrowly missing Len's head as it crashed onto the floor. Miraculously, none of the Misfits made a sound. For a few seconds, the beeping of the alarm stopped. In the silence, Odin leaned forward and took the amulet. "This," he proclaimed, "will help the cause!"

Behind him Tommy said, "What cause? I thought we just wanted money."

Josh said, "Hurry up!" And then the alarm started in again, monotonously beeping.

"OK." Odin admired the beetle amulet. "I've got what I wanted. Let's go."

When Odin was at the door, Len stood and shouted, "Hey Butte Boys, you shouldn't be taking that amulet. It's not just a hunk of gold."

"Shut up!" whisper-screamed Bennu. "You're going to get us all killed!"

"Look, it's the Bartho-boy." Josh threw his loot bag over his shoulder. "Just as I remember him, short and stupid."

"Leave the amulet here, Odin. All of us say so." Len motioned for the other three Misfits to stand up. Lizbeth got part way up, but Bennu stayed low.

"I don't think so." Odin seemed angry about something besides the presence of the Misfits. "We'll talk more next time." He and his brothers sprinted out the door.

From the place where the Misfits now stood, they could hear noises down the hall where the McKenzie Boys had gone. "I'm not afraid to use this!" Odin shouted. Then they heard a gunshot and a new voice, "There's a fire!" Then footsteps came pounding back toward them.

Odin ran into the exhibit. "You know, this whole thing reminds me of where we left off. 'Cept this rock is on fire!" He held the amulet away from his body. It glowed hot, steam rising. Odin tossed it painfully from his left hand to his right. "I'm gonna finish the job."

Odin cocked his arm and threw the amulet with all his strength. "We'll see how you like the 'more' this thing does." The scarab rocketed mightily toward Len, radiant and hot. Instinctively, Len reacted like the Little League catcher he had been; he held out his mitts. He cradled the amulet with both hands, pulling it to his chest like the last out of the World Series.

Then the Misfits were gone.

CHAPTER NINETEEN
COMMISSIONING THE COMMISERATION

It is superstition to put one's hope in formalities;
but it is pride to be unwilling to submit to them.

BLAISE PASCAL, *PENSEES*

 Unlike his first trip to Welken, Len was awake. He stood exultant, intoxicated by the victory over Odin, shining from his own courage, hoping someone would notice his outstanding leadership. The amulet glowed but did not hurt his hand.

Although disoriented by his transport from the museum and his unfamiliarity with where he was, Len had the presence of mind to say, "Some catch, eh?" to anyone ready to praise him.

Bennu slapped him on the rear like athletes do. "You're Pudge Rodriguez, Johnny Bench, and Yogi Berra rolled into one."

Len noticed Bennu's sarcasm, but he didn't care. He wanted to strut around, put on the lotion of false humility, and bask in silky-smooth glory. Tut, tut, it was nothing, everybody. Please, less applause; I feel self-conscious. I will, however, be happy to recount my masterful accomplishments as long as I have breath.

Given how the grand room they were in took his breath away, Len realized he might not get very far. Though awestruck by the size of the place, by the gold fixtures and burning lamps, he tossed the amulet up and down in his hand as if it were a baseball. No one seemed to want to play catch just yet. Then he noticed four marble doors in the middle of each wall. "Where are we?"

"It's called Ganderst Hall." Angie waved to it and half twirled. "Isn't it fabulous? We're underground in a kind of extravagant cave. Behind one of the doors is the Tetragrammaton."

Then the greetings began.

"Piers!" "Mook!" "Prester John!" "Angie!" "Sutton!" "Bennu!" "Alabaster!" "Lizbeth!" Although the entire company seemed electrified, nobody yelled, "Len!"

"Welcome, good friends!" Piers held his arms out warmly, his smile wide and inviting.

"It feels sooo good," said Lizbeth, "so solid to be back." And she flexed her substantial biceps.

Vida Bering Well sniffed a teary-eyed welcome. "I've been positively kleenexed since you were dewelkenized. I feared I might not ever get to smoochify another misfitted cheek."

"Well, we have returned," said Bennu, who appeared to Len to be keeping his feet on the ground with difficulty, "though we don't exactly know how."

I did it, roared Len internally. I snatched the amulet, and now I don't get any credit.

As the other three Misfits caught up on news, Len slunk off. He pouted but at the same time felt overwhelmed by the grandeur of Ganderst Hall. The four marble doors beckoned to him. He wanted to open each one. He ran his hands over the carved woodwork in the chairs, tables, and paneling. The craftsmanship went far beyond the primitive quality he had been expecting.

Not how I'd do my room, he thought, but there's no denying the beauty. Then again, how in the world did all this stuff get into a cave, and why? Why waste all this beauty where only a few could see it?

Then he looked up at the vast vaulted ceiling. No stalactites hung into the cavern. Near the top, two openings let in sunshine. Some fifty feet up, these windows, like the hall's eyes, illumined an interior dome. What's more, the light revealed a ledge on the opposite side of the top of the dome. Neither windows nor ledge would be any more than curiosities if it weren't for their obvious artistic construction. These were not natural wonders. An etched-in-stone frame surrounded the windows, and a short golden railing shone brightly on the overhang opposite to it, as if people might stand up in it.

How? thought Len. There are no doors. And what is the point of that ledge?

Bennu rushed over to Len, interrupting his survey of the room. "We'd like you all to meet Len. He's awake now and wants to help—well, at least *some* of the time." Muffled snickers accompanied the greeting of Len, who took Bennu's comment as a cheap shot.

"Maybe we should hang the blighter!" jeered an angry guardian. "Draw and quarter him!"

Len looked startled.

"Why do that?" asked Terz.

"Because then I could give all four of you a portrait! Honk! Honk!"

When Bennu laughed at the guardian's silliness, he did a perfect backward somersault like astronauts do in weightless space. His glasses fell off. After he examined them for damage, he put them in a zippered pocket of his black windbreaker. That reminded Len of changes, so he ran his fingers into his own longer, bushier hair. Then he noticed that his shirt felt too small.

"Although the stalwart Zennor Pict wished for your health with a purer heart," Sutton Hoo bowed so that his blond beard curled up from his chest, "I am most glad to see you standing so surely on your own two feet, Len."

Finally, a little respect, thought Len.

Sutton shook Len's hand in his frightening large one. "Though I did not mind doing what needed to be done, I will not miss carrying you through tunnels and hallways."

"My cousin labored well and hard on your behalf." Zennor gestured to Sutton with his staff.

"And Zennor also bore your weight without complaint," said Sutton.

"Thank you," said Len, anxious to stop this mutual admiration dialogue. "Don't worry. You guys can have some time off."

Having been raised in early twenty-first century Skinner, Oregon, Len was prepared for an answer of "sure, whatever." Instead, he heard, "We gladly do as we are called."

Len replied, "Sure, whatever."

Lizbeth walked up to Piers. "Before we make plans, I'm wondering— when did you come here to Ganderst Hall? Weren't you in the alder grove? What has happened since we were gone? And how did we end up here? Why didn't we go to Circle Stand like last time?" Len liked to hear her speak so boldly.

"We arrive where we are needed, do we not?" said Piers. "And, we hope, where we are needed is also where we want to be. When wound and medicine meet, then the healing can begin. So. You might recall that you returned home not from Circle Stand but from the alder grove, where we caught the glimpses. I invite you to discern if where you are is where you want to be."

⚬∿⚬

To Lizbeth, the voice welcomed them as fully as her grandmother's arms, as tenderly as the sweep of her grandfather's finger on her chin. When Piers said, "The healing can begin," Lizbeth's fears faded. Details mattered less than being with him, with all of them, in this time and place.

Lizbeth rested for a moment in this recognition—then broke the spell to look around as he asked—and she saw that the high-backed, thronelike chair she held was one of fourteen in a circle. No one sat in a chair. In fact, none of the Welkeners even touched a chair. Lizbeth sheepishly removed her hand.

Angie spoke as her body moved in and out of translucency. "Talking about the alder grove reminds me, I'd like to thank Miss Zizzonte." As Angie became less visible, Lizbeth caught a glance at Bennu's discouraged eyes.

"She sacrificed like a mother in childbirth so we could be reborn into our own world," continued Angie. "How is she doing?"

"You are right, Angie." Piers lost his jovial expression and gripped the chair back in front of him. "Miss Zizzonte gave painfully for your sake. She used her very being to stretch the light, which is a worthy task for all of

186

us. Yet Miss Zizzonte did more than this. I know that you do not want to hear it, but she gave up her life. Holding the light so wide for so long took too much out of her. She could not pull the light within herself again."

"Then I don't ever want to go back." Angie showed as much anger as she ever did. "I don't want to cause death. I don't want more Miss Zizzontes on my conscience. And I'm sorry, Piers, but I feel cheated. Why didn't you tell us?"

"In Welken, we do as we are made. Glimpses stretch and share the light. They know who they are. You did not take her life. She gave it away—and not only for your sake—but for Welken's sake and Soliton's, even for her own. Whether you see this fact or not, it's part of a larger truth, that some kinds of dying can be closer to living."

"No!" Angie started to cry. "She was free and beautiful, and now she's dead. Dying is not living."

Lizbeth went over to comfort Angie. With her arm around Angie's fading shoulders, Lizbeth also felt the weight of the painful revelation. At the same time, she thought that sometimes life *does* require a death. Hadn't she been told all her life that the freedom she enjoyed meant that sometimes soldiers needed to die? And she also knew that good habits required dying to laziness. Lizbeth took some solace in the fact that for once even Angie struggled to submit to Welken's ways.

"Perhaps you'd like to know," said Piers, "that Miss Zizzonte's last words were also a gift, another riddle. It went like this:

Of all the deeds that you must blame
Don't forget to see the same.

"We are wise to attend to these words, for the inklings of glimpses have a way of serving others in good time. Perhaps we'll understand more in the days to come. So. For now we should learn from our friends who have returned from strange and different lands."

Len turned to Lizbeth. "So, *we're* the ones from a strange land?" She noticed him kneading his thighs.

After Lizbeth explained her dream about Akhenaton, and Len the family's link to Kieran Barth, and Bennu the Eye of Horus, and Angie the attic exhibit with knights and sarcophagi and the scarab, Piers smiled. "I know why you've come to us just now. You were inspired to search and you searched. You were given visions to see and you saw. You obeyed, and that also means you worked hard. But I must admit, I don't understand the part about—what did you call them?—Ken and Barbie."

The Misfits laughed.

Then, at Piers's instruction, the Misfits and Welkeners sat in the fourteen chairs in a circle, while the guardians stood behind alternately praising and criticizing the arrangement. Finally, they sat in silence. After a while, Lizbeth felt the gravity of Morphane's wrath push them all down. Piers added to the weight. "Somewhere in Welken, a beast of hideous mysteries walks—devouring life and gaining strength. Whose friend will next fall victim to Morphane's glare? Whose mother? Whose child?" His words caused many to slump over. "Swift are the paws of Morphane." Piers waited and then added softly, "Swifter yet is the mind of Soliton. So. In Welken."

"Of Welken," came the resounding reply.

Piers put both hands in his lap. "A storehouse of knowledge has yet to be shared, but without Gandric's guidance, we may miss its fullness." He turned to Len on his right. "May I have the amulet?"

That's it? thought Len. That's all the thanks I get?

Reluctantly, Len handed Piers the golden beetle, the scarab that he now knew had made its way down from Akhenaten to Caesar to Cleopatra through the exiled pharaohs and the Egyptian Coptic church for centuries until it was discovered in Kieran Barth's attic and made known to the Misfits by Miriam Rashid.

"Len, in this place, while you slept, we learned of many things. Of greatest importance, we entered a room through the east door, over there. Inside, landscapes graced the walls, but in the back stood a vanquished grace, the home of the four tiles that make up the Tetragrammaton. These tiles, each with a symbol of a beast from our folk tales—an ox, a falcon, a lion, and an angel—were taken some time ago. Our friend Gandric told us that these were held in by a golden beetle."

He paused, as if he thought these words explained everything to Len.

But Len was still wondering why no one acknowledged his feat and what any of this had to do with their lives in Skinner and how the other Misfits could act as if nothing happened, even though they just got zapped out of a museum and into a fairy-tale underground hall. He barely heard Piers. "What'd you say?"

"Len, hear me now. I will return the amulet to you, and I want you to say whatever truth you think must be said. A truth will push to get out, and you must not resist it. Though speaking the truth may hurt, withholding it will hurt far more."

"Maybe that's why that McKenzie idiot threw it at me," said Len. "I couldn't get why he would go to all the trouble to steal it, and then give it up without a fight. I don't think they were real big on the truth."

"Here is the scarab, good friends." Piers held the scarab high for all to see. "The Misfits have brought this golden beetle here, they say, from a place where old things are stored. It was passed down, they say, for generations, kept safe by their own guardians, protected from enemies, until they were drawn to it. They say they brought it here, but I say it brought them here. The amulet, one piece of the Tetragrammaton, has been returned."

While the Misfits looked at each other in bewilderment, the Welkeners cheered, honked, and clapped with joy. Jacob Canny Sea thrust a dagger into the air. "We've been lotterized! We've been sweepstaked!" Then another round of applause filled the cavern.

Terz held his hand up to get their attention. "Far be it from me to dampen a celebration, for I so enjoy our spirits united in happiness, but what does this mean? What do we know of this amulet? Maybe we should put it aside while we study the Book of Quadrille for insight."

"You may be right to be cautious, Terz," said Piers. "But there is something in the amulet itself that affirms its purpose. See it glow as I hold it. It speaks. Or rather it calls out of the bearer things that should be said. I will pass it around, and you will learn what I mean."

Piers returned the gleaming scarab to Len. This time it burned him a little, but he did not flinch. As he wondered what Piers could mean about "calling something out of the bearer," he felt foolish holding a golden dung beetle while everyone stared at him. All these events made him think. He felt an idea coming to the surface like an air bubble rising steadily through the water.

While waiting for this truth, his mind wandered back to days in elementary school during recess, when all the boys would line up against the side of the fourth-grade classroom to be picked for teams. Scott Benesch and "Mighty Joe" Quinn were the captains as usual, selecting the best athletes one by one until one boy, the smallest boy, remained, Len. Anger and shame filled him as it had so many recesses and lunchtimes before. He could see Scott and Joe arguing about who would get stuck with "the runt." Len shouted to the phantoms in his mind, I'll show you someday! He burned with revenge fantasies. He burned with hot embarrassment and loneliness. He burned because—suddenly he realized—the amulet glowed red in his hand. Abruptly aware again of the group in Ganderst Hall, sensing the sweat on his brow bead into leaden drops, he cried out, "I hated them! I hated being last! I hated watching those golden boys get all the attention . . . and I hate it still!"

Though the tears came to the brim of his eyelids, they did not flow down. Len sucked them back on the inside, and breathing heavily, he wiped the sweat from his forehead. He had no idea why he said what he did or what it had to do with the amulet or Welken or Morphane. All he knew was that a sea-born coolness washed over him. And he felt deeply good and whole. The amulet's heat faded.

"You spoke well," said Piers, subtly acknowledging what he had not yet directly stated, that holding the amulet created a crisis, a test of willfulness and truth-telling. "I knew you would, for you carried the scarab into Welken."

Relaxed that his turn was over, Len watched the others. From hand to hand, the amulet passed with varying results. Ellen Basala's test lasted less than a minute. Without any strain she took the golden beetle, closed her eyes as if waiting for the truth to be written on the screen of her mind, and calmly said, "Prester John annoys me. But I love him anyway. I love him."

Then Zennor Pict stood tall and announced, "My sweet Jarrow lives!" Vida Bering Well held her tongue while dancing a Deedy jig in the center of the circle. During her curtsy, she said, "What matters in life is a good hokeypokeying." When the amulet came to Terz, he cupped it top and bottom like he was about to shake dice. Instead, he sweated through a serene smile, uttering only the phrase, "I love to serve." After passing the scarab along, Terz sat on his hands.

Pressing the amulet to her heart, Angie closed her eyes. Len braced for the looniest response. "I see Percy curled up ever so peacefully beside Mom in the Adirondack chair that looks out to the Wilder. Mom writes a line or two, pets Percy, scribbles out a word, and pets Percy again. She lifts her head majestically like the royal queen she is. Looking grateful and satisfied, her eyes find me. I think she sees me where I am. 'Mom! I'm over here! Can you see me?'" Far from ashamed of her, Len wished Angie would keep going, but the glow of the beetle faded. Angie held the amulet out for Bennu.

Lizbeth saw the hesitation in Bennu's hand. For all his poetic powers, he constantly worried about saying the wrong thing. Maybe, she thought, all poets do. In this case, she knew he might feel forced to say something embarrassingly romantic about Angie.

Bennu squeezed the amulet tightly. To Lizbeth, the tension in his face departed instantly and a soaring smile replaced it. His grin swept up as high as it could reach, and then his mouth opened, his head tilted back, and he laughed. What ecstasy was this? Lizbeth wondered. Winning the P.O.E.T.S. top prize? Beating all his friends at any computer game ever invented? Having Angie say she liked him? She did not know—but, like everyone else, she smiled and then laughed with him.

Bennu's spirits seemed to rise and rise until he rose too. He levitated above his chair, and then, fifteen feet above the chairs, he flew in a circle. Later, he told Lizbeth that he imagined he was having an oft-repeated dream, himself as Superman flying over Skinner, swooping around, waving to friends, and enjoying the view. He said that he saw his house by the Lewis River. And he saw Angie in the backyard next door, sitting in a chaise lounge reading Charlotte's manuscript. That's when he yelled out, "Hi, Angie!"

From her chair in Ganderst Hall, Angie called back. "Hi, Bennu. You don't have to shout. I'm right below you."

Then Bennu broke out of his dream and opened his eyes. He lost altitude and—as Lizbeth and others held out their hands to catch him—he missed them all and tumbled clumsily to the ground. Still smiling widely, he returned to his chair. He handed the amulet to Lizbeth. "You'll be fine, Liz. Go ahead."

Almost instantly, Lizbeth traveled in her mind through her own childhood. She kept going back through the years, not cartoon-style like in her library dream but more like time-lapse photography in reverse. Smaller and smaller she shrank until she lay in her crib at about six months old. Her father and mother hovered over her. They talked to her more genuinely than she had ever heard them. "There she is, Martin," said Darlene, "the girl you've always wanted, perfect in every way. I love to touch her velvety skin."

Martin looked with great longing. "I know. She's so cute. I don't understand how any parent could ever abuse a child. I will never stop loving her. I hope she always knows what she means to me, especially when she becomes a teenager. I remember. I was so worried about how I looked."

Truths poured into Lizbeth, about her parents' affection for her, about how blessed she was to have grown up never truly doubting their love, and most surprisingly, about how her parents weren't just obstacles to her plans but real people with strengths and weaknesses like anyone else. All Lizbeth could do was weep and mumble quietly, "I know now. I won't forget." As the light from the amulet diminished, she passed it along to the last in the circle besides Piers, Alabaster Singing.

Lizbeth had heard the great anticipation that accompanied each passing of the scarab. What truth would next be told? What secret knowledge would be revealed? But now what could happen with the amulet in the hands of Alabaster? How could she *speak* the truth? Would she act out her message like charades? Would the amulet reject her as a vessel because she could not talk?

Alabaster calmly placed the scarab in her right palm. Her left palm also was open, as Lizbeth put it, "ready to receive." The golden beetle brightened in her hand, first a yellow shimmer, then a golden glow, and finally a beaming orange that seemed to pulse through her hand. As Alabaster sat there, lips unmoving, seemingly unfazed by the power of the amulet, her left palm began to glow as well, yellow, then gold, then orange, shining with as much illumination as the scarab in her right palm. No perspiration appeared on her serene brow.

The twin orange brightnesses pushed their light upwards, sparking and spitting like a roman candle fireworks display. Up and up the autumn colors rose, building on each other like the brilliant light beams in the Window under the Mountain. They rose as high as her cheeks, and higher still they grew. Unperturbed, oblivious to the tiny skyscrapers of light in her hands, Alabaster sat without moving, as silent as the stone for which she was named, until the fiery columns curved together into an amber arch, framing her dark, clear, untroubled Nezzer face.

When Alabaster opened her mouth, Lizbeth's eyebrows shot up. Alabaster began the natural movements for speech, and all present leaned toward her. Then without struggle or stutter, Alabaster uttered sound. Before the gathered, grateful ears, Alabaster Singing sang. Her wide-ranging voice, melodious as a meadowlark, filled Ganderst Hall. Past shock, beyond amazement or disbelief, Lizbeth found herself experiencing adoration. This heretofore silent voice, this sound with unquestionable mastery of volume and pitch, tone and quality, made Alabaster Singing the diva of divas.

Then the beauty of her song changed. The sprightly trills and lush arias transitioned gracefully but undeniably into darker, minor tones, flowing into a somber, brooding melody. More remarkable yet, Alabaster sang these lines:

> Morphane, Morphane, has no home
> O look, he licks old Gandric's bones
> And swells the size of empty moans
> Each face he saw he then did steal
> And made of heart and soul a meal
> Yet Morphane is a spinning wheel
> O Morphane's mind's a spinning wheel.

In seconds, the arch disappeared, deconstructing itself back into columns, then orange pyres, golden embers, yellow lights, and finally just the shining amulet, unchanged in Alabaster's hand. Alabaster looked at the others as stone faced and mute as ever, beautiful in her silence and serenity. A contented smile added to the sparkle in her eyes.

After the awe settled, murmurings and interpretations erupted once again. Lizbeth listened to dismal prophecies, anxious calls to action, and brazen claims of superiority and infallible victory. For her part, Lizbeth hoped never to leave the circle.

Terz suggested that the amulet be buried for safekeeping. "What if Morphane finds this treasure?" When he gestured, Lizbeth noticed marks on his palms.

Piers quieted the crowd as he took the golden scarab and held it up for all to see. The amulet remained unchanged in his hand, though Lizbeth was sure she saw the beetle itself quiver. To the circle of fourteen and the leaderless guardians, Piers held up his hands. "So. I am told it is time. And now, Lizbeth, Len, Bennu, Angie, come." Piers moved his chair so that a way out of the ring was possible. The others watched as Piers led the Misfits through the east door, past the wrought iron second door, and into the small room containing the Tetragrammaton.

Remembering the mysteries within and the helplessness she felt last time, Lizbeth approached with caution. Crossing the threshold, she studied the images in the frescoes, which seemed more familiar than before, but she could not put her finger on the reason. The elegant chiseled words also remained obscure. Piers led them straight back to the Tetragrammaton, to the empty shield. Its violated surface stared back at them. Where the sacred tiles should have been, only the silhouetted profiles of the mythological beasts remained. However, this time Lizbeth recognized their relationship to these profiles. Somehow, in Welken, she had evolved several steps closer to an ox, Bennu a falcon, Angie an angel, and though he denied it, Len became more leonine.

Carefully, Piers pushed the golden scarab like a puzzle piece into the oval in the middle of the quadrants. The amulet's glow intensified, at first brightly illuminating the empty spaces the tiles once filled.

Then two strange things happened. The middle legs that were flush on each side of the beetle lifted themselves off and stretched out and grabbed the horizontal bar of the shield, as if to say, "Here I'll stay. I will not easily be moved." Then, as the Misfits watched in wonder, the surface that held the tiles retreated, moving inward until the four holes were so deep that their back walls could not be seen.

"Do you remember which opening held the ox tile, Lizbeth?" asked Piers.

"Yes, the top left." She swallowed hard in anticipation of his next request.

"Put your hand into the hole, Lizbeth." Piers reassured her with his hand on her shoulder. "Do not be afraid."

"I don't know about the afraid part," she said, "but I'll reach in because you said so." Slowly, she moved her right hand into the opening, suppressing thoughts of spiders and centipedes, sticky legs and poisonous bites. When her hand was in just past the wrist, she felt a buggy thing walking on her forearm. "Yuck!" she said as she whipped her hand out. No insect could be found. While rubbing the offended spot, she peered into the hole, hoping to see a nonbiting, nonpoisonous, friendly Welken bug. As far as she could see, the quadrant was empty. Then she noticed something moving by her face, at the threshold of the opening. It was a leg of the scarab. With two of its feet clinging to the shield, the remaining four groped for the absent tiles in each empty space. "Glaaah." Lizbeth stuck out her tongue. "I don't like creepy insect legs even if they do belong to golden-sacred-amulet-scarab-beetles."

She changed to her left arm so she could push it against the wall away from the beetle's foot. To her surprise, her hand kept going in without finding the back wall. Reaching in deeply, she nearly touched the front with her shoulder. This put her face about three inches from the annoying beetle leg. Then she didn't care. "Wait, I feel something."

"Bring it out," said Piers.

With trepidation, Lizbeth removed her arm from the stone sleeve and held up a tiny ornate box, latched securely, with oxen symbols painted on all sides. "What's this for, Piers?"

Ignoring her, he turned to Angie. "Angie, it is your turn. Find what awaits you in the Tetragrammaton."

Angie reached in more quickly than Lizbeth and came out with a small vial, tightly corked and containing some clear liquid.

Len was next. He pulled out a dull cloth, neatly folded and held together with twine. "Cool special effects, but this thing doesn't look like much."

Finally, Bennu's turn arrived. Cautiously, he inched his hand down the rock-hewn corridor.

"Get goin'," said Len with irritation. "Nothing happened to us. Nothing will happen to you."

"OK, OK." Bennu's eyes bulged in concentration. Then he closed his eyes, took a breath, and pushed his hand in. "Piers?" His voice contained some panic. "There's nothing there. I can feel the back wall, but there's no pouch or vial or anything . . . Wait. I feel something. It's not on the bottom. Actually, it's not attached to anything. It's just floating. There, I think I've got it. It feels wobbly like jello, but floppier, like that slime stuff you can buy. OK, I've got it." Bennu pulled his arm out. Slowly, he opened his hand to reveal . . . nothing but his palm. "Did I drop it?"

"Don't move," said Angie, "or you *will* drop it." When she grabbed the underside of his hand to steady it, Bennu looked up from his hand to her eyes, but she kept staring at the unseen gift. Then she pressed toward his palm with one finger. The finger met resistance before it reached the palm. "It feels like an invisible caterpillar."

Bennu whispered, "And you are like an invisible—"

"It is time," said Piers, calmly, firmly, in precisely the same tone as his last pronouncement. "So." Lizbeth saw that Bennu lingered in Angie's hand as long as he dared and then moved back. With a sweeping gesture, Piers motioned for the Misfits to go first out the east door back into the center of Ganderst Hall. He shut the door behind him. The light pouring in from the "skylights," together with wall sconces, provided ample illumination. Even so, all the guardians held candles with both hands in front of their black robes, as if in a vigil. They had moved the chairs against the walls so that the center of the hall was clear.

On the way to the center, Len pulled Piers aside. "I have this idea. I mean, I'm not even sure why I'm telling you this. I'm not really sure why I should care about everything here, or why I'm in Welken—but, here's the deal. I can't believe Morphane's it, the whole problem. It doesn't make sense. He couldn't have taken the tiles."

Piers stopped walking. "Len, you say more than you know. We are all wise to reckon the breadth and depth of the evil sprung upon us."

"OK. Well, yeah, I'll keep a lookout too." Len wasn't sure that what he said made any difference. He resumed walking to the center. "What's going on, Piers? It looks like a memorial service out here." He inhaled the waxy smell.

"I suppose you could say that we are remembering something." Piers hid his hands in his tunic. "All traditions take us back. But these candles glow in anticipation of a solemn commissioning. The guardians know we must now face the evil outside once again. We must put up a shield against it."

"Sounds like a good idea," said Bennu. "So when do you lead everyone out of here?"

"The commissioning is not for me, Bennu; it is for you—you and the other Misfits and your new friends from Welken."

"And what about you?" Lizbeth looked crestfallen. "Won't you be coming with us?"

"No."

This one word fell like a brick, crushing Len's hollow twig of trust.

"Terz and I have other work to do. You remember the letter from Aelred Broonsees—the one we call Bors—and our friend Sarah Wace? We must try to find them. That is our task."

"Why don't we come with you?" asked Lizbeth.

"Angie knows why," said Piers, "and so should you by now."

Already, the shadowy Angie knelt near the center of the hall, facing the south door. "I've told you, but it was too hard for you to believe. The destinations foretold by Kieran Barth are now affirmed by Welken's circumstance."

"C'mon, Angie," said Len. "Speak English."

"Len, you should know. You saw me in the attic room. I put you with the saying, 'in the north, justice,' because you like to be right all the time."

Piers motioned to the doors. "Please, take your places. Jacob Canny Sea and Vida Bearing Well, stand behind Angie, facing the south door.

Lizbeth kneel to the west. Mook and Alabaster, join her. To the north is you, Len, accompanied by Prester John and Ellen Basala. That leaves you Bennu, as you know, east, with Sutton and Zennor."

Bennu looked perplexed. "But, Piers, the east door leads only to the room we just left, into the vault for the Tetragrammaton."

"Kneel, Bennu, and you will see. Do you know which direction you are being asked to walk?"

"Yes, Piers."

"Then you know enough to take a step. You will learn how to take the next step after you take the first." He waited for silence. "Good friends, you have come a long way, but you are only at the beginning of your journey. For now you know who you are and why you've come." He walked around them, hands raised as if in benediction. "Before you is work both mysterious and grave. You must find the stolen tiles of the Tetragrammaton and return here. Without its goodness whole, we cannot hope to prevail over Morphane.

"True, you travel lightly, only three to a group. Not an army really, but souls prepared for battle nonetheless. And you should know, I won't be far. If you meet Morphane, do this: Think deeply on me. With all the power of your will, hold my image before your face in your mind, and you will be safe, for Soliton has reckoned it so.

"Now, accept the memory of my touch." Len watched as Piers bent over Angie, Jacob, and Vida and clasped each head as if he were pushing in some secret wisdom. After some tremulous blessing seemed to pass from Piers's fingertips, he spoke quietly to the south-facing group. "In the south, grace. Angie, Jacob, Vida, keep your hands open to receive. Though Deedy daggers might come unsheathed and Angie's vial unleashed, do so only as you must. Angel, listen close for the wisdom."

Len admired Angie's kneeling trust, her readiness to listen to and obey this remarkable Piers. Len flashed on his mom's line about Wise Dominic, "the sagiest sage I know," but he struggled to give himself over to this kind of submission.

Piers walked clockwise to Lizbeth. "In the west, power. You know it's true, Lizbeth." She relaxed noticeably when he touched her head. "Wield your oxen power well. Lizbeth, Mook, and Alabaster, you may employ

Nezzer arrows or the locked box as you see fit, but listen for mercy. Do not seek revenge."

He walked on. "Len, I now come to you."

Terrific, thought Len, here comes the crowning of Sir Leonard the Welken Boy.

Piers put both hands on Len's bushy hair and dug his fingers in until they touched his scalp. It felt tingly and good to Len, like a head rub a dozen times better. "In the north, justice. Go with righteous certainty. Len, Prester John, Ellen, be not swift to draw your swords or open the covered gift. Lion, my word to you is wait, wait."

Seems like this place finally starts to get interesting, thought Len, and I'm told to be patient.

Moving over, Piers placed one hand on Bennu and the others behind him, touching both Sutton and Zennor. "In the east you three bring peace. Let it spread as wide as your hearts will allow. But do not use your staffs alone or the secret gift from the scarab to bring the peace. Falcon, watch, watch, and be brave."

With this last command, Piers stepped to the center of the twelve and was joined by Terz. Each group looked outward, ready to open the door that seemed to have chosen them.

Piers gave the last instructions softly. "Rise. You know your task and your direction. Find the tiles. Go."

As they stood, all four doors opened simultaneously. A chill wind brushed Len's skin, making him nervous and alert and suddenly wary of danger. Piers and Terz said, "In Welken."

While the others replied, "Of Welken," Len only mouthed it.

Wrestling with thoughts of comfortable backyards, the Lewis River, Weyerhauser High, and the next family dinner, Len and the other Misfits of the commissioned Commiseration marched soberly toward the Ganderst Hall doors. When Len reached the magnificent sculpted marble of the north door, he paused. Against his flimsy trust in Welken's calling, a stiff, thick doubt gripped once again. And he was gripped, too, by a desire to look one last time at his friends. He turned around, and Prester John and Ellen stepped aside. As if rehearsed, Bennu and Lizbeth nodded at each other and at Len. No sleight of hand from Piers could have reassured him more. He smiled at each Misfit and waved, wishing he knew a more profound gesture. Across to the south, he waved larger, as if his movement would make Angie more visible. A blur in the background told him that the translucent Angie waved back. Then she glowed, and he saw her wave plainly.

I must be crazy, he thought. And he put his foot forward, taking his first step onto the threshold of the north door.

CHAPTER TWENTY
ABU'S TOO TRUE

Use what language you will, you can
never say anything but what you are.

RALPH WALDO EMERSON

 The afternoon turned warm. Sitting in her chair in the backyard, Charlotte felt the heat mining its way into her veins. Her thoughts turned to steaming sands, sleepy-eyed camels, and dusty pyramids. Later, she awakened in a dazed state, with something in front of her blocking the sun.

"Hello, dear." Her neighbor Darlene must have come through the gate from the Wilder. "I got so worried about you sleeping back here that I brought over some sunscreen, instant iced tea, and a spare umbrella. You should be careful about the sun."

Charlotte rubbed her sore neck. "I know. You're supposed to wear Arabian headdresses and do whatever Abu P. Cockles tells you to do."

"Oh, Charlotte, I don't think I know anyone as zany as you are. No wonder you're a writer. I just hope you aren't getting heatstroke."

"I'm fine, Darlene. Thanks so much for your concern."

As Darlene left through the gate, Charlotte wiped her mouth and then wondered if she'd been drooling in her sleep. The wet spot on her shoulder confirmed it. Then she poured out the phony iced tea, dropped the sunscreen on the lawn, and moved her chair into the shade. She was ready to begin.

CHAPTER FIVE: Ollie Ollie, Camel's Free

Percy adjusted his pince-nez and faced the freshening breeze. "Bones, ol' buddy, you doubted me. You didn't think I'd get us onto the fastest ocean vessel ever to slip into a slough. But all I can say is 'Good-bye, Virginia. Hello, Cairo.' We'll be there in two whips of a whippoorwill."

"Yes, Perce, I quite—"

"Anchors can wait, my friend," he said as he pointed out to the sea, "until we've sailed that wild blue yonder."

"Percy?"

"Yes, First Mate Bonesy. What's on your mind?"

"We're still in the harbor."

Eventually, Percy proved to be right about the speed of the *Queen Celeste*. At full throttle she charged through the sea like a fat Amazon River tourist getting chased by piranhas.

In the brig of the *Elephantisimo*, miles ahead of the *Queen Celeste*, Ollie prattled on remorsefully. "Mama, I am not a good boy. No, no, no. I *would* be good if I just didn't keep being bad. But, you see, it's not me who's making these bad decisions. It's not my fault, truly it isn't. I'm a victim. I'm a tragic victim of a tragic past. I'm being controlled by some inner madness that hasn't let me go since I was just a little pup and my daddy ran away. I'm practically forced into stealing! It's a disease I tell you. It's not my fault!" Ollie buried his head in his hands, sobbing.

"C'mon, Ollie," said the guard, "ya shouldn't a' otter talk like that."

"I shouldn't a' otter? That's a good one, Mr. Guard Man. I feel better already: 'Hey, Mama, I shouldn't a' otter done that!' Woo-wee, that's too much."

The *Queen Celeste* gained so much ground on the *Elephantismo* that they both arrived in Alexandria at nearly the same time. While the brig's guards led Ollie to the local police, Percy and Bones stepped onto Egyptian soil. Bones's gratefulness that he now stood on stable land was soon replaced by his misery in the desert sun. What took his mind off the heat was the waiting guide, Mr. Abu P. Cockles, who attracted the detectives' attention with the prearranged signal, four exposed tail-feathers, each with a blue-green spot staring at them like the Eye of Horus. He greeted Percy and Bones with two kisses to each cheek and an American handshake.

Abu grabbed their luggage. "Hoo-hoo, all is made ready. Dominic sent a telegram. I followed instructions. First, we take an up-to-date aeroplane to Cairo."

Which they did.

"Then we kick out chickens sitting in our seats and take economy train past Memphis."

Which they did.

"Then go to next stop, hoo-hoo, what Americans call 'middle of nowhere,' no? Now our friendly camels will take us to the pyramids."

Arabian headdresses securely fitted, Percy, Bones, and Abu set out for the pyramids on gangly desert steeds. The camels, after ungracefully tanking up on water, brayed in protest at the little whips that stung their hide. Percy adopted the cockeyed persona of an Arabian cowboy. He sang:

> Home, home on the sand,
> Where the dromedaries are grand,
> Where seldom is said, "A rain cloud up ahead,"
> And the dates fall all day in your hand.

His robes flowing in the wind, Percy sat up tall on his camel's hump, as if a film crew were following him, and rode the snorting bronco over the burning dunes.

Bones, not exactly the nomadic type, tried to get comfortable in the saddle, but his short legs made balance difficult, and the scorching sun burned holes in his stable temperament. "I don't like to complain, Perce, but a basset's idea of adventure is checking the lettuce for snails."

ॐ

In Cairo, on the way down the gangplank, Ollie tried to explain his shenanigans to the policeman by his side. "I was going to put all of Hammy's things in a museum. His medals belong there with Mrs. Markle's golden beetle brooch, which I would have donated just after I showed it to Mama."

The policeman kept walking toward the jail cell. He tried to plug his own ears, but the handcuffs wouldn't let him.

"I hope you collect the reward for me," continued Ollie. "I hope you buy your family a new house, then some good will come from my life of crime."

"What?" said the startled policeman. "A reward?"

"It's all on this poster I have in my pocket." Ollie reached in with his handcuffed hands and pulled out a newspaper clipping.

While the policeman read it intently, Ollie slipped out his picklock, slipped out of the handcuffs, and slipped out of sight.

"I don't see anything here about a reward," said the policeman. "Looks like a nice recipe for lorenzo dressing, but that's it." He lowered the newspaper. "Hey, where'd you go?"

ॐ

A few hours had passed when the three-camel caravan stopped to rest at an oasis. They dismounted. Never had five scrawny palm trees looked so good to Bones.

Abu acted like the temperature was seventy degrees. "Hoo-hoo, the trip is only four short miles, and today we

204

don't even have a sandstorm. What you Americans call 'skip and a jump,' no? Mr. Bones man, I gave you the very happiest camel in the herd."

"Have a swig from my canteen, Mr. Malone." Percy did leg bends to loosen up. "Now, Abu, we need to form a strategy. As the brown book says, 'Don't throw the logs from your own eyes to the pigs.'"

"Hoo-hoo, so funny, you Americans. OK, we go to a fake door in the pyramid—all pyramids have them for the gods—but it is really a real door, not for the gods but for those who know the secret entrance." Abu pulled out a map of the pyramids and turned it several times. He walked his fingers along their route, then put the map away—all so quickly that neither Percy nor Bones could get a good look. "The secret entrance, hoo-hoo, is in the secret door by the secret stone with the secret key and the secret opening! All very secret!" In his hushed excitement, ten tail feathers popped out involuntarily.

"I just love these mysteries, don't you, Bones? Moving panels, strange symbols, magical potions, and all that. One, two, a word that's true. Three, four, a secret door."

Flat on his back in the shade, Bones moaned, "The heat, the heat."

"Don't go 'ten plagues' on me, ol' boy. Dominic wouldn't give us a bigger bone than we can chew."

Abu slapped his belly as if he'd just eaten a five-course meal. "Rest is good, yes? Now let's get back in the saddle again, where a friend is a friend, as Americans say, no?"

Soon they were at one of the triangular tombs. Percy examined the rough stone and announced, "Impressive. Severe. Old. And I'm not just describing you, Abu."

To Bones, every stone in every pyramid looked the same. But then Abu approached a false door, the place where priests and relatives would leave food for the visiting gods. Above the stone molding of the low door were four small holes, into which Abu rolled gems from a pouch: a diamond, ruby, emerald, and sapphire. At this, the false door became a real door, shook faintly, and opened with a creak.

Inside, Abu lit sconces on the walls and carried a lamp around the room, showing Percy and Bones not a dusky old tomb but a well-maintained throne room, a vision more extravagant than Percy had ever seen in Versailles or Rome or the Taj Mahal. Bones, of course, had never seen anything grander than the dogwood blooms in May. On the walls, elegantly painted murals, still vibrant with color, told stories.

Abu strutted around the room, occasionally preening in the mirrors. "Don't miss the carving on the throne chairs and the overflowing jewel boxes."

"It's all very pretty," said Bones, "but what is the point, Perce? Why are we here? Shouldn't we have tailed Ollie instead of coming here first?"

"Remember, Bonesy. Fours, fours, my kingdom for some fours. We've been dealt a hand, let's play the field."

The recollection did little good—not because the clue was meaningless but because *everywhere* they looked there were fours. Four walls, four murals, four thrones behind which were four chests of riches.

Percy held his pince-nez close to his eye. "I do wish I could read hieroglyphics, Bones. After Latin, Greek, and Hebrew, I had to leave time for badminton and bridge."

"Ah," called Abu. "I am your guide at your service, remember? I know something about these murals."

"That is convenient, isn't it, Bonesy?"

"The story is told of Aki-hatten—he's the pharaoh looking at the sun, over there—how he knew his kingdom was crumbling, so he decided to hide his treasures to preserve his descendants. Little mummy joke, no? His queen, Nefertiti, looks at him from the opposite wall, probably to be sure he takes the trash out after dinner. Hoo-hoo! The final verse at the end of the story says:

THREE SUNS RISE TO FOLLOW YOU
BEFORE THEY SET YOU FOLLOW TOO.

We've been waiting all these years to discover its meaning."

Charlotte stopped writing.

This is so weird, she thought. The three suns and the one. I can't help thinking of Len. Lately, he's seemed out of sorts with everything, even with Angie and Bennu and Lizbeth. As a short guy he's had such a tough road, and now, this sullenness.

She rubbed her neck.

I think I did get sunburned. I hate it when Darlene is right.

"Maybe we should poke our way through the jewelry boxes," suggested Bones. "Maybe something will jump out at us."

"Really, Bones," said Percy, "I don't think they're spooked. They're just filled with oodles of gems and gold and coins and maps and things."

A voice broke in from the door to the tomb. "How convenient!" It was the familiar voice of Ollie Ollie Otterson. "I know you'd love to run your fingers through those necklaces, but isn't that just toodly-too bad!"

Ollie swaggered into the tomb with three grumpy-faced ruffians, all waving sabers and rifles. "So glad this charming map led me right to the spot. Mama taught me to follow directions, and then she gave me this map as a test of my abilities." He tossed the map aside. In a cowboy voice, he added, "Tie them up, boys, one to a chair, and help me saddle up these jewels, will you?" Then back to Otterese: Dearie, dearie, doodles, there's just bunches of baubles here. Mama? You know that itsy-bitsy Rolls Royce you've been wanting? Well, I'm going to get you three—with different colors to match your moods: black for blaming Daddy, white for praising me, and red for making strawberry and crayfish pie, my favorite."

"Hey, Otterson," grunted the grimiest thug. "You want all four trunks? We can't lug 'em all back in one trip, y'know. Too heavy for the camels."

"Not to worry your handsome seven-day stubble, dear lad. We have plenty of time. We'll be leaving Perkins and Company to watch over the other three trunks while we take this one to your sweaty friends in Cairo. You're happy to help out, aren't you, Percy? Thanks ever so much!"

With characteristic haste, the slick burglar scampered out the door, into the desert heat.

♈

After pulling at his ties to no avail, Bones slumped. "Oh, Perce, I just thought of something serious. My neighbor is going to get tired of watering my garden. I wonder how long before she gives up on me and abandons the crops to every buggy vice. How the worm turns!"

"Don't worry, Bonesy, 'all's well that the cooks don't spoil.'"

"Hoo-hoo," said Abu, "you Americans have a funny way of being humorous."

"All's well," continued Percy, "because of a trifle our delusional Ollie forgot. Cats have claws . . ."

PART FOUR
THE SOUL OF ADVENTURE

CHAPTER TWENTY-ONE
On the Thresholds

As . . . the maker and molder of thyself, thou mayest fashion thyself
in whatever shape thou shall prefer.

GIOVANNI PICO DELLA MIRANDOLA, "ORATION ON THE DIGNITY OF MAN"

 *The journey came to a place of many crossroads. Scattered to the four corners of Welken, the Misfits and Welkeners faced enemies fiercer than they could have foretold. Indeed, I feared for them. I knew how they labored in their souls. I can tell you this: new voices would be heard, voices for help and voices for hurt—and some that were hard to discern.*

The Master watched what transpired from the edge of the alder tree grove. He saw the white bone on the hill, clean and bright in the freshly turned soil. Though he realized that the bone provided a warning about rushing through the river of light in the Window under the Mountain, the Master did not care about what happened to Gandric.

He cared about something else. He studied an animal licking the bone with its sandy red tongue, an animal that caressed the bone paternally, remembering the scent, mourning for the loss of one of his kin. This animal, Morphane, threw his writhing head to the sky and roared. The terrifying scream, cold and wild, moved from a low rumbling agony to a fierce, high-pitched snarl. The voices locked inside him added their cries, making Morphane's howl unnatural and multiple, a discordant screech of haunting proportions. From behind him, Morphane's army, his brood of vacant bodies, the horde, added their chorus of despair, grasping desperately after their true voices.

Abruptly, Morphane stopped, as if listening for his echo through the valley, and then he ran down the hill. At blurring speed, Morphane lurched toward the alder grove of glimpses. Though fast, Morphane darted back and forth, unable or unwilling to follow a direct line. The Master knew that though the trail did not zigzag, Morphane's mind did. His perilous face, the moving, sucking thing that gave him power, had swallowed so many selves that he could barely contain them. As he possessed them so they possessed him, speaking to him, confusing him, leading him to madness. Alabaster's song was right; Morphane's mind spun like a wheel.

Crudely, Morphane rumbled into the wood. Even more clumsily, the horde descended to join him. The obedient creatures spread out as their net allowed. They sniffed bark and tore up leaves. They trampled through bushes and chased after any living animal, sometimes destroying it, sometimes absorbing it onto their bodies.

No glimpses stirred.

Patiently, the Master drew his conclusions. He respected the awesome power of this beast, yet he saw Morphane as all belly, all instinct, with no subtlety or strategic deception. The next meat mattered, nothing else. And his horde, he thought, grew in numbers but not in effectiveness.

Arching his back, Morphane thrust his head again to the heavens. But this time no roar emerged, no piercing double scream split the silence of the grove. Something was different. Morphane sensed something else was there. His nose, faster than his eyes, picked up the presence, and he turned to face the intruder, if Morphane's roiling sea of heads could be said to face anything. The Master knew he had been discovered. With confidence, Morphane strutted forward. He did not charge. Then the Master did what only he could do. He walked into the open and straight toward Morphane. The great beast slunk close to the ground, ears forward, tail down in submission.

The Master was no intruder. Gently he put his arm around Morphane's neck, pulled close to him, and whispered instructions slowly and carefully, almost lovingly, into Morphane's waiting ears. When the

Master finished speaking to Morphane, the great beast sat on his tail like a docile pet, his front legs stiff against the leafy forest floor. The Master withdrew his arm from around Morphane's neck and looked into his eyes. He looked and was not drawn into his destruction. The Master loved that he could stare into the roiling face of Morphane without being absorbed into that tumultuous prison.

Then the Master turned his attention to Morphane's army, the bodies that mindlessly followed him after Morphane had swallowed their souls. Linked to Morphane and to each other by an invisible web, the drones stood aimlessly. Some scratched the rocks or sticks attached to them. One pulled at dead blackberry canes affixed to its hip.

The Master thought about the one drone that Morphane threw into the fire in Chimney Cave. He also knew that Gandric's body had failed to defeat Mook. He wanted better service from this army, these shuffling bodies, this horde. So the Master called for them to gather together. In their webbed connectedness, the bodies huddled closer, forming a semicircle behind Morphane's waiting hulk.

In mock solemnity the Master blessed the drones with a hand held high and a smirking laugh. Then he stepped between Morphane and the horde. Holding aloft the wispy tendons, the nearly invisible membranes that linked the horde with the selves swimming in the sea of Morphane, the Master shredded the web. Morphane moaned—and the drones echoed him. But the Master pushed them apart. Then he motioned for the drones to move even closer together, to pile in on each other, to act as if they could merge. He touched their grasping collectivity, and then they did merge. The bodies collapsed in on themselves, fell into each other, shrinking into a tighter, denser single entity. All the bodies buckled into the center, groaning while they still had heads, until at last Morphane's army had condensed into a blobby mass the size of only three human bodies.

As they sunk into their own vortex, instead of looking like a more solid, crowded block of bodies, they blended, chameleonlike, into their surroundings. Gradually they blurred together and adapted to the background. They faded. In this amorphous form, the thing did not become invisible; it imitated its environment. Then, like one huge tank tread, it rolled slowly over the landscape, changing into images of grass, boulders, even trees. The bodies that made up Morphane's army had become a shape-shifting wheel.

The Master waited until the raging metamorphosis settled down, until no groans could be heard. Smiling, the Master stepped up to touch the illusion of a bush created by the condensed horde. He touched it. Though realistic to the eyes, it felt soft and pliable.

Then the Master took the wheel to another level of transformation. He poked and smoothed the chameleoned bush in his own hands. As a skilled potter to the willing clay, he sculpted a human form, first its trunk and then its head and arms. As he did, he spoke to the substance as if he were a teacher coaching his students. Finally, the Master withdrew his hands and stood back to size up his creation. It was a crude but complete image of himself, his grin sweeping maniacally across his duplicated face. Then the chameleon-gel seemed to understand. It took up the sculptor's craft from within, and altered the body's features, refining the form until it stood as a mirror-reflection of the Master. The Master bowed to his image, and the golem bowed back. Grabbing his sides, the Master laughed richly into the trees. The joke was just too good. And his image copied the revelry.

The Master composed himself and stared deeply into the eyes of this perfect copy. Then he placed his hands on the phantasm's head and closed his eyes. As the Master pressed his hands against the flexible head, he imparted knowledge. He gave to the changeable beast images and voices, even memories.

With somber resolve, the Master removed his hands. "You are the fruit of Morphane's vine. You are the new life born from the power of the Tetragrammaton. And your name shall be Malleal, for your gift is resemblance. Now, Malleal, behold your own power." The Master smiled as if he were showing off his pet's new tricks. "Vida," he commanded quietly.

Instantly, Malleal reshaped itself into the image of Vida Bering Well. Then even more ghoulishly, the image spoke. "I've been hot-potatoed once again!" it said, squatting down in a characteristic Vida posture.

"Zennor Pict," said the Master, with a casual wave of his hand.

Rising swiftly, the Vida image stretched into a Zennor image and spoke in his deep compassionate voice, "Is there some way you could allow me to serve you better? I am only a herdsman, and you are full of grace."

"Prester John."

Again the blobby stuff moved until it had conformed to the taller, more angular nobleman from the Highlands. It said, "This reminds me of the time I saved a regiment by impersonating a mountain goat bleating in the night."

At this the Master laughed again, slapping his thigh several times in sheer delight. After recovering, he walked over and put his arm around "Prester John," as he had earlier with Morphane. He spoke bluntly to Malleal, issuing instructions and directions. Aloud, he said, "Go." Malleal shifted out of the image of Prester John and into more immediate sights: sword fern, decomposed bark, a willowy young alder. Treading lightly on the trail, the conforming thing rolled away until it reached a fork in the path. Then, as the Master had commanded, it divided in half.

Malleal's journey, two of them, had begun.

The Master perched himself on a smooth, flat boulder, pulled out some bread and jerky from his knapsack, and proclaimed to himself that this meal was a feast fit for the gods. He looked over at Morphane. "Don't be disappointed. Your time will come."

༏

His hands on the doorframe, Len hesitated. From the outside it looked as if he were bracing himself so he could boldly confront whatever might resist him past the threshold of the north door. But inwardly, Len knew that his muscles flexed against the doorframe to keep him from going in. How could he fight for Welken when he really wanted to be home, skateboarding, ripping various heel flips? Then again, how could he deny the mass of hair that flopped to his shoulders and his compulsion to give needed advice?

Prester John grabbed one side of the threshold and leaned in toward Len. "Ah, yes, I know what you're thinking. All thresholds speak to the irreversible choices we make. Once a path is taken, once a mark in the soil is made, we risk spoiling the tender places in our hearts heretofore protected from the vanities and vices we might encounter on this journey. It is wise to ponder before a threshold, for on the other side dreams may be broken."

"Actually," said Len, "I was just thinking I had to go to the bathroom."

Prester John sat down to wait with Ellen. "The young warrior is shrewd. He considers every liability before a battle."

Soon, Len returned, a little short of breath. "I'm ready. It's not like there's much of a choice; so in we go." Looking down at his skater shoes, he knew that here, in Welken, at the threshold of some quest, he was in fact a poser.

The north door opened into a stairwell curving upward to the left. Polished limestone walls reflected the lantern's glow so well that daylight would have done little to improve visibility. Though darkness was not a threat, the angle of ascent created one. Almost immediately the path turned into torturous steps that soon had Len's knees aching and his calves shaking. But he could see that this was not true for Ellen. She bounded from step to step, as sure-footed as a bighorn sheep. Her balance and strength irritated Len, whose steely will to win all contests was never more present than when challenged by a female.

Len leaped up the winding stairs, his fluidity of motion contrasting with Ellen's more precise jumping. The unspoken competition continued until Ellen stopped to look back at the one she was sworn to protect, the sovereign lord of the Prester Highlands, Prester John. He huffed and puffed many leapings back.

Prester John waved her off. "Don't . . . worry . . . about . . . me. The rear flank . . . is a noble calling . . . My sword is poised . . . to pierce the hide of any enemy . . . who might attempt an ambush."

Ellen sighed. She got Len's attention, then motioned with her thumb to Prester John. She seemed disappointed to have to pull out of the competition. Len looked behind her to see Prester John using his sword like a cane to help himself up. "I'm going to wait for His Elegance, Len. You go ahead. We'll catch up."

Without answering, Len pounced up the next series of steps as they circled around, his thighs feeling hot but muscular. He lunged upward, sometimes pulling himself up by his hands. On a landing out of Ellen's line of sight, Len stopped to rest. He rather enjoyed this springing sensation and its result of ascending three or four steps at a time. Then an impulse came that startled him. He wanted to lick his own hand. He put his hands in his pockets to resist the temptation.

I will not start lapping milk, he thought. I will not sleep twenty hours a day. I will not chase and tease helpless prey. Well, maybe. Depends how cute she is.

From his vantage point on the landing, Len guessed that he was now near the top of Ganderst Hall, perhaps even with the dome. As he looked around, his lantern revealed three openings. Two solid wood doors with iron rings stood side by side. He pulled the handles to no avail. Directly across from the locked doors, a passageway opened up, the only real option available to them. Unlike the limestone stairwell, this level corridor possessed black onyx walls. Dimly, maybe a hundred yards ahead, a light shone like the headlight of a train. Len figured it must be the way out. For reassurance, he reached into his pocket and felt the cloth-covered gift from the Tetragrammaton.

Without waiting for the others, though he could hear Prester John's labored breathing, Len ran into the ink black tunnel. He didn't know why he ran. Was he trying to get away from these Welkeners—or Welken altogether? Was the light too alluring to resist?

He did not stop to think. He just ran toward the light. Head down, he pounded the tunnel floor for maybe thirty yards. When he looked up, a solid rock wall blocked his path. To keep from charging right into it, he slid feet first as if stealing second base, onyx chips flying and tunnel dust momentarily hindering his vision.

Ellen had reached the landing. "Len, are you there?"

"I'm in the black tunnel." His voice sounded dead against the walls.

"Len, I can barely hear you!" shouted Ellen. "Prester John wants to rest, to further 'embolden his desire for sacrificial service,' he says. We'll join you soon. Don't go far."

Not much chance of that, thought Len, as he gave his full attention to the rock face before him.

After standing, Len noticed that the wall did not stretch from floor to ceiling. In vibrant colors swirled together like vanilla ice cream and orange sherbet, the weathered stone created shapes both fanciful and severe. A looming cliff perplexed him because it seemed too large to fit into the low-ceilinged tunnel. The proportions weren't right. At the top of what appeared to Len more and more as a mountain than a wall, a tower stood. Whether natural or Welken made, Len could not tell, it seemed so far away.

But the tower was right there in the tunnel. And he saw something alive near the tower. Something moving.

This must be a miniature city, Len thought, with little gremlins running around. Maybe I can be the tall one for a change, a regular Gulliver in this orange-sherbet world.

Thus inspired, Len reached toward the gremlin, hoping to pull the little guy out by his collar. Instead, his hand passed right through the tower. Panicked, he felt around, desperate for something solid, something to tell him his eyes weren't deceived. He thought for a second he might fall over. Gradually, his eyes focused beyond the tower, and he could make out the light he'd seen before at the end of the tunnel.

Prester John spoke from two feet away, startling Len. "What are you doing, may I ask?"

"Don't sneak up on me like that!" Len felt that his hair must be standing on end.

"Perhaps you shouldn't charge ahead and leave yourself without the benefit of soldierly experience and impeccable character."

"Well, OK, Mr. Soldier Man, what would you do if you found an imaginary rock wall in front of you?" Len paced in the short width of the tunnel, afraid to walk into the vision before him.

"I so enjoy these make-believe military questions, but don't you think we should proceed down this tunnel? I dare say my lantern won't hold out forever."

"What do you mean, make-believe? I'm talking about this genuine rock wall illusion right in front of me."

"So you want me to speculate on the reality of an imaginary wall?"

"Yes! I mean this image here."

Prester John drew his sword to prepare for the invisible enemy. "I have the keenest eyesight in all of the Highlands—except for perhaps the Great Anuba whose sight is also inward—and I see nothing blocking our march to victory." He turned his hunched figure back to his loyal subject. "Do you, Ellen?"

"I see no vision. Your Eminence has once again discerned wisely."

"This is stupid! What's the point of a wall only I can see?" asked Len.

Prester John returned his sword to its scabbard. "If I were you—and I'd much rather be me—I'd study this rock wall carefully. Perhaps you are to learn something vital and lifesaving. My recommendation would be to describe it to us."

So Len did, orange sherbet and all.

"No doubt about it," said Prester John, "your image here is an exact replica of the Wasan Sagad, the last outpost between the Highlands and the vast uncharted Wasteland. The sandstone tower rises out of the desolate but colorful canyon you ably describe."

"What is the Wasteland?" asked Len.

Ellen held her lantern up like a butler in a horror movie. "No one knows for certain. We know it is hot and barren and that to get to the tower is a grueling ordeal. Not many bother. To keep going beyond the tower is pointless. Though some say the Wasan Sagad is a monument worthy of a pilgrimage, the Wasteland is worthy of nothing."

Len tested the illusion a few more times, passing his hand through it as if he were Helen Keller touching water for the first time. He kept expecting the colors to pool in his hand. Reluctantly, he walked through it.

As the three pressed on toward the opening, Prester John recounted the legend of the Wasan Sagad. "Centuries ago, Highlanders say, all the land beyond the Great Alpine Reef was as fertile and beautiful as Welken today. Some say that Welken itself was larger then, too, extending east through the Wasteland and beyond. In those days, many enjoyed traveling for weeks and months behind the Reef. One man so wished to celebrate this paradise and to provide a way station for pilgrims that he built the colorful tower you saw in your vision. His name was Wasan Sagad.

"Wasan Sagad lived in the tower, providing hospitality. As long as Wasan lived, a faithful community in the tower protected the life in the valley. When he died a new host for the tower, a new Wasan, was needed. This new leader was also called Wasan Sagad—and so it went for generations, the old Wasan passing on responsibilities to the younger Wasan, until one day, still generations ago, no younger Wasan came forward. Slowly the region wasted away and everyone left. Springs dried up.

Animals starved to death, and plants shriveled unto dust. The land that was beyond imagination became the barren world we now call the Wasteland. All that remained of Wasan Sagad was his tower, and so it is named for him."

"What do you think, Ellen?" Len trudged forward. "Is the story true?"

"It's possible," she said. "The tower is there. I have seen it from a distance. Some say cisterns for water remain. But I have not been all the way out to the Wasan."

"Ouch," said Len. He bumped his head on the unforgiving stone and sat down to rub the bump. "Is it my imagination, or is the tunnel getting smaller?"

"I've been hunched over for some time." Prester John rubbed his neck. "But I did not want to speak of the creeping agony in my lower back. Highlanders are the last to complain, especially about back pain that surges through the spine in blinding flashes. We simply would not draw attention to ourselves by mentioning—"

"Wait," said Len. "The opening isn't as far away as it looks. It's just smaller." He got on all fours and crawled gamely over the onyx shale on the floor. When he reached the three-foot opening, he blocked the light from Prester John and Ellen. Len crouched down and poked through. Then he stood outside on a path that sloped steadily downward. Prester John and Ellen joined him.

All three faced the northwest. In the shade of the mountain, they looked out past the shadows to the light of the setting sun flickering on rock formations farther out. Shining like a lighthouse in a sea of frozen ships, the Wasan Sagad captured their attention. It was just as Len had seen in the onyx tunnel, just farther away, too far to see any people.

Nevertheless, they received a greeting. Though the peak of the day had passed, waves of heat swept over them and stole away the coolness of the tunnel. As bright and beautiful as the tower glowed, fear upon fear layered quickly into Len's consciousness. Heat. Barrenness. Rocks. Heat. Death. There was no denying it.

The terrible Wasteland called their names.

CHAPTER TWENTY-TWO
A Full Compass of Doors

Every man has a right to risk his own life in order to preserve it.
Has it ever been said that a man who throws himself
out a window to escape from a fire is guilty of suicide?

JEAN JACQUES ROUSSEAU, *THE SOCIAL CONTRACT*

 When Angie took her last look at the other Misfits in Ganderst Hall, she could tell by their searching eyes that they had a hard time finding her.

I am a vapor, she thought, a ghost. Like every kid, I used to dream of being invisible. But now that I'm really there or close to it, I'm not sure I like it. At least I can also flicker with light. I'd hate not to be seen at all.

She turned back to Vida. "I feel like I'm walking just past sunset but never fully arriving at night. I've been 'twilighted,' as you might say."

Vida grasped Angie's hand.

But I'm worried, Angie thought. What if I get stuck as invisible? Or what if I disappear into nothingness? And yet—it is all good so far. Who am I to question what has not yet happened? I will take the next step, as Piers said, grateful that my footprint can be seen by all. Hmm, I guess I *have* become a bit of an *airhead* now.

Finally, Angie grabbed Jacob's hand also, and together, they crossed the threshold of the south door. Then Angie let go. Of course, she knew where she was. The south door opened into the tunnel that led to the back of Chimney Cave, the scene of their first encounter with Morphane.

They began to retrace their steps. Vida Bering Well and Jacob Canny Sea stayed close behind her.

Jacob held a lantern into the familiar passageway. "I've been stalagmited here before, and the memory is particularly claustrophobed."

"Don't be so pessimized," said Vida. "As my Auntie May Reeding Well used to say, 'When life scurvies you, lemonize it.'"

Angie put up a hand. "Wait. I see something up ahead, I can't quite make it out, but I see a lot of blue. It looks alive somehow."

"What's she visulating?" asked Vida.

Jacob shrugged. "I don't know. All I see are kettles of blackification. Angie, what's it look like?"

"Oh, Vida, Jacob, I can see it now. It's the wide ocean swirling in turquoise loveliness. And there's the sand. It feels warm just looking at it, and there's a single rowboat floating near the shore. I feel drawn to it. Jacob, Vida, let's go. I think we're supposed to get in the boat, maybe row out to that island. And look at that island. Its cliffs are so forbidding, pinnacles that cut the sky like shark's teeth. Maybe the tile is there. Hurry!"

Angie moved toward the lapping waves, reached out her hand to grasp the boat, and then, to her surprise, found herself still in the cave. Quickly, she turned around and could see the ocean and rowboat again, only in reverse because now she was on the other side of the scene, a vision that was like a movie projected onto a screen in the cave, only there was no screen, just the image, and no movie projector. If she focused in the distance, she saw Vida and Jacob standing in the tunnel with their lanterns, the blues of the ocean playfully coloring their faces. Angie walked back through the image and met them just inside the south door.

"What do you think it means?" Angie asked.

"What *what* means, Angie?" Jacob sounded worried. "If you being invisible ain't enough for our poor little einsteins, now you say we ought to columbus what we can't see no matter how hard we squintify."

Angie pressed her hand in and out of the scene. "You really can't see the waves?"

"Not a droppified bit," said Jacob.

"Nor me," said Vida, "and the only island I know with cliffs like you steinbecked is Justice Island, so the boat must be in Mercy Bay, a good day's trekkification from here."

Angie felt upset that the Welkeners could not verify her vision. "Then let's keep moving."

Up the tunnel they marched. With the comfort of knowing where they'd arrive, the time sped by until Angie bumped up against a dead end.

"Hold the light a little closer, please," said Angie, who in the dimmer light could not be seen at all unless the flame shone right next to her. Jacob and Vida feared they might step on her feet, so they lagged behind until she glowed into sight. "This must be the back of the fireplace," she said. "Let's move the smaller rocks and then see if we can move the big one."

Jacob kept his hand on his dagger. "Oh, dear. At times like these, my knees get all wobblerated and I earthquake from head to toe."

"Steady, Jacob Canny Sea," said Vida. "We Deedy dwellers know how to quarterback our options."

After pulling off the stacked rocks, all three leaned against the left side of the circular stone and tried to push it to the right. With less effort than they anticipated, the stone rolled away. Then to their surprise, light from the room blinded them.

They lowered their heads to duck under the top of the opening and saw the cold remnants of a fire. As their eyes adjusted, they stepped into the fire pit and stood up, lifting their heads to take in the familiar walls of Chimney Cave.

But instead of sconces and broken stools, they saw an elaborately furnished dining room, including a massive oak table about four feet wide and thirty feet long. From the twenty-foot ceiling hung banners with family crests and other royal designs spaced evenly so that looking up, Angie thought of huge venetian blinds.

Vida put away her daggers. "Well, I'll be magicianated!"

"Cool!" said Angie, too awestruck to say anything else. She examined the detailed carving on the backs of the chairs, each one unique, some displaying pastoral landscapes and others battle scenes. Both walls of the long sides of the room contained eight expansive stained glass windows, arched at the top. Before Angie could study the images in the glass, her sense of urgency overtook her. "Where are we?" She did not really expect an answer.

"I'm quite libraried with the place." Jacob thrust himself up so he could sit on a broad windowsill. "We're in the Long House of The Village, the politification of Primus Hook."

"Should I know what that means?" asked Angie.

"I beg your christification, dear Angie," said Jacob. "Of course, you wouldn't. This is called the Tholl Table of Long House, where the wordly wars are waged so that we don't get napoleoned so easily. Piers presides over the goings-on."

Vida stood on the seat of the head chair. "Here's where we were electionated to help. The sitters at this table decided Jacob and I could lewisandclark with the best Welken could offer."

"I'm glad that you are good lewisandclarkers," said Angie, smiling, "but I'm wondering how we got here, in this room. And *why* we are here? Are we to protect these treasures? Or is the tile hidden in this room somewhere?" Angie leaned into the bay of a stained-glass window, its colors delicately illuminating her indistinct features.

"I'm hunchinated to the bottom of my blood pumper." Vida put one foot on the table. "Everything in the room seems to send my peepers to the outside, to hubble the view as best I can." She hopped off the chair and led Angie and Jacob Canny Sea to two tall stained-glass doors. She turned the handles and pushed the doors outward, revealing an open veranda capable of holding dozens of people. "When I was toddlerated, my dear old mother, Sally Aryoo Well, brought me here to learn of Welken's wonders. I was positively vistafied. See the gander for yourself."

Angie's dim outline, like the distortion of heat rising from asphalt, glided over the terrace. Once at the railing facing south, she saw the ocean's deep blue set against the sky's fainter hue and said, "Mercy Bay, right? And out there is Justice Island. That, I think, must be where we're headed." Between the veranda and the beach lay the town, Primus Hook, filled with thatched-roof cottages and shops and, on the outskirts, farmland. "It's so beautiful, so peaceful."

"Don't forget, Angie"—Jacob pushed his open hands on the top of his dagger handles—"Into this splendorated scene, Morphane has villained us."

Angie pointed toward town. "Oh, look."

Down below, on the steps leading away from Long House, a little girl scratched a stick across the rough surface. She drummed on the steps, then balanced on one like a tightrope walker.

Leaning on the railing, Angie studied the little girl. She seemed as cute as any girl Angie had ever seen. Actually, the more she watched, the more Angie thought that she *had* seen this face before, maybe when she baby-sat for the Taylors. The girl's irrepressible smile beamed under the graceful canopy of her feathery blond hair.

Twirling, the girl danced off the steps and sat on the ground, her skirt flopping down to cover her legs entirely. She raised her head sharply toward the three on the veranda. She seemed to motion to them, as if to say, "Come down here."

With no hesitation Angie ran from the veranda down the steps toward the girl.

Jacob cupped his hands over his mouth like a bullhorn. "Wait! Stop! What's all the ferrari?"

⚮

Poised at the west door, Lizbeth reviewed her growing sense of confidence. Instead of cursing her body, she relished how it was made and what it could do. She felt as if she were admiring a graceful athlete, not stubby ol' Lizbeth who would belt a home run but then clomp around the bases.

In her inner dialogue as she paused at the door, she imagined explaining her new feelings to her mother. It's like this, Mom. Suppose we were driving, and in front of us, a pickup truck blows out a tire, veers off the road, and crashes into a drainage ditch. We pull over to help, but when we get to the truck, the driver is sitting up. He tells us that he's going to be OK, but that he is so grateful we stopped that he wants to give us $10,000. We protest, but he says he has millions and can't give it away fast enough.

It's like this in Welken, Mom. Though terrible things happen, somehow I think it's all going to work out.

What if, continued Lizbeth to herself, the very thing we believed would hurt us turned out to help us? What if the thing we thought was our enemy turned out to be our friend, but only if we had the courage to call it that by name? What if my body turned out to be a gift? What a great cosmic joke! Yeah, totally cosmic.

Mook twirled an arrow impatiently. "Excuse me, Lizbeth, but shouldn't we get going? You seem frozen in the first step."

"It's often the hardest one." Lizbeth smiled sagely and brushed off her overalls as if this task were the reason for the delay. "But you're right. Let's move on."

She looked back at Mook and Alabaster, turned forward, and crossed the threshold. I am home, she thought, really home.

That sentiment took on added meaning when their first step splashed into a few inches of water on the floor of the passageway, reminding Lizbeth of the wet Northwest.

"No problem," she said. "I'm used to walking through water." She kept going with one hand against the left wall.

Soon, the inch of water turned into five, and their feet stuck to the murky bottom with each step. Then, Lizbeth noticed the reason for the water. Up ahead on the right, nearly blocking their way, a waterfall splashed into the tunnel with fire-hose force. Pushing herself off the wall, Lizbeth sloshed over closer. She saw even more surging water coming out from an alcove. Her legs in water to midcalf, Lizbeth enjoyed the exhilarating spray.

She waved Mook and Alabaster over to her. "Fantastic, isn't it?"

"I wouldn't put it that way," said Mook.

"Don't you feel refreshed?"

"I'm glad you do. To me, it just means my shoes will not dry out for days and that our journey will be slow."

"No, no, no, I don't mean the creek. I mean the waterfall. I love the pounding water and the mist in my face. And look there!" She pointed at the base of it. "A young boy is standing in his canoe. He's looking downriver. He sees something. Now he looks scared, really scared. He's losing his balance. Whoa, he fell into the current. It's taking him downstream. We've got to help him." She strode through the water as best she could. "Mook, Alabaster, help! The river's got him!" She dove at the boy and then surfaced. "I missed him. But look, there he is. He bobbed up. He's resting against something standing in the water. Oh no. Oh no! Mook, the thing in the water. It's Morphane! And the boy is looking right into Morphane's face! Boy! Don't do it!" She plunged in again, stood up, and turned around frantically. "Where'd he go? Mook, do you see him?"

"What waterfall, Lizbeth?" Mook held his lantern where Lizbeth was looking.

"What do *you* mean 'what waterfall'? I'm talking about the boy. Didn't you hear me? The waterfall is deafening."

Mook pushed through the water to stand by her side. "To tell the truth, I was going to ask you why you were shouting."

As Lizbeth stood flabbergasted, Alabaster sloshed through the water straight for the waterfall. Before Lizbeth could stop her, she passed through the bubbling base of the waterfall unfazed. Lizbeth turned to Mook looking shocked. "What happened? Where's Morphane?"

Mook took Lizbeth's hand. "Walk with me toward your waterfall." While Mook strode through the water on the floor, head held high, red and gray hair flowing down his back, Lizbeth ducked to keep from getting wet. She struggled mightily to ignore the evidence her eyes could not deny. Yet nothing splashed against her face. The lantern did not dim.

"You are in Welken." Mook paused. "Visions appear. You can see a waterfall that we cannot. Although the image may be a gift, we must discern to be sure it is not a deception. Tell us more about the place."

Lizbeth described what she saw, especially the craggy horseshoe rim. "What good is a vision of a boy meeting Morphane? I don't want to know that someone is swept away to die!" Alabaster consoled Lizbeth with a hand on her shoulder.

"Your dream will be important later," said Mook softly. "I'm certain you saw Alta Nez Falls, near our home. Maybe what you saw is the future. For now, use your worry to keep us moving along."

"Ouch!" Lizbeth felt a pain and realized Alabaster might think she was talking about her hand still resting on her shoulder. "No, not you, Alabaster. I think I got bit underwater."

Alabaster lifted Lizbeth's leg out of the water, pulled up her loose overalls, and held the lantern up to it. Then Lizbeth started screaming and tore into her leg. Alabaster passed her lantern to Mook and gripped Lizbeth's leg so hard that she stopped flailing. With calm but firm movements, Alabaster pushed Lizbeth's back against the tunnel's wall and pulled her left leg out of the water by the heel. Wrapped around Lizbeth's calf was something part snake, part leech. The creature was clamped onto Lizbeth's leg, like a centipede with spiky teeth instead of legs, each incision drawing blood.

Painstakingly, with Lizbeth screaming as much from the idea of it as from the teeth, Alabaster peeled off the sucking basilisk. For just a moment, Alabaster held the snake-leech above her, as if offering it to the heavens, and then she sliced it in half with her knife, blood dripping into the water below them. Mook held one of the two remaining lanterns close to Lizbeth's leg. The serpentine bites left a crude tattoo.

"Not poisonous," said Mook. "We haven't seen many of these until recently. We're sure they've increased since Morphane appeared."

"Let's get out of here." Lizbeth couldn't get her leg to stop shaking. "I need to get walking on the leg, get the blood flowing—while I still have it—and we're supposed to find a tile, not waste time in some rising creek."

In the dimmer light, Lizbeth and the two from the Nezzer clan pushed through the water for a hundred feet or so. And then it was waist deep. As Lizbeth winced from her wounds, Mook held his quiver of arrows above the water with his elbow.

Lizbeth stopped. "I don't like this. I was just starting to feel like maybe I wasn't the most doomed person on the planet, then I get attacked by that sea monster, then this rising water. Mook, what are we to do?"

"Piers told Bennu to take the next step he knew to take. Shouldn't we do the same? Do you know the next step, Lizbeth?"

"Yes, but so what? Each step leads to deeper water. Then what? We swim. I don't like it. I'm afraid."

"What is the next step, Lizbeth?"

"It's one step further into this stupid cave!"

"Then, come, you get in the middle. Let's face it together."

Too frightened to feel embarrassed, Lizbeth took Alabaster's hand with her right and Mook's with her left. Strength seemed to multiply a hundredfold. With the two remaining lanterns reflecting off the water, the west-door questors took the next step simultaneously.

As they did, all three lost their footing, and the lanterns filled with water. Mook, Alabaster, and Lizbeth fell on their backsides down, down, down, through the most spectacular waterslide of all time.

Skeptically, Bennu returned to the ornate east door. Bolstered by the muscular, positive presence of Sutton Hoo and Zennor Pict, he relaxed and enjoyed the idea that above the others he had won the assignment to lead these two men of moral and physical integrity.

Piers must have singled me out as a leader, he thought. Then he thought some more. Maybe Piers has the *least* confidence in me so he put the two biggest and strongest Welkeners in my group. Oh, well, either way I'm glad they're on my side.

Despite this advantage, he had to begin his quest for the Tetragrammaton tile by entering a room that didn't lead anywhere. It was a dead end. Unlike the other three doors, the east door boasted a tooled iron gate in addition to the marble door itself. While the marble door opened out, the gate split in half and swung in on its hinges. When the two parts of the gate met, a wrought-iron scarab held them together.

Bennu studied the symbols on the gate before swinging up the beetle clasp and pushing it open. The closed gate paralleled the Tetragrammaton itself—four quadrants, two on each side of the gate. In addition, the border of each quadrant possessed several "buttons" that covered the larger welds, buttons that contained the same image, a beehive or a turban or some kind of whirling dervish. Now that he noticed them, these buttons seemed to be everywhere. Then, out of the corner of his eye, he thought he saw some motion on the gate. One little beehive spun like a tiny tornado. When he turned to focus on the button, nothing moved. Then his peripheral vision caught something again and his direct vision missed it again. Since so many buttons hung on the borders, the effect of the spinning images unnerved Bennu, making him dizzy. He pulled his hands out of his black windbreaker and steadied himself against the gate. Then he pushed it open.

Inside the room, Bennu felt helpless. "Now what? We've already been here."

Sutton tugged on his beard just below his bottom lip, "Aye, but these paintings remind me of something."

"Indeed." Zennor tugged on his beard under the chin. "The color looks as fresh as dew on the Durrow moors."

Great, thought Bennu. All we need is a PBS commentator. "What does all of this mean? How can we be getting any closer to the tile?"

He studied the landscape and saw whirling buttons. Then he looked back to the door and saw more of them.

"I am not as discerning as my loyal friend, Sutton," said Zennor, "but what if the fruit in those trees means we are to think of other golden globes, the sun perhaps?"

Sutton nodded. "A good beginning, Zennor, a right promising start."

"What makes it a good start?" Bennu's irritation over his vision was noticeable. Then he caught himself. "I'm sorry to be rude. I'm just frustrated by these spinning buttons. I think I'm getting seasick."

"How can that be, Bennu?" asked Sutton. "We are as landlocked as anyone can be in Welken. And what's this about spinning buttons?"

Whirling with nausea, Bennu barely realized that Sutton claimed not to see these whirling pests. All Bennu wanted now was relief. Like a sleepy truck driver, he shook his head to try to flick away the blurriness. But the visual confusion remained. He closed his eyes—but his head spun all the more. He searched for a stable spot, a fixed point on the horizon somewhere. Yet the tornado-inspired tormentors chased him peripherally until he thought he should go blind or mad. Finally, one space on the wall provided visual solace, a three-by-seven-foot rectangle. In a few seconds, Bennu could focus again.

Within the frame, a simple rural scene contained finely painted details: men plowing fields, women baking bread in outdoor ovens, children playing on dirt paths. Behind the village, a sliver of land, a jetty perhaps, curled into the sea like a giant claw. To Bennu's surprise, Sutton and Zennor recognized the landscape easily.

Zennor pointed excitedly. "That's Kells Village just east of Durrow Wood. It looks like it was painted from Wroxeter Bluff. It's a right fine view from there."

"And that hut above my finger is where my fair Gildas goes to trade mutton," said Sutton. "Just recently she bargained well for salt, honey, and a broadax."

Bennu's eye followed the road through the village to the jetty in the sea. The curve of the claw of land reminded him of something, so he walked closer to this section of the painting, grateful he could do so without the mini-tornadoes in pursuit. Sharp contrasts of light on the water and the dark, barnacled boulders caught his eye. He was so close to it he could see a few brush strokes on the surface.

He jumped back and said, "Whoa." The curve of the strip of land on the sea came into a special focus for him until an eye stared back at Bennu's eye. It was the Eye of Horus, and the curve in the land matched the curve in the line under Horus's eye.

Bennu pointed to the claw in the water and asked, "What's this?"

Sutton said, "It's called Goffer's Spit. It's named after a village troubadour who used to come to town to tell stories. Some were true. Some were not, but all rolled together they make up the memory of Durrow Wood. Goffer had only a few teeth. When telling tales, he mashed his gums and scrunched his eyes into any manner of face he wished. Children followed him 'cause his words hooked so deep he could fish right into your heart—and then you'd be gettin' pulled whichever way he chose. No one's seen him for years, so we guess he got swept out to sea durin' a storm. The village took to callin' that whisper of land Goffer's Spit. He was a right lathery orator."

"That doesn't explain the Eye of Horus part," said Bennu.

"The eye of what-us?" asked Sutton.

Bennu looked down. "Oh, nothing. I don't suppose you see anything unusual on Goffer's Spit?"

Sutton studied the wall. "No. Just rocks and tide pools and that little girl bendin' over to tie her shoe. There, she's done. Aye, that's a good painting!"

Bennu looked again and saw the girl walk down a path. He did a double-take at Sutton and Zennor, and they all noticed that everything inside the spinning border pulsed with life. Sheep ate grass. Smoke from the chimneys swirled upwards until it gradually disappeared into the heavens.

Bennu tried to collect his thoughts by looking away, but the spinning buttons everywhere else forced him to stay within the frame. "Now what. Here's a living painting three-by-seven feet. So what? What are we supposed to *do*? Hey, wait a minute. I know something three-by-seven feet. A door!"

Bennu searched for the doorknob or some key. He pushed his hand into the scene . . . and it kept going. His other hand followed, and then forgetting that he wasn't supposed to be brave, he stepped fully into the wall. Instantly on the other side, he found himself on a grassy knoll overlooking the pastures below. He felt a light breeze and smelled kelp from the sea. He pushed one hand back into the room and crooked a finger for the others to follow. Zennor and Sutton slipped in behind him, leading with their massive staffs. The three looked around and at each other in sheer delight.

"As sure as that Goffer did spit," said Sutton, "we're home!"

"Ha, ha!" Zennor held his staff over his head in triumph. "That's a right handy way to travel!"

"Aroooo!" Sutton sung like a wolf. "I think I see Kew and Patrick down there! And isn't that Drumonia who walks with a basket on her head? You can be sure all the men of Durrow will watch her every step. Bennu, let's run. Maybe I can introduce you to her. Drumonia is as fair as they come, that is, saving the fairest lady of them all, the handsome Gildas, whose arms await me. What am I saying? I'll run whether you keep up or not. I've got a baby to be seein'. Charge!"

Using their staffs to aid their footing, Sutton and Zennor raced down the hill, happily trampling wildflowers with every step. Bennu took off after them. As he ran, he felt the invisible gift from the Tetragrammaton jiggle in his pocket. It started to come out. Afraid to lose it, Bennu stuffed it back down, but in the bouncing down the bluff, it wiggled up and back out. With every adjustment of the gift, Bennu lost ground on Sutton and Zennor. Exasperated, Bennu grabbed the thing as firmly as he could and returned to the race.

Into the wind he sped until, suddenly, like a hang-glider pilot, his feet, still churning, left the ground. Bennu sailed boldly into the sky, sans hang glider, sans parasail. Bennu flew. Arms outstretched, downhill, into the wind, Bennu stayed aloft, happily aloft, even at times skillfully aloft. Soaring past Sutton and Zennor, he added his delirious scream to the cheers of his friends. A screech was more like it, the high-pitched gravelly screech of a falcon.

CHAPTER TWENTY-THREE
SNAPPY ESCAPADES

With the catching end the pleasures of the chase.
ABRAHAM LINCOLN

"No, that won't work," Charlotte said to herself. "If Ollie takes the camels, how will Percy and Bones get out?" She rose from the Adirondack chair to do what she usually did when she felt stuck. She deadheaded flowers, snapping off the faded blossoms with her fingers. Marigolds, petunias, pansies, anything would do. Snap. Snap, snap.

Her husband, Jeff, waved to her from the back porch. "How's it going, dear?" Charlotte looked up at him with narrowed eyes and steely jaw. "Maybe not so good, eh?" he said. "I won't say, 'Writing a book is like pulling teeth.' That would be a bad dentist joke, so I won't say it, OK? I don't want to be a bad dentist, do I? Ha!" She threw a dead marigold flower in his directions.

Suddenly, she stood boldly upright, struck a Eureka! pose, and ran back to the chair. The dam broke furiously. Flooded with words, she wrote furiously, trying to get the waterfall on paper before the tap slowed to a drip.

CHAPTER SIX: Chasing Percy Chasing Ollie

By the Mews," exclaimed Percy, enjoying Dominic's phrase, "looks as if our hands are fit to be tied."

"Perce," moaned Bones, "our hands *are* tied. I thought

you said you could do something about it."

"Tut-tut. A watched rope is never foiled, my friend."

In no time, the ties that bound were slashed and cast aside by Percy's clever claws. Then Percy darted over to Ollie's discarded map and snatched it up. He squinted, put on his pince-nez, and squinted again. He turned it ninety degrees to the right and tried again.

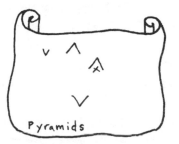

Just when he looked as if he recognized something, he turned it ninety degrees to the right again, the way spatially impaired navigators will do to keep the road and the map lined up. Percy turned his back to the door of the tomb and held the map up into the light. That's when he noticed the painted eyes on the opposite wall reflecting the sun's rays, glistening in their gold mascara.

"Ah!" Percy said with authority. "So that's it. So. So. So."

"So, what have you got, Perce?" asked Bones.

"It appears"—Percy stroked his chin—"that this map is indecipherable."

Abu P. Cockles, their loyal guide, laughed, slapped his knee, and pushed one of his feathers back into place, "Hoo-hoo, good joke. You Americans know how to push one's leg, no?"

Bones looked out the door into the desert sun. "Time's a' fritterin' away, Perce. I don't like the thought of Ollie galloping across the sands. Why don't you let us give the map a try?"

Percival P. Perkins III, detective cat, deducer without parallel, champion figure-outer, handed over the map and sat with his back against a wall by the door, as dejected as one would likely ever catch the flamboyant feline. As Abu and Bones pointed and theorized, Percy mused aloud while pacing inside the room of riches: "What would Wise Dominic say if he could see me now? Would he say I'd failed in one ear and out the window? Would he be as mad as someone long in the tooth? Would he say that Ollie pulled the rug out from under our own eyes? Oh, Dominic, Dominic, would you tell me my efforts are not worth a tinker's nose to the grindstone? Wait a minute, Bonesy. Wait a flea-bitten minute. Don't you see, that's it! Dominic is in my head as we speak, so to speak."

Bones looked up from the map. "What have you got, Perce?"

Percy's voice showed no lingering traces of self-doubt. "Here it is, Bone of my Bonesy. My mutterings about ears and teeth and eyes and nose—four parts of a face. It's an image, waiting to help us. And I think I know whose."

Grabbing the map from Abu, Percy walked over to the sunlit mural with the shining gold. Placing the map over the profiled face, he shifted the map around until four pyramids on the map aligned with the eye, ear, mouth, and nose. When he did so, he could see a crack in the wall that ran from the teeth up the face between the eye and the ear. After tracing the crack with a pencil, Percy pulled the map off to reveal a trail leading out from the pyramids and toward the Mediterranean coast.

"And look here!" Percy kept the pencil going above Alexandria. "This seems to go up and up in the shape of the Greek letter sigma, and the pencil catches on four spots along the way."

Not wasting a minute, the ever-resourceful Abu led the inspired detectives to a camel stable nearby.

"Our guide is as lucky as you are," remarked Bones to Percy.

"Come now, Mr. Malone. What's luck got to do with it?"

They paid the owner with a handful of jewels and were soon clumping over the sand, Bones in the rear, complaining about his rear. In no time the pursuers retraced their steps back to the train. After dropping off the camels to a friend of Abu's, they rode the rails, sweating past Cairo, through Tant'a, and finally to Alexandria. Here, at the end of the line, having fulfilled his orders, Abu bid adieu. Much hugging and kissing of both cheeks. Hoo-hoo.

Bones squatted on the ground Egyptian-style. "I dunno, Perce, I don't see how we're supposed to find Ollie. It's like trying to find a carrot seed in a pumpkin patch."

"Just the right insight, Bones, and as the brown book says, 'Not a moment too good to be true.' Where would we find our missing otter of a carrot seed? In the most attractive pumpkin patch around, the local bazaar."

✒

O h, Mama, my mama." Ollie surveyed the throngs at the bazaar. "So many pockets, so little time. My fingers get so twitchy, Mama. There they go toward that stuffed purse over yonder. I try to control them, but I can't. Oh, fingers, come back. You shouldn't a' otter do that. It's no use, Mama. All I can do is tag along for the ride."

Ollie slithered up to a bulging handbag and flipped through the contents as if they were files in a cabinet. Talking quietly to himself, he examined the items. "No to the souvenir pyramids, yes to the silk scarf, no to the porcelain alligator, yes to the ceramic trivet thingies, no to the pictures of grandkids—"

"Yes to jail." A voice from the crowd greeted him, and then out popped Percy. "All the loot from the pyramid wasn't enough for you, eh?"

Ollie stuffed the priceless trivets into his coat while lamenting his fate. "Oh, Mama, my destiny is cheated again!"

"I do believe," said Percy, "you like the hunt better than the capture." Percy and Bones leaped toward Ollie. "But I don't at all mind capturing *you*, old boy."

Just then Ollie threw a handful of coins high in the air in Percy's direction. Percy caught one deftly while the others fell to the ground, inspiring a mad scramble in the bazaar that effectively cut off Percy and Bones from Ollie. By the time they pushed through the crowd, Ollie's "toodly-too bad" had long since faded into the hubbub of hundreds of shoppers.

"Curious," pondered Percy, "Ollie looked right at me when he tossed those coins."

"He had to look somewhere, Perce," said Bones.

"No, there's something more in this. His eyes bore a message, Mr. Malone. I don't know why, but they seemed to say, 'You want to chase me, Percival P. Perkins? Here's something for you to chew on.' Hmm. What could it be, Bonesy?"

"I have a cheese sandwich in my bag."

"No, no, no, Bones. What about this coin in my hand? It's imitation ancient Roman, with Caesar's head on it. What could Ollie be telling us? Oh, the worm turns over in his grave."

"The worms in my garden have nothing to do with Caesar, Perce. They do provide good fertilizer for romaine lettuce, and that can become a nice Caesar salad."

"Wait a flea-bitten minute. I know you're going to say I'm one marble shy of a full deck, Mr. Bones, but I think I've discovered where Ollie is headed."

"To my garden?"

"Oh, please, Bonesy. It's much closer than that. To Rome! The old burglar is headed to the city of seven hills."

"Rome? You can't be serious, Percy. How will we find him there?"

"Just take the next step. We know that much. As the brown book says, 'All's well that the cooks don't spoil.'"

Exhilarated, Charlotte dropped her pen and stared out the gate into the Wilder. She fancied Percy and Bones walking into her backyard looking in the bushes for Ollie.

Percy strolls up to her and says, "Dear lady, have you seen a nasty otter hiding somewhere?"

Bones points to a slug trail around the flower bed. "You might not realize it, but we bassets have been gardeners for generations in Virginia." As he leans over to look at the petunias, Angie is by his side conferring quietly with him.

"Hey, Charlotte!" yelled Jeff from the garage. "What's for dinner?"

Poof. Everything vanished. Charlotte noticed a light breeze fluttering through the lilacs and two lizards doing push-ups. Above the last of the golden primroses, the box hedge leaves glistened like tiny oval mirrors in the sun. Straining to see if she could catch Percy's tail exiting through the back, Charlotte blocked the afternoon glare with her hand. Then she rose and walked to her faded petunias. Snap. Snap, snap, snap.

CHAPTER TWENTY-FOUR
FATAGAR

Everyone will be salted with fire.

MARK 9:49

 From the platform at the exit of the north door, Prester John looked longingly at the tower called Wasan Sagad. "So lovely in its own right, yet also a beacon, a moral lighthouse testifying to what awaits those who ignore the laws that govern life and death. In the fading light of day, the Wasan Sagad calls us to remember." A tear fell across his manly cheek. "We are to remember what Great Anuba wisely said."

"It's a rock," said Len flatly, hands in his back pockets.

"What?" asked Prester John, startled by Len's interruption.

Len brushed off tunnel dust. "We're looking at a bunch of rocks piled on top of a bunch of other rocks. No more, no less. What's the big deal? It's a deserted bed-and-breakfast. Business got slow, and the place closed down."

"Dear me." Prester John took a step away from Len. "You are uninformed *and* unimaginative. Ellen, what are we to do with the dreariness of this boy?"

"I suspect—," said Ellen.

"I am not a boy!" roared Len, his short mane standing on end then relaxing. He bared his enlarged leonine teeth.

"I was going to say," Ellen measured her words, "that we should find some shelter before we have no light left."

Prester John saluted her. "Yes, of course. But let us be sure to walk with hearts hardened against any beauty along the way. We'll call it Len's method." He stormed off down the trail. Ellen gave Len a now-look-what-you've-done grimace and followed her prince.

Len shook his head, as much at his own irrepressible indiscretion as at Prester John's sentimentality, and tagged along behind.

With the tower a few miles away, the Northern Company, as Prester John had come to call the three of them, did not like their circumstances. "The Wasteland might dance colorfully at sunset," he said, "but it makes for treacherous traveling. I fear we may discover beasts whose dispositions match this climate."

Soon the luminous rock formations appeared ghoulish and intimidating. They walked from the exposed platform to the sheltered trail they could see below them. In the twilight they walked in the general direction of the tower, assuming that the tile awaited them there.

Once down in the narrow path, Len felt like a rat in some giant's maze. The canyon was only three feet wide in places, striped in shades of coppery orange rock, all six feet high or higher. At various bends in the trail, wind-carved sculptures looked to be tottering above them, evoking images of monsters or predictions of tumbling boulders.

After just a few minutes in the maze, from somewhere in the distance, they heard a swirling, swishing sound.

"I'm thirsty," Ellen said. "Let's find that water."

"A cool lemon jingle with frothy mint topping sounds ever so appealing." Prester John acted as if an inn were around the next corner. "But I suppose simple, fresh water, the elixir of the gods, would salve the palate."

"What water are you talking about?" asked Len.

Ellen kicked a rock as she picked up speed. "Can't you hear it getting louder? We must be getting close to a waterfall."

"I hope so." Len tied his sweatshirt around his waist.

His hope, that virtue so easily confused with naiveté, dried up in the next minute because the flowing, rushing water they heard turned out to be a raucous sundowner wind. In the low light they could see the dust swirling ahead of them, down the long stone corridor. It paused as it rounded the corner at the opposite end of the corridor, appearing almost human, almost willful in its movement toward them, as if it deliberated how to maximize impact. Down the narrow canyon with no exit the wind blew, sweeping along debris. Sand and gravel pummeled the trapped threesome. Tiny grains stung their heads and necks—any exposed flesh. Len wrestled his sweatshirt back on.

The grit flew into every opening, down their shirts and into their shoes. They did their best to cover up, but they were unprepared for this kind of enemy. Swords meant nothing to the whipping reinforcements that came. Sand, sand, and more pelting sand. Into the ears, into the eyes, pushing and prodding at the corners of the mouth, tapping, rapping, on the base of the neck, at the eyelids, blasting like shotgun shrapnel on ankles and wrists. Len's scalp felt as if lice had invaded, crawling without resistance across the hairy landscape.

Then Prester John found a small alcove in the canyon wall, maneuvered Len and Ellen into it, and he covered them with his tall frame, keeping his back to the wind.

No one spoke. There was neither the moisture to do so nor the will to risk sand between the teeth.

After a blistering twenty minutes, the wind subsided. Groaning with each unfurled limb, they rolled away from the wall and slowly stood up in the desert night. In gratitude, Ellen and Len dusted off Prester John's backside, the discharged sand from his sleeves forming neat cones on the rock floor. Where exposed, his skin shone red and sore.

Prester John's dry tongue flopped in his mouth. "No need." He scarcely could whisper. "I . . . serve with . . . no thought of repayment."

More delicately than usual, Ellen placed her fingers on his lips, asking for silence. The half-moon beamed above them, not smiling as a crescent or disarming the dark with its fullness. Its incomplete face reflected their mood: half defeated, half exhausted, half doubtful. Unlike the Highlanders, who would have added half victorious, half resilient, half certain to this list, Len's lunar disposition was full, full of resentment and fully ready to return to Skinner.

These are not my problems, he told himself repeatedly. Why should I suffer for these comic book characters? What difference does it make? Who cares about some stupid tile? And this hair makes me so hot. And everything has sand in it, my ears, my mouth, my eyes. Everything feels dry and raw.

Yet they plodded uncomfortably forward in silence. Once some sand shifted to a spot in Len's shoe that required stopping, but otherwise they trudged gamely on. To their credit, they did not complain. Len did not want to waste the moisture in his mouth.

They walked and walked, Prester John reasoning that they would not want to move during the heat of the day. Though he would be willing to carry both of them, he added, perhaps it was wise to march on as long as they were able.

Len didn't think he had much choice. What are we supposed to do, he thought, go back? Wait for heat, heat, more heat? Sit down until someone smart enough to travel with a canteen came along?

After more dusty plodding, the narrow canyon walkway widened, and then it opened dramatically into a generous, flat plateau. In the half-moonlight, they had a hard time finding the path, so they spread out to look for evidence of a trail. On the right, Len spotted a darker surface that shone brightly against the white. When he recognized what it was, all he could think of to say was "Wahoo!" Unabashedly, Len ran into the water, shoes and all. Though his mother's fears of parasites raced through his mind, Len suppressed them and drank and drank again. When he looked up, Ellen and Prester John were doing the same. Len believed he could feel the water trickle through every inch of his body. He imagined he could hear his parched cells cheering.

After agreeing that Ellen could wash first in the shallows protected by reeds, Len and Prester John turned their backs on the pool and awaited their turn. If he had rafted past skinny-dippers back home, he would not have considered averting his eyes. It was half the fun of rafting. But here, Prester John's noble code seemed right, and he had no more trouble being disciplined than did Prester John. Strangely, this action also had the effect of making him think more highly of Ellen. When she finished, Len and Prester John shed their clothing and washed out the sand.

Afterward, Prester John pulled on his high boots and pointed out the top of the Wasan Sagad reflecting the moon above the colored cliffs. "Four hours' walk, I'm guessing. Maybe less if we retain our normal pilgrim-warrior courage."

As a kind of bedtime story, Prester John told how he, as a young impetuous prince, was molded into the completed kingly presence who stood before them today. Ellen whispered to Len that everything had returned to normal.

Normal? To Len, the word stuck at the fulcrum of his mind, leveraging his future. What was normal about walking in a Wasteland toward the Wasan Sagad with two strange Highlanders? How could normal be attached to magic amulets, shaggy manes, and a bundled gift from the Tetragrammaton?

❧

In the Wasteland after dawn, Len learned how intensely the smoldering heat rose with the sun, degree after degree, never satisfied, never diminishing, pushing the whole landscape into a bulging thermometer ready to blow. The flame troops from the sun then swept over the ground in suffocating waves, a blitzkrieg of burning air firing down on their vulnerable little Northern Company. And then they started walking. In the next hour, the ground and air assaulted them as if directed by some devilish field marshal. And then it got hotter. And hotter.

Their powdery tongues clacked against the roofs of their mouths. Dry, dry, everything dry. Parched throats ached. No saliva. Rocks. No living thing. The little sweat that didn't evaporate trickled down, sadistically reminding them of water, water falling, water near but unattainable, slipping down their backs as undrinkable as sand.

Silent as the stones themselves, the threesome walked step after step toward the Wasan Sagad. With steady persistence, they hoped to reach the tower before the worst heat of the day.

To Len, the worst heat was not later but now, the eternal now, every single second he existed on this path. The radiator of his mind bubbled over: Who in their right mind goes to Death Valley in the summer? And once there takes a hike in the heat of the day, on the sand dunes, on the hottest day of the year? Idiots, that's who! And I'm the biggest idiot for being here at all, for agreeing to help Welken. But then, when did I agree to anything? I came here unconscious the first time. All I did was catch an old bug from Egypt the second time. I don't want to die of heat stroke or skin cancer so that Piers can find his magic tile. And this stupid hair. It's like wearing a wool beanie and scarf to the sauna. I didn't ask to be transformed.

"Hey, watch out!" shouted Prester John after Len walked right into him.

"Sorry," said Len. "I guess I was lost in my thoughts."

Ellen licked her lips so she could speak. "Getting lost is not a good idea, in your mind or on the way. If you're not careful, the sun will bore a hole right into your head. The sun is a fiery demon telling you to give up your soul, to rush into the furnace and sleep in its fire."

"She's right." Prester John draped a cloth over his head. "If not for my iron grip around their sweaty wrists, two of the Highland's finest protectors would have baked in a sandpit."

"I'll try to keep focused," said Len. "But if we're here any longer, I'll never look at 'baked goods' in the same way again."

Ellen wiped her brow, leaving copper lines on her forehead from the dust. "I see that the day is not yet hot enough to melt your humor."

After another mile of sedimentary hallways, the maze once again opened out, and they saw the Wasan Sagad spiraling magically toward the sky. Below the tower, green leaves shouted happily to them of liquid relief. This time they entered the water, clothes and all, for Prester John reminded them of how quickly the sun would dry them out.

In the deliciously wet pool, Len brought up the question they had been too preoccupied with the heat to ask. "What do we do now that we're here? I'm hungry, and I want to get out of this place."

Prester John pointed to the tower. "All we can do is bravely ascend. Maybe the tile awaits us in plain view. Maybe it will be delivered to us by a wizened hermit whose eccentricities endear him to us. Not all quests lead to dragons and treasures and maidens. Sometimes you simply obey and move on to the next adventure. Then again, when I was just a lad, I slew a fearsome sea creature that attacked our boat off Point Refusal. In the tumultuous rain, I slashed and stabbed and hacked the monster. The crew could not believe their eyes and I—"

"Hush."

"Don't stop me now, Ellen. I think Len finds the tale instructive."

"I said nothing, your Elegance."

"Hush, I said."

This time Len could tell that the woman's voice came not from Ellen but from the reeds at the edge of the pool closer to the tower. "You are in danger. Do not let him find you."

Against the brightness of the water's surface, the speaker's body was difficult to see. Len did not struggle over what course of action to pursue. He plunged into a freestyle stroke, cutting the distance between them in half before the voice called again, making him stop so he could better listen.

"Do you not understand? Quiet yourselves. And leave. The Wasan Sagad is no sanctuary. You do not want to meet Fatagar. Every syllable of his name brings pain. Go. Go now. Do not enter the Sagad." Keeping her face hidden, the woman exposed her arm in the sunlight. She shook its ragged thinness, and the chain holding the fetter around her wrist rattled. Before she slipped from view, she leaned briefly into the light.

Len saw a woman perhaps twenty-five years of age, in shameful rags, whose haggard lines said she raced toward death. Throwing himself again into the water, Len swam as fast as he could toward the shore. When he stood in the shallower water, he turned back to the Highlanders. He saw Prester John, with his head bowed, weeping, and Ellen's tight jaw more resolute than ever.

Len quoted Prester John. "Sometimes you just obey and go." Panting from his swim, he sloshed to the shore, just in time to see the ragged woman glance back to the water before she slipped through an opening at the base of the tower.

So much for beautiful maidens, too, thought Len.

"Len, wait!" whisper-shouted Ellen.

Len straightened his water-soaked pants and adjusted his shoes.

Prester John swam furiously after him and then stopped. "Len, don't go. I have a plan." He hurled himself again into the water, his long limbs contracting and shooting out like a water strider.

Len stood one foot in the water, one on the shore. A scream from the tower entryway cut through the heavy, hot air.

"Wait!" Prester John pulled himself up in the waist-high water, halfway to the shore. "There are two kinds of bravery, Len. One says yes and one says no. By the Great Anuba, I plead with you to say no. Wait!"

Len stood on the precipice of this decision, between cautious wisdom and spontaneous action. The sun seemed to add its voice to the debate: "You are here in this hot place, in *this* desert, *their* Wasteland, not yours."

Then the sad woman screamed again.

In the split-second-that-can-change-your-life, Len bolted up the trail to the door. Awkwardly in his wet clothes, Len approached the archway. He heard someone being choked. As his eyes adjusted to the darkness inside, he heard muffled gasps from down the hall. He ran, conscious of every step, every breath, every shadow that could mean destruction. A room to the left. An opening. The sound of fist on flesh. His hands raised like paws ready to strike, Len charged into the room. He saw the woman on the floor, a dagger at her throat, the rusty chain on her irons held by a guard.

At her side crouched a creature as much reptilian as human, with pebbly lizard-like skin and bulging horny toad eyes. His muscular neck and shoulders sat on a body loaded down with lumps and layers of fat. He grinned smugly. Sharp spikes and nubby bumps protruded from his skull, giving him a look of having just been shocked or frightened.

"I'm Fatagar"—he ran his tongue across his upper lip—"and you are mine."

Squatting next to the panting woman, Fatagar leaned back on his own fat until it touched the ground, providing him with a kind of built-in blubbery chair. He rocked gently in his own fat as he motioned for two of the nearby guards to release their weapons from the woman. Rising to his full height of four feet, Fatagar stretched so that a few layers of flabby skin unfolded, revealing a gummy grey mold that looked to have been composting since his last bath eons ago. The stench gagged Len instantly, making each breath feel like an irreversible contamination.

Fatagar's presence was not subtle. Sometimes evil is hidden, masquerading behind flattery and happy handshakes. Other times evil forsakes anything resembling a disguise. To Len, Fatagar was closer to the latter, true to himself, a creature in whom there was a perverse integrity.

"You are t-terribly d-daring." He smacked his tongue off the roof of his mouth as if he were lapping up some forbidden delicacy. "I like d-danger t-too. *Tck, tck.*" To his guards, also reptilian though taller and thinner, he said, "Lock him in here, with the others. Feed him. His strength will be useful. *Tck, tck.*" His shiny tongue carefully dabbed his lips, stopping shy of the crusty corners of his mouth.

On his short, conical legs, Fatagar teetered up a dank winding stairwell that Len guessed led to the upper tower. As the guards turned the key in the door locking him in, Len wondered how someone so apparently weak as Fatagar could control a group of people. Power, he thought, is not only taken by force. Then he returned to the immediate. Where was he? How would he get out? Who was he with? How could he have been such a moron? Why was he stuck in a stupid cell in a stupid place called Welken? Len remembered Piers's charge during the commissioning to "Wait, lion, wait." He didn't like the sound of it.

The woman he had come to save spoke in the same whispery voice she'd used by the pond. "Thank you, anyway." Her eyes alternated between glazed dullness and alert awareness. "I'm sorry to have screamed. I tried not to. But when the dagger pierced my skin, I could take the pain no longer."

Len grimaced at the bloody wound on her neck. He tore a piece off his T-shirt and crudely cleaned the mess. "Who are you?" he asked gently. "Why are you here at the Wasan Sagad?"

"The first question is easier to answer than the second." She coughed. "My name is Adal Gabrian. I came here some time ago, years I suppose, from the Prester Highlands. I wanted adventure and solitude so I made a pilgrimage to see if the stories about the Sagad were true. I stumbled into this tower nearly dead from the heat. Fatagar found me and fed me. How many years have rolled by since then? I don't know. I remember pain and work and disgust, but not days or weeks. The Wasteland fog holds everything in its grip. It smothers the land and gets into your mind."

"Strange, my time here has been blurry, too, for different reasons. But I see what you mean. The heat takes over everything, just like fog."

"No, I'm talking about the real fog. I feel the tingly coolness most of the time."

Len studied her sweat-stained rags and, in the stifling heat of the cell, wondered what she could be talking about. "So, who is this Fatagar?"

"Fatagar." Adal paused, coughing again. "Every time I hear his name, I gasp. What will he do to me this time? Fatagar is . . . he is what you see. His ugliness goes all the way through. I've heard he is a failed military leader, maybe court-martialed by Prester John. Some say he came here to show others he was fit to rule. 'How can I lead,' he likes to say, 'without followers?' If I obey him, I see less grief."

"Why don't you run away?"

"What would I eat? What would I drink? I get scared and shake all over if I don't stay close. Besides," Adal yawned, "I like the cool feeling. But leave me alone now. I'm sleepy." She hacked out a deep cough and turned her head.

"Don't go to sleep yet, OK? I want to hear more."

"Talk to the others. I can't stay awake."

Others, thought Len, what others? Then he heard a clacking of keys from outside. He hoped Prester John and Ellen had come after him.

At the bottom of the door, a partition slid open and a tray of mush appeared. In his disappointment Len slumped to the floor and put his head against a wall. Then, to his surprise, the "others"—prisoners so lifeless he hadn't noticed them in the shadows—became animated. Near skeletons all, they rushed to the tray, grabbed what they could, and gobbled it down. Smiles of satisfaction glistened in the dim light.

It's disgusting, thought Len. How could they grovel like this? I won't lower myself. And yet, I am hungry. I do need something to keep me going. What if I don't get water? What if I end up a slave for this beast, this Fatagar?

Suddenly, he felt himself wanting to cry. Self-pity welled up. Despair overflowed, but not tears.

In ludicrous contrast to his depression, the fettered prisoners began to sway, some with their arms around each other. Driven by internal melodies, the prisoners shuffled and danced as energetically as their frail bodies and dangling chains would allow. Occasionally two dancers locked arms and swung around, or a group formed a circle and stumbled together in tragic glee. Len would have laughed had he seen the movie version, but here he was in a humid cell watching the delirium descend, he thought, like a nightmarish fog.

CHAPTER TWENTY-FIVE
Waiting and Wanting

If pleasures are greatest in anticipation,
just remember that this is also true of trouble.

ELBERT HUBBARD, *THE NOTE BOOK*

 A fog. Adal's fog, the fog of the Wasan Sagad. Of course, Len thought, the prisoners' food is drugged.

He jumped into the middle of their trancelike dancing. "Hey! Adal! Everybody! Stop eating this. It's tearing you down, don't you see?"

Some responded to his plea with dreamy waves and smiling stupor. Most ignored him. The dancing gradually slowed and then stopped. Arms plopped around each other and legs intertwined. These tragic pilgrims collapsed on a dirt floor in the slave tower called Wasan Sagad.

Frustrated, Len stuffed his hands into his pockets and paced back and forth, reliving the decision that led him to this predicament. The rashness that haunted his eighteen years returned, a ghost that wouldn't slip back into the shadows. As a toddler he "had to" ride his Big Wheel in the street like the older kids. A neighbor nearly ran him over, not seeing him because his trike was so low to the ground. In fifth grade he "had to" try a water ski trick that he saw on TV. Fourteen stitches later, his chin came back together again. Junior high found him mouthing off to anyone who called him short or skinny or anything he could take offense at. "I *had to* defend myself," he would say. "I couldn't let them get away with that garbage." Looking back on his life, Len now saw that more often than not what he actually "had to" do was restrain himself. He'd always told himself that his feistiness was his strength, that he needed spunk to survive as a shrimpy kid, to drive himself, to prove himself. Isn't this feistiness what drove him right now to say, "I have to get out of here. I have to help Adal"?

At the same time, he thought, how can I stop saying I *have to?*

Conditions in the cell gave little hope that anything would soon change, "have to" or no. In groups of three or four, doped-up prisoners lay in various positions of uselessness, like overripe fruit rotting on the ground. Flies, rats, moldy straw, and their own waste added to Len's disgust. He walked over to a small window in the door.

Maybe Prester John was right about waiting, Len thought. Maybe I shouldn't have rushed in.

Then Len noticed on a shelf across the hall, a twinkle of light, a tiny pulsating beacon that made him think about how close he was to the tower's entryway. He could not see the outside; the glimmering light might be coming from it. But no, the light was too small, too focused. Maybe it was a bit of glass reflecting the light from outside. In the dark hallway, this tiny flickering reminded Len of the North Star. He felt curiously affirmed in this image, that he would somehow navigate his way through this trouble, that Fatagar would not be his end. You might say that he caught a glimpse. And then he looked closer.

Wait, thought Len. It *is* a glimpse!

Across the hall, housed in a tiny cell, tied with the tiniest of ropes, a glimpse gasped and flickered tenaciously.

"Hey, glimpse!" shouted Len, knowing full well that he wouldn't be able to hear the glimpse even if it answered. He hoped for the response of a buzz or some blinking, something to corroborate the memory he had of glimpses in the alder grove. Nothing happened. Hands in his pockets, Len shrugged off the unbuzzingness and searched in his own cell for some way of escape. He felt the small package Piers had entrusted to him in the room of the Tetragrammaton and turned it over in his hand.

I should find out what's inside, he thought. Careful there, Len, you don't want to drop it. OK, how am I supposed to open this in such low light? There's a knot that needs to be untied. Here goes. Uhn. What's the point of such a tough knot if I'm supposed to use this in an emergency? If I could just get my fingernails into the twine.

For all of Len's impatience, he was remarkably tolerant doing tedious work. Methodically for several minutes, he gently tugged and wiggled the twine until finally the knot gave way. He congratulated himself.

Who says I'm not patient? I'd like to see Angie try to undo that knot. Actually, I'd just like to see Angie.

In the dimness of the cell, Len unwrapped the gift and held up the contents, a stone smaller than a ping pong ball but rough and lumpy. He rolled it over and felt its sliminess. When he cut it with his fingernail, its gritty surface seemed to yield. He held it up to any light he could find. As best he could make out, the rock was black and slick.

Terrific, he said to himself sarcastically. My "extra special" gift is coal. Big stinkin' deal. Maybe coal is like money in Welken, but it's nothing to me.

Then aloud, he said, "I'm still stuck in this hole, and all I've got is some idiot Tetragram-a-thing to show for it."

"Then why not let me see the r-rock?" Fatagar's voice slimed through the crack in the door as it was being opened. Lanterns in hand, two of Fatagar's guards approached Len with their hands out. Fatagar smiled, his sharp teeth gleaming in the lantern's light. He sat on his fat, the round sides rising to the height of armrests. Sitting in his portable throne, Fatagar awaited Len's response as if he were a gentleman.

"No!" said Len, "You can't have it." Yeah, right, Len thought, good move. And how am I supposed to keep you from getting it?

"Why would you want an old r-rock?" Fatagar plucked a stick out of his pocket and crushed it between his teeth.

"Same reason *you* want it," said Len, lying. He had no idea what this reason could be. What he *did* know was that Fatagar must have some reason for wanting it, and some reason for not telling his soldiers to take it from him. He must be afraid of something, thought Len.

"Tell you what." Len pointed across the hall. "Trade me that glimpse for it."

"Ha, ha, ha." Fatagar's explosion of laughter rolled him back on the ball of his body, and then he bounced back up to his flabby throne. "You are a strange one. Ha, ha, ha." Fatagar snatched a fresh stick from his pocket, stabbed a cockroach, and ate it. His spikes glowed softly.

Len thought all was lost. Fatagar would approach, grab the lumpy coal, and then chew Len to bits with those sharp teeth. Maybe he would butt him against the wall with those knives on his head.

"You are stupid," said Fatagar. "I will gladly give you this worthless glimpse. *Tck, tck.* You, guard, bring the glimpse over here."

Len held the coal piece hard, worried that he'd made the wrong decision. "How do I know you'll make an even exchange?" The coal felt warm in his palm.

"Just explain your terms, runt."

Len thought, Where do *you* get off calling *me* a runt?

But he said, "OK, let me into the hall. You can put a guard on both sides of me, but far away. I'll take the glimpse with me. Then I'll roll the coal to you. Once you've got it, you move the guards and let me go, agreed?"

"I like these t-terms. You are shrewd but not unreasonable. I like that." Fatagar spat a cockroach leg onto the cell's floor.

"If you agree then go ahead, put the glimpse down, and back away." The guard did so, and Len picked up the tiny cage, loosened the clasp and held the glimpse in his palm. "Hello," he whispered. "Are you OK?"

"I think so. A little weak, but I'll make it."

Len walked out of the cell and whispered to the glimpse, "Give me a fingerhold of light."

By the time Len was a safe distance from Fatagar's guards, he had looped his left pinky into the light emanating from the glimpse's tail.

"C'mon, glimpse, I need more light."

The glimpse groaned and pushed.

"T-time to pass the stone to me," said Fatagar firmly, licking his lips.

"OK, Fatagar, here's my part of the bargain." Len held up the gift with one hand and kept pulling on the light with the other.

"Now!" shouted Fatagar.

Then Len rolled the rock down the hall to the grasping hands of the squatty beast.

251

Tongue drooping lustily out of his mouth, Fatagar scooped it up and laughed again. "You idiot boy! *Tck, tck.* You don't know what you've g-given up!"

"Neither do you!" Len pulled hard on the glimpse's light, stretching it, tugging at it, nearly tearing it. Though it only took seconds, to Len the widening seemed to take forever. With the glimpse's eyes rolling back in his head, Fatagar laughing ever more hideously, and the soldiers running down the hall, Len stepped into the circle of light. Squeezing in, he slid his hips, then his torso and then his shoulders through, until only his head remained. His last vision of Welken was of Fatagar cradling the coal in his right palm and pointing it at one of the slaves. Fire shot out of it, burning her arm. Wherever he pointed, the coal produced a shot of fire. Fatagar pointed at Len. The fire came.

And Fatagar laughed.

In the alder grove, the Master finished his meal, sucked his fingers clean, and slipped off the rock. He saw Morphane tossing his head pigeonlike, each snap registering some pain from within. The Master almost pitied him. Almost. Instead, the Master called the beast over and ordered him to sit. Scratching him under his chin, the Master asked him to open his mouth.

Then the Master grabbed a huge bottom canine tooth in each hand. As Morphane lowered his mouth gently, the Master leaned back, held on tight, and stared hard into Morphane's writhing countenance. He wanted to take inventory. Coursing like backwards waves, faces rose from the depths of Morphane's chamber. When the eyes looked out of Morphane's sockets, for a split second they seemed to see and remember. The Master recognized them all. First, a military guard came up. He had the look of failure, of remorse for his inability to protect those he'd pledged to preserve. Then a lady-in-waiting slid by Morphane's eyes as if she were remembering a physical struggle. These eyes called out for rescue.

Then came Sarah Wace, the one Piers read about in Chimney Cave. Her gentle beauty could be detected even as it stretched in agony beyond its delicate boundaries. The Master smiled. He saw her eyes blink as they passed Morphane's portals to the outside. She appeared too grieved to look, too wounded to suffer anew the source of her disembodiment. Faces and more faces rolled by, all tortured, all miserable. When Morphane bowed as if to say he had revealed all he possessed, the Master shook Morphane's jaw in disappointment. He yelled at him and cursed him for not showing Bors, for not having captured Bors. The Master could not understand it. They had both been there in Skane Lodge. In disgust, he released his grip and sat on the ground. Morphane did not bury his head in guilt. He just waited. And twitched his head.

The Master had not counted on this, nor on the mounting confusion in Morphane's mind. Each soul he possessed added to the weight on Morphane's already imbalanced scale. He was becoming less himself, whatever perverse predator that was, and more *them*selves. In one sense Morphane was no longer a thing but a group, no longer a he but a they. The Master spoke to this assembly, this body of conflicted wills churning in a schizophrenic tempest. He told them where to go and what to do.

Morphane got up and ran on his massive paws. He heaved himself forward, down from the alders, down through Durrow Wood, through the brush, on and off the trails, crossing creeks without bothering to find boulders for dry passage. The Master watched him go down as he had been instructed, down through the gently sloping foothills, down past Skane Lodge, down toward the Nez River.

Angie slowed her descent. She figured the girl playing below must be important, yet Vida kept yelling at her from the veranda of Long House. "Wait! Hold your horsification! Have a little good samaritan!"

"Don't worry!" Angie raced down and watched the stone steps so she wouldn't fall. "I'll wait for you at the bottom!" Then she saw the girl skipping away with her hands behind her back. Angie almost tripped. Then, with renewed resolve, she nearly flew over the remaining steps.

Just before she reached the bottom, Angie glanced over to see the child turn and run toward the houses nearby. Then she poked her head out toward Angie as if to say "Here I am, catch me if you can." Angie's legs ached from jolting down the steps. She looked back toward Vida and

Jacob. Awkwardly, they maneuvered their way down and down. They were only at the halfway mark.

Angie cupped her hands and yelled up to the Deediers, "I have to go! She's getting away!"

Jacob stopped on the midpoint landing. "So what? We shouldn't divorcify!"

But Angie pretended she heard nothing. Clenching her fists, she ran after the girl behind the shop. Just as she reached the back corner of the building and peered around, she saw the girl speeding around the other side.

And so the game continued. Don't catch me, please catch me. Serpentine, between buildings, through back lots, down alleys, Angie chased this remarkably fast little girl. And each step Angie took made it difficult for her to forsake all the previous steps. Angie felt that she must catch up, that some mystery would be resolved when she caught her.

Playfully, down the main street toward Mercy Bay, through the grain store and the fabric shop, the girl scampered away from Angie. At times she giggled, her luscious hair flowing behind her.

Perhaps she knows the way to the tile, thought Angie. She's so beautiful, she must be good. Piers must have sent her so I'd chase her to some significant place.

From behind a tree, the young girl poked her head out and waved at her.

Then Angie heard Jacob call after her, "Wait, Angie!" Jacob and Vida were running straight down the street. "What does this juvenile barbieness have to do with the tile?"

Angie felt torn. "I don't know yet. I feel I must follow this girl—and my intuition is always right." Angie ran ahead. When she couldn't find the girl, she pounded her thighs in frustration. For a moment, Angie's own exhaustion nearly made her give up the chase. For a second, she doubted her reasons for following a mysteriously tireless child down the main street of Primus Hook.

Then, "Over here." Standing on the edge of the beach, the girl waved. Giggling, she turned and ran toward the water.

Angie pushed through a narrow break in some blackberry bramble, wincing as the thorns scratched her legs. She forced her way past the last few canes and noticed lines of blood on her calves. Angie half ran, half tumbled over the uneven sand. She fell once and, looking up, could not see the child. She slammed her fist into the sand.

Then she saw the girl bob up in the surf. Angie got up, sand clinging to her new cuts.

The girl swam out to a wobbly rowboat and pulled herself into it.

By the time Angie reached the water, Jacob was running to the edge of the sand. "Angie! Come back. Don't navy it out, I'm telling you."

Angie felt the cold water around her ankles. "You don't have to come. Wait here."

Turning away from Vida and Jacob, Angie dove into the ocean. The salt stung her wounds. She used the pain to make herself swim harder. Her pulse racing from excitement and exhaustion both, she reached the side of the boat, threw her hand up, and clung to the edge. Resting momentarily, she looked back toward shore.

Jacob and Vida waddled into the water. Though awkward on shore, they swam gracefully and quickly, like sea turtles.

Vida raised her head. "Angie, don't be gamblifying. You don't know the odds."

Jacob shouted, "Don't get in the boat. Listen for the wisdom, Piers said!"

But Angie listened to the boat rocking in the water. To end the suspense, she knew she must get into the boat and talk with the girl.

A playful voice giggled. "Let me help. I can pull you in."

Almost faint, Angie accepted this invitation, and offered her one hand. The lovely child grabbed it with both of her own, clamping tightly around Angie's wrist. The girl's hand felt wonderfully reassuring. As the girl pulled and said, "Up we go," Angie's wet hair in front of her face kept her from seeing the girl well. Then Angie flopped over the side and rolled into the boat. The girl tumbled back into the bow. Angie, on all fours, faced away from the girl, toward the shore.

Just then Jacob and Vida shouted again at Angie. Swimming hard, they were only fifteen feet away.

The little girl whispered from behind her. "Use the vial."

Too tired to think about how this innocent child knew the secrets of the Tetragrammaton, Angie obeyed. She reached into her pocket and pulled out the tiny bottle. In a daze, Angie yanked off the top and poured one drop onto the sea. She corked the vial and returned it to her pocket. She then balanced on her knees in the bouncing vessel. As if she were kneading bread, Angie pushed and pulled the air in front of her. Corresponding to the motions, a swell grew between the boat and the Deedy dwellers. Then Angie raised her hands and pushed, causing the wave to crest and carry Jacob and Vida safely back to shore.

Angie sat on the seat by the oars, and the girl sat on the smaller seat in the bow. "Let me look at you," Angie said.

The face she'd chased across the town and into the water smiled at her. Angie examined the luminous blue eyes, the high cheekbones, the milky, freckled skin that must have caused Primus Hook villagers to talk about how many heads this girl would one day turn.

Her own eyes wide in amazement, Angie realized that she was right. She did know this face that produced awe and desire and envy. She knew it because she'd seen it thousands of times, in the mirror. The little girl was Angie at eight years old.

"What's going on here?" said Angie, out of breath once more. "Why do you look like me?"

Little Angie ignored the question and from her pockets produced two bracelets. "I have presents for you. See? I'll put them on you." She leaned forward.

Too stunned to resist, Angie allowed her "younger" self to slip the bracelets over her hands. She spun the bracelets, then rested Angie's hands on the oars. Instantly, the bracelets moved and grew and fixed themselves to the oarlocks, trapping Angie there.

Angie could not believe what was happening. "What are you doing? What is the meaning of this?"

"I guess," said little Angie, "you could say that you caught your self and now your self has caught you. At least, that's what I was told to say."

In shock, Angie saw her little twin begin to shake and wobble, remaking herself out of Angie's childhood shape and into one of Morphane's conquered souls, into the chameleon-gel that had been infused with images after being separated from Morphane, into the part of Malleal that the Master had sent to the south to capture Angie.

"And now, Angie," it said, "we need to go back to the Master." The thing took the vial of liquid out of Angie's pocket, poured a drop into the sea, and caressed the air until a single wave bore the boat aloft and carried both guard and prisoner out of Mercy Bay and to the east.

But the tile, thought Angie, and Justice Island and Jacob and Vida. What have I done?

The boat cruised on the wave, spraying water in Angie's face. When she closed her eyes, she remembered the rain of her first moments in Welken, in Circle Stand. And in this shower that blended with her tears, she wondered how she could possibly live up to her calling: "In the south, grace."

CHAPTER TWENTY-SIX
SINGING THE LAST VERSE

Upon such sacrifices, my Cordelia,
The gods themselves throw incense.

WILLIAM SHAKESPEARE, *KING LEAR*

For Lizbeth, Mook, and Alabaster, sliding down a water-fall inside a mountain was no water park. The rocky bottom, the dark, and the unknown end of the rapids left Lizbeth flailing around for something to grab. She tried to find some hope to grab, as well.

Then she screamed. Her first scream echoed into a large cavern; the second failed to overcome the din of crashing water. Soon, the three slid down a steep shaft of tumbling river. Lizbeth cried out for help, but her mouth filled with water. Falling feet first down the water-fall, she pumped her legs and arms as if running in place. She really thought she would die. Utterly helpless, she groped for something to cling to. She imagined herself with her neck broken, floating head down in a pitch-black hole in a land far from Mom and Dad and her own safe bed.

Then she splashed into a pool. She bobbed up, flailed about for a moment, then caught her breath and floated, finally calming down. She yelled for Mook and found that he was close enough to grab her hand. Then the speed of the water picked up rapidly until holding on became impossible. First Mook, then Alabaster, then Lizbeth swirled into a whirlpool, around and around, funneling them steeply down.

Shot blindly into a tube, Lizbeth screamed again. The tube wound through horseshoe turns and straightaways. A banked turn nearly flipped her upside down. Without knowing if the next rushing dip would take them left or right, she worried about whiplash and low stones that might strike her.

Then Lizbeth remembered that she had been taught how to go down a water slide. You were to lie down and fold your arms against your chest. Though this position made her feel vulnerable, she clasped her arms and let go of the need to protect herself.

Through the bowels of the Great Alpine Reef, they spun, slipping along the smooth, waterworn sides. In her submissive state, Lizbeth relaxed and began to dream, first of swirled ice cream and then of curly-Q straws and roller coasters and rafting in the rapids. Then she saw herself floating in the clouds blissfully. Drifting up beside her came her father, Martin. He held out his hand. She took it, and they soared through the puffiness together. Lizbeth saw him smiling at her as if to say, "You're going to be OK." Lizbeth chuckled in her dream because she imagined he also said, "Bobsleds in the sky. Hurry, while supplies last." He let go and waved good-bye.

Then on the other side of Lizbeth's dream, her mother, Darlene, slid up feet-first, a straw in her mouth, chaise-lounging through the air. One squeeze from her hand and she, too, was off, fading into the clouds, petting Sniffles, who was curled up on her stomach.

From overhead Piers himself drifted over. With typical solidity and compassion, he said, "So." Then he started to slide away.

"Don't go," called out Lizbeth.

"Don't worry," Piers said calmly. "All's well that the cooks don't spoil."

In the tube shifting right and left, Lizbeth shook herself awake. Dreams, she thought, are so bizarre.

Then Lizbeth heard Mook scream up ahead. Her own scream followed as she shot out of the tube and into the air. While fumbling in the nothingness and hollering for help, she *saw*. She wasn't sure what she saw, but light came from the direction she was flying toward. Before she could focus, she belly flopped loud and hard into the water below.

When she surfaced, she laughed. Relief rushed through her in a wash of tingling joy. Treading water, she checked her limbs gratefully. Then she called out, "Mook! Alabaster!"

Mook shook his head, his foxtails flying. "We're here! We survived." They embraced.

"If only I had known"—Lizbeth panted heavily—"I would have enjoyed the ride." Funny, she thought, that's true for my whole life.

After swimming to a shallower part, Lizbeth stood with the others to collect herself. She blew her nose, pushed water down her sleeves, and announced that she was fine. Mook said the same, and Alabaster nodded.

Mook drained the water out of his empty quiver. "It looks like the river has led us out. All we have to do is find a way to that daylight."

"Yahoo!" Lizbeth threw water into the air and then splashed Mook.

"Yes," said Mook, "this is a good thing."

Alabaster Singing smiled and pushed them toward the closest shore of the pool, on the left side of the opening as they faced the light.

From there Lizbeth could see that getting out would not be simple. In front of them loomed one last gauntlet, the final thrill on this ride of rides. The mouth of the cave formed a perfect proscenium arch. From the dark theater where the three caught their breath, they watched the action on the stage outside. Brilliant vine maple leaves hung over the opening, a backdrop for the jays and woodpeckers that fought over their food. A black-tailed squirrel poked its head toward them and then scurried down a branch and out of sight.

Mook looked troubled. "I don't like what I see. The water in the pool fills up the opening as it flows out. The river crests over the whole exit. How are we to know what awaits below or how strong the river moves?"

Lizbeth twisted the bottom of her shirt to get water out. "We can't know, but how is this any different from anything else we've done? Shouldn't we just get into the river and trust we'll survive?"

"I suppose we could. But this decision is different. Before, we had no choice. Now we need to examine our choices. We are no less trusting for reasoning our way to a safer path." He pulled at his braids, squeezing water out of them.

Alabaster Singing had not been reclining like the others. Walking around the limited shore to examine every vantage point, she scrambled atop the highest rock in the cave, back toward the waterfall that shot them into the pool. She pointed across the water to the right side of the arch.

Mook climbed up next to Alabaster to see for himself. "Yes, Alabaster, I see it too. Lizbeth, there's a spot where the lip is exposed, a place a little higher where we might be able to get out. I can even see small waves hit the rocks."

Mook scrambled back down. As he reached Lizbeth, she pointed back up to the rock. Mook turned just in time to see Alabaster, the steady and unspontaneous one, dive off the rock and plunge into the cold pool of water. Lizbeth, worried about the depth of the pool, leaned over the water. Then Alabaster surfaced. She grinned back at them as if to say, "Chicken!" and swam toward the dry spot.

Taking up the challenge, Mook and Lizbeth stepped into the water. But while they were still wading in, Lizbeth noticed Alabaster splashing close to the opposite shore. Lizbeth looked at Mook quizzically and kept wading in.

Suddenly Alabaster went under.

"What's she doing?" wondered Lizbeth aloud.

"I don't know." Mook moved into deeper water. "I'm not used to seeing her like this."

"What *is* she doing?" asked Lizbeth again, this time more anxiously. "She's been down too long. I don't like it." Lizbeth got ready to launch into the water.

Mook gave Lizbeth his bow and quiver. "You wait here," he said as he surged into the water.

Then Alabaster surfaced. Gasping for air, she slapped at the water, at something, at anything, at everything. Her mouth in a silent scream, she struggled with an enemy beneath her.

And then Lizbeth saw them. Basilisks. The eely demons climbed over each other to get at Alabaster. Hundreds of them. The lapping waves into which Alabaster swam teemed with them, their blackness shining in the light as they flipped up out of the water, their teeth searching for something to pierce. One wrapped around Alabaster's right forearm like an Egyptian bracelet. With both hands, Alabaster tore off one that slithered around her knee.

"Mook, stop!" cried Lizbeth. "Don't go!"

He did not hear her. In a panic, Lizbeth tried to think of what to do. Alabaster tossed another serpent from her and then another, but still they came and still she tore them off. She tried to climb out of the water. Then Lizbeth saw her backside, nearly covered with dozens of teeth sunk into Alabaster's blameless skin. Blood flowed over the blackness of the basilisks.

Unaware of the danger, Mook sped toward the rocky exit. Lizbeth had to do something. Blood spilled down Alabaster's arms, from her side, and now, from her neck. Her legs must have been covered. And soon Mook would be too.

Lizbeth couldn't think of what to do. What good was oxen strength in a river of giant leeches? Through her tears she struck her chest, calling out, "No, this can't be happening!" She stabbed one hand into the other, hoping the pain might help. She slapped her sides and pounded her fists against her thighs.

And then she felt it. The box. The gift. The power of the Tetragrammaton entrusted to her. Shaking, she pulled it out of her pocket and flipped open the lid. Surely a genie would appear—but no. Inside was dirt, ordinary dirt.

Yet in that split second she knew it couldn't be plain soil, not if Piers had entrusted it to her. She took some out, snapped the box shut, and threw the dirt on the shore. She didn't know what else to do.

Then she said, "Do something . . . in Welken, of Welken, go!"

In a flash, the dirt recombined and built itself up. It formed and shaped and expanded and constructed itself into the image in Lizbeth's mind. A bridge emerged, arching over the water from the shore to the dry spot above Alabaster. Lizbeth ran over the bridge.

Now she knew what to do with her strength. Leaning over the side, she easily pulled Mook to safety, one basilisk attached to his foot. Frantically she dashed to Alabaster, ripped her out of the churning beasts and set her down on the bridge. Only stripes of Alabaster could be seen underneath the clinging basilisks. Without care for Alabaster's skin, only for her life, Lizbeth and Mook tore at these enemies. They ripped them from her throat and back, from her arms and side. They pulled more delicately at the two sunk into her cheeks and forehead. Crying, Lizbeth yanked. Eyes aflame with rage, Mook flung the terrible leeches back to the pool.

And the basilisks bit them too. Their needle-sharp teeth stabbed whatever flesh was available—fingers, palms, wrists. Lizbeth and Mook shook them off as best they could, wincing in pain. But they didn't stop. They couldn't stop. They yanked until their hands were raw.

Then with Alabaster's legs still partly covered, Lizbeth motioned for Mook to stop. She had noticed that Alabaster wasn't breathing. While Alabaster's lifeblood trickled out from punctures all over her body, Lizbeth cupped the Welkener's head in her hands and breathed into her mouth. For several minutes she pushed her breath into Alabaster's lungs, praying for life each time, hoping that the breath would not escape through the holes also. Again and again she breathed and waited and breathed and waited. Mook kneeled helplessly beside her. Then Lizbeth shook Alabaster. "C'mon," she whispered. "C'mon!" she yelled. Then Mook's hand, hard and sure and compassionate, gripped Lizbeth's arm until she stopped.

Lizbeth turned to look at Mook. His face, as plain as ever, streamed with unrestrained tears. Alabaster was dead.

Mook and Lizbeth embraced, their shoulders heaving in sorrow from the pain. Shaking, Mook and Lizbeth created a sanctuary for their grief. They held tight to Alabaster's memory, her fading warmth, her sacrificial spirit, her truth.

And when they let go, they knew they were releasing Alabaster Singing, too, saying good-bye to her silence and the security of her presence. Alabaster had sung her last song.

Silently, they finished the task of removing the remaining basilisks. As if Alabaster could feel the pain more than before, they pulled the teeth out tenderly, killed the demons, and flung them back into the pool. With only one remaining around Alabaster's ankle, Lizbeth rose and walked off the bridge to the edge of the pool. She closed her eyes and clenched her fists against her sides. Harshly, punishingly, she raked her fingers through her streaming black hair. Her pulse heightened. As she walked into the water, she boiled inside like the churning beasts themselves. Then she erupted in molten rage, grabbing basilisks, tearing them apart, and reaching in for more. Ignoring the risk, she stomped and ripped the leeches, enjoying every death, determined to kill them all, though of course she could not. Holding one above her head, she stretched it till it snapped, its blood splattering her face.

A voice came from behind her. "Lizbeth, no." Mook firmly held her shoulders. "Even now, in our sadness, Piers's words carry us to safety: 'Wield power well. Do not seek revenge.'"

Of all the words that could be spoken to her, these were the ones Lizbeth least wanted to hear. Not when she deserved her anger. Not when her hate could be directed at such a perfect object of evil. "Why?" She turned her bloody face to him. "Why should I stop? Can't I fight the snakes that killed her? Can't I show my friend what I should have done sooner? Can't I show Alabaster that I love her?"

After two labored sighs, Lizbeth dropped her hands. She walked out of the water and collapsed again in Mook's arms. One last basilisk pierced her calf. She let the pain sink in. It was the least she could do for Alabaster.

When calm again, Lizbeth grabbed Alabaster's feet, and Mook took her arms. Carefully, they climbed down the rocks and out to the grassy area below the mouth of the cave. Mook rummaged around for branches and reedy twine out of which he fashioned a carrier he could drag.

Lizbeth finally realized the implications of his actions. "But, Mook, why not make a regular stretcher so that I could help bear the weight?"

"You have your own weight to bear, Lizbeth. I must return Alabaster to her family so they can prepare her for the Rising Ceremony. You must fulfill your task. You must find the tile. You must go alone to the place below Alta Nez Falls, to the place you saw in your vision."

"You can't be serious, Mook. I'm supposed to go alone? Me?"

"Yes, Lizbeth. And you should know that there will be no discussion here. As a Nezzer, I have no choice but to follow our ways. As one who was called to Welken, you have no choice but to stay true of voice. We can both honor Alabaster's death in this way. I will return to you as soon as I can. Now listen, I know this area well. Stay on the path that follows the river down. From there you will know what to do. Lizbeth, you are here because of who you are and what can be done through you. Go to it. In Welken."

Silence.

"Lizbeth, in Welken."

"Yes, Mook. You are right. Of Welken. But I want you to take the box. You can use it to make your path smooth. Please, Mook. I'll feel better about you carrying Alabaster if you take the gift."

Mook nodded. Holding the gift in his hand, he gave Lizbeth a hug.

In minutes, their paths diverged. Lizbeth found a pontoon bridge that allowed her to cross to the east side of the river, so she could head south. Mook dragged Alabaster on the carrier on the west side of the river.

You have your own weight to bear, Mook had told her. She knew that he meant the weight of the mission, the weight of finding her portion of the defiled Tetragrammaton. Now with every step taking her farther from Mook, the weight of attempting this task by herself pushed on her shoulders like a yoke. Around her neck the yoke pressed, until in her trek toward the falls, she plodded oxenlike, tramping in a furrow. She felt the weight of her own weight.

Alone once more, she thought. Alone is the story of my life. Every time things seem to be working out, they're crushed, just like this leaf below me, just like everything gets crushed by every two-ton step I take. Piers said to listen to the mercy. What mercy? Alabaster is dead. I don't want to listen. I keep hearing her screaming silence.

Nose toward the furrow, Lizbeth had not noticed how far she had walked nor how close she now was to the falls. When she finally felt the mist and heard the roar, a power beyond self-pity claimed her attention.

She listened to the sound of the waterfall. It pushed her to consider issues outside of herself: how to get to the base of the falls, how to find the tile, and what danger might await her. She liked these practical questions.

Walking along the banks of the Nez River, Lizbeth thought of the Lewis behind her house, the smooth flowing water that rippled gently over rocks and posed a threat only to those ignorant of the frigid spring thaw. But here, as the water reached the falls, the innocence of the Nez broke over the edge of a hundred-foot cliff.

In some situations, thought Lizbeth, going to the edge means going over the edge. One has to pay attention.

She stood for a while to appreciate the surging water and the dancing mist. She watched the sparrows circling with mud in their beaks. As if her spirits weren't agitated enough, the crushing rhythm of the water accelerated the thumping of her heart. Each step down took her closer to some battle, no doubt, closer to a new crisis. She imagined the tile resting on a platform with ancient booby traps blocking her path. Would the poison arrows get her? Or quicksand? Would she be brave enough, agile enough to get the tile? With the water pounding on her pounding heart, Lizbeth stopped near the base of Alta Nez Falls to catch her breath, to keep from hyperventilating.

Then she saw the boy.

Back turned to her, the boy lay motionless, the river lapping gently up to his waist.

Now what? thought Lizbeth. It looks like I'm too late. Maybe if Alabaster hadn't been attacked or if I had thought to make the bridge sooner, I, we, could have made it here in time. Now what am I to do with a boy ravaged by Morphane?

With as much speed as the slippery, mossy rocks allowed, Lizbeth made her way to the level shore.

But maybe he survived, she thought. Maybe I can help him.

Then Lizbeth saw the boy stir. He pulled himself up, then flopped back down on the loamy shore and moaned.

Lizbeth bolted toward him. Sloshing into the water, she rushed to his side. She knelt. Frightened, she turned him over to see what harm had come to him. Her vision seemed sharper, larger. She noticed every detail, the Nezzer hair with foxtail tips, the scar on his right shoulder, his long eyelashes, and his warm, limp body.

Good, she thought, the body's not grown cold. And he's breathing.

She checked for wounds or broken bones. Dragging him a few feet out of the water, she saw some moss stuck to him. She knelt again by him in the gravelly sand. His unconscious face scared her. Trembling, she touched his cheeks, then, though she worried she transgressed some unspoken boundary, she pulled up his eyelids. The irises and pupils looked dull, drained of life, drained of any vibrancy or color. She stared into the gray orbs, and she knew what had happened.

But she didn't have time to move. Morphane's roar from ten feet away electrified her. Morphane! Nothing could have made her feel weaker, more helpless, more alone. And she felt stupid for having walked right into his trap, a trap she'd been warned about.

Morphane stalked Lizbeth and growled. Even worse, the captive chorus of screams could be heard in his own menacing snarl. His claws raked the ground. He had planted and watered, and he came for the harvest now. He stretched out a paw toward Lizbeth and took a step. He was in the hunt.

Quickly, Lizbeth looked up at him and back down. She knew she shouldn't look—but how could she not look? In that very instant she remembered the stories of Sutton and Zennor, how only blind Bebba survived, how looking at Morphane was the thing *not* to do, the thing that would be your last decision. She tried to trust this knowledge. She hadn't thought it would be so hard to avoid looking at what disgusted her.

Yet Morphane demanded attention. Death paw upon wounding claw, Morphane came closer, and he called to Lizbeth. How could she not look? His prisoners were asking for help, weren't they? And how could she avoid his lunging bite if she didn't look?

Eerily attractive, his voice caught and turned her heart. He came within five feet, then he howled. She kept her head down—but, she thought, what did it matter? Absorb me or devour me, what is the difference? He slammed his paw against the ground as if it were a fist, a monstrous gavel at the Day of Judgment. Lizbeth closed her eyes and turned away. He roared louder than before, louder than the falls. His roar said *I am here, and you must give yourself to me.*

Don't look, she told herself. Don't add to his army. Hold, hold, hold firm.

Then the boy moved. He sat up and grabbed both of Lizbeth's arms. His dull eyes widened. He squeezed her hard. Sickened, Lizbeth broke out of his grasp, slipped, and accidentally looked full into Morphane's face. She felt tricked, yet now she had looked. Tired, startled, defeated, Lizbeth stared. She saw the horrible roiling faces. She felt her own face, her very self, her soul, tug inside her. She felt herself severing, her deepest attachments unraveling. A rope inside her stretched and frayed and tore.

No, she wailed to herself. This can't happen to me. I'm strong. I'm strong as an ox. I'll hold back. I know what happened to the others. I can use that for strength. I can believe what I was told to do and not do.

In a furious battle of wills, Lizbeth and Morphane pulled against each other. Like an arm wrestle one knows one is losing, Lizbeth strained against her enemy. She resisted, but she knew she could not overpower him. Inch by inch, she faltered. Inevitably, she thought, her face would course through Morphane's torturous muzzle. She held and did not hold. Still she fought. She dug in the heels of her will and yanked in this soul-stretching tug-of-war.

Then she remembered. In Ganderst Hall, in the moments before they left for separate journeys, Piers had told them, "If you do meet Morphane, think deeply on me."

Turning from direct resistance of Morphane, Lizbeth concentrated on Piers. She imagined his face, his confidence, his fearless countenance. Yet she realized immediately that she could not do this and maintain the battle with Morphane's will. To hold one meant letting go of the other. To turn toward Piers meant turning away from resisting Morphane's suction. She decided. Against all common sense, she let go. And then her body relaxed. Her eyes refocused. She let herself look in Morphane's direction—but she tried to see only Piers. She envisioned his face on the face of Morphane.

She looked so hard for Piers that she no longer saw Morphane. She saw a garden somewhere far away, and a sign that said "Endel Inn." She felt near to Piers, that he must be close by. But then, frightened and unknowing, Lizbeth felt herself somehow substituted for Piers, *in* him, *in* his body, *in* his mind. From inside Piers, she could tell that he had fallen to his knees and given himself over to her agony. He accepted her fear and, concentrating his whole self, tried to look through it.

At the same time, she could still dimly see Morphane's face. But Piers was there, too. He seemed to know that she needed him to switch, to be part of her also.

In that instant, space meant nothing. Though miles away from Lizbeth, Piers's image leaped onto Morphane's face, rising from nostrils to ears and above. Instead of Lizbeth's face, Piers's image rode the contours of Morphane's head. And Piers, at the Endel Inn, writhed on the ground. Lizbeth saw both places of suffering. She could feel Piers's body jerk around and tear at itself. Piers held his switching face in his hands. And Lizbeth knew that though his image leaped, he could not be enslaved into Morphane's prison. His body wasn't there. He would recover. He understood the surrogate life.

Into this bewildering moment, Piers screamed, and then Lizbeth saw something inside, something else swirling in the contrariness of space and time. She didn't know who or what it was, but it spoke. She felt a presence near her, in her ear, from inside Piers. It wasn't Piers's voice, yet the voice said, "Run!"

Lizbeth's eyes flashed open. All at once she knew what had occurred. Morphane, preoccupied with Piers's image but unable to keep his soul within, no longer noticed Lizbeth. She tried to stand, but the boy held her legs firmly. Without trouble, Lizbeth slapped his hands away and obeyed the voice.

She ran.

CHAPTER TWENTY-SEVEN

How Many Eyes Does It Take to See?

The deeper problems . . . come less from the unscrupulousness of
our "deceivers" than from our pleasure in being deceived.

Daniel Boorstin, *The Image*

 Gliding down from Wroxeter Bluff as Sutton and Zennor ran below him, Bennu smiled broadly. Over the rocky, treeless promontory he flew. Soaring, flying, sailing, he sensed he was not merely *using* the wind; he felt he had *caught* the wind and held it like a baton. Effortlessly he conducted music through the sky, pulling up, swooping down, turning. In these glorious aerial minutes, he praised the copper-colored lichen on the boulders and the gently flowing spring that trickled down the north side of the bluff. Sutton and Zennor seemed to him the noblest friends anyone could know, their beards flowing back as they ran.

If only Angie could see me now, he thought.

Wanting to stretch out his fingers in front of him like a superhero, Bennu returned the blobby mass, the Tetragrammaton's offering, to his pocket. Instantly, he plummeted. The air punished him as he fell helplessly toward the rocky hillside. In a ball, with his back to the ground, Bennu pushed and fumbled against the pressure until he found his pocket. Finally, he straightened out enough to dig into it. As he gripped the gift tightly, the substance oozed between his fingers. Then he pulled up as though weightless. Chest forward, arms out, Bennu regained control and, trembling, landed at the base of the bluff as gracefully as his weak knees permitted.

He sat down, hung his head between his knees, and tried to catch his breath. He watched a line of ants bump against his feet. Looking up, he saw Sutton and Zennor near him, about fifteen feet up from the base of the cliff. They threw their staffs to the ground below and spidered backwards down the last steep rock face. Because they were large men, their agility impressed Bennu. Then the two Durrow woodsmen retrieved their staffs and ran to Bennu's side.

"Yours was a right amazin' acrobatic feat," said Zennor, panting.

Sutton leaned on his staff. "Aye. You looked like a great bird I once heard about, called Lord of the Eagles in one of Goffer's tales. He was master of the sky and saved the village from a dragon."

Bennu kept his eyes fixed on the ants. "Glad you liked the show. As Vida would say, I feel all wobblerated. It was fun while it lasted, but now I have a headache."

"Ah, the bird is weary from his flight," said Sutton. "We can wait."

Bennu tried to sound brave. "I'm fine. Let's go. Walking will help settle me down."

"Good work, lad." Zennor slapped Bennu's shoulder with his huge Durrow hand. "You're a right solid warrior."

"I dunno about that." Bennu stumbled forward from Zennor's pat on the back. "But I can keep going for now. Lead on, you two. Let's get to Kells Village. A tile is waiting for us somewhere."

Soon the three strode down the gently sloped hill and into a forest that lay between them and the town. The grasses on the hill flopped about in the breeze, flashing shades of emerald and chartreuse so vibrant that only stands of yellow mountain daises could steal away Bennu's eyes. Along the path, Sutton and Zennor told stories about Kells, how the inhabitants enjoyed the simplicity of hard work, good food, and great affection for each other. Sutton said that little had changed over the centuries. Zennor added that little needed to. Those in the Durrow knew their peace rested on the practice of honoring all in their community.

Not long after they entered the forest, they passed cottages tucked cleverly into the landscape. In one dwelling, four aspens stood at the corners of the house, and key branches had been trained to connect along the sides. Their leaves flickered like green silver dollars. No one appeared to be at any of the homes.

Sutton stopped and offered some pine nuts to Bennu. "It's right disappointing you won't meet the Craigs. They have a rare generosity. No traveler fails to rejoice in their presence. Just when you're ready to thank them for their mercies, they tell you of all you've given them."

"And the Shannons aren't here either," said Zennor later, pointing with his staff to a cottage with a thatched roof, round windows, and a ladder climbing high into a crow's nest lookout in an adjoining fir. "I hope we see them in town. They have a way of saying with their eyes that they know you deep and true and that you're loved as fiercely as Kells village defends itself from enemies. Not that we have many enemies."

Bennu thought, no wonder my Ganderst Hall door says, "In the east, peace."

Toward the edge of the wood, just after they came to a clearing from which they could see Kells Village, an elderly woman sat on a stump. Zennor and Sutton exchanged troubled glances that, in turn, troubled Bennu.

"What's the matter?" asked Bennu.

"That woman is Bebba the blind." Sutton's face fell with sorrow. "Mook spoke of her back at Chimney Cave. She told about the wounds of Morphane and the mystery of her own survival. Just saying this much returns a right sorrowful ache in my heart. I'd be glad never to see or think about those husks again."

Zennor stroked his beard. "For all Bebba's blunt words, she means to serve. Some don't like her 'cause she seems to come round more when grief gathers at the door. We'd best heed what she says." He put his staff on the ground in front of him and pulled against it, like he was punting on a river.

Before either man from the Durrow could announce their arrival, Bebba said, "Sutton Hoo, is it?" Her pale globes shone in the light. "And Zennor Pict? Ah, two of Durrow's best, that I know. And who's the stranger silent by your side?"

Bennu wondered how she knew he was there, for indeed he had been silent. He turned to face her, and the sun caused him to squint.

Zennor gestured more broadly than normal, as if this would help

Bebba see. "His name is Bennu. He's a visitor not just to Durrow Wood but to all of Welken."

"I see," said Bebba, though she didn't. "I'll tell you this. Bennu's heart races like a rabbit chased by a fox, but it's not from meeting Bebba the blind." With eyelids stretched open, Bebba made a ghoulish face. "It's not from journeying he knows not where. He fears a calamity to come—and I know what it is.

"Morphane howls wherever he is, and the sounds reach deep into the land. Bebba has heard them. Even now, all Durrow families are in Kells. Those who've lost kin to Morphane want to know why. Why has Morphane come to the wood? Why did he rob the joy from this mother or that father and not another?" She bowed her head for a moment and then raised it quickly. "Morphane! The evil one! I spit on him!" And she did, the splat on the ground nearly hitting Bennu's foot. "Who has let him in? Yes, this is the question the Villagers ask. And they have found someone to blame. Dinas Tintagel and her sons, Illtyd and Kew, speak in the streets to hungry ears. They know, they say. They say it is the Whithorns, Elmet and Marthen, the father and mother of Drumonia the Beautiful."

"But why?" Sutton pleaded with his huge hands. "What has Drumonia done?"

"Drumonia upset the peace, they say. Drumonia drives the men mad and the women into envy, they say." Bebba stood, as if in her full height she bore some resemblance to Drumonia. "She knows all the arts of the forest. She is good and kind, and her neighbors could bear all this if she were not more lovely than all who've ever walked the Durrow." She followed a scar on her neck with a finger. "Bebba cannot see Drumonia, so Bebba cannot tell. I know not of the kind of beauty that feeds the eye."

Bennu thought, Ain't that the truth.

Bebba cocked her head in his direction. "But I did hear a raging pestilence of jealousy." She leaned forward on her walking stick. "Bebba hears and Bebba knows. Perhaps it matters not, but Drumonia hasn't let anyone court her, including Kew Tintagel, the chosen son of those who raise the feud." Bebba thrust her stick over her head and shouted, "May Morphane die from a thousand arrows. He is a destroyer!"

Without returning a word, Sutton, Zennor, and Bennu marched off toward the town. Bebba had the last word. "I know how you leave," she said just before they were out of earshot. "Bebba knows the walk that says 'we come to rescue.' But Bebba hopes it will not come to this. You are only three, and more suffering will come before you have set the crooked things straight."

Ignoring the shallow streams that crossed their paths now and again, the three ran out of the trees and to the edge of the village. From a distance, they heard a commotion and sprinted toward the noise. Bennu lagged behind a little, and Sutton waved at him to catch up.

As they approached the crowd, Zennor told Bennu that it was Illtyd, the son of Dinas Tintagel, the brother of Kew, who was speaking the loudest. Illtyd said, "Good neighbors of Kells, the shadow of Morphane spreads over the wood and into our homes. After centuries of peace, suffering and death have come." He stood on a wooden platform in the middle of the town square. "I have said it before, and I will say it again. Drumonia is the cause. She has stirred the passions of many and brought pain to our village. Some who went searching for a way to win her heart did not return. Who brought Morphane upon us? I say Drumonia!"

"My heart grieves to accuse anyone from Durrow Wood," said a middle-aged woman. "But my heart suffers more for the emptiness in our cottage." She stepped onto a tree stump. "All death has a cause," she continued. "Morphane killed our only son, Patrick. And someone invited him in. Someone set son against son. I charge Elmet Whithorn's daughter, Drumonia!"

"Wait!" said Marthen Whithorn, Drumonia's mother. "I, too, hate the evil of Morphane. But Drumonia has done nothing wrong." Some in the crowd tried to shout her down, but Durrow courtesy prevailed. "Some say she is more beautiful than any in Kells's history. Even if that is so, her only crime is that she has not yielded her hand to a suitor—yet." This last word appeared to awaken a new view in the crowd. Marthen gathered her apron in her hands and pleaded with it. "Must these disappointments point to a flaw in Drumonia? I offer you a different cause, one with better evidence." She waited for silence then took a step into the crowd. With each line she spoke, she turned to a different mother or father. "Who has seen Morphane and lived? Who came so close to Morphane as to touch him . . . to hear the dying cries of our own villagers? Only one person. Only one. Bebba the blind."

"But she is an old woman!" shouted one in the crowd.

"No matter. She opened the door. You can be old and do that!"

"But she always curses Morphane!" yelled another.

"What better veil to hide her wickedness?" said Marthen.

Sutton widened his stance. "I cannot believe what I hear: spite and hate in Kells Village, with all love for truth cast aside."

Dinas Tintagel waved for and got the floor to speak. "Bebba frightened Illtyd and Kew when they were younger. She seemed right pleased with herself for giving them nightmares."

Marthen stepped up next to Dinas. "You see, there is a pattern of dark choices. We must find Bebba!"

The crowd pounded their feet and staffs on the ground and called out in one loud voice of agreement.

Sutton screamed over the din. "Stop! Please, good friends, we just came from Bebba the blind, and she is right troubled about—"

Many in the crowd raised lances and staffs. They shouted Sutton down.

Marthen motioned for the right to speak. "I saw Sutton and Zennor come from the path leading to the bluff. Bebba must be there!"

When the tide of villagers surged forward, Sutton and Zennor stumbled backwards. They held up their hands as if they were wizards about to send a wave back to the sea. But the wave swept easily around them. In seconds, Sutton and Zennor stood alone, except for Bennu.

"We have to go protect Bebba," said Sutton.

Bennu put his hands on his hips. "Yes, of course, we should go."

"No," said Sutton, already walking back up the path. "You aren't trained for this kind of battle."

"Sutton is right, my friend," said Zennor. "Besides—you must find the tile. Go seek it. We will catch up to you."

Without waiting for an answer, Zennor and Sutton turned away from Bennu. In full stride, their staffs pounding the trail like pile drivers, the Durrow pair ran to save Bebba from the wrath of her good neighbors.

In the center of Kells, Bennu stood alone. He looked up the path at the rising dust and back to the suddenly quiet square. The snapdragons

275

surrounding the platform had been trampled.

Some hero, he thought. Some messiah. Actually, some misfit.

Kells had become an instant ghost town—and Bennu the apparition who haunted the streets. He walked down the main thoroughfare. Doors had been left flung open. In one home, Bennu saw smoke from hastily snuffed candles curling into the air. A few children ran out to close shutters.

Yes, thought Bennu, batten down the hatches, put the horses in the barn. Big bad Bennu has arrived, the guy who can't even help an old, blind woman.

Shoulders slumped, Bennu walked the length of the main street. He felt the salty sea breeze calling for his tears. Staring out at the waves crashing on Goffer's Spit, he sat on a rock and watched the sea wash over mussels and anemones and then recede and reveal them again. Bennu wondered how they survived the battering.

He closed his eyes. Images came and went. Sutton saying no. Blind Bebba in trouble. Piers sending them off. The McKenzie Boys. Angie. He pictured the two of them together, holding hands on a beach in the Caribbean, St. Martin's maybe. She whispers in his ear, "It's always been you I've wanted, Bennu. Only you. Why did it take you so long to see my love?"

Yeah, right, he thought. As if the most insightful, beautiful girl on the planet would be thinking about me, Bennu with his dumb glasses and hook nose. Why would she want to be with someone who never feels at home? Now I suppose I should look for that stupid tile.

A voice startled him out of his fantasies. "The smells of the sea come waftin' along, doon't y'know." Bennu turned to see an old man pointing toward the ocean. "Out there, a spirit knows what kelpy smells we need." His crevassed face told Bennu the man had spent years out in the open. He struck a dramatic pose and said,

> There are secrets in the sea,
>
> Too many to be told.
>
> Sailors will tell ye,
>
> "Let them be, let them be,"
>
> But about these secrets, be bold.

"The sea, young lad, has tales to tell, doon't y'know."

"I suppose it does." Bennu stepped back to size up the thin old man. Slightly stooped, the man crooked a finger to the ocean, revealing wiry arms beneath his tunic. His bald head and a long gray beard that flowed down his chest gave him the look of a sage.

Exposing the wide gap between his two front teeth, he spoke again. "Tell me, lad, what's your business here? I know these parts—and some have called me a prophet, doon't y'know."

"No, I don't, and I don't know that I should be telling you my business."

"Ah yes, 'tis wise to be cautious, lad. Once, when I was your age, I made a terrible mistake being rash. Yes, I did. Tried to grab an arrow comin' at me with my bare hands, doon't y'know. The thing is, I nearly done it. I grabbed it by the feathers and slowed it down a'plenty—but not before the arrow landed straight between my two front teeth and pushed them apart. See!" He pointed to his gap and laughed wheezily, leaning back until his hip bones showed through his tunic.

Bennu felt glad to have a little company, now that the old man seemed harmless. "What you say sounds as logical as the Window under the Mountain or flying Oregonians."

"Ore-whatians?"

"Forget it." Bennu threw a rock into the surf. "I've heard more stories lately than I know what to do with."

"Stories, y'say?" The old man stroked his long gray beard. "Ha! I've got more stories to add to yours. That's what I do. That's what I am. Goffer's the name, and that"—he pointed to the wisp of sand and rock running into the ocean—"that's my spit!" He leaned back to gather strength then snapped his head forward, flinging his own spit fifteen feet where it hit a rock with a splat. At the sound he wheezed his squeaky laugh again.

"You're Goffer? The storyteller? I thought no one had seen you for a while. Where have you been hiding?"

"Here and there." He poked in the sand with his cane. "I was gettin' too many folks followin' after my every move. A prophet's no good unless he's got some mystery about him, doon't y'know. In the meantime I've been collectin' stories like a hen does her chicks."

Benny felt bold. "Then maybe in all your stories, you've heard about stolen property, some kind of valuable tile that was taken from its rightful place and brought out here." With the word "tile," a flush of shame swept over Bennu like a shadow from a cloud suddenly blocking the sun. But, he wondered, didn't Piers also say, "Be brave, falcon, be brave"?

Goffer paced back and forth in the sand, his sandals and cane leaving deep imprints. "Hmm, you're worried about Morphane, aren't ya, lad?"

"Yes, of course, isn't everyone?"

"Indeed, like sailors staring down a squall. Morphane's a story that keeps a crowd awake, doon't y'know? He's a fearsome beast, beautiful in his own way but terrible and cruel. He could yet rule the day." Back and forth, Goffer paced. "This tile that you desire, is it magical?"

"I believe so." Bennu nervously ran his hand through his wavy hair, torn between the desire to speak and the fear that he should not. "I don't know exactly what it does, but I do know that the right side wants it right away."

"So you feel stuck, like a barnacled rock—and the tide's risin'."

"I suppose so."

"I hear a story comin' to me. I remember something from the Book of Quadrille."

At this, Bennu's head shot up in recognition.

"In the Book of Quadrille," Goffer continued, "there's a story that begins on land and ends on the sea. Come, shall we walk out on my own spit?" He smiled broadly at this repeated joke. "I like to move when I tell my tales, doon't y'know."

With a glance toward town to see if Sutton and Zennor were returning, Bennu turned to follow Goffer onto the rocky strip of land.

Goffer balanced well on the rocks, rarely needing his cane for support. In the inlet of water protected by the natural jetty, anchored fishing boats swayed gently. Bennu remembered that from the air, Goffer's Spit bore the outline of the Eye of Horus. They were walking now on the eyebrow.

"Long ago, before the Kells and other places had grown into towns," said Goffer, "the Quadrille tells of a time when misery had come to Welken. The early Welken folk knew evil was out there, but there's different types of knowledge, doon't y'know. A great lathery fog—like this one rollin' in right now—covered the land." Goffer faced the incoming thickness that grasped at the rocks like huge treading paws. As his beard fluttered in the misty breeze, a seal barked in the distance.

Goffer stopped a moment, then walked quietly on the sandy beach. Gulls squawked their ugly song and fought over the remnants of a crab that had died on the beach in the night. "Creatures came into Welken from a foreign land. Two on land and two from the air. They traveled through Welken to the center of the peninsula, where a giant tree stood, a fig tree large and full of fruit, a tree that told the folk that all was well. The creatures fell upon the tree with a vengeance, gnawin' at its roots, peckin', stompin', chewin' furiously. Welkeners crowded around but did nothing. They watched and watched and watched."

Goffer paused and climbed atop a boulder in the center of the eyebrow. Bennu looked back toward Kells and saw below them the "eye" in the Eye of Horus, an island of sand on which a dozen sea lions bellowed to them.

Goffer walked on. "These creatures hacked at the roots of the tree till it grew weak." Goffer spat on the ground and squished his spit with his cane.

Bennu could hardly believe what he was hearing. Four creatures? From a foreign land? Maybe Goffer *was* a prophet. Yet these foreigners seemed bad for Welken.

Though the fog dampened all, Bennu began to sweat, wiping drops from his forehead. He didn't like being a fulfillment of prophecy.

A seal near the shore barked loudly.

"Didn't any Welkeners protest?" asked Bennu, wondering why he asked a question that accused himself.

"I can only say what's in the Quadrille, doon't y'know. I wouldn't stretch the truth wider than the space in my own teeth." Goffer smiled.

Bennu returned the smile, nervously. "OK, go on."

They passed the skeletal hull of an old ship partly covered in sand.

"Then the four creatures looked up from their gnawin' and hackin' and went off in different directions. In time, a furious storm drove the fog away. The rain came down like the Nezzer Falls, floodin' the countryside. A gale came up and drove the rain like hailstones upon the helpless Welkeners. Still they watched the tree. The wind rushed over Welken like a mighty hurricane of destruction!"

A wave dashed on the rocks below.

Bennu wondered, if Goffer is talking about the four of us, then we are hurting Welken. How?

"Weakened at the roots, the mighty tree fell with a roar heard all over the land. Many were injured or killed in its falling. The Welkeners that were left unhurt charged after the foreign creatures. In all directions they fled, mobs seekin' revenge."

They were nearing the end of the spit. A primitive lighthouse stood before them.

Bennu didn't like the implications of the story. All could be coincidence, he told himself, but his experience in Welken told him otherwise. The story says that the Welkeners should not have watched. But Piers told me to watch, to be observant and careful.

As they made their way around the building on a narrow path between the rocks and the lighthouse wall, gangly pelicans hovered and then dove speedily for food. Two seals perched on a guano-covered rock barked into the fog.

"The Welkeners captured them all, doon't y'know." Goffer tried to push the fog out of his face. "The Quadrille doesn't talk about the battles fought to secure the intruders, but it does tell about what happened to them."

"Yes, go on," said Bennu, his sweat feeling clammy on his skin.

They walked to the very end of the spit, and facing the open sea, Goffer said, "The Welkeners said good riddance to these four by tyin' 'em up and castin' 'em off in a prison ship with one sail. The wind was fine that day and carried the betrayers of Welken out to sea never to be seen again, except . . ." Goffer stopped here and held his hand over his brow as if looking for part of the story in the churning waves.

"Except for what, Goffer? I'm not sure I like your story, but you can't leave me hanging like this." Bennu felt the fog swirling around his feet, enveloping him. "How does it end?"

"Strange as it sounds, the dream ends with one of the flyin' creatures returnin'. How she got away we don't know. But the Quadrille says this, that she came ridin' toward the shore, on the crest of a wave!"

Goffer pointed to the sea. There from out of the fog, came a rowboat propelled by a single undiminishing wave.

As it came near, Bennu recognized the outline of the person bound to the oarlocks. He cried out, "Angie! Angie, are you OK? I'll come get you!"

Yet he could not. His feet were stuck.

Goffer kept telling the story. "So old Goffer says, 'Let this dream be a lesson to you. Don't watch! Don't wait! Welken must learn to do as it pleases, and those who resist should be punished. Someone is comin' who will set things right. His name is the Master!'"

Bennu turned from Angie to Goffer. The old man's face changed quickly into a hideous visage, the face of one of Morphane's servants. Bennu looked down to see that his own feet were held fast, not by the enveloping fog but by "Goffer's" own legs that had melted and reformed into large, binding fetters. Struggling in this trap, Bennu twisted around, kicked against "Goffer's" grasp, and fell to his knees.

"Don't come up here, Angie!" he shouted. As he wrestled against his bindings, Bennu turned back and saw the lighthouse behind him. Off shore, a lone seal barked plaintively into the mist.

After dragging the rowboat onto the spit, the changling that had been "little Angie" released the real Angie from the bracelets and carried her to Bennu. To the two Misfits' amazement, the impersonator of Goffer and little Angie melded back into one creature, Malleal the Resembler. Without speaking, Malleal took the hidden gift out of Bennu's pocket and wrapped one arm tightly around Bennu and another around Angie.

"I'm sorry, Angie," Bennu said. "I suspected something, but I just kept listening to the story."

Angie turned her translucent face to Bennu. She did not speak, but her drooping head told Bennu that she too had failed. Her glow pulsed faintly.

With Bennu's gift of flight held firmly, the beast rose in the sky. From below, no one could see Angie's tears fall, evaporating before they hit the landscape below.

Malleal screeched, not like a falcon riding the winds, but like the last gasp of a cornered creature, the sound of the fear of death.

CHAPTER TWENTY-EIGHT
RIDDLING WHILE ROME TURNS

*Coming to recognize you are wrong is like coming to recognize you
are sick. You feel bad long before you admit you have any symptoms
and certainly long before you are willing to take your medicine.*

NORMAN MACLEAN, *YOUNG MEN AND FIRE*

 As Fatagar's laugh burned in his mind, Len closed the glimpse's ring of light with a yelp. The fire shooting out of Fatagar's hand had nipped his fingers hanging on the rim. The hole snapped shut, and Len bumped to the ground. He rubbed the burned spots, ignoring any motherly advice he'd heard to the contrary.

Len found himself on a sidewalk near a busy intersection. Disoriented, he sat and tried to get his bearings. He wondered if any time had passed since he'd left Skinner. Maybe it was like the first time. Maybe the McKenzie dolts were still in the museum. No matter where he put his focus, his mind kept returning to his recent choices and his empty stomach.

When he was in Welken, all he could think about was getting out. But now that he was out, he wondered why he'd ignored Prester John's warning and why he'd made a glimpse suffer.

As the journalist in his head asked probing, difficult questions, he tried to turn his attention elsewhere, anywhere that might provide relief. He looked around and realized he was on the corner of Amazon Parkway and Pershing Avenue, just two blocks from his house. Jumping up, he pulled his cap out of his back pocket and put it on backwards. He brushed off any remaining Welken dirt and rubbed his hunger pains.

Yet Welken could not be so easily dismissed. Though it was a pleasant seventy-six degrees in Skinner, Len's sweat-soaked shirt looked as if he'd been lifting rocks all day. Then there was the troubling circumstance of where he reappeared. He was not at the museum. Just then, Trevor Marshall, a freshman at Weyerhauser High and one of the best skaters in the area, sped by, riding the curb and doing a heel-flip as he said, "What's up?" to Len.

"Nothin." Len tried to cover his sweat with his arms. As Trevor rolled by, Len noticed his T-shirt. It said "London" on it and was imprinted with England's lion rampant regardant breathing flames. Then he walked by the Enquists' house on Pershing and saw the sign by the door, "Welkommen." The "omm" seemed to drop out as he did a double take. Then he thought of the name for this area of town, Four Corners, and how, on this street years ago, Angie fell off her bike, hit her head, and started talking out her dreams, those otherworldly tales of paradise.

Stop it already, Len thought. Then he added aloud, "It's no use." Shrugging his shoulders, he summed up his struggle in the last way he ever thought he would. He muttered, "In Welken, of Welken."

Looks like I can't get out of Welken even by coming back home, he thought. And now—the problem is that I can't get Welken out of me. What an idiot I am! Now I've got to go home and get a car or a bike and go back to the museum. And how am I going to explain why I'm alone? I know, I could say I caught a red-hot amulet, and it transported us to some fantasyland stuck in the Middle Ages. And then some horny-faced guy named Fatagar was going to lock me up and turn me into a desert slave when I got away and left my friends there. Yeah, right.

Soon he approached his front door.

So far, so good, he thought, no one in the front yard.

On the porch's step, Percy soaked in the sun, facing the rays with closed eyes.

"Hey, Percy." Len announced his arrival with deceitful cheer. "Hey, you feline furball." He stopped to pick him up, sat on the step, and turned to face the sun himself. "You don't know this, Percy ol' pal, but we have plenty in common. Yessir, I'm the king of cats, myself, and don't you forget it." Len scratched Percy behind the ears and rubbed his backend until it rose and his tail stiffened in unashamed satisfaction. Then Percy turned over, four paws to the sky, and let Len pet his chest. "Well, Percival P. Perkins, detective cat, I guess I'd better see if I can get through this mess." He let Percy in as he opened the door.

Seeing no one, Len tiptoed to the kitchen. Still no one.

Feeling victorious, he went to the fridge, drank milk out of the carton, put the carton on the counter, grabbed a handful of Oreos, and left the bag open.

And Angie says I can't be quiet? I'm practically as invisible as she is.

Percy meowed from a kitchen chair. "OK, catmeister, I'll give you some more attention." Percy flopped over onto Charlotte's latest chapter, "Maps for Chaps." Len glanced at the title, popped two Oreos in his mouth, scratched Percy in the hollow triangle under his chin, and heard his father arguing with his mother. "You're too soft on him, Charlotte" was all Len needed to hear. He tiptoed out to the garage.

After hopping on his mountain bike, Len headed for the museum. He'd only pedaled a few revolutions when he saw Darlene in front of the Nefertis' house. Outfitted in matching garden gloves and apron, she weeded the front flowerbed. Her boombox blared with an oldies station.

She waved to him. "Yoo-hoo, Lenny, do you have a minute?"

Len squeezed his brakes, breaking a cookie in his hand. "I guess, Darlene, but . . . uh . . . I am in a bit of a hurry."

"I'm glad you came by. Martin and I have to leave on an emergency business trip. One of his clients wants to talk about his many brilliant slogans. Anyway, would it be OK if Bennu and Lizbeth spent the night at your house?"

"Sure, no problem."

"You *are* a dear, Lenny. Thanks!"

"Yeah. Bye." Len readied one pedal high and gave it a push. Before he got too far, he heard Darlene sing along with the radio, "Why can't I be a teenager in lo-ah-ove."

I can give you ten ranked reasons, thought Len. *Whew. Now I don't have to explain why Bennu and Lizbeth aren't here, at least not to the Nefertis. I still can't believe I left them. I'm such a jerk. I'm not sure I'm fit to be a Misfit.*

Len's internal jabbering continued as he rode his bike, finding inspiration from various houses and cars that reminded him of past failures. About fifty yards from the museum, a car behind him honked to move him back into the bike lane. Len swished quickly back and stopped, his right foot resting on the curb.

That's when he saw the Ford LTD.

How did they get out? wondered Len. Why haven't they been arrested?

As the LTD drew closer, Odin leaned his head out the window. "You're a slippery piece of work, Bartholomew. One minute you catch that stupid rock. The next minute you're up here on your stupid bike." He brought the car to a stop on the opposite side of the street. "Next time, we won't let you go."

As Len braced himself to take off, he could see Josh in the backseat digging through the stolen museum stuff. "I don't remember you 'letting' me go, Mink. Seems to me *you* were in a hurry to leave *us*."

Odin shook his head. "Always quick with the jokes, aren't you?" He put the car in park. He opened the door. "Maybe you'll regret them in a minute." Odin got out of the car.

Then the sirens came.

Odin stepped back and reached through Josh's open window and into the backseat. He pulled out the bag of museum treasures. "I didn't like giving up the amulet to you." He rummaged through the bag. "You're indebted to me now."

Tommy leaned over from the passenger's side. "C'mon, let's go!"

Odin opened the driver's door. "Let's just say I want you even further in my debt." He flipped something in the air over to Len. "Hey, maybe the cops will find you and think you took all this stuff. Happy explaining."

Startled, Len dropped his bike to the ground and caught it. As the McKenzie Butte Boys drove off, Len looked at the round disk in his hand. It was an ancient coin with a military figure on one side. Len would have stared at the coin for a long time except for the sirens that grew louder. At about the same time, a cop car raced in the direction of the McKenzie Boys and a fire truck barreled right by him, toward the museum. He watched the truck stop in front of the museum's bell tower.

When Len looked up at the museum, it seemed strange. He'd seen it hundreds of times, but today the bell tower looked different. He put the coin in his pocket and stared at the tower, framing it with the right angles of his fingers and thumbs. Then he squinted at it. Like a trading card hologram, two images flipped back and forth, first the bell tower, then the Wasan Sagad. Fatagar stood in the balcony at the top of the Sagad, leading prisoners by their chains. Then the bell tower came back into focus. Len saw smoke. Then Fatagar squeezed the coal piece. A thin rope of flame lashed Prester John on the back.

Len opened his eyes wide and saw the museum bell tower again. In it, flames darted around the interior walls. Security guards fought the blaze with fire extinguishers. Passersby gawked and pointed. Shouting to the crew below, a firefighter on a truck's extension ladder stretched closer and closer. The flames curled up to the wooden ceiling, chasing the guards away with heat and smoke. Coughing, they stumbled down the tower steps.

The fire moved swiftly to the center of the open tower, to the beams holding the glowing bell. Like a flaming ax, the fire chopped away at the beams, at the ropes that secured the bell in the rafters. Then the water came and smoke clouded the scene. From the force of the water on the flames, the bell itself rocked. Back and forth it swung until the huge clapper struck its side in a kind of victory clang. The sound reverberated over the noise of the water and the trucks, down to cheering onlookers, and somehow, mysteriously, down to Len. The bell pealed beautifully—and the firefighter just kept water on it. Len wished that every fire could be doused with such a triumphant declaration.

Then Len hopped back on his bike and pedaled hard. Without poking around to find out how the fire got started, he found the Skylark, threw his bike in the trunk, and slipped into the vinyl front seat. As he started the car, all he could think about was that rather than escape from his troubles by coming home, his problems had multiplied. Every minute in Skinner told him he should have stayed in Welken. Every second felt like an hour's betrayal, a week's worth of abandonment. But he didn't know how to get back. What was he supposed to do . . . find another secret amulet? And then there was the explaining to do. What could he tell his mom and dad about why the others weren't in the car?

After driving home, Len, still sweating, flung open the door into the kitchen from the garage. His parents were at the dinner table. "Hi. Car is now here resting peacefully. It's not really 'the car,' or 'the Skylark.' It's too basic, so it's just Car. Car is happily dripping oil onto the garage floor. Hey, great, dinner."

"I know you think we have no cause to ever worry about you," said Charlotte, "but until you get your own car—"

"I should take care of yours. Yes, Motherrr."

"You look terrible." Jeff picked meat out of his teeth. "What have you been doing?"

"Well, I . . . *we* have been playing mud football."

"Did you think of maybe getting out of those clothes before coming to the table?"

"Actually, Dad, I didn't think you'd want me to eat dinner naked."

Jeff sighed.

Charlotte said, "Do you know anything about all those sirens? They sounded like they were heading downtown."

"Yeah." Len grabbed his fork. "There was a fire in the bell tower of the Wasan Sagad. It was so cool."

Jeff gave Len the why-must-everything-be-difficult squint. "The Wasan Sa- what?"

"Oh, I'm sorry," said Len, blushing. "I meant the museum. Just a little nickname we dreamed up. Anyway, the bell actually rang while they put the fire out. The crowd cheered. Very exciting. Could I get those potatoes from you, Dad?"

"Sure," said Jeff. "By the way, where's Angie?"

"She and Lizbeth went to do something. I dunno exactly. They were talking about an overnight, maybe in the Wilder someplace."

Charlotte frowned. "She'd better check in first. Sometimes I wonder how that child makes it through a day. She can be so spacey."

"She's not a child, Mom. She's sixteen. That's where you should begin." Len shoveled in heaping forkfuls of fruit salad, finished his last eight ounces of milk in one throwback of the head, and got up from the table. "Thanks for dinner. I gotta go do some stuff in my room."

As Len left the table with a loud belch, he heard Jeff say to Charlotte,

"And we thought they were exhausting when they were toddlers."

Happy that his parents were appeased for the moment, Len went to his room and flopped onto his bed. He looked at the coin, played video games for a while, looked at the coin, got bored, looked up Roman coins on the Internet, got bored, closed his eyes to rest for a while and, unable to nod off, got bored.

I guess I'll take a shower, he said to himself. Some losers might think I stink.

As the sweat and soil from Welken ran down the drain, he remembered for the first time another shower, the rain in Welken, something about a ledge, waking up, sliding down a slick embankment. Ouch. He rubbed the tender spot as he washed his hair.

Stepping out of the shower, he thought, if the museum tower and the Wasan Sagad overlap, what else does? Where in Skinner is Ganderst Hall, Chimney Cave, and the rest? I wish I'd been awake for all of it. Piers didn't have much of a chance to fill me in. I guess I didn't really want to get filled in either.

He looked in the mirror. Fingering his own face like a mother monkey searching for bugs, he popped a zit. To Len, everything seemed to be coming together—the past, present, his inner world and outer world. And then there were *other* worlds, like Welken.

The whole universe is a giant smoothie, he thought, with all kinds of flavors blending together. And the speed of the blender keeps increasing, and the froth is spilling out.

He popped another zit.

Len put on clean new clothes and his old stinky cap. He decided to brave the living room again. No one was there. "Out on a walk" read the note on the refrigerator. Percy meowed at the door. Len leaned over and petted him, but Percy made it clear that his affection for Len in this moment was strictly utilitarian. He wanted outside. Len opened the door.

As Len turned to check the pantry for a snack, he saw his mother's manuscript spread out on the kitchen table. He didn't recognize three of the chapters, "Ollie Ollie, Camel's Free," "Chasing Percy Chasing Ollie," and "Maps for Chaps."

Len tucked the chapters under his left armpit, grabbed a Coke and a glass with ice in his left hand, and snagged a bag of chips with his right hand.

No problem, he said to himself as he kicked open the door to his bedroom and stepped over the laundry all over the floor. I might as well take my mind off my troubles while I wait for the others to return.

He propped up two pillows against the headboard, bounced onto the bed, and read. Occasionally, he swept potato chip crumbs off the bed and onto the carpet.

When he finished "Chasing Percy Chasing Ollie," he set the manuscript down in his lap. He had enjoyed the escape from the pyramid and the pursuit of Ollie. But now, his adrenaline rush told him he had done more than read an entertaining story. He pulled the coin out of his pocket and studied it again.

Could this be Roman? he wondered. If so, why did Odin throw it to me? How many coincidences is a person expected to survive in one day without going crazy?

Unable to find an answer, Len kept reading.

CHAPTER SEVEN: Maps for Chaps

On the boat to Rome, Percy turned the ancient coin over and over in his paw. Staring at the Mediterranean whitecaps and then at the sigma-shaped route he traced off the pyramid's wall, Percy paused to flip the coin in the air. He caught it, looked at Caesar's head, and put it back in his vest pocket.

"No matter how many times I fret my noggin' over this one, dear Bonesy," he said with a sigh, "I end up thinking, 'You pays your money and you takes your bad penny.' Nothing like the brown book to help out in time of need."

Len thought, I wish it were so easy for me.

Soon, Percy and Bones were running into the Colosseum arena expecting to find Ollie. The place teemed with tourists, many of whom paid a fee to don gladiator garb and pretend they were fighting for their lives. One of them was a helmeted

Ollie. "Aha," he said, "now we'll find out if Mama trained me right." He thrust a sword at Percy.

Percy poked back with a spear. "My dear Ollie, you don't think for a second you can outduel me, do you? Why, I'm full of vim and victory! I'm as fit as a fiddler! I can do the minuet in forty-five seconds!"

Ollie slashed at Percy repeatedly, causing the detective to back up and nearly trip.

"Where's a lion when you need one!" muttered Percy. "This is the Colosseum, isn't it?"

Just when Percy twirled a net above his head, preparing to toss it over the jousting burglar, Ollie threw his sword in an arc above Percy. Ollie's sword met the net after Percy released it and forced the net down on top of the cat, the sword stabbing the net into the ground.

"Toodly-too bad!" Ollie giggled as he ran out of the Colosseum.

Bones helped Percy get out of the net. "Perce, lookit here. On the hilt of the sword. Something is tied on. I've always wanted to get a message like this."

Percy straightened his vest. "It's a riddle, Bonesy:

Mr. Nick's first names were ever so bold.
Marshall Umster, they were, or so I've been told.
Join him for a stein, and you won't feel so old.

Len stopped here to figure out the riddle. He put the manuscript down as he recited, "Marshall Umster Nick," over and over to himself. He couldn't figure anything out—and he hated the fact that his mom could outwit him. He looked at the coin for a clue.

He thought, I'll have to tell her that this is way over her readers' heads.

CHAPTER TWENTY-NINE
Revolutionary Insights

You! You chameleon!
Bottomless bag of tricks! Here in your own country
Would you not give your stratagems a rest
Or stop spellbinding for an instant?

HOMER, *ODYSSEY*

 From the bedroom window, Len heard Percy meow at the back door to be let in. "Don't worry, Percival. I'll be there soon enough. Just after I finish this chapter."

"Well, Marshall Umster Nick makes no sense to me," said Bones. "We might as well be looking for a single bratwurst in all of Germany."

Exactly, thought Len.

"That reference inspires me, Mr. Malone. Marshall Umster Nick is M. U. Nick, which sounds like Munich if you put it altogether. That's where he is—and the 'stein' must be telling us to go to the famous Beer Garden."

"They grow beer from seed in Germany, Perce?"

"No, no, no, my wide-eyed canine friend. You'll see."

Aw, c'mon, Mom, thought Len, that's ridiculous. Even Piers wouldn't figure that one out.

Percy meowed again, louder.

"OK, Percy, hold on a flea-bitten minute! I'm going to finish this Perkins chapter." Len paused. "Sheesh. Too many Ps."

> In Munich's Beer Garden, as if on cue, Ollie stumbled up from behind them, his feet unstable and his speech slurred. "If it ain't my good friends Pershy Perkins and Monesy Baloney."
>
> Percy confronted him. "I hate to see you like this, Ollie. I think you just lost your 'gentleman burglar' status."
>
> "Dearie, dearie, doodles," said Ollie, his eyelids at half-mast. "You schnoops can be show cruel, show cruel." Then, Ollie reached into his knapsack and pulled out a bottle of wine. He shouted, "Free wine! Bordeaux, 1915!"
>
> About twenty wine lovers surrounded the trio, grasping after the green bottle. In the tumult, the bottle bounced from hand to hand until the red contents glugged out onto the floor.
>
> In the commotion, Ollie slipped away, and Bones slipped on the wine.
>
> As Percy came over to help Bones up, the basset hound wrung wine out of his back pocket hankie. "I hope we get another chance at him."
>
> "I think we will, Mr. Moses Baloney." Percy spied a wine-soaked note on the floor. "Another riddle, I presume, and not a moment too good to be true. Here it is, Bones:
>
> > I fill up a tower till it's snug as a rug.
> > I'd say no to a dame as much as a bug.
> > You won't find me here till you put down your mug.

Len stopped again, determined to decipher this clue. He got up, went to the bathroom, listened to Percy meow with greater fervor, came back, flipped the coin in the air, read the riddle out loud twice, paced back and forth with the manuscript in his hands, yelled, "Be quiet, Percy! I'll let you in when I'm good and ready," rapped his knuckles against the top of his head as if he were knocking on a door, and finally, thrust his fist into the air with an enthusiastic "Yes! I got it!" He sat up on his bed and returned to his place in the story.

"Even a simple-minded farmer like me can get this riddle, Mr. Perkins," announced Bones with aw-shucks pride.

Thanks for the boost to the ego, Bones, thought Len.

"Yes, quite so," confirmed Percy. "As the brown book says, 'The bird's eye view catches the worm.' From our perch, we can see that 'I fill up a tower' must be the Eiffel Tower and 'no to a dame' must be Notre Dame. So off we go to the Paris of France, but surely this scoundrel is laying a trap."

En route by train, Percy and Bones studied the map. Rome, Munich, and Paris all lined up with the notches on the sigma. If the map held true to form, they would soon be crossing the English Channel.

"But why?" Percy persistently inquired. "Why not just say, 'Meet me in London, if you dare' or some such folderol?"

❧

In Paris, between Notre Dame and the Eiffel Tower, dozens of booths and entertainers vied for Percy's attention and Bones's spare change. A drama troupe reenacted scenes from the French Revolution. Marie Antoinette, sporting a massive blond wig, marched up to a makeshift guillotine. The rebels put Marie's head in a slot below the raised blade. They locked the wooden top piece around her neck. "Liberte!" the actors shouted. "Liberte!" the crowd repeated. Then, the executioner released the blade from its terrible height. Flying down as fast as a dive-bombing falcon, the blade shone in the sun not like a cardboard prop but like polished steel.

Swoosh, it ran down the channel! Swoosh, it cut through the neck of Marie Antoinette, her head dropping into a basket!

Bones could hardly believe his eyes.

As the crowd cheered wildly, the headlock was raised, and the headless Marie Antoinette, to the amazement of no one except Bones, stood, her neck stump pointing awkwardly to the sky. Clumsily, her arms reached up and fumbled with the buttons on her dress. Soon, the bodice was flung open to reveal, of course, the real head of the actor playing Marie. The crowd exploded again into cheers.

"I'm so relieved," said Bones. "They had me going for a second or two."

Percy flicked one of Bones's overall straps. "They had you going for every pea-cotton minute. And look, Marie Antoinette is Ollie Ollie Otterson!"

Men from the crowd grabbed Ollie and hoisted him onto their shoulders, cheering all the while, "Long live France!" Clearly enjoying the attention, Ollie told his bearers to giddyap, and so they galloped him away from the Virginia duo. As Ollie sped ahead, he threw a paper airplane at the detectives. Unfolded, it read:

"Mama, they wander across the sea bridge."
"Don't worry, my Ollie, just go to the fridge.
It's stuck in the kitchen up there on that ridge."

Len pointed to an imaginary map in front of him. "Now, the sea bridge has got to mean the way to cross over to England. Percy already said as much."

The other Percy, the housecat who sounded more annoyed with every passing minute, meowed and meowed. Len thought he could hear scratching noises on the door.

"Don't get all worked up about it, Percy. Sheesh! No wonder we named you Persistence. I only have a few pages left."

Making furrows in his hair with his fingers, Len resumed reading.

"The sigma map," said Percy, "takes us over the English Channel, so that must be the sea bridge."

Two points for me, thought Len.

> Percy measured spots on the map with his fingers. "If my sense of distance is as impeccable as usual, that last notch on the map must be a place *below* London. Bones, what do you think?"
>
> "Well, I . . . I—"
>
> "Bones, this is no time to play pirates, but hey, you've given me a splash of inspiration. A famous lord who descended from a pirating family set up a fine house in which the chef was required to chop and cut with scabbards and daggers instead of traditional cutlery."
>
> "His name wouldn't be Mugg, would it?"
>
> "Bones, you're as smart as all the tea in China. How did you know?"
>
> "The last word in each riddle, Perce. They spell 'Old Mugg Ridge'!"
>
> "I always knew some of me would rub off on you. Yes, that's the place named after the pirate One-Leg Mugg, about an hour or so south of London. I learned it all when studying the life and times of Jolly Roger. Off we go, then."

Len heard Percy's meowing increase in volume and intensity. From his bedroom window, Len could see the back door. Percy was clawing his way up the screen.

That little guy *really* wants in, thought Len. His meowing is beginning to sound vicious. "Have some patience, little guy! That starts with a *p*, too, y'know."

CHAPTER THIRTY
MANORS AND MANNERS

Tyger! Tyger! Burning bright
In the forests of the night
What immortal hand or eye
Could frame thy fearful symmetry?

WILLIAM BLAKE, "THE TYGER"

 ike a haunted mansion in a bad movie, the house on Old Mugg Ridge dominated the skyline. As Percy and Bones made their way up the stone steps to the front door, lights flickered on and off throughout the house, creating an illusion of lightning that spooked Bones noticeably.

Percy patted Bones on the back, scaring him. "No need to worry, my chum of chums. I've read Hawthorne and Poe. These buildings are always more or less than meets the eye."

Percy pressed the doorbell.

A smartly attired butler opened the huge oak door and addressed them.

"Good evening. My name is Jeeves. The lord of the manor has been expecting you."

"Good show," replied Percy, as usual falling helplessly into the local dialect. "Would you be so kind as to take us to the old chap?"

"Right this way, sir."

Up a grand circular staircase they went, turning round and round till they were even with the chandelier that hung in the central opening.

Jeeves bowed. "The master of the house requests your presence inside."

Once in the room, Bones and Percy noticed they were in a finished attic. Two dormers let in a little light, but otherwise the room was rather dark. On opposite walls, two suits of armor stood at attention. Across from the windows, two painted mummy cases stared into the light as if looking for the next pharaoh. A box on an old chair occupied the center of the room.

Whoa, thought Len, this is really too much. Did we tell Mom all about the museum? I don't remember. How would she know? Then again, why aren't the mummy cases facing each other? Where's the amulet?

Percy strolled over and poked at a knight's helmet with a claw. "Curious place, Jeeves. Just why are we here?"

"The master of the house desires for you to translate a verse for him. It's in several languages: Latin, maybe Hebrew, even a few hieroglyphics."

"I see. And what will the master get for all my trouble?"

"It appears, sir, that the verse will lead to some great discovery. I believe it involves a book he is writing, sir."

Bones whispered in Percy's ear.

"My question exactly, Bonesy. I say, Jeeves old boy, why should I do this—outside of my own humble generosity, I mean?"

"The master has instructed me to tell you that if you don't translate the verse, you'll never leave this room alive, sir. Pardon my rudeness, gentlemen. I am only following orders, such as they are."

"Well, Bones, we have been issued an ultimatum. I do so enjoy these challenges, don't you? Better a little crust with your toast, I always say, eh, Bones?"

"Sounds like as much fun as a plague of grasshoppers. You're not going to give in to Master Ollie are you?"

Percy took off his derby and scratched his head. "Yes, I am. These kidnapper stalemate thingies can be annoying. Better just get on with it."

"The master will reward your willingness to help," said Jeeves. "He is an honorable fellow, a good chap really."

Percy bopped his derby back on. "All right, then, torpedo the dams, full speed ahead."

Bones moaned, and Jeeves handed Percy an old parchment.

C'mon, Percy, thought Len, you're smarter than this. Bones, talk him out of it.

"What's the verse mean, Perce?" asked Bones.

"Well it's not exactly elementary, my dear Bonesy. But it is straightforward. All except the Hebrew, which is straightbackward. Let's see, invert the squiggle on the cursive *L* and remember that the blinx tells us to add two to the previous number. Yes, I think I've got it:

First to the right you'll find twenty-four
Left then to ten, then spin some more
After twelve to the right you can open the door.

Percy stood there, as satisfied as a cow munching on tall grass. "Ho hum, 'twas nothing. Please, no more applause."

"Jolly good translation, sir." Jeeves brushed some lint off of his satin lapel. "I'm sure the master will be quite pleased by this." Jeeves walked to the box on the chair in the middle of the room. It was a small safe. After spinning the lock deftly and turning the handle, he smiled broadly, reached in, and pulled out a rolled map. Then he picked up a solid gold pin shaped like a beetle. He held it lovingly and slipped it into his coat pocket.

Now you've really messed things up, Mr. Perkins. You've played right into Ollie's hand. And you found a gold beetle? What's going on here? How could Mom *not* know? I'm going to ask her as soon as she comes home.

Percy let out another angry meow, this time sounding wilder, more like the stray alley cat he once was. He meowed and yeowed and reowed. He wouldn't stop.

"All right already!" shouted Len with anger. "I'm coming! You are such a pest."

Muttering to himself about houses in England and cantankerous cats, Len strode quickly to the back door. Head down in anticipation of Percy's entrance, he put his hand on the knob. "OK, you stupid cat, maybe now you'll shut up."

When he opened the door, Percy wasn't there.

Something else was.

A huge, snarling mountain lion faced him on all fours. The cougar bared its teeth and uttered a low menacing growl. Len stiffened and did what always frustrated him in the movies. He just stood there staring at the beast, paralyzed, one hand on the door, the other on the door molding.

Do something! yelled the audience in his mind. Shut the door!

But Len, hands shaking, didn't move. The cougar's growl grew more piercing, its body tenser. The scab on Len's head throbbed.

Then the puma cocked his head and roared loud and strong and terrible. He was so close, Len could smell his breath. He smelled the wildness of it, the scent of the predator. And, somehow, this scent awakened him out of his paralysis—and into a kind of instinctual response. Contrary to every rational thought that sped through his brain, Len flung the door completely open. With both hands facing the cougar, fingers curled forward and muscles taut, Len roared back.

Gathering up all the power he could muster, Len threw back his head and answered the snarling beast. Len growled and scraped the air. His voice thundered into the night.

And then the roar of the cougar stopped.

The great beast turned and ran to a towering cedar in the backyard. Treating the trunk like a huge scratching post, the mountain lion raked its claws deeply into the bark. It turned back to Len, narrowed its eyes, then bolted for the open gate leading to the Wilder.

Len reverted to paralysis. He stared at the empty yard, his fists clenched and his toes pressing forward. A normal, heart-stopping fear descended upon him. He thought about how he'd gone face to face with a mountain lion in his own safe backyard. And he realized how close he'd come to getting hurt, how foolish a risk it was to attempt to outroar a cougar.

And another fear grew, that all this senselessness made sense, that he was playing a role in some grand story, that Welken mattered, that events in his life were not arbitrary and inconsequential, that he was discovering who he was and what he was made to do.

Len's body finally caught up to what had happened. Shaking, he did not know how much longer his knees would support him. His arms seemed incapable of rising above his waist. He closed the door and walked back to his bedroom.

Though weary, all he could think was that he must find something that would help Piers and the Misfits.

I need to get back, he thought.

More than ever, Charlotte's manuscript appeared to him as a prophecy, a map, a secret code. He could not explain it, but he could read it. A few pages remained.

Bones tugged on an ear. "I'm not at all sure you did the right thing, Perce."

Jeeves butted in before Percy could answer. "Of course, he did the right thing, sir. I have the gold, and you have my master's gratitude that says you can go free."

"See, Bonesy," said Percival P. Perkins, "as the brown book says, 'All's well that—' "

" 'Otters don't spoil,' " interrupted Jeeves again. Slipping deftly out of his butler's costume, Ollie pulled off his mask and grinned at the stunned detectives. Then Ollie moved to the door. "You two *are* free to go. Mama taught me to follow the rules. There's just one itsy-bitsy hitch. You have to find the way out. You can't pick this lock, no sir, and the room has a funny little way of getting smaller. Old Mugg used to call it 'The Swallower.' Clever, eh? If you can't get out, well, gobble, gobble, that's just toodly-too bad!"

Ollie shut and bolted the door, laughing all the while.

Inside the attic, things were not so cheery. The sound of grinding gears startled Percy and Bones. Below the tall dormer windows, a spiked wall emerged and moved steadily toward the mummies.

"Aw, Percy, I don't want to die like a pincushion."

"Now, now, old boy, chin up, ears down, nose to the wind, what what. Ollie may have betrayed us as Jeeves, but I'm guessing his clue is right about a way out."

The gears brought the wall toward them, foot by foot, ever closer, ever more threatening. The sharp spikes shone brightly.

Percy struck a bold pose. "We could wedge the armor against the wall. Pip, pip, old boy, let's go!"

Percy laid down one suit and Bones the other. Then they waited until the spiked wall, now only six feet from the mummy wall, reached the medieval wedge. The wall stopped. It groaned. Percy noted the burning gears.

"Ah," he remarked calmly, "like a bat out of the frying pan."

Then, as if a twig, the legs of the armor snapped, and the spikes came steadily on. Five feet to the mummies. Four feet. Percy and Bones grabbed the knights' broadsword and ax and jammed them in as stoppers. Those snapped. Three feet. The wall easily pushed the safe along.

"Percy, I just want you to know you've meant more to me than a ripe tomato in July. You're the best friend a dull ol' basset ever had." Bones wiped his tears with his ears. "Goodbye, Mr. Perkins."

"Nonsense, Bones," said Percy with a twinkle in his eyes. "Quick, open the mummy cases and get in. Maybe the spikes won't pierce the outside."

Percy and Bones opened the cases as best they could,

pushing against the spikes. To their surprise, there were no mummies to throw out. Bones imagined the magician's assistant in the box, the sword thrust in without hurting her. Simultaneously, he and Percy squeezed in and closed the lids.

But the spikes came on and crushed the mummy cases like termite-demolished logs.

By this time, of course, Percy and Bones were long gone, sliding down Old Mugg's ridiculous attic laundry chute until, plop, their screams were stopped by the dirty clothes in the basket in the garage. When Percy stepped out and pulled boxer underwear off Bones's head, they both turned to see Ollie backing up in a dandy Rolls Royce. Then Ollie sped away.

In two shakes and a whiskered sprint later, Percy hotwired the three-wheeler Morgan still in the garage and raced after Ollie. When the Rolls came in sight, Detective Perkins honked the horn and turned to his friend next to him. "Ah yes, Bonesy, don't you think there's a certain charm in that nasty thief? I even like the way his name rolls off the old wagger. Ollie Ollie Otterson. Ol-lie Ol-lie Ot-ter-son."

In a flash, Len became tense. He repeated Percy's last line. Then, he threw the manuscript aside and jumped up. "That's it! I don't want to believe it, but it must be true." He began to pace back and forth in his room. Then he darted back to the dresser, studied the map Percy used, reread the last page, and sat on the edge of his bed.

What should I do now? he thought. What *can* I do? I have to go back. I have to warn the others. He ran his hand over the bedspread, pulling off the pilled fabric and tossing the little balls onto the carpet.

Just then Percy meowed again at the back door. Len's hair stiffened, and goose bumps electrified him all over. He collected the manuscript pages.

Ominously, summoning the depths of primal courage, Len walked out of his room and toward the back door. A second face-off raced through his imagination, but this time with a different outcome: a ravaged Len carted off to the cougar's tree for a late night snack. He put the manuscript back on the kitchen table and went to the door. He turned on the outside light and peeked through the curtains.

No cougar. He looked down at the cement doorstep. Percy looked up and meowed.

Gratefully, Len opened the door and picked up the noisy cat. "Am I glad to see you, Mr. Perkins. I was beginning to think you were eaten by your cousin, Mr. Puma." Len examined the backyard while petting Percy's orange fur.

Maybe I imagined everything, he thought. Maybe I was daydreaming on my bed. How could there be a cougar in our backyard?

Then he saw massive paw prints in the lawn, leading toward the cedar. Len looked out toward the clawed tree. He noticed something shiny, maybe a slice of moonlight reflecting on wood where there was no bark. It glistened, intriguing him. Like a child, he felt that he *had* to know, he *had* to discover what glowed. Cautiously he stepped out of the house, his heart pounding.

The shiny spot flickered brighter with every step. He stared at the light—and he thought that it couldn't be just bare wood and moonlight. It was too bright, too extraordinary. There were colors. And they were moving.

At the tree, Len dropped Percy, who meowed and rubbed against his leg. Cautiously, his nerves poised for another attack, Len studied the shiny sliver. On the surface it was just an unnaturally bright claw mark, a place where the cougar dug deep into the tree. Len held his hand to shield the moon and streetlight from illuminating the gash in the bark. The claw mark shone brighter still. Gently, Len slipped a finger into the indentation. He felt no resistance. He slipped a fingernail on one side of the sliver and another fingernail on the other side. He tugged a little, and the sides gave way. Then he licked his lips.

Slowly but firmly, Len pulled and tugged at the borders. The light grew larger and brighter. Soon, he could put his hand inside. He tugged some more and peered inside. He could see Welken! Against the solid tree trunk, the light became fluid. Len stretched it larger yet and twisted it around. Adjusting his eyes to the objects in view, he realized he was seeing Welken from above, seeing Durrow Wood and the Great Alpine Reef to the north. Scanning the countryside, Len saw the Endel Inn to his left, the Nez River well up ahead, and to the right a path leading to the Window under the Mountain.

With excitement, Len realized that the zigzag trail mirrored Percy's sigma map.

By accidentally leaning on an edge, he learned he could influence what he saw. He grabbed the window like a steering wheel, and when he dipped and turned it, scenes changed and zoomed in and out. He pushed it over to the Endel Inn and saw Piers walking away from the building. "Hey, Piers!" he shouted, "I know what's going wrong!" But Piers did not respond.

He shifted the window down so he could zoom in lower. Like a pilot, Len maneuvered the opening here and there, searching for the other Misfits. There! He spotted Lizbeth running hard, maybe over to the Endel Inn, maybe higher up into the wood.

Where's Bennu and Angie? He steered the hole with more and more skill, looking out to Deedy Swamp, Primus Hook, and Mercy Bay. Feeling increasingly frantic, he pushed and tugged on the hole till he lost control and it snapped shut.

He jumped back. "Shoot! I can't have lost it! C'mon! C'mon! Where's the edge?"

He wiped his sweaty hands on his pants and went back to the light. He found the crease and spread it apart, this time more easily. Once fully open, the window's vantage point was higher up in the sky, about fifty feet above the ground somewhere northeast of the Endel Inn.

Just when Len was about to push down to get closer, a huge mass flew right beneath him, startling him so much that he nearly let go. Holding steady, he pulled up just a little so he could focus on these birds. But he didn't see birds. Instead, he saw Bennu and Angie being carried under the arms of some flying monster.

"Bennu! Angie!" he screamed. "Ah, it's no use. I wish I could tell them who, who—wait, I have an idea. I'll play the spy."

Hovering ten feet above, Len maintained his pursuit, deftly steering the window-wheel. Finally, the creature landed and whisked Bennu and Angie away somewhere in the woods between Skane Lodge and the face of the mountain range.

Len pushed down. He saw pine needles in the cover of a thick stand of evergreens.

X marks the spot, he thought, just like on the map.

Stepping into the passageway, Len heard the needles crunch against his feet. Before letting go, he stuck his head back in and took one last look at his yard and house.

Percy meowed near the base of the tree.

He appeared to be smiling.

PART FIVE

TO MAKE THE WELKEN RING

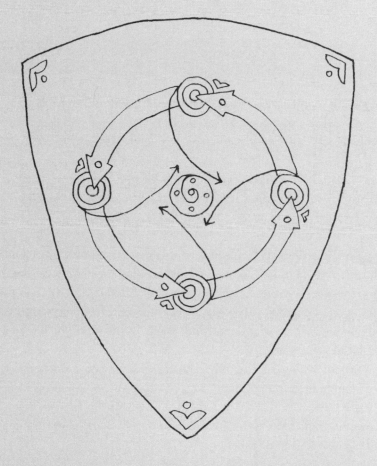

CHAPTER THIRTY-ONE
SWITCH

Love you? I am you.

ATTRIBUTED TO CHARLES WILLIAMS

 *Pain upon pain, failure upon failure, the suffering grew. In your world, I heard some say that water flows where it will, as if nothing could be done to resist the tide, or that troubles would eventually float away like so much flotsam and foam. But in the valley I traveled, I saw the water keep rising, threatening to become a flood. Yet what concerned me most were the events I knew to be coming. So many, so fast, so perilous.*

Crumpling onto Welken soil, Len rolled over and over until a fallen pine tree stopped him. This time he did not hit his head. The smell of skunk cabbage from nearby made him wish he'd at least hit his nose. Standing up, he attempted to get his bearings. All he knew was that he should be somewhere near Bennu and Angie. In that faith, he hid behind some bushes and waited.

Without really noticing what he was doing, Len crouched down, more leonine than ever. As he brushed his short mane out of his face, he felt his senses on alert. He kneaded his knees with his fingers. Ready to pounce, he sniffed the air for information, for aromatic clues that might register in his library of scents.

He smelled pine sap, then the skunk cabbage again, then something he had trouble deciphering. It was heavy and sharp-edged, a slicing, disturbing odor, something decaying. Then he knew. He smelled evil. He never thought a moral stance could be so palpably sensed, but this pungency struck his nostrils hard, stunning him. He leaned backward like a fighter eluding a jab. He remembered what Angie had told him, something from a letter Piers read in Chimney Cave. Bors had warned about the rancid odor of Morphane growing sweet.

No worries there, thought Len. The stench is real bad, worse than old tuna fish, worse than the decomposing rat I found last winter in the garage. I might gag to death. Maybe it's the thing that has Bennu and Angie.

Before he could decide what to do, Len heard a tramping noise from down the trail. He slunk deeper behind the bush and hunched over on all fours. If he'd had a tail, it would have been twitching. The steps churned closer. He hunkered lower yet, onto his belly, and narrowed his eyes. He prepared to pounce but drew in another long draft of the scent. Then he saw who it was. "Lizbeth!"

Lizbeth stumbled and caught herself. "L-L-Len?" She stood there panting, looking unsure.

Len rose from his hiding place. "It's OK. It's me, over here."

"Oh, Len, am I glad to see you! You scared me half to death."

"Good thing. If you kept going, you might have found the other half. Lizbeth, you won't believe what I've been through."

"Don't be so sure." Lizbeth gave Len an awkward hug. "I've been learning to believe all kinds of things lately."

"Yeah, well, Prester John and Ellen and me, we ran into this despicable toady-guy named Fatagar and—what am I saying? We don't have time to swap stories. Bennu and Angie are up ahead, I think, held prisoner by some flying thing. And it really stinks too. I mean literally."

"I smell something, too, but it's not all *that* bad."

"Well, my nose must be working better or something. Let's get off the path and out of sight. We need to figure out what to do."

"What are the options?" Lizbeth wiped sweat from her brow.

"Just go after them, I guess." Len looked down and fiddled with some pine needles. "I don't have the gift I got at the Tetragrammaton."

"You don't? Why not?"

"I'll tell you later. You still have yours, then? What does it do?"

"It moves dirt around. Pretty handy, really. I saved Mook's life with it, but then I gave it to him when we split up." She started to get choked up. "Alabaster Singing, she—"

"Great, we have no weapons." Len sat, his chin in his hands.

"Well, maybe we have one," said Lizbeth. "Remember when Piers said to think about him if we got in trouble? It works. I was about to get swallowed up by—"

"Shh, I'm getting a whiff of that stench again. From over here."

The two Misfits moved. Holding themselves so quietly they cringed at every crunch of a twig, Len and Lizbeth followed Len's nose. About seventy-five yards from where they found each other, Len led Lizbeth off the path to an opening in a grassy hillside. From a distance the open space looked like nothing more than a shadow on a knoll. Up close, it resembled a short mineshaft with an earthen overhang shielding the entrance.

They paused.

"They're in there," said Len. "At least 'it' is in here. Can you smell it?"

"Yeah. But either I can't smell it as well or I'm just willing to put up with more than you."

"Probably a little of both."

She pulled her hair back and adjusted her overalls. "Let's go."

With a courage born of fear and ignorance, Len charged through the opening, Lizbeth following. Immediately, Len knew this was no ordinary passageway. First, the fetid smell rushed them in oppressive waves. Then, sounds assaulted them. They heard not the voices of Bennu and Angie being tormented, not the dragging of chains or the slithering footsteps of rats, but words; single, hollow utterances that seemed to come trembling from the walls themselves.

"Unworthy."

"Shameful."

"Worthless."

Len looked to Lizbeth for support. But what he saw amazed him even more. Lizbeth walked on all fours, and horns emerged from her head. She had become an ox. Then he looked down and saw that, unbelievably, he walked the earth with paws. He shook his mane. He switched his tail. And, just as astounding, he hardly noticed when he had changed. He felt natural walking on all fours. Clearly, his leonine and her oxen qualities had moved from soul to body. With these transformations complete, Len the lion stared wide-eyed and disbelieving at Lizbeth the ox.

All this power, Len thought, is rippling through my amazing muscles. It's almost worth enduring this wretched smell. But what now? I suppose I can try to help Bennu and Angie as a lion—but how can I communicate with Lizbeth?

Just then, Len heard Lizbeth inside his mind, the way Piers sometimes spoke to them. "Len," she said, "can you hear me, or am I just making cow noises?"

"Yeah, I can hear you, but if you prefer, I could moo."

"Stay focused, Len. We've got to find Bennu and Angie."

"That's what's so great about you, Lizbeth. You know when to be all business, even when we just got ready for the zoo. OK, fine, we'll keep going."

Accidentally, for he was not yet at ease with his own bulk, Len brushed up against a wall. "Whoa, the wall moved, Lizbeth. I'm getting totally creeped out."

Then the hollow voices renewed their chant:

"Weaklings."

"Incompetent."

"Hated ones."

Len roared back. He didn't mean to, really. It just came.

Lizbeth poked him with a horn. "Stop it! We're not going to surprise anyone by roaring."

"Sorry." Len's tail slunk down.

Then, the dank tunnel opened into a kind of designed living space, not a cave. The smooth walls bore huge images of kings and queens, faded paintings of some old Welkenian history. Two lanterns illuminated the room.

Glad to have the stench fade somewhat, Len strolled around the room on his huge padded paws, examining the frescos. One king wore a

Celtic kilt and a pharaoh's headdress made out of feathers. A queen stood in full armor like Joan of Arc but held a sling for stones and wore a crown that resembled an American pioneer bonnet.

Lizbeth gestured toward one with her horns. "Too weird."

"Yeah, like the painter flipped through our history books and created a mishmash."

"Do you think these four are us, Len?"

"Don't be ridiculous. Why would you say that?"

"Well, everywhere we go in Welken, there are messages about us, like we used to be here or that someone knew we were coming." She looked up at one of the queens. "Maybe I'm wrong, but Wise Dominic said to pay attention to fours."

"I know. Finally, I'm paying attention."

As Len studied the painted king closest to the entryway, the king's lips became three-dimensional. He whispered, "Destroy."

Quickly, more of the king came to life. From the entryway, the fleshy sides of the tunnel crept along the painted walls of the ancient room, taking on the images as it covered them. Then the king emerged from the wall, alive, or, at least, moving like a giant marionette. It threw one arm around Len's lion neck and muzzled his dangerous mouth with the other.

As Lizbeth set herself to charge into the king, a painted queen popped off the wall, shouted, "Defile!" and blocked Lizbeth's path. The queen grabbed Lizbeth's horns, twisting her oxen neck back and forth.

Without expression, the animated paintings dragged Len and Lizbeth deeper into the room, through an arched opening and into a cold, limestone cell. Torches burned, and the smoke rose through a hole open to the sky.

Against one wall stood a cell of iron bars, like an old zoo cage. Into it the king threw Len and locked the door. Toward the opposite wall, the queen took Lizbeth, pushing her head into a heavy wooden yoke chained to the wall. Once the top and bottom parts of the yoke were fastened together, the queen joined her husband at the door. In unison they accused once more, rising in volume with each word.

"Unwanted!"

"Unimportant!"

"Cursed!"

When they left, Len paced in his cell, rubbing his flanks against the bars. Across the room, Lizbeth tugged on the chain until the heavy yoke hung like a barbell across her neck. Before long she lay down and sighed.

Then Len noticed they were not alone.

In a birdcage hung on the wall to Len's right and Lizbeth's left, a falcon clutched a rod and occasionally snapped his head in an attempt to throw off a hood covering. Opposite him, illuminated by two torches, her wrists and ankles held by wide leather straps, an angelic creature lay weeping, her two pale blue wings faintly visible. A blindfold covered her eyes.

Len recognized these forms instantly. "Bennu! Angie!"

"Len?" said Bennu from under the hood. "I heard a commotion in the room, but I never guessed it would be you."

Angie lifted her blindfolded head. "Oh, Len, are you here to rescue us?"

"I wish. But I'm in a cage, and Lizbeth is stuck in a yoke chained to the wall."

"So you are a lion, and Lizbeth is an ox?" said Angie. "As strange it sounds, that doesn't surprise me."

"And you, Ang," said Len, "we can't see you well, but you now have wings."

"Really? I don't feel all that different."

Bennu rocked on his perch. "Of course, you don't. You didn't have as far to go as the rest of us."

"Is this really the time for sappy compliments?" asked Len.

Lizbeth snorted and stomped a hoof on the ground. "Let's get back on track."

"I don't get it," said Bennu.

Len pressed his nose between the bars. "What don't you get?"

"Don't you see? This place, this prison, has been waiting for us, just us, with special ways to hold each of us, individually. Morphane couldn't have done this."

"I know," said Len.

"Wait, you two, wait." Angie rose to her knees and pulled against her leather ties. Her whole body shone as brightly as Len had ever seen. "Do you hear it? Something is coming to my ears not as sounds but as an image."

"I don't hear or see anything," said Lizbeth.

"Don't talk." Angie pulled her bound hands toward her chest in an imaginary hug. "I keep seeing the ginger cat with the warm green eyes."

"Don't go cosmic on us, Ang," said Len. "We need you."

She cocked her head. "The ginger cat, the one who listens to you if you speak, like I did there at the tree houses, the one who—"

Angela.

Angie froze. Len heard it, too.

Angela, Leonard, Elizabeth, Horace, I know you are here and I know your fears. What you do not know is that The Welkening is coming. The Welkening! So hurry. So. One word is all you need. One word will guide you.

"What word, Piers?" asked Len. "How will a word help?"

Lizbeth, remember the day on the Nez River? asked Piers. *Remember what happened before you ran?*

"How could I forget?"

Piers's voice faded.

"Piers," said Lizbeth, "speak up."

Piers's voice came as soft as a waning sunset. *One word. One word is all you need to know: Switch.*

"Piers!" yelled Lizbeth. "Piers, come back!"

As his voice slipped over the horizons of their minds, no one spoke for a moment. Then Bennu said, "Switch? Switch?" His words mimicked the short, snapping moves of his head. "What does he mean by switch?"

"Sounds like a kid's game," said Len. "What's the point of that? I'm not in the mood for games. I'm feeling pretty stuck." He dragged a claw across three or four bars.

"I'm not sure what he means." Lizbeth's tone of voice sounded to Len wearier than her words. "But I do know this. Somehow when I was about to be taken by Morphane, Piers and I switched places. I don't know what happened exactly, but I felt like I was inside his head. Then, suddenly, I realized that Morphane was distracted and I could get away. Maybe switching, whatever it is, is just part of the way Welken is set up. But I don't see how thinking about Piers now would do us any good."

"This probably sounds dumb," said Bennu, "but remember when we used to play that storytelling game we called 'switch'? One of us would begin a story, then switch to the next person."

"And that's supposed to help us?" Len tried to restrain his sarcasm. "I don't see how."

Angie fluttered her wings. "I think I do. Listen. One thing we can still do while we're tied up is imagine stories. Maybe that's the kind of switching we're supposed to do."

"I know what I'd like," said Lizbeth. "I'd like to switch places with you, Angie. Anything to get out of this yoke. It weighs a ton."

Len's tail twitched back and forth. "If you could do that, that would be something."

"I feel a story coming," said Angie. "Here's what I see: Piers is coming over to me. He whispers to me that the voices are wrong, that I am not shameful, hated, cursed. Instead, I am wanted, loved, blessed. Then he takes my hand. The bindings mean nothing to him. We walk lighter than air over to Lizbeth, but we're held up. Why? I'm not sure. Wait. I can't get in. Somehow, Lizbeth needs to leave."

"I'm working on it." Lizbeth pawed at the ground with one hoof. "It's hard to believe I can move anywhere with this yoke weighing me down."

"Just close your eyes and see it, Lizbeth," said Angie. "Your imagination isn't in the yoke. Tell a story. Piers comes and unlocks the yoke. And I have a hunch we should all do this at once. Everyone, tell your story. Switch!"

Len assumed each Misfit wove a tale about Piers walking up, reaching out, and helping. But when he tried, he remembered all his own flippancy, his anger and doubt, his ridicule of the others. He walked to the wall, away from the bars. Slumped over, he buried his head in remorse under his massive paws. If lions can weep, Len did so. When he pictured Piers, the Welken leader threw off his cloak and pointed threateningly to him and reminded him that he had abandoned Prester John and Ellen. Len could not imagine Piers opening the door. He couldn't imagine Piers opening his arms.

Then he felt a nudge.

Poking Len with his beak, Bennu squawked, "Switch, switch. I need to get in."

Len arched his back and raised his head. He saw Piers opening the cell door with both hands. Dumbfounded, Len couldn't tell if he was dreaming or telling a story—or if a story was being told to him. "Come, Len," Piers said, his palms open in welcome. "It is your turn to switch. All you are and all you've done must come. For Angie's sake, come. For Bennu and Lizbeth's sake, come." Meekly, Len rose and walked out of the cage, his tail sweeping the floor behind him.

The next thing he knew, Len couldn't move or see. Blindfolded, with all four ankles bound together with leather straps, Len realized that he had literally switched into Angie's place. In seconds, Len shredded the straps and clawed off the blindfold. Then he saw that the other Misfits had likewise switched. Angie, her neck inside Lizbeth's yoke, easily slipped out of the ox-sized hole. Lizbeth exploded out of Bennu's birdcage, his cloth hood spinning for a moment on one horn. In a much larger birdcage, Len's cell, Bennu flew between bars too wide to hold him.

Len said, "Let's get out of here. Don't hesitate. Run."

"Meet you outside," said Bennu. "Angie and I will go up through the skylight."

Len and Lizbeth charged out of the cell, past the kings and queens, and into the tunnel. As the rancid walls groped out toward them, they kept straight ahead, Len first because he was faster. Paws and hooves pounded swiftly down toward the exit.

Len guessed what would happen next. The light to the outside started to close up like a shrinking lens. As the fleshy walls came together, he leaped claws first through the gap, brushing against the slimy stuff. It could not hold him. He landed outside on his front paws and turned back for Lizbeth. She lowered her head and rammed the opening with all of her speeding bulk, gashing the shrinking wall with her horns.

It gave way. Skidding on the grass outside, Lizbeth struggled to maintain her balance and finally fell onto the ground.

Before he recovered, Len saw the entryway to the prison churn around, draw itself together, and pull itself off the interior walls. It molded and shaped itself into a wheel. In shock, Len looked over to Lizbeth. She was no longer an ox; neither was he a lion.

"Just as we thought!" shouted Bennu down to Len and Lizbeth. He stood on the hill above the door, not as a falcon. Angie stood by his side without wings. "As soon as we landed here, we changed back."

"The thing in front of you is part of Morphane," said Angie. "We don't know how, but it can change into any shape, even us. It's what brought us here. It told me it calls itself Malleal the Resembler. We've got to get away from it."

Then Malleal rolled toward Lizbeth. Aghast, Len watched Bennu leap off the hill, a ten-foot drop-off. Instantly, Bennu changed back into a falcon and dove at the monster. He swiped with his talons, right where Lizbeth had gored it. Malleal stumbled as it rolled, and fell over. In its own way it heaved and sighed, as if trying to catch its breath.

Bennu landed on his talons that swiftly changed back into feet. After Angie joined them, all four Misfits cautiously watched vacant faces come and go on Malleal's fluid surface. Then they merged into the landscape.

"It felt great hurting it," said Lizbeth, "but now, I don't feel so good."

Angie put her arm around Lizbeth. "All the more reason to hurry."

Turning back toward the path, the Misfits resolved to go toward the mountains, to Ganderst Hall if they could find it.

CHAPTER THIRTY-TWO
A KISS OF FIRE

For, it was to be seen with half an eye that he was a thorough gentleman, made to the model of the time; weary of everything and putting no more faith in anything than Lucifer.

CHARLES DICKENS, *HARD TIMES*

 For the first time during their stay in Welken, the Misfits observed a sunset. To their left, beyond the Nez River, the sun's last yawn sent colors stretching into the sky. Yellow hues glistened on the horizon as orange plumes shot softly into the drifting madras. Soon, the night would come on, and the vulnerable, heart-pounding dark.

Lizbeth tried to keep her thoughts on the path and the Misfits' mission, not on the forest noises and the silhouettes of gnarled trees. "You won't believe what happened to me. Mook and Alabaster and I were knee-deep in water when I saw a waterfall up ahead. But they didn't see it. Then we stepped right through it and felt nothing, like it was a movie!"

"Me too." Len held up his hands as if to say wait. "I saw the Wasan Sagad—this tower in the Wasteland, and—"

Angie interrupted Len silently. She glowed. In the growing darkness, she cupped her wings toward the path, and they shone enough bluish light to guide their steps.

Len darted into the blue light and turned around. "We've got to hear these stories one at a time. I think I should go first. What I learned could affect us any minute."

"You always go first, Len," said Lizbeth assertively. "And you always have a good reason. You'll probably ignore what I say as usual, but I think I should tell you what happened to me. It matters more than you realize."

"C'mon, Lizbeth, how is that possible?" Then Len paused and dropped his shoulders submissively. "Y'know, Lizbeth, you're right, I do throw my weight around—such as it is. You go."

Lizbeth was so unaccustomed to being deferred to, especially by Len, that she blushed. She wondered what could have possibly brought about this kind of behavior in Len. "Thanks, Len. The worst of it is very bad. Alabaster Singing is dead. There were water snakes—basilisks they call them—they had teeth all over. I used the gift I got, but I was so slow getting to her. Typical clumsy me. The basilisks bit her everywhere. It was terrible."

Bennu put one hand on her shoulder. "Oh, Lizbeth, I never thought anyone would die. And to lose Alabaster . . . Remember her song in Ganderst Hall? Her words filled me up. I can't believe she's gone." Bennu stopped. "Can we wait here a minute?"

Without answering, the other Misfits stood by Bennu. They held hands in silence. Then Angie's glow dimmed, and her tears fell to the ground. The tears shone as they dropped, gathering on the path into tiny pools of light.

ॐ

Len felt himself feeling certain things for the first time. He tried to picture himself in Lizbeth's place, watching someone die, trying to help, not being able to help. Then he heard a voice.

I have a message for you.

Len squeezed Angie and Lizbeth's hands. "Did you hear that?"

"Yes," said Lizbeth. "I heard someone say, 'I have a message for you.'"

The voice came again. *You must keep searching for the tiles.*

"Piers, right?" said Bennu.

"Shh," said Lizbeth.

I know you are weary, but the food of success will revive you. Up ahead you will come to a fork in the trail. Len and Angie, go to the left. Before long

319

you will come to a giant cedar in the middle of the path. Look for a tile there.
Bennu and Lizbeth, go to the right. You will see me waiting for you.

"But, Piers," shouted Lizbeth. "Without Angie, we can't see!"

No answer followed.

"In Welken, of Welken," added Lizbeth clumsily.

In the silence that followed, they stopped holding hands.

"I don't like this," said Bennu. "Why do *we* have to walk in the dark?
I don't like this at all."

"You don't like a lotta things," said Len, immediately sorry he'd said it.

Bennu pushed Len. "Hey, you've got Angie for a lantern."

Lizbeth stepped between them. "We don't have time to argue. You
heard Piers. Bennu and I go to the right. You two take the left. Angie, we
haven't heard from you."

Angry about his anger, Len kicked the path in disgust.

"Well," Angie said, "I don't see the cedar."

Lizbeth gently shook Angie, as if trying to awaken a sleepwalker.
"Angie, we aren't even at the fork yet. Of course, there's no cedar here."

"Oh," she said faintly, her wings fluttering enough to scatter the light.

"C'mon, Angie," said Len. "We need you to help us find the way."

Angie closed her eyes as if she were looking for the cedar on her eyelids. She opened them, cupped her wings, and started walking. The light
illumined tiny white flowers in the grass at the edge of the path.

After a short while, the Misfits found the fork. Bennu said, "See,
we're going to be fine." As Lizbeth and Bennu moved out to the right,
Angie directed her light that way for a few steps down the trail.

⣿

With illumination, Len and Angie walked hard, then jogged. When the
path took a downward turn, they broke into a run. Then Len became a
lion, transforming as fast as a hand becomes a shield when something is
thrown at the face. In her angelic form, Angie flew just above Len, dodging the occasional overhanging branch but keeping a beam focused ahead
of Len's surging paws.

"I don't see it," said Angie.

"That's OK," said Len. "It'll come. Let's keep going."

320

Len ran through a break in the trees and then uphill. On the rise the path circled back around to a hollow. Len stopped and panted heavily.

"I don't see it," said Angie.

"I don't either. It should be around here, shouldn't it? Piers tells the truth, right?"

"Of course. But I'd feel better if I could see it, be sure of it in my mind, picture it as Piers would want me to, with him waiting there for me in his green vest."

"Piers wears a green tunic, Angie. Wait, I smell something, something fresh. Shine your light over there to the right. Those trees there in a line like they were planted. There's one in front. I see the cedar."

As Len bounded over a fallen willow trunk, he motioned toward an enormous cedar, its outline shimmering against the star-jeweled sky.

Angie followed, looking troubled. "Where is it? I only see the line of trees you say are behind the cedar."

"Really? It looks just like the one in our backyard. Wait a minute." Len lifted his head and roared. "I know why you don't see the cedar. It's all in Percy and Bones. I'm so stupid. I should have thought of it right away. We've got to get out of here. Hurry!"

⚮

Lizbeth had asked Bennu if they could hold hands, in part to calm her nerves, in part to have something to hold when one of them tripped. And she did, stubbing her toe. "There's got to be an easier way." Lizbeth acted as if she had some real option available to her.

And then she remembered that she did. She became an ox. Bennu changed, too, and perched himself on her back while Lizbeth clumped down the trail. Crushing the smaller twigs that would have troubled her human feet, Lizbeth boldly pushed through the darkness. They rounded a sharp bend, and the path descended steeply to the right under overhanging branches. They reverted to human form so they could duck under the branches, and then below them they saw a campfire blazing. Someone bent over the fire to throw a stick on. He turned and waved to them.

Bennu leaned forward. "It's Piers!"

They scrambled downhill as fast as they could by the light of the campfire. Piers smiled. Just before they came up to him, another familiar face came out of the darkness to greet them.

"Lizbeth! Bennu!" said Terz, "I've missed you so much." He hugged them both. "I'll bet you've had enriching adventures at every turn. You've kept a sunny attitude, I hope."

"Terz," said Lizbeth breathlessly, "being reunited with you and Piers is just so awesome. I'm sure everything's going to be great now."

"I'm sure it is too," said Terz, "but then I always am." He laughed a little at his own expense, then led them over to Piers.

Bennu smiled broadly at Piers, thrusting out his hand for Piers to shake. As Lizbeth sidestepped over to receive a hug from Piers's other arm, she looked at Bennu's hand. To her horror, Piers's hand was growing over his, overtaking it, enveloping it. Bennu screamed. Then Piers's other arm spread over Lizbeth like a net, stretching into smelly tendrils of rope. Piers wrapped his substance around Bennu and Lizbeth until they gagged from the stench.

Bennu coughed. "So, if this isn't Piers," he said, "who are you, Mr. Terz?"

"Oh, I'm Terz all right, the one and only, optimistic Terz. I've always been me, charming little me. But I'd rather not be called Terz. I prefer to be called the Master."

When Terz closed his eyes, the glow from the fire created grisly shadows on his face. "Sometimes I can scarcely endure the ecstasy." He inhaled Malleal's flesh slowly and deeply. "The aroma of conquest, so sweet, so delicious. I understand now the warrior's lust for the battlefield, the thrill of a wide field of corpses." He opened his eyes to see that Malleal had grown over the two Misfits, had enclosed them in a netlike prison cell. Bennu and Lizbeth pulled on the net. "You shouldn't trouble yourselves," he said condescendingly. "You won't get out like you did before."

Lizbeth put her face up to the net and suppressed her gag reflex. "Terz, what are you doing? Why are you capturing us? I thought you were one of us, but you're a traitor. You make me sick!"

Terz stepped up on a tree stump, making him almost nose to nose with Lizbeth. "Dear girl, how pale my flaws before the brightness of your folly."

Lizbeth stopped yanking on the net and sat glumly in the fetid cell.

The betrayal added to her sense of captivity. She thought, How could someone we trusted want to destroy us? How could Piers not know? If he knew, why didn't he do something? And what should we do now, become suspicious of all good things? Or did we miss some signs along the way? I don't know what I'm supposed to learn from this. But maybe there's nothing to learn. We're just trapped. That's all.

She looked at Bennu sitting on the ground. "Get up. We've got to try harder to get out."

"What's the use?" Bennu scratched at the dirt with a stick.

"Get up!" Lizbeth hit Bennu in the shoulder. "We've both been given tools we haven't even used yet."

"What tools? Terz has my air gift and your box of power dirt!"

"I know!" Then she said softly, "But I have horns, and you have a beak made for shredding."

Bennu faced the net. Once he changed into a falcon, he gripped the rope with his talons and tried to sever the lines with his beak. Malleal shuddered slightly as he did. And the whole cage trembled when Lizbeth thrust her horns through the holes and shook her head violently. Yet the net held; it simply yielded a little and held.

Lizbeth watched Terz circle the fire, all the while muttering to himself. Then he ran back to his prize hostages. Curiously, to Lizbeth, he did not seem surprised to see them as ox and falcon. "Hmm, hmm, hmm," he said, "things are working out nicely. Oh, you two will come around. You'll see that all of this is necessary to bring about a New Welken, a Welken with fewer rules, with less need for deference. Now, let's see, what should Master Terz do next? I so dislike waiting. In the meantime, you two should just enjoy this peaceful moment."

As Terz walked toward his knapsack, Lizbeth tugged at the net, hoping to discover a weak spot or to wear the beast down. But Malleal always snapped back, making the Misfits' maneuvers futile. So they changed strategies. Bennu took to nibbling on one small strand while Lizbeth smashed a section with her hoof. As she did, the net pushed down on her back and snaked a tentacle toward her head.

Then Lizbeth saw above her head the tear from her earlier attack at the mineshaft. She lunged up and dug her horn into the wound. Malleal emitted a lone high-pitched scream. It retracted and loosened its grip on Lizbeth's hide.

Then Bennu said, "I'm nearly through this first thread, Lizbeth. It's just so hard to grip, and the taste is disgusting."

Terz sat down next to the knapsack. "You Misfits don't appreciate the world-changing things I'm working on." Then he shook the contents on the ground. "You must be in here, you little gifts of the Tetragrammaton. Come to Terz."

Bennu severed one strand and managed to poke his falcon head through the hole, but he couldn't get his wings free. "Help," he said. "This thing is choking me."

Lizbeth flailed away at Malleal with her horn. He seemed to loosen his grip around Bennu's neck.

Then Lizbeth felt overcome with urgency. She realized that at this moment, everything teetered on a precipice. Bennu leaned out but was nearly strangled. She stabbed toward a fatal blow but risked becoming further enmeshed. And there was Terz, scrambling to find the powerful gifts of water and air from the Tetragrammaton that Malleal had stolen from Angie and Bennu.

Just when Lizbeth thought that things could not look bleaker, a fierce, howling growl cut through the night. It roared of terror and strength, an angry, scathing call for vengeance and blood, a furious sound rising and rushing toward them.

Terz turned hopefully to the sloped path above the fire. Lizbeth's shoulders fell. She withdrew her horn and looked over at the Bennu. "It's Morphane," she said.

Racing down the hill, the great beast came, nearly flying under the willowy branches above him. Lizbeth's heart stopped as she scanned up the trail. But something wasn't right. He wasn't large enough. Then she saw a light above, a crisp, cool beam emanating from two vibrantly blue wings. It wasn't Morphane. It was Len, in the fullness of leonine fury, and Angie, racing to the aid of their friends.

The smile on Terz's face quickly fell. He fumbled through the scattered contents that covered the ground. Lizbeth saw him toss them around: socks, a spool of thread, a hunting knife; every item except Angie's water vial and Bennu's air powers.

Terz glanced up. Len bounded out from under the branches and ran straight toward them, his teeth glistening in the firelight. Terz looked down again and sorted through things in haste. "I'm supremely confident." He looked up again, discarding items haphazardly. Angie's beam glowed white. "I'm the Master . . . of so many things." He turned more frantically to the items before him, throwing off a red woolen cap, some rope, a tin cup. Then he pulled to his chest a floppy fabric and twine package. "Ah, just as Malleal gave it to me."

He shot his head up again, just in time to be bowled over by Angie. He held tight to the package. As she swooped around for another pass, Terz crawled back to the scattered materials, grasping the knife.

"Over here!" Lizbeth shouted to Len. "Get Bennu out, then come back to me!"

Chest heaving from the long run, Len looked at the net. His paw shook from exhaustion. Deftly, he slipped a claw into a strand torn by Bennu and tugged. Bennu flew out.

Lizbeth pointed with her horn. "Over here, it's the place I hurt before—at the mineshaft. Maybe both of us can rip it open."

Len lurched toward Lizbeth but did not move. Then Lizbeth saw that Malleal had encircled his hind legs. Len clawed at the ropelike fetter and then stretched out to see if he could reach Lizbeth's damaged opening.

Len roared. "How can we get out of a prison that moves? By the time you get free, I'll be trapped."

"You're right. Let's wait a second, and maybe we'll think of something."

Above them, Bennu screeched righteously and circled above Terz. When Angie shone her light into Terz's eyes, Bennu dove. Talons extended, he blindsided the distracted Terz, tearing at his shoulders through his thick coat. Terz popped his fist back to smack away the falcon. Bennu careened off, regrouped, and swooped again. He dug with his talons. This time Terz screamed. He dropped the knife. As Bennu flew up and away, Terz watched him ascend, and he ducked several times before Bennu even began his next dive. Then Angie's right wing clipped him under the chin and knocked him another step away from the knife. Terz groped around after it.

"Come!" Terz shouted to Malleal. "Come! Do something." He swatted the air, swinging wildly to fend off the dive-bombing Misfits. Bennu drew blood on Terz's forearm. Terz dropped the gift momentarily, examined the blood flowing down to his hand, and then picked up the package again. He shook his wrist as if to cast off the pain.

Lizbeth cheered for Bennu and Angie, and then struck at Malleal again. She missed. At Terz's command, Malleal started shifting forms. It released Len and Lizbeth and slunk back into its original shape, a wheel, only now it was more damaged. Haltingly, it rolled toward Terz.

"Not a wheel!" Terz looked up from wrestling with the knot on the package. "A monster! A beast with nine heads! A living claw!" Malleal the Resembler rolled awkwardly forward, stopped next to the fire, and took on the image of the flame.

"Yes, fire!" Terz scooted toward the knife on his knees. "Be fire!" He grabbed the gash above his wrist and winced in pain. Then Angie stormed toward him, and Len and Lizbeth charged. Malleal blazed enough to brighten the sky but did nothing else. Bennu rose and screeched a victory cry. At the zenith of his ascent, he turned, tucked in his wings and bolted down behind Angie. She knocked Terz on his back, causing his coat to fly open. Then Bennu dove in and struck Terz's chest. His talons tore. Bennu held on and stabbed with his beak.

Shrieking, Terz punched Bennu away. He forced himself up again on his knees. With Len and Lizbeth nearly upon him, he scrambled forward, grabbed the knife, and popped the tie. Ignoring his bleeding chest and arm, he threw open the cloth and stirred the invisible substance with his finger. A whirlwind grew upward and swirled above him.

Afraid, Lizbeth stopped—and Len did too. Then Terz twisted the funnel harder, and it rose mightily into the sky, blowing back Terz's short, thick, brown hair. Lizbeth saw that Bennu and Angie hesitated in midair. They struggled to hold their positions as the wind increased.

Squinting now against the gale force, Terz held the corners of the cloth and tipped it over toward Angie and Bennu. The wider top of the funnel followed the downward pull of the tip, spinning violently. Terz steered the cyclone skillfully, sending Bennu tumbling helplessly out of the battle zone, feathers flying. Angie, too, could not resist the raging wind. Her attempt to get under it left her flat on the ground, relentlessly pummeled by the whirling air. Face down, she tucked her wings as tight as she could to her body. Terz concentrated his efforts on her. He held the base of the tempest like Zeus, gleefully punishing those who didn't appreciate his deity. Tilting this way and that, the wind obeyed Terz's manipulations. He slammed the top edge of the cyclone repeatedly at Angie's head, pounding her into the grass.

Then Len and Lizbeth slipped around behind Terz's unprotected backside. As she trotted, Lizbeth saw Terz play with the wind's power. He reached out one hand to caress the base of the funnel, to feel the energy he controlled. He let his hand bounce off the whirling wind. Then he must have sensed danger behind him. As he jerked around to see what was coming, his caressing hand instinctively clutched what was nearby. It was the cyclone. He plunged his hand in up to his wrist. While the surface wind repelled, the inner suction pulled him fiercely. Terz tried to leverage against the cyclone with his free hand, but then it too slipped into the vortex.

Standing now with the base of the cyclone dropping to his feet, Terz had no choice but to face the driving whirlwind. He leaned back to avoid its force. With both hands enmeshed, he could not lean far enough. He strained against it with all his might, his skin and clothes taking a pounding, and his exposed wounds getting cut up by the daggers of the spinning wind.

Angie looked up from her suddenly becalmed place in the grass. To Len and Lizbeth, she yelled, "Now!" But Lizbeth was already pounding toward Terz, Len behind her. She slammed her oxen body into Terz, knocking him clean out of the cyclone. The jolt broke the cyclone from its source, the gift from the Tetragrammaton that had been entrusted to Bennu. The twister rose into the sky and quickly dissipated.

Without pause Len switched into his human form and picked up the substance and the cloth. Lizbeth, panting, changed back as well. She found a string among the strewn knapsack contents and bundled the blobby gift back into a tidy package.

In the meantime Bennu reverted back into his regular body and held Terz until Len came over with some rope to tie his hands behind his back.

"You shouldn't crush my pride like this, you Misfits," Terz said. "You won't like me when I'm truly angry."

By the time Lizbeth made it over to see if Angie was OK, the angel was spreading her wings out full and ruffling the feathers until they all slipped back into place. "Look for the vial," Angie said, "the water vial that I received." She brushed the dust and dry grass from her clothes and hair. "It's cold and fluid and icy and surging and warm." Lizbeth noticed how her hair seemed as knowledgeable as her feathers, rearranging itself into cascading blond neatness. She brushed back her own hair with her fingers.

The Misfits kept their distance from the still burning Malleal. Lizbeth repacked the knapsack.

"Eventually, I'll win," Terz said. "The optimists always do. I don't doubt myself. All I have to do is think positively, and I will achieve my goals."

Bennu turned to Len. "Can you find a rag to stuff his mouth?"

"If you knew what I know," Terz paused and winced from his cuts and bruises, "you'd let me help you find your true selves. That's what it's about really, just being yourself."

"Hurry up!" yelled Bennu. "I want to let go and rest."

A roar responded to Bennu.

"You don't have to impress me, Len," said Bennu. "I *know* you're the king of the forest."

Len's voice shook. "I didn't say anything, Bennu."

Then they all heard it again, only louder, a low grinding growl, a halting, cackling roar that enlarged whatever pit lay in their stomachs.

This time, the real Morphane had arrived.

From his knees, Terz called out to him. "That's it, my pet, come to the Master."

In disbelief, Lizbeth looked at Terz and then back at Morphane. She thought, how could Terz be lord over Morphane? Wasn't Morphane the danger on the loose?

From the other side of the fire, opposite the path that the Misfits had come down, Morphane stood tall. Legs straight, tail switching, Morphane cocked his head toward Terz. The golden fur on his shoulders tensed up and then relaxed. He seemed confused. He acted like he knew he should go to the Master's voice, but that something else competed for attention. He walked slowly, haltingly. As the sea of faces swirled over his, Morphane grew more unstable with every step. He shook his head wearily, as if this tactic might dislodge these parasites that wore him down.

He bounded around the edge of the fire towards Terz. About every third or fourth step, he stumbled or thrust his head off to the side awkwardly or spun around to attack some invisible intruder.

Lizbeth's sense of triumph fell like a stone. Confused or not, Morphane was an unleashed terror, a threat more frightening than his enormous girth. Unconsciously, she changed back to an ox, and she saw that the others had switched back to their Welken-shapes also. Unfortunately, as a falcon Bennu could not hold Terz down with only his talons around the rope. Terz ran toward Morphane, and the Misfits gathered by the knapsack.

"We can't charge directly," said Len. "We can't fight Morphane while staring right at him."

Bennu landed on Lizbeth's back. "C'mon! We have to think of something to do!"

No one admitted it out loud, but Lizbeth knew they had panicked. In the uncaged roar of Morphane, they'd heard the caged souls, their voices desperate and aching for help. This unrestrained suffering caught them off guard. Instead of running away or attacking, they watched.

Lizbeth would say she couldn't help it, any more than she could take her eyes off the glimpses or the river of light. Welken's good was too good not to enjoy—but its evil was breathtaking also, even the sight of Morphane nuzzling Terz.

His bindings discarded by Morphane, Terz stroked the monster's neck and chin, and Malleal shifted from fire to wheel and rolled over to join forces. Terz shouted to the Misfits. "Don't be dismayed! It's inevitable that I rule. You'll see. All will be well when you accept the New Welken. Come. Look into Morphane. You will see the blazing truth of your own future." He fingered the wound in his chest.

Then Terz faced Morphane himself, as if to model his suggestion. His eyes wide and welcoming, Terz, standing as tall as he could, stared directly into the display roiling over Morphane's ears and eyes and nose. He seemed to invite the power to do whatever full surrender would permit it to do.

And still the Misfits watched.

Terz leaned over. His face met Morphane's nose to nose. Then, unbelievably, it went in, not detached like the others, not tormented over the terrible beast's features, but inside, as if he had dipped his head underwater to see what lived beneath the surface.

The Misfits gasped.

Then with a flourish, Terz whipped his head back and ran his fingers through his stubby hair. Morphane licked his Master on the chin.

To Lizbeth, Terz looked different. He seemed taller and stronger. But she couldn't tell if his eyes glowed because they reflected the fire or if they possessed some new power within. Lizbeth wasn't sure if now this face, like Morphane's, contained a trapped soul flowing over the shape of his rage. But she felt sure that Terz had more fully crossed some canyon he'd only dreamed of crossing before. His countenance had changed. It was as if he'd paused at the banks of sorrow, filled his cupped hands to the brim, and swallowed. He did not shudder. He did not bend over and wretch. He drank, and to him, it must have tasted good.

While the Misfits reeled back from this sight, the unholy trinity came at them. As Malleal rolled along the edge of the fire, Terz walked straight ahead, and Morphane swept out to the left to outflank the Misfit's escape.

When Lizbeth turned to flee, she heard a voice so rich and true, it slapped against the images of Terz that had dulled and overwhelmed her.

"I grieve," Angie said, hovering above them. "I grieve."

Under the blue light shining from her wings, Angie opened the vial she had lost in the boat on Mercy Bay.

Len changed back into his human body and searched frantically through the knapsack. "We've got to find a canteen of some kind. Angie needs water. She needs something for the power to act upon."

The flame rolled closer. Morphane's paws, twice the size of Len's, turned the soil with every leap. Terz, in the middle, eyes glistening intensely, charged forward on his short, squatty legs. He didn't seem to mind the gashes on his chest and arm.

"Hurry!" Lizbeth shouted to Len.

"I grieve!" said Angie, this time with a tremble. Lizbeth and the others looked up. Angie poured one drop from the vial into the palm of her hand. And then her tears fell one by one into it. She began to sob freely, and these tears dripped straight down into her waiting hand. Once more she whispered, "I grieve," then she dropped the vial, and Len caught it. She held her palm to her mouth and blew, scattering the tiny drops.

The moisture gathered quickly and multiplied. A misty rain became a pouring rain, and the pouring became a solid sheet of water, a torrent that plunged down between the Misfits and their enemies. The sheet buckled as it hit the ground and crested into a mighty wave, crashing upon Morphane and Terz and Malleal. The three lost their balance and bobbed up and down helplessly in the rising flood. Sweeping out to the east, the water carried the betrayers of Welken out and away.

Angie fluttered down and sat with her arms around her knees. Her tears kept flowing.

CHAPTER THIRTY-THREE
RETRACING, RE-ERASING

Selves act in ways that choose their bodies, but bodies also create the selves who act. We can observe more of the first process than of the second; how bodies create selves is scarcely understood at all.

ARTHUR W. FRANK, *THE WOUNDED STORYTELLER*

 Heading, they hoped, toward Ganderst Hall, the four Misfits made their way back up to the main trail. By the time they got there, they had shaken off their battle nervousness, and just as a bright moon rose above the western horizon, Angie asked Len to recount what happened after he met Fatagar at the Wasan Sagad. As he did so, he felt doubly exposed, for he told of his shameful escape. A short while later, another moon followed, smaller and reflecting a bluer light.

"I can't believe I left Prester John and Ellen with that toad." Len threw up his hands. "I guess I should say that I *can* believe it. I'm selfish all the time. Anyway, it was back in Skinner that certain bizarre connections came to me.

"First I went to pick up the car at the museum. By the time I got close, I realized that nothing had happened the whole time I'd been in Welken. The McKenzie Boys were just getting out of the museum. I don't know how they escaped. They drove up to me, and Odin flipped some ancient coin to me, just like Ollie did in Mom's story."

Lizbeth nudged him. "Ollie did what?"

"Oh yeah. Mom's written more chapters. Anyway . . . when the Boys

332

left, I looked up to see the bell tower of the museum in flames. Then somehow it switched out, and I was staring at the Wasan Sagad. If that wasn't enough, that night I was reading Mom's latest chapter at home, with no one else in the house. Percy was at the back door, meowing to get in. I kept yelling at him to shut up. Everything started overlapping, like one of those see-through kid's books. In Mom's chapter, Percy and Bones caught up to Ollie in England at a run-down mansion."

"How'd he get there?" asked Bennu.

"It doesn't matter," said Len. "What am I saying? Everything does. Anyway, after more meowing from Percy, I finally opened the back door. A bona fide snarling cougar was there, not Percy. Even weirder, I scared it away—well, that's the short version—and I went back to my room to finish the chapter. At the very end, Percy says 'Ollie Ollie Otterson' real slow, sounding out the syllables. That's when I heard Terz's name—in the middle syllable—and I realized I had to get back to tell you, that I wanted to get back, not to be a hero but to make up for all the stupid things I'd done. Then when Angie and I were looking for the cedar, I remembered that the cougar had scratched our cedar. So I told Angie we must have been double-crossed by Terz, and we came tearing back to find you."

Angie pointed out that the smaller moon was so cute she half expected him to wink. "I know," she said to the man in the moon. "I know what awaits. I will stand in the fire and will not be burned."

Len squinted at the moon. "Angie, if you don't stand in a fire, you don't have to worry about it. OK, fine, have your little moon-fire story. Lizbeth, tell us about switching with Piers."

Lizbeth couldn't explain how the exchange worked. "But something just as mysterious happened when I was in Piers's head. I'm sure someone else was there, that someone was trapped in there. I've been worried about it ever since."

Then Bennu and Angie told their tales, about how they ended up together on Goffer's Spit and were captured.

"I don't know about you guys," said Bennu, "but all this talk makes me miss Sutton, Zennor, and the others. I hope they're OK." While Angie said, "Me too," Bennu grabbed at some tall weeds he expected would snap off easily. They didn't, jerking him back a little.

Yet Len knew that *his* traveling companions were not in good shape. Before he could say so, Lizbeth spoke. "Well, Alabaster Singing isn't OK." She held her forehead in her hand, eliciting a consoling hug from Angie, and she wiped tears from the corners of both eyes. "Mook said something about a Rising Ceremony. I hope it's real."

"Maybe we're just seeing them on their good days," said Bennu, "but Welkeners seem to agree about important things more than we do back home. In Skinner, I dunno, everything gets confused."

"I know what you mean, Bennu," said Angie. "Back home, we argue all the time about how to live, and then pretty much do what everyone else is doing, even if it tears us apart. But here, I can *see* what's good, I can *feel* it, *hear* it. In Welken if I let my wings become a sail, I can catch the currents of the true and beautiful." She leapt up and circled around them in the air, her white gown reflecting the moonlight.

Len came back to a question he thought the others were avoiding. "But what about the tiles? We're marching back to Ganderst Hall—we hope—as if we've been victorious, but the plain fact is we're returning with *less* than we took from the Tetragrammaton. Fatagar has the stone of fire, and Mook may still be in Nezzer with the earth-moving stuff. How can we do what we're supposed to do when we haven't done what we were supposed to have done?"

No one answered Len.

✿

Up ahead and to their right, the morning sun peeked over the mountains' tallest points and fell like a curtain on the Welken stage. In time a drape of light found the trail, and then all the Misfits bathed in its warmth.

That's when Len saw him. "Hey, look, someone's there. Let's be careful. It could be another trick." Len watched as Bennu and Angie flew over the figure sitting on a tree stump, circled once and landed. The two Misfits hugged whoever it was. "Not fair," said Len to Lizbeth. "Why can't lions fly?"

Lizbeth raised her eyebrows and broke into a full trot. "Piers!" she yelled. "We're coming!"

334

Once they arrived, Lizbeth hugged Piers, but Len hesitated. "How can we know you're the real thing?"

Piers looked tired. "Like you, I've been walking all night. Along the way, I have learned of Terz's betrayal."

Len stepped closer, checking Piers out up and down, looking for some sign of deception. "And you could be that Malleal thing in disguise."

"True enough." Piers held out his hands like a magician showing nothing up his sleeve. "Yet this is one of the risks of trust. Somehow we are to be shrewd and innocent at the same time. It's not easy. I had my suspicions, but I wanted to trust Terz. I wanted to believe my ideas more than the truth. Still, it's better to risk trust than to play the skeptic all our days. It grows wearisome, no?"

"Are you asking me?" said Len.

"No, I am reminding myself." Piers held out his hand to Len. "Come, I have much to tell. The Welkening is coming. I have been telling many others to gather at Granite Flats. You should know too."

Len took his hand and squeezed hard. He let go and smelled his palm. Nothing. "Yeah, the Welkening. Guess we'd better get up to speed on that. And we've been walking too. A break sounds good."

Everyone sat in the morning sun. "The first thing you must know is that Soliton has been speaking more frequently and more plainly than ever."

"Who is Soliton?" asked Len, trying not to assert only his skeptical self.

"Soliton is Welken's Maestro. He takes our feeble tunes and turns them into strong and loving melodies. He is the one behind and the one in front. He is the ever-teaching Tutor, the intervening Watcher, the compassionate Mender. Most of the time, we see him as the Becomer. And once our eyes grow true, we recognize him as the Weaver. But, of course, I say too much and too little at the same time."

"You're making me look like the master of clarity," said Angie. She laughed.

"Perhaps this will help. When I was a boy, I heard stories about Soliton, about his arrival in the land, about his oversight of Welken's ways, about his various appearances to Welkeners over time. One is called The Magic Lantern.

"After months of rain, when the ancestors of Sutton and Zennor and Bebba lost hope of ever again seeing the sun, a massive mudslide separated certain shepherds from their herd. As the rains continued, a boy named Gwion was awakened one night by a lantern shining by his head. Gwion followed the light to the mudslide. Guided each step by the lantern, Gwion found solid footing over the slippery terrain until he found the herd. He stayed with them, guarding them for weeks until the villagers could safely create a new trail and lead them back home.

"Deedy Swamp and the Prester Highlands and Primus Hook each have their own stories. Soliton might appear as a lantern in the night, a wolf to chase away intruders, or as was the case in Primus Hook, a silent beggar who confounded an ambitious thief. He's the Becomer. He becomes what gains an audience to those who will listen.

"And here's what I must tell you. Though I've never seen Soliton, I have known enough to keep walking, to keep making my way through Morphane's destruction, past Gandric's death, and Len's—well, the way he left Prester John and Ellen. But I don't feel the same way anymore."

"Do you mean," said Lizbeth, "that the betrayal of Terz has made you want to stop following Soliton?" She shook her leg nervously.

"Far from it." Piers leaned in. "After you left I saw Soliton, at least part of him, the part he became to me." The morning's rays reflected brightly off his boots. "I was in the room with the Tetragrammaton, and I noticed that the paintings on the walls seemed real all around."

"Yes," said Bennu, "I saw that too."

"I could see down Wroxeter Bluff toward Kells Village and the lapping waves. To the south I could make out the sloping hills and the smoke from the evening's fireplaces that rose from Primus Hook. Then I thought I had lost all sense of time and had been there all night, for the next thing I knew I smelled the ocean breeze and shielded my eyes from the dawn breaking over the sea.

"Only, the sun rose too quickly. It soared up to its peak in a few seconds, and if that weren't enough to trouble me, it suddenly came at me, blinding me with its brightness. I staggered back. Then I knew. It was Soliton. And he spoke to me. He said, 'I have been waiting . . . and more than that. So.'

"'So,' I said back, too full of awe to say more. At the same time, I felt invited to be there, so I looked full-faced into the flashing orb that hung about a foot above me. Soliton's light shone on me and into me. As I looked at the light, I was amazed at what I saw. A whole city seemed to be living in Soliton. I saw faces smiling and animals running through open pastures. Soliton seemed to be always moving yet always at rest. And then he sent out images to me. Most of them went back in as fast as they came out. Then the light flickered, shrunk back, and I could tell that it now shone out of a lantern. The lantern was held from behind by someone. As the light faded back, I recognized his head and clothing from the windows in Long House. He had a cape that seemed to be made of dusty sunlight and sewn together with a mossy thread from the forest. The figure was a man with a cougar's head, and I took him for Donic the Seer, the diviner, the interpreter. Here is the first revelation: Donic is the one from the past I would most want to meet. So now you see why Soliton is called the Becomer. And then Donic the Seer said, 'Piers, prepare for The Welkening.'"

Bennu scratched the dirt with a stick. "This is a lot all at once, and Piers, we still don't have the tiles. Do we have time for this?"

"Time is gathering up. It's heaping and overflowing."

"So, then, what is The Welkening?" asked Len.

Piers stood. "In some places, the Quadrille says that The Welkening is like a fire that melts away what's crusted up and covered the real, or it's a healing rain after a wounding drought. In other places The Welkening is said to be a wind that catches everything up and puts things down aright, or it's the whole land swaying about until all settles out, the things too high finding their way to the hollows."

"I'd like to say, 'Oh, I get it now,'" said Len, "but I'll have to take your word for it, Piers. Whatever it is, I can tell it's important—at least that you think it is. That's enough."

"And about Soliton," said Angie, "what more can you say?"

"For now, I will tell you what he told me. Here is the second revelation. He said, 'You have fulfilled your tasks well, Lord of Primus Hook. You have submitted to be transformed, and transformed you have been.

You've chased the dreaded ones across the lands, from flesh to book and back to flesh again. But the greatest test awaits. Now you must lean on what's within, not just your own strength and wisdom, not just your trust in Welken's ways, but also in the sadness you carry in you.'

"I said to Donic, 'I'm never far from it, m'Lord—from him, I should say. When the time comes, I will gladly lean on Bors, my friend and brother who dwells within me. He is here, ready, bones of my bones.'"

"What?" asked Len. "Bors is within you?"

"That's not all. Donic said that the amulet would—"

Len shot up and pointed. "Piers, everybody, look."

From out of the wood to the south, Morphane came, with Terz and Malleal riding on his back.

Piers said, "Go."

Instantly ox and lion, with the knapsack secure around Lizbeth's neck, Lizbeth and Len rushed down the trail toward the Great Alpine Reef. Piers stayed with them. Bennu and Angie flew above them, keeping equal pace.

Len called over to Lizbeth and Piers. "Should we stop and fight?"

Lizbeth answered. "I don't know. We can't get into the knapsack unless we change back. I'm afraid Morphane will reach us before we can do anything. Maybe we can shake them."

"It's worth a try," said Piers. "At some point I will try to lead them off your trail. Just keep going."

Len easily outpaced Lizbeth. When he looked back to see how she was keeping up, he saw Angie swoop down from behind Morphane. Bennu also buzzed them, screeching ominously. They could not dislodge Terz and Malleal. He also saw Morphane gaining on them. Despite his helter-skelter gallop and the distractions of the flying Misfits, Morphane surged powerfully over the ground.

"OK," shouted Piers, "you two head into these woods. I'll try to lead them into the open trail. Don't worry about me. I'm headed for the Window under the Mountain."

"But, Piers!" yelled Lizbeth.

"Lizbeth, there's no time for debate. Remember, all's well that the cooks—"

"Don't spoil. I know."

Piers ran off to the left. Len and Lizbeth peeled off into the trees.

⋆⦜∿⦜⋆

In seconds all knew that Terz did not take the bait.

Len glanced behind. "That didn't work. And now we have even less time to get into the water vial." His mane flowing, Len motioned with his head to the right. "OK, Lizbeth, maybe we can lose Morphane in these thicker trees. He seems to need a lot of space to run." Trampling over fir cones and the soft-needled floor, Len dodged trees and almost enjoyed his slalom around the thick trunks. But he could tell Lizbeth struggled to keep up. He slowed down. "C'mon, Lizbeth, you can do it. Already we've gained ground."

But she couldn't. Morphane charged right up to Lizbeth's heels for a few lefts and rights. Len tried something more dramatic. He took two turns he thought would be all Lizbeth could handle and more than Morphane could muster. It worked. Morphane shuffled too wide on a turn. Terz must have hit something, for he screamed. Len bounded ahead. He skidded around a tree to the left and accelerated through the brush. Lizbeth lost her footing on the same turn. Len saw that she tottered and nearly caught her horns on a low branch, but she lowered her head and blasted through it. Soon she was back behind Len's swaying tail.

Morphane must not have made the turn at all. The next time Len looked back, he saw Terz on the ground holding his knee and Morphane on his haunches licking his paws.

In minutes the four Misfits reunited as Len and Lizbeth came through the dense trees and out into a long open meadow that ascended gradually to the face of a mountain. Relieved to have, for now, escaped Morphane, Malleal, and Terz, Len let out a roar and stopped at a small steam to drink. He didn't rest long.

Run.

The word felt unmistakable and firm.

Run. Now.

They all heard it at once.

Run. Now. Quickly.

339

"OK," said Len. "OK. But where?"

Run quickly. Come to me. Keep coming.

All he knew to do was to maintain the same direction, to run, no matter how tired, toward the mountain. So across the meadow they all charged, looking this way and that for something familiar, some signpost, some reassurance of the right direction.

From behind them they heard Morphane's familiar chorus of terror. He was out of the wood. For all the Misfits knew, he would be gaining on them soon.

Running side by side, Len and Lizbeth trampled the tender meadow floor. Angie raced through the sky directly above Len, and Bennu flew above Lizbeth. All four kept equal pace.

As if rent open by Morphane's roar, the grass gradually parted, and Len and Lizbeth found themselves on two parallel, gravelly paths. Up ahead about two hundred yards loomed the smooth slab of the mountain, as flat as if a giant guillotine had fallen from above, leaving a clean, stark cut.

Run. Run hard.

Len spoke back to the voice. "Yes, but where to? Straight into the wall?"

Run. The Welkening is near. Run.

"Look up ahead," said Bennu. "I see tiny windows, two of them."

Look for the keys. Run.

"I see the windows, Bennu," said Angie. "But what about Len and Lizbeth?"

"I'm running," said Len. "I'm running, but I don't see any keys! I don't see any doors. The wall is coming up. We're almost there. What are we supposed to do?"

Find the keys. Run and find the keys.

"What keys?" said Lizbeth. "What doors?"

Len could see the openings for Angie and Bennu.

"I think I can just fit into mine," said Bennu.

"Me, too," said Angie.

Run, came the voice, *run. Bear down harder.*

Len looked at the granite wall, just fifty feet ahead. He saw a faint outline at the end of his path, and another etched line awaiting Lizbeth.

"Hey. I see what could be a door. But we're going to die. I don't have a key. It's solid rock. We don't have the tiles. We've failed!"

"No," came a voice. But it wasn't Piers or Soliton. It was Angie. "I see it now, Misfits! Keep going! *We* are the keys!"

In the next second Angie and Bennu slipped into their keyholes above, and Len and Lizbeth broke into the face of the mountain, the doors giving way in precisely the shapes of the charging Misfits' bodies.

CHAPTER THIRTY-FOUR
A SENTENCE OR TWO FOR OLLIE

I shall tell you a great secret, my friend.
Do not wait for the last judgment. It takes place every day.

ALBERT CAMUS, *THE FALL*

 Charlotte went to the backyard and paced. Few things got her more worked up than her husband and her son fighting. Her stomach churned. Her heart raced enough to get her to swear off caffeine one more time. Escalation, she said to herself. Those two can take a minor disagreement and crank it into a full-fledged argument in just seconds. Something needs to happen. Sometimes I wish there'd be a huge cataclysmic event that would wake up these hot-headed males. I also wish they could work a little harder at building bridges.

Then Charlotte picked up her yellow pad. She had her own conflict to resolve.

CHAPTER EIGHT: Bridge Over the River Cry

Ollie looked in the rearview mirror of the Rolls-Royce. "Dearie, dearie, doodles, my eyes spy two guys on the fly. Oh, I shouldn't have stopped to count all my loot, Mama, but you taught me to keep track of everything I steal, and I am a good obedient boy." Ollie pulled the stolen goods close to him and patted the bag as if it were a long-lost friend.

Percy and Bones, goggles securely attached, bounded down the road in their speedy three-wheeler Morgan. Percy threw a red scarf around his neck so that it blew dramatically behind him. "That Ollie made a big mistake, Bonesy. He couldn't resist taking the more expensive Rolls-Royce, so here we are catching him. We'll be on his bumper in two whips of a whippoorwill."

Bones folded his ears so they fit snug under the goggles' strap. "By the way, Percy, aren't we on the wrong side of the road?"

"Actually, no, my droopy-eyed friend. In England what we call the wrong side they call the left. It's not about politics, old boy, just British loopiness. As the brown book says, 'Don't count your chickens before they cross the road.'"

Ollie twitched his paws back and forth on the steering wheel. "Mama, I've got to get to the pub Beer and Karth before those nasty detectives catch up to me. I need to meet Kelly Karth there and trade these ceramic trivets for some genuine green-smelling money. That old tomb raider says the trivets will complete his collection—and I'd so much like to see him unload his riches in our direction. It's enough to make an almost reformed otter almost change his mind."

Just then Ollie steered his massive Rolls-Royce onto a bridge. From the other side, a convertible Jaguar barreled at him in the same lane, driven by the utterly oblivious Reggie Longswallow, his long pink neck sticking up well above the windshield. Ollie saw him and blasted the horn, but the silly flamingo only waved and said, "Cheerio." Ollie yanked on the wheel, and the lumbering Rolls teetered abruptly to the right. It crossed the other lane and hit the guardrail with its fender, and one headlight broke. As Ollie pulled the wheel back to the left, the Rolls crossed the bridge and stormed off the road, curling down and crashing against a boulder next to the river. Then it burst into flames.

Percy and Bones watched the whole fiasco from behind. After they barely missed Reggie's head as it leaned out of the Jag at a ninety-degree angle, they crossed the bridge just in time to see Ollie leap out of the Rolls, his pants on fire.

"Well, Bones, I guess we could say, 'Liar, liar, pants a-pyre.'"

"Oh look, Perce, Ollie jumped into the river to put out the fire. But, wait, the current is sweeping him away!"

"Good thing the road follows the river. We'll just keep pace by the by. Nothing like watching a schemin' thief bob up and down in the drink."

Floating on his back, Ollie reached under the water to scratch his singed behind. Right away he realized that the burned hole in his pants exposed his entire bum. "Oh, Mama, how mortifying. The sacrifices I must endure to win The Most Adventurous Best Burglar Award. At least I had the brilliance of mind to snatch the loot. Now I can put it on my chest and keep it dry, such a guy am I. Whoa, what's this? A waterfall! Oh, Mama, thanks for the swimming lessons!"

As Ollie fell over the short falls, Percy and Bones stopped the Morgan so they could run out to the riverbank. The drop landed Ollie into the churning water, where he tumbled around for some time. When he finally popped out, he looked like a rat that had taken a spin in a washing machine.

Percy tried to get his attention from the shore. "Ready to

throw in the towel, Mr. Otterson? It's the only way to get high and dry."

Ollie plopped against a rock in the middle of the river and looked inside his loot bag. "You haven't caught me yet. Mama taught me to finish what I started." Ollie pulled out of the bag the ceramic trivets, the only thing that had not been lost in the waterfall. He put the trivets in one coat pocket and the bag in another.

Bones nudged Percy and chuckled. "By the way, Ollie, I'm not at all sure your new pant design will catch on in Virginia."

Ollie slipped into the water. He floated on his back in the current, while Percy and Bones climbed back into the Morgan. Soon a roar could be heard over the Morgan's engine. A much longer waterfall approached.

Percy stopped the car. "He's an ingenious lad, Bonsey. But now he's in a pickle that's fit to be tied."

As Percy and Bones made their way to the shore, Ollie flew over the falls, literally. Holding his empty loot bag as a parachute, Ollie drifted down and away from the waterfall.

"Oh, Mama, ain't I clever? Even as those nasty detectives are trying to ruin our fun, they don't know I'm planning to float right back to burglar reform school. They don't know . . . Whoa, what's happening?"

Just then Ollie's loot bag sprung a leak, and the air escaped faster than Percy could say, "Bones, old boy, for a fat bird, Ollie don't flap much."

With an unceremonious galumph, Ollie landed feet first up to his thighs in a mud hole next to the river. The ceramic trivets fell out of his coat pocket just out of his reach. Unable to run, Ollie slumped his shoulders dejectedly. "Oh, Mama, you gave me the fastest feet in the whole U.S. of A., but here I am stuck like a cedar in a sawmill. The blades are coming, Mama, the blades are coming!"

"Oh, Ollie," said Bones, "I'm not anything as sharp as all that. But I do know how to tie your paws together. It's just too bad I don't have any way to hide your heinie from the sun. You could get a rude sunburn."

While Percy took a picture, Ollie began to cry huge burglar-that-got-caught tears.

"Don't worry, Ollie," said Percy, "we'll tie a coat around your waist before the bobbies arrive."

CHAPTER THIRTY-FIVE
SOLITON

If there when Grace dances, I should dance.
W. H. AUDEN, "WHITSUNDAY IN KIRCHSTETTEN"

 After exploding through the wall, Lizbeth finally skid-
ded to a stop. She couldn't believe she wasn't hurt. She
couldn't believe so many things. Here she was, back in
human form, back in Ganderst Hall, her mind spinning.
Yet, curiously, time seemed to have slowed its revolutions. Lizbeth brushed herself off, then saw Len in
human form doing the same. She checked to see that the knapsack was
still around her neck and looked for Bennu and Angie. She found them
resting on the platform above her, the one with the gold railing that jutted out opposite to the skylights she'd seen before. Somehow, in this slow-
motion moment, she knew that Morphane would not be coming through
the keyhole. After all, neither he nor Terz would be the right fit.

She looked over to the east door, the only source of light within the
Hall. She thought Piers might come out of the room or a giant amulet or
the floating orb of Soliton. She didn't think she was quite ready for that.
He was too high, too holy, too intimidating. A shadow filled the doorway,
and Lizbeth flinched. The shadow came toward her, step by step, eventually becoming exposed to the light. To her utter astonishment, Lizbeth
saw Emily Stedman, her best friend from second to eighth grade, until

Emily moved away to the Midwest. Emily smiled and held out her hands.

Lizbeth studied her, entranced yet baffled. Finding no good reason to deny her senses, she accepted Emily's offer and gladly hugged her. This girl seemed just like Emily. Lizbeth felt as comfortable as if the two of them were sitting on her front porch. All that mattered now was Emily and their friendship. "I've missed you so much. When you left, I had no friends who saw in me what you did."

Emily stroked Lizbeth's hair. "Oh, Lizbeth, you don't need to say it like it's in the past. I saw then and I see now what you're made of, especially your compassion."

They sat and talked for a while. When Emily stood and walked back to the east door, Lizbeth did not run after her. She felt content. She kept waving good-bye until someone grabbed her hand.

It was Bennu. "Lizbeth, the most amazing thing happened. You won't believe it."

"Oh yes, I will." She saw Angie and Len standing next to Bennu. "I had an amazing thing happen, too."

"OK," said Bennu, "you tell yours first."

After Lizbeth spoke of Emily Stedman, she realized she told the whole story without shame, even the tenderest parts.

Then Bennu rubbed his eyes. "As soon as I flew down, I saw someone sitting in a Ganderst Hall chair. I thought it was Len, but as I got closer, I thought, This looks like Dad. He was younger than he is now—no bald spot—and he seemed more relaxed than I think I've ever seen him. He got out of his chair and put a hand on my shoulder. We talked for a while, and then he said, 'Remember that spelling bee you won in sixth grade? I was out of town on business, but I spent the evening writing you a letter about how proud I was of you, not for winning the award—I would have loved you anyway—but because you were my son.'

"I said, 'Why didn't you give me the letter, Dad?' He said he was embarrassed. Then he looked into my eyes and said, 'I didn't yet realize that my love for you was not as obvious to you as it was to me.' Dad said that. Can you imagine?"

"I was brushing off keyhole dust," Len said, "when I felt someone helping me. I looked down and saw a lamb. I thought, Whoa, haven't you ever heard about the lion and lamb thing? Then she said, 'You have preyed upon me most of your days.' I thought of a sarcastic comment but didn't say it. I said, 'Yeah, I know.'

"Then this lamb kept talking. She said, 'But look at what has happened to you. Len, you can now be with me without hurting me, without chasing me away with your shredding words.' Then she changed, I mean, her faced changed. I saw dozens of faces, some I'd ridiculed in the past, some I didn't recognize. None of the faces looked mad at me. Then she said, 'This is your future, lion. These are the friends who will welcome you because you will be so welcoming to them.' I said, 'It feels good to be here with you.'"

"I was still on the landing," Angie said. "I saw four strings of light reach out to grab my arms and legs. They pulled me off, and I fell down and down, deep and deeper into some mystery. I saw a city, and everyone in it seemed to know where they were going and why. At the gates of the city stood a griffin. It said to me, 'You know about the fire.' I said, 'Yes.' The griffin said, 'You will need to protect your friends. The fire will not harm them, but more troubles will come, and they may waver.' I said, 'I will shield them with my wings.' And then all I could think of to say was, 'I will remind them of the ginger cat and his warm, green eyes.' Then we flew around the city, and I landed here, next to you."

In the short silence that followed, Lizbeth looked each Misfit in the eye. All of us, she thought, all of us are beaming.

Len pulled up a high-backed chair and plopped into it. "What's happened to us? We used to go to school and listen to music, but now we're seeing visions, listening to griffins, and talking to lambs."

No one answered him.

"I mean, it's a good thing. I know that now. But what are we going to do about Morphane coming? Shouldn't we get some defenses ready or something? Where's Piers? And what really happened to us just then? Was it some Tetra-matic magic or something real?"

Lizbeth listened to his questions without anxiety. They were worthy questions, she thought, questions that needed attention—and though she could not begin to answer them, she did not feel troubled. "Len, The Welkening is coming. Everything will be set right."

"I suppose. But that doesn't mean we just sit around."

"He's right." Just then Piers came through the door that led to the guardians' quarters, the door they had all passed by on their way to the tunnel tentacles and the Window under the Mountain. He looked nervous.

"Piers!" Lizbeth ran to him. "I was just feeling relaxed. But your face makes me worried."

He put his arm around Lizbeth and walked to the others. "I see the keyholes you've come through. I'm glad for that, but I know what remains—of pain and battle. What has been set in motion will march until its feet move no more. There will be weariness and struggle and death. Yes, I can see a certain bliss in you, Lizbeth. I can tell that Soliton has been here."

"Actually," said Bennu, "I didn't see a small sun rising or that Donic guy. I saw my dad. Explain that."

"Good friends, Soliton is the Becomer, and he became for each of you whatever love required. Your task is to learn why love required what you saw. I saw Donic the Seer. Soliton is forever the same and always changing. His wisdom is to show us that part of his being best suited for who we are and who we will be. Since he acts as love requires, we see what we are ready to see, those qualities we have in us to understand. More or less will come as we grow into the bodies and souls set out for us."

"Will we ever see him for all he is?" asked Lizbeth.

"I expect that's possible. But it's more than I know just yet. And for now, we must prepare. We must get ready for The Welkening. Outside, the others are coming. I know they are. Mook promised me that the Nezzer Clan would mourn for Alabaster as they walked. And Bebba the blind knows the way. She will bring Sutton and Zennor and those from the Durrow, even Illtyd and Marthen. Yes, I know they quarreled. That is past, and they are coming. The place of the keyholes is Granite Flats. As other Welkeners come to fill the place, we have our own work. Come, let's walk to the Tetragrammaton."

Once through the east door, Len scratched his head and faced Piers. "Piers, Lizbeth might be feeling blissful, but I'm torn up. On one hand, I have so many questions. On the other hand, all I can think is 'Can we hurry up?' I mean, Morphane has got to be outside by now. Terz is probably out there lying to everyone about a New Welken. I'm confused. If everyone outside is getting ready for a battle, why are we inside chatting?"

Piers nodded. "Your sense of justice serves you well, Len. So does my admonition to 'Wait, lion, wait.' Time is as important as you suggest, but speed is not always the best use of it. This might be a good moment for a few questions; but remember, not everything that might be explained can be explained, and not everything that can be explained should be explained."

"So I should just be a good soldier? That's not been my forte, as you know."

A lantern brightened the room from behind them. "Piers speaks truly." The lantern was lowered, and the Misfits could see the head of a cougar on the body of a man. "I am Donic. I am Soliton. I will hear you now."

Len's eyes widened and froze. Then they moved as if going down a list he had been keeping. Lizbeth looked at him as if to say Don't. But Len said, "OK, I've wanted to know, why do glimpses die when they help us? And why did the bell tower become the Wasan Sagad? What does it mean that we are the keys, and what is The Welkening?" Len stopped, then added, "I have other questions too."

Lizbeth grimaced in disappointment. She felt that Len was reverting to his cranky old self.

"So," said Soliton-as-Donic, pulling his cape around his shoulders. "So it is. In this moment, I can only begin to provide answers. I will say this: that all we can offer at any time is ourselves—as keys—not just to the doors but to these questions. Keys are made to fit a lock, to let one in or to keep others out."

"I'm not sure what that means," said Len. "But maybe all that really matters is that we didn't find the tiles, that we failed."

"The answer is that, though you didn't find the tiles, you fit the lock. I have a question for you. What made you a key?"

"I don't know. Were we born that way? Did I try to become a lion? I don't know. And Donic, Soliton, I probably sound rude, but if you have so much power, why don't *you* do what needs to be done? Why don't you fight Morphane and Terz? Why don't you become a key and recover the tiles?"

The bottom of Donic's cape curled under and lifted itself up. Just before it withdrew entirely into the lantern, Donic's cougar head peered out of his hood. "I have a task, and you have yours. Mine is to see that Welken's ways are loved and followed. When all good purpose is united, the sound peals bright and clear. You might say we are all here in our own way to make the Welken ring."

The lantern moved through the room and over to the Tetragrammaton. Its glow diminished, and then it looked to Lizbeth like an ordinary lantern. When the golden beetle amulet placed there by Piers caught the lantern's light, its legs came alive and reached into the empty spaces.

Then Piers seemed worried again. "So it is time. Place your hand in the hole where your tile should go. Remember, you are the keys."

Lizbeth, Bennu, Len, and Angie leaned into their respective places in the Tetragrammaton. Inside the openings, their hands became hoof, talon, and paw—and Angie's hand remained unchanged. Then Piers said, "The Tetragrammaton receives the four of you as substitutions for the tiles. Your presence allows me to do what I must do." Piers then leaned into the middle and took the amulet from its appointed place. It squirmed in his hand, its legs grasping for something to hold.

Instantly Piers backed away as if overwhelmed by its weight. Sweat appeared on his brow, and he used both hands to support the scarab. He stumbled away from the Tetragrammaton. As the amulet glowed through his fingers, Piers acted as though heat were surging up his arms and deep into his body.

In a whisper Piers said, "The Welkening is a reckoning. It is an unveiling of hidden acts, of deceptions and cruelties. It is an undoing of all that must be undone. It begins with fire."

Lizbeth and the others pulled their hands out and followed Piers back into Ganderst Hall. The amulet glowed red-hot in his hands. Piers clearly suffered. Lizbeth came along one side to hold him up, and Bennu helped from the other. Lizbeth felt the heat. She couldn't understand it. If the scarab hurt those who withhold a lie, as they had been told during the commissioning, why would Piers be in pain? What did he need to unveil? But he *was* in pain. He acted like the amulet's fire surged through him, testing him, searching for a lie, some malice, some pretense.

Piers had trouble standing. He closed his eyes and bowed his head, sweat dripping down his face. Lizbeth and Bennu each used both arms to steady him. Then he shook uncontrollably.

Haltingly, they walked through Lizbeth's keyhole, into the sunshine and onto Granite Flat.

Lizbeth braced Piers up and looked around. She had been so intent on running through the keyhole she didn't even notice the area before. It was a large clearing, an area without vegetation, filled with granite rubble that must have crumbled off the mountain. The paths to the doors were smooth, as was much of the open area, but boulders formed a wall around

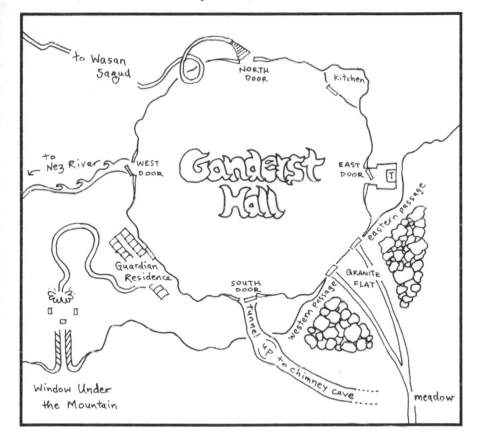

most of the clearing. Except for the Misfits' trails to the south and two narrower openings at the base of the cliff, to the east and west, the place was like a large amphitheater. Many Welkeners sat on boulders. Some milled around nervously on the flat. Lizbeth searched for Mook.

She found Terz.

He stood on a boulder partway up the wall to the west. Sutton and Zennor stood near him. Since he had the attention of the crowd, no one noticed the five of them come out of Ganderst Hall. Terz raised his hand. "I've come to offer you hope, my friends." Then Lizbeth saw Jacob Canny Sea and Vida Bering Well slap each other on the back.

Lizbeth was about to expose Terz when Piers, his eyes barely open, said, "Let him speak for the moment. All will be revealed. All will be undone." Lizbeth stiffened at this request.

Len came close to Piers. "Why can't we get the unveiling going? I'd love to see him undone."

"Don't be so anxious, lion. *All* will be undone."

Then Lizbeth saw Mook on the opposite wall. He slipped his bow off his shoulder.

Terz smiled through every word. "I predicted you'd all amaze yourselves at how fast you could get here."

Mook pulled an arrow from his quiver.

Terz walked over to the end of the eastern wall, next to Lizbeth's path. "Tell you what, why don't we all move away from the opening in the rocks here. We all want to be ready to give Piers a proper welcome when he comes, don't we?"

"Please, Piers," said Len. "We shouldn't wait any longer."

"Hold steadfast, lion." Piers breathed heavily. "Help me to sit."

"Terz!" Mook's stern voice shattered the lighthearted mood. The Welkeners turned toward him as they backed off from the entrance, obeying Terz. Mook gestured with his bow. "Why are we here?"

"Right now, we are about to applaud our faithful leader," Terz said, "if only you'll change that negative tone in your voice."

Sutton could be seen and heard above the crowd. "Mook, what's the problem?"

Mook strung an arrow in the bowstring. "Tell me, Sutton, why are we here?"

"To do as Soliton bids," he said.

"Yes, I know," said Mook, his voice as tight as Lizbeth had ever heard it. "But what is it called?"

Terz held out his hands in a brotherly offering. "Please, must we express all this anger?"

"You do not answer, Terz," said Mook, "because you do not believe it will happen."

"Bebba knows why we're here!" The blind one hammered her stick on the rock floor. "Bebba knows—"

Terz interrupted. "Well, I—"

"Bebba will not be silenced by anyone, especially by the beast whose lips taste death with every lick. Bebba says we are all here, ready with weapons and resolve. We have come for The Welkening!"

Then, a loud noise rumbled up from the path. Lizbeth heard the sound of giant paws running through gravel. She looked at Piers for help, for permission to scream out what she knew. His eyes rolled back.

Then Morphane charged up the path and into their midst. Each time she saw him, Lizbeth felt stunned by his size. She screamed along with everyone else. In the chaos, Lizbeth saw Terz nod his head as if his expectations had been fulfilled. She yelled out, "He's a traitor!" But no one heard her over the cacophony.

Then Morphane growled louder, unleashing his chorus of dread, and he bounded to Terz's side. The Welkeners were hushed by this. Then in shuffled the drones called Morphane's army. Lizbeth realized that Terz must have turned Malleal back into the webbed bodies that followed in Morphane's wake.

With the other Misfits, she yelled and waved her arms. Then she saw Mook aim his arrow.

All eyes were on—but not looking into—Morphane. Welkeners climbed up onto the rocky walls, parting for Morphane as the Red Sea. And Morphane strode this dry path, shaking his head and growling, straight toward Piers and the Misfits.

"It's too late, now," said Len. "We're the ones who'll be undone."

Lizbeth held Piers's head. "He's coming, Piers. You've got to do something."

Piers's lips were blistered, his face ashen. He tried to speak, but nothing came.

Ten paces away, Morphane faced the tormented Piers.

Then Piers let go. Lizbeth felt his arms give way, and she turned to grab the amulet as it fell. But the amulet clung to him. The scarab's feet grabbed tight as Piers opened his arms and trembled violently.

Morphane came. The Misfits shielded their eyes. They looked at Piers. Lizbeth tried to push his arms back into position. And then in an instant, the heat left Piers. Like one whose fever had just lifted, an exhausted Piers opened his eyes and said, "Bors, you have done your work. Now the amulet can do its work." He held the glowing amulet above his head and then placed it on the ground.

The amulet shook. Its body quivered, and then the scarab grew. Its six legs merged into four and added muscle and mass. Through the golden shell of the beetle, hair sprouted—and a flowing tail inched out the backside. Now two feet tall at the shoulders, then four, the scarab grew a neck, a thick powerful mammalian neck, and a huge head lurched out from that neck. On its four new legs the scarab-beast stood, six feet tall when it raised its head, that massive flesh and skull, with its daggers for teeth. The head leaned back and roared a gruesome, curdling growl that set the very stones on edge. Then the head came down, and the beast's claws dug into the ground, and the whole body contracted its muscles for its first deadly pounce.

As the Misfits stared in terror, all could see that the scarab had become another Morphane.

CHAPTER THIRTY-SIX
ONE LITTLE WORD SHALL FELL HIM

Those who'll play with cats must expect to be scratched.
MIGUEL DE CERVANTES, *DON QUIXOTE*

 Len dropped to one knee. "I can't believe it. Everything comes down to this?" His eyes stayed focused on the beast, but his tone drifted to despair. "Is it possible we've been duped all along—first by Terz and then by Piers?"

The newly created beast rumbled the beginning of a roar. He kept it idling in the back of his throat, as if poised for a sudden, violent outburst. He walked to the center of Granite Flats.

Len's hands shook. "Do we run or fight? Why doesn't anyone say anything?" He guessed the others had given up, so his voice dropped. "How could we defeat two Morphanes, anyway?" He stole a glance at the barely conscious Welken leader.

Piers lifted his head slightly. With Lizbeth supporting him, Piers whispered so softly Len could not hear. Then he passed out.

Len surveyed the scene. Like Colosseum goers, most of the Welkeners had climbed up on the bouldered walls, yielding the center arena to the two beasts. A few ran away. While Nezzer folk drew arrows, Jacob and Vida pulled daggers and hid behind large rocks. Zennor raised his giant staff. No one took charge.

Except Terz. "The moment of victory has arrived. Two Morphanes will ensure the bright future I was telling you about."

As the Morphanes slowly circled around head to tail, Terz walked out toward them, his head barely visible above their backs. "You can see my lack of fear." He gestured broadly like an experienced orator. "I have seen a new day for Welken. I have studied fresh ideas, my friends, and though I knew I'd be resisted, I bravely aligned myself with the coming revolution. Welken's ways are changing, and we need to change with them."

Len's right hand became a lion's paw. He saw Lizbeth lay the unconscious Piers down. Horns started to emerge from her head.

Terz smiled. "Years ago, when I was a guardian in Ganderst Hall, I learned the lost languages. I read the ancient books. Oh yes, I've changed since then. The other guardians wouldn't know me now. But I remember that prophecies indeed foretold a Welkening. And they also spoke of a hopeful voice of authority."

In the center, just a few feet from Terz, the newly created beast snarled louder, holding on to the edge of a roar. "I know you are ready, my friend," said Terz. Len saw the beast's face roil backward, but without any captured souls staring out. Amid the rumbling tension, Morphane's troops shuffled closer to the center, their weariness hanging like white flags limp in surrender.

Terz boomed his message. "I want to lead you into Welken's future, the New Welken, a place of greater honor and influence. We will order ourselves and then take New Welken's ways to other lands. And you can be a part of this mission. Morphane is not a destroyer. He's just a tool, just the means for tearing up the worn-out rules. He will bring our differences together into one brilliant mind. With one purpose, one voice, one will, we can truly improve our lives. And now there are two of these tools to help us."

Terz forged between the one Morphane's head and the other Morphane's tail.

"Captured revolutionaries are called traitors," he said, "but successful rebels are called founding fathers. I will be all of this to you. I will be your father and mother, your sister and brother."

Bennu crouched behind Piers, as if the motionless leader were a barricade. He whispered to Len, "Terz sounds so certain."

"I'm not sure that's the issue," said Len. "Look at Terz. Do you want *him* to be your father and mother?"

Terz turned to plead his case to those from the Durrow. He gestured for them to come down to join him. A few started down the boulders.

Then a voice called out from above. "Wait!" From twenty feet above, Angie circled in flight. "Terz asks you to trust him. And some of you wonder if you should. But some of us have already seen his betrayal. We've seen how he uses his gifts to entice and abuse and destroy."

Even the two Morphanes stopped posturing to look up at her.

"Deceivers come in many disguises," she said. "Some please the eye like poison oak. Some sweeten their speech."

Terz turned to the crowd. "She is an outsider. She is the one not to be trusted!"

Angie swooped lower. "I have seen what happens to those who set themselves up on thrones! A fire is coming, hot and unrestrained!"

Len felt confused. He thought the fire had already come, in the heat of the amulet.

Then both Morphanes grumbled louder, a tremulous warning that Terz seemed to accept as his fanfare. His eyes sparkling, he said, "Look here, everyone! I'll show you what I mean. I'll show you why you should join me as we triumph today. Arrows and swords will not stop us. Two Morphanes is more than enough. Watch!"

Terz turned to the older Morphane. He held the beast's mighty jaw like it was a bowl, and then he dipped his head into the fluid faces. Though Len had seen him do this before, it was no less horrifying this time. He watched the Welkeners stare in disbelief and hold their weapons. Len feared a wilder, more empowered Terz.

Lizbeth gently shook Piers. "Wake up. We need you."

Len broke away from the sight and, as a lion, raced into Ganderst Hall, grabbed the knapsack in his teeth, and ran back to the others.

Terz pulled his head out of Morphane's faces, his eyes glowing brighter than the last time, his expression full of determination and power. Three warriors from Deedy Swamp were clearly impressed and moved in for a closer look. Others gasped. Then the newer Morphane turned out of the circle and faced Terz in the center. He shook his head once to the left and then once to the right. Len felt that he could interpret these feline motions. He thought the beast acted like it was his turn, as if Terz had been neglecting him, as if the time for the old Morphane had expired and now it was time to show what he could do, time for his reign. The beast paced before Terz, his tail switching.

Terz patted the monster's nose. "I am the Master, over one Morphane and now over the other. Welkeners, I am worthy of your allegiance."

Grabbing the knapsack out of Len's mouth, Bennu, still in human form, pulled out the contents and searched through them. He showed Len he'd found the water vial.

"Watch again, friends," said Terz. "This next Morphane will give you an inkling of what's to come." Eyes aglow, Terz squared around toward the animal. He bowed. "I wish to have a second helping of Morphane, and we will all become one mind."

The new Morphane submitted. He hunched down on the gravel so Terz could be over him. He lowered his head, as if inviting Terz to drink deep.

So drink deep he did. Terz leaned into the beast's face. Len thought for sure that Terz's power would multiply, that he and the others would now have two Morphanes and a stronger Terz to fight.

Instead, Terz's image leaped off his face and transferred onto this Morphane's muzzle. Terz reached out in horror as if to grasp his self before it slipped away. Then his agony came. Terz's face flashed onto the beast's face—and traveled up, his eyes blending into his nostrils and then flowing up to his ears, up and over, slipping back into the new Morphane's walking, breathing prison. Helpless, mind-torn, Terz's body writhed on the ground. It flopped and twitched till the torment passed. Then his body stood once again, eyes vacant, gravel embedded in its pant legs and on his hands. Husks of skin, Terz's fingers, fluttered in the breeze like wide blades of grass.

Lizbeth shook Piers harder. He moaned in response.

"Angie, get down here!" shouted Len. Then, to Lizbeth and Bennu, he said, "This must be The Welkening. What are we supposed to do with Piers asleep?"

Bennu gave his answer. His fingers trembling, he worked at the tie around the package of willful air. Angie flew down to the Misfits and took the water vial from Len. Welkeners took up arms. The Nezzer clan aimed their arrows once again. Deediers unsheathed daggers. Kells Villagers raised overhead their spears and swords and clubs.

Then Len's countenance fell. Into the center of the flat ran a small Welken child, a Highlander. She ran out toward the two Morphanes. "What are you doing?" Len yelled. "The archers can't shoot now!"

Piers groaned and held his head in his hands.

"C'mon, Piers," said Len, "it's The Welkening."

The first Morphane frantically thrust his head back and forth, as if fighting an invisible foe. The girl ran right by him and over to his web of followers, who had flopped down at the base of the eastern rock wall. Repulsed, the girl ran back to the center, sobbing. Holding out her arms, she made it back to the rubble wall and was swept up by Vida Bering Well. Then the other Morphane bellowed to the sky with a roar. That was all Len needed to hear. "Bennu, untie the knot! Angie, pull out the cork!"

"No," said Piers, his voice weary but sure. "This is not The Welkening. Much more will come. Much more is needed to come. For now, hold the gifts. There must first be some devouring. This new beast, his name is not Morphane. It is Ferodor. He comes with the fiercest of loves."

The massive beasts faced each other and turned their low, curdling threats into teeth-baring roars. They circled around and strutted toward combat, sizing each other up, negotiating, but not toward compromise. Len knew more than the others; here were two snarling males in a contest for dominance.

Ferodor growled again, a nasty, shredding sound that rose louder, stronger, clearer than Morphane's voice. When Ferodor's head lurched up for another roar, Morphane leaped, diving for a rear flank. He missed. The younger beast jumped to retaliate—but the older darted away, scattering rocks in his wake. Then Ferodor chased and snapped at Morphane, drawing blood on a back paw. Red spots darkened the pale stones. He ran Morphane up the wall near the western opening, scattering a few Deediers. Then Morphane turned quickly and swatted at his attacker. Ferodor leaped clear over him and onto the center stage of Granite Flat. The younger beast ran Morphane back and forth, pushed him and pushed him; yet, to Len's thinking, he could not quite get around in front, to face off head to head, teeth to teeth. The animals slid over the gravel and stirred up dust. Morphane panted hard. Then he dashed for a southern opening, but Ferodor swooped up and down a wall to block his path. He ran him back into the center, up the eastern wall, and over the backs of huddled and ducking Welkeners.

On his next leap to ground level, Morphane stumbled, and Ferodor slashed him across the back, drawing stripes of blood. The two tangled for a furious moment, rolling over once, but Morphane broke free, wounded now on the neck as well as the back. He ran toward the Misfits. Unscathed, Ferodor tore at the earth to catch up. Fully extending himself, he pounced and sunk his teeth into Morphane's left hind leg with his teeth. Morphane roared in agony. He turned back to shake off his attacker, but Ferodor did not let go. Then Len heard the bone snap.

Shrieking a dissonant cry, Morphane tripped and collapsed in a heap, blood flinging to the ground from his back and neck, his broken leg dangling uselessly. He tried to get up to run on three legs, but he could not. He flopped down, struggled up to sit on his haunches, and faced his mirror image.

"The first part will happen now," whispered Piers. "Sometimes truth comes devouring."

Ferodor strutted over to the front of the old beast, face to face, muzzle to muzzle, roiling prisoner to roiling prisoners.

Morphane looked down submissively, but Ferodor demanded his attention. He stomped one paw on the ground and opened his mouth to roar. To Len's surprise, no roar came. A clear audible sound could be heard, yet it wasn't the beast's growl. Into the silence came a speaking voice, the garbled voice of Terz. As he made his pass over Ferodor's muzzle, he issued forth one word. Terz's eyes glared out from Ferodor's globes, then he delivered a single syllable.

"Crave."

Though a whisper, Len heard it, and he knew others did, too.

Morphane looked up greedily toward his Master's voice.

Piers said, "Morphane's been invited to gorge himself, to feast upon his own heart."

Morphane and Ferodor stared at each other. Then Morphane's image, his tangled face of others' faces, rose. It began its voyage over to Ferodor's waiting muzzle. But Ferodor's eyes had locked with Morphane's as well. His image also lifted off and over, floating toward its destiny. Somewhere in the mystery of space between them, the two images met. They merged. They roiled together. Detached, these countenances twisted and pushed against each other. They wrestled to return and to receive. Unleashed, they craved, they ate, they consumed, and were consumed.

In that battle of wills, that mutual theft of identities, both monstrous bodies flailed on the ground. Morphane and Ferodor fell on their backs and lashed out blindly in the air. As granite dust flew, the beasts screamed as only wild things can. They howled. They yelped, translating the fear of death into each utterance.

With their images thoroughly enmeshed, both bodies ceased struggling, rolled over, and sat up facing each other, facing their suspended images. The bodies inched closer till their front paws touched. Then, without resistance, they gave themselves up to each other. Each acquiesced to the tugging and ravishing of his own soul. Images of faces entered and exited each other's muzzles. They floated in between. Then the beasts leaned in, and their legs touched.

Unable to resist each other's gravity any longer, Morphane and Ferodor pushed into each other. They trembled as they merged, their tails twitching in pain against the rocky floor. They fell into each other. They rose across the emptiness and roiled in the air. They wholly lost themselves, and then they imploded.

Into the absence Piers said, "The devouring is finished. Morphane's craving is over."

Like a crystalline blanket, a thin veil covered the scene. Len tried to look through it for the remains of the two creatures. As the veil dissipated, he saw on the granite floor not two beasts but the golden scarab shining in the sun, and beside it, four gleaming tiles boasting the images of an ox, a falcon, a lion, and an angel.

CHAPTER THIRTY-SEVEN

THE SILENCE, THE TALK, THE FURIOUS FIRE

That which is grows, while that which is not becomes.

GALEN, *ON THE NATURAL FACULTIES*

 The ensuing quiet ached with life. It rose in strength to the edge of its own cliff and teetered precariously. In its free fall, Lizbeth realized that the absence of the roaring beasts left a presence just as palpable. She changed back to human form. Her eyes fixed on the tiles, she walked cautiously toward them. She stopped, looked back at Piers for reassurance, and kept walking. He and the other Misfits followed her.

She shielded her eyes. The gold scarab dazzled her as its own light joined with the reflection of the morning sun. The Welkeners seemed unable to move and unwilling to break the silence. Lizbeth knew they were waiting for permission from Piers, perhaps even for a judicious word from someone as unlikely as a Misfit. Tenderly she knelt next to the amulet and the tiles. She waved a hand over them, as if they were too holy to touch.

Visibly weak from his own battle, Piers sat beside her. He nodded, inviting Lizbeth to let the quiet crash upon the ground of her own words. "Why?" she asked. "How? When? What does it mean that we have been searching for the tiles, and they were in Morphane all along, that they *were* him?" The more she said, the more stirring and murmurs she heard from the Welkeners.

Slowly, Piers leaned over and picked up the ox tile. "I was not sure at the beginning. Even a few moments ago I was certain only that Morphane's life, his creation, was born in the guardian's freedom." Piers ran a finger over the ox image. "You probably noticed the guardians had no weapons. They were not asked to protect the Tetragrammaton by force. Most of their power came from the choices they made in the light of all they had learned and from their ability to help others see this wisdom."

"Do you mean," asked Lizbeth, "that any of the guardians could have taken the tiles at any time?"

"Oh, there were hindrances to such an act, ways of living together that made certain choices easier or more difficult."

Len picked up the lion tile. "But then one day, without resistance, Terz just came in and ran off with the tiles and created Morphane?"

"In Welken," said Piers, "in Ganderst Hall, these decisions are at once as simple as you suggest and far more complicated. A hundred years ago, even fifty, the decision would have been unimaginable. The guardians would have put it thus: who would trade a life of good purpose for a week of dishonorable power? But, as Gandric explained, smaller yearnings and leanings added up over the years, until the reminders on the walls no longer reminded. In the end, the few loyal guardians had no more influence than a grain of sand tossed into the wide open sea."

"What's crazy to you," said Bennu, reaching for the falcon tile, "seems like every day back home. Who would trade dull goodness for a week of getting what they want? Just about everybody."

Piers put his hand on Bennu's shoulder. "But who called goodness dull? Only those who've abandoned their true home cannot find room for the adventure of loving well. Should we prefer quarreling to peace, jealousy to contentment?"

"Not when you put it that way," said Bennu. "It's just that most of us back home would rather be famous and rich. I don't think we'd be very good guardians."

Lizbeth heard more shuffling. She thought she might not have much more time to get an answer. "Piers, the thing I want to know is, what do the tiles have to do with Morphane?"

Piers pulled himself up with help from Len and Lizbeth. "Let me see if I can relay what Soliton told me." He held up a hand to keep the Welkeners from interrupting. "The tiles allow whoever holds them to enflesh the most willful part of their souls. This means that the tiles become whatever their possessor most deeply desires. Morphane was not a creation from Terz, as if he were an artist. Morphane was what Terz had become on the inside; Morphane embodied how Terz thought and what he wanted."

Lizbeth looked down. "When you think about it, that's more than just a little scary. I'm not sure I want to know what the tiles would make of my desires."

"Every moment you are in Welken, Lizbeth, you should fear that less and less."

"Piers," said Len, "while we're on the topic of 'becoming,' the whole business makes me think Morphane was like Soliton in reverse. Y'know, Soliton becomes, as you say, whatever love requires, but Terz, well, his desires 'became' Morphane. Soliton gives and gives images that are needed. Morphane sucked images in, destroying, killing, leaving behind empty husks."

"You're beginning to sound like Bebba the blind," said Bennu.

"Speaking of," said Lizbeth, "shouldn't we be seeing how the others are?"

"You wear well the yoke of compassion," replied Piers. "Yes, we should look after them. But if you haven't noticed, Angie has already been at work."

Lizbeth felt bad. She had been so preoccupied with her questions, she hadn't even noticed Angie wasn't there.

Piers picked up the amulet and told the Misfits to take their respective tiles. He called Angie over to get hers.

Then someone moaned.

Lizbeth took her first good look at the Welkeners encircling them. She hadn't thought about what Morphane's demise meant for his released prisoners. But now she could see all over the rocky plain that they had returned to their bodies. Though more obviously themselves than they were before the battle, they were still deeply hurt. Lizbeth saw wounds bleeding as if they had just occurred. She wondered which Welkener received a gash from her. Feeling responsible, she ran around, searching for the one with this injury. She saw all manner of suffering. Since at their swallowing, most of these Welkeners joined to aspects of their surroundings, these now dropped off. Lizbeth saw on the ground sticks and vines, even animal parts: a rabbit paw here, a half a snake there. The worst of it was seeing where the Welkeners had parts of themselves turn to husks that stayed behind. Open sores remained, some, she guessed, life-threatening.

Why did I talk so long to Piers? she thought. How selfish. But didn't he know? Why did he talk so long to us? I'll never understand.

The moans and screams of the former army moved Lizbeth to despair. She saw that though some were worse off physically, all had been ravaged by the trauma of entering Morphane's mind. All lived the sorrow of being twisted into different shapes and being separated from the fullness of themselves. Some held life by the thinnest of threads. Some had no strength to hold on to much of anything.

Lizbeth and the others, including the rest of the Welkeners, tended to these aching bodies as best they could. Some Welkeners gathered sticks for splints. Others tore garments into strips for bandages. While Lizbeth cleaned and consoled, she watched Piers. His satchel open and the healing oils in his hands, Piers ministered to them one by one. It was just like back in Chimney Cave. Sometimes his ointments had immediate effect. Sometimes his whispered words seemed to be enough. Sometimes he instructed those around him how to care for those he revived. She saw Jacob and other Deediers scurrying about. Vida came up and said she "nightingaled" and "redcrossed" everyone in her path. Lizbeth pulled blackberry canes off one Welkener's arms. Next to her, Angie brushed off the gravel that had clung to the legs of another. Ten yards off, Sutton wept, his shoulders shuddering. Lizbeth ran to him and held him. He said he saw the maimed face of the child whose husk he had seen near Circle Stand.

It's just so sad, thought Lizbeth. Even if all of these bodies recover, they'll never be the same. They'll be missing hands or toes—and maybe what's worse—they'll be scarred forever on the inside.

She tried to help a shepherd from Durrow Wood get comfortable. "I know it must hurt," she said, "but we can be Misfits together."

From behind her, Piers came up and patted her on the back. He moved in front and smiled. Then Lizbeth saw a Welkener approach Piers.

Though he, too, had seen his image flow over that treacherous muzzle, he was not as hurt as the others. This one had found the wherewithal to sit up, brush off his pants, and rest his head on his knees.

The man moaned and held his ribs. "I shouldn't a' done that. My mistake. I'm going to need some time to recover my pride." He looked at Piers, who was on one knee and ready to offer him a drop of elixir. Terz shook his weary head. "Oh, Piers, how will you ever forgive me? That was one doozy of a ride. I can tell you one thing. I've learned a lesson."

"What's that?" replied Piers, his voice stern.

Terz stood as tall as he was able, his frail body still shaking. With resolute eyes, he looked over Piers's bent shoulder, past the other Welkeners attending to the worn and wounded, past the wall of boulders to the western entrance by the granite face. Terz's eyes, dull and drained when Lizbeth first saw them, suddenly came alive. "Never give up, my friend. Never submit to a single worrisome thought. Never give up, not in a cold bitter wind, nor even when things seem to go up in flames all around you." He lifted a finger toward the face of the mountain.

Lizbeth did not think Terz's confession sincere, but she did believe the fire in his eyes. When she looked over to the western passageway, where Terz pointed, she saw literal flames shooting out from behind the rocks.

Terz held one arm high. "Never give up, especially when you have warmhearted friends!" He swept his hand across his body from head to toe, bowing in welcome to the source of the fire.

"What is it, Piers?" asked Lizbeth.

"It is the beginning," he said. "Go find Len and bring him to me."

Not taking her eyes off the flames for long, Lizbeth darted among the Welkeners looking for Len. She hated waiting for what was to come. She hated what came even more. Out from the narrow passageway walked slaves in chains. They were greasy with sweat and burdened down by poles they shouldered. They pulled a carriage into view. On it sat Fatagar, and flames flared out from the coal in his hand. Lizbeth stopped. She saw the fire arch into the open air and hit the slaves in front. She pitied them. Under a crude canopy, Fatagar bobbed up and down in his own blubber. He laughed.

Lizbeth saw Len and ran to him.

"It's Prester John," said Len, angrily fighting back tears, "and Ellen. They didn't do anything wrong."

Jerked around as his wide berth was yanked through the rock walls, Fatagar sent a stinging lash of flame onto Prester John's back.

Fire, thought Lizbeth. Piers said The Welkening would begin with fire. But why would Fatagar have it?

〜〜〜

Len felt Lizbeth tug on his sleeve. "I'm supposed to take you to Piers," she said.

"I left them once." His guilt gnawed at him. "I'm not going to leave them again." Guilt kept chewing, and he ran to escape its teeth. "I want a closer look." As Len weaved between Welkeners, Lizbeth stayed with him. He scrambled up the front of the western rock wall.

"Look out!" Len heard Mook's voice and ducked. Then he looked back to see an arrow in Terz's left shoulder. The Master crumpled in agony to the ground, holding the shaft with his right hand, a look of disbelief on his face. Other Welkeners readied weapons.

Fatagar ordered his carriers to drop to one knee. "D-do so gently," he said, knocking the closest ones on their heads with his walking stick. Though Fatagar's enormous weight still pressed upon their shoulders, the slaves seemed glad for this respite. Len changed into a lion, but then the tile fell out of his paw. He looked to Lizbeth to pick it up.

"Fine," she said, "but we need to get back to Piers. I'm sure you'll do more good if you do what he wants you to do."

Len uttered a low guttural growl, not at Lizbeth but at Fatagar and at his own mistake. He imagined Fatagar on the journey here, how he must have tormented Prester John and Ellen, and how these Highlanders must have also suffered under the weight of knowing they were delivering Fatagar closer to his ambition.

"Ha!" Fatagar called out to the crowd. "Prester John thought he could b-banish me to the Wasteland. What d-does he think now?" He stood and shook off his sweat like a dog.

A few slimy drops hit Len. He roared and bared his teeth.

Fatagar laughed. He pointed the coal at him, singeing his mane.

369

Lizbeth brushed at it to be sure the fire was out. Then Fatagar turned and directed a line of fire at Prester John. The nobleman flinched under the blast, but held his head up as if scanning the crowd for allies. Len changed back to human form and tried to get his attention. When Prester John started to nod in acknowledgement, Fatagar burned him again on the back of his head. Prester John bent down to dodge the flame yet kept the platform steady. He tried to raise his head again. Fatagar's flame prod anticipated his move, searing his back once more. Eventually, Prester John stayed down, and he dropped his head in submission. Len realized that with Prester John and Ellen in the front, the Welkeners dared not send their arrows to strike Fatagar's rolls of mildewed flesh. They could not charge Fatagar, and neither could Len.

Len climbed higher on the wall. He looked over and saw soldiers filing in behind Fatagar. The spikes on his head gleaming sharply in the sun, Fatagar said, "I want the other t-treasures." He wiped dripping saliva off his lips. "I know about the T-T-Tetragrammaton. Terz has told me about the other magic you have like my fire. Give them t-to me, or I'll burn your friends." He crunched a stick with his steely teeth.

With Fatagar's threat still echoing in the amphitheater, Len heard something overhead, and he ducked. Several Nezzer arrows flew above him and down into the western opening. As he scrambled to safer ground, he heard soldiers below him cry out.

Furious, Fatagar blasted Prester John and Ellen. No longer able to endure the pain and hold the poles, they let go. The front end crashed down. Fatagar slid off on his own blubber and bounced to a stop. He grabbed Prester John and Ellen before they could duck under the carriage.

"Len!" shouted Lizbeth. "We have to find Piers!"

"OK," he said, back in human form and taking his lion tile from Lizbeth. "But this better work."

As the two Misfits ran away from the front, they saw Welkeners surge forward in battle. More arrows flew overhead, and some half-dozen Kells Villagers clambered up the east wall and threw spears. Deedy dwellers scampered atop the western wall and tossed spinning disks. Though none hit Fatagar, many struck the soldiers of the Wasan Sagad.

Almost to Piers, Len looked back at the disgusting tyrant. Fatagar's anger seemed to cook his own flesh. His spike tips glowed red. He held the firestone with both hands. A huge explosion followed. Len could hear swords and daggers drop to the ground. Fatagar seemed to press his entire will into the stone. Then he opened his palm and released a raging wall of fire, a fearsome blaze that swept out like an autumn brushfire. The crackling firestorm began slowly. It blazed into the air above Fatagar, and then it billowed out like a hellish canopy, out over the walls, out over the flat. Into the inferno Fatagar yelled, "Burn!"

And the fire came.

Piers said, "It is time."

CHAPTER THIRTY-EIGHT

THE WELKENING

A gift that has the power to change us awakens a part of the soul.
But we cannot receive the gift until we can meet it as an equal.
We therefore submit ourselves to the labor of becoming like the gift.

LEWIS HYDE, *THE GIFT*

 The fire rolled out over the Welkeners, bright orange at the center and frayed black along the edges. Then the heat came. Len felt it like the sun in the Wasteland, pushing down, baking and smothering as it descended.

Piers whispered to the Misfits. "Good friends, now we will see who is true of voice. Hold your courage close, for The Welkening is here." He did not shield himself from the fire. "Len, take all four tiles and cover them in your hands. Then search inside your soul for your strongest, best desire. Feel this longing deeply, Len. See it. And trust me. The time for waiting is over, lion."

Len collected the tiles quickly and held them. He thought of ice and snow and frost. Nothing happened. He knew immediately these were surface desires, not the deeper ones Piers asked him to call up. The heat made him think of Adal in the Wasan Sagad. He thought of the McKenzie Boys, then Soliton's lamb, then how he'd always been chosen last, if he'd been chosen at all. He remembered his commissioning, how it felt so sure and true. Then he knew what he wanted and willed it. He looked up. Still, the flames came. He saw fear in the Welkeners' faces. He knew all anyone could think to do was to run, but the flames came too fast.

Len felt his desire was the best one, and he thought he could exercise trust. Into the fire he yelled, "In the north, justice!"

And the flames swept down like they were burning a hillside in the sky. They blazed and crackled. Len saw Bebba the blind cover her head and huddle on the ground. Would they all be burned alive? He stood as long as he dared—and then he saw, just before the blanket of fire engulfed him, someone standing nearby. It was Angie. She smiled at him, faced up to the flames, and announced, "Do not fear!" Len tried. He looked up and saw the center of the inferno flash out like a bomb. Len covered his eyes with his hands—and then the flames reached his head. The fire rushed over him hot and heavy. It curled down his arms, flashed over his waist and down to his feet. The flames licked his shoes in its blazing fury.

Len braced himself for the pain. He cocked the trigger of his scream and held his breath for the scorching obliteration.

But it did not come. He felt only pleasantly warm. He removed his hands from his eyes and looked around. Astounded, he watched the fullness of fire crawl over him. He felt no pain. It was the same everywhere. The flames cascaded down, seared their worst, yet no one was consumed. Len thought surely Death would come, but if he had come, he had left empty-handed. The flames did not burn.

In the wildly orange and yellow place, Len studied the battlefield. Welkeners rose from the ground and stood into the flames. Even the weary ones got up, the sick and wounded Welkeners, those who'd been in Morphane's prison. They seemed stronger. Instead of destroying, somehow the flames cleaned and refined. They restored. Then Len realized he had received what he wanted. Justice came in the fire.

Then there was Fatagar. Len looked over to the face of the mountain. Though he kept squeezing the tiles, he watched the orange glow dissipate. And then he saw that Fatagar, burned clothing and all, carriage on fire, still lived. Len didn't know what to do next.

He didn't worry for long.

One of Angie's wings brushed against him. He watched her fly above him, right through the remaining fire. Fatagar saw her too. Looking bewildered yet angry, he clutched the firestone once more. A flare thrust out in her direction. It pushed aside the waning fire and climbed up toward her blue wings. Calmly, she uncorked the water vial, poured out all the water, and put the vial in her belt. In the center of the unburning flames, Angie opened her hands and called the water to her. It heard her. The water stopped its descent before it hit the ground, as if it were listening for wisdom. The water pursued the living auger that was Angie.

Len pulled Lizbeth and Bennu next to him. Standing arm in arm with them, he said, "If she could get rid of Morphane with a few tears, what will she do with this waterfall?"

The water grew in volume as it flowed up. When it reached her feet, she tapped it back down and stood on it. The water curled over and became a cascading fountain, spreading outward in all directions. Len let go of Lizbeth and Bennu. The three of them held their hands open to the falling drops.

As Angie danced on the fountaintop, the showers came down, extinguishing the lingering flames. The flowing water doused Fatagar's flare and sent harmless steam rising into the open sky. Len felt refreshed, exhilarated, even joyful, like he would in the first rain after a hot spell or, better yet, after a long drought. The splashing drops felt like an unexpected mercy had come to heal the land. And then he remembered Angie's commissioning, "In the south, grace."

Through the rain, when Angie turned her back in a pirouette, Len saw Fatagar try again to press his flames toward her. Len called up to warn Angie. She appeared not to hear him. All the while, the cool water flowed and flowed out and down. Then Angie faced Fatagar, raised her arms, and the water surged forth in greater volume. At first, the harder rain felt good to Len. He looked into it and let it wash over his face. Then the drops began to hurt. The fountain gushed and became a torrential outpouring.

As the water pounded the ground, Len's joy vanished. He searched for cover and found none. He held his sweatshirt above his head. The rain sprayed down as out of a fire hose. The fountain became a river, and a deluge flashed upon them. Like a burst dam, it crashed over the ground, collecting and rising into a flood. It came up to Len's ankles, then his knees, then his waist. He couldn't figure out why it didn't flow out to the south. The water overtook everything. It came and came, filling Granite Flat as if it were a basin for a lake, rising up, higher and higher, threatening to drown everyone. It lapped against Len's neck. As he treaded water, he saw that Lizbeth and Bennu were doing the same. He couldn't see Fatagar or Prester John or Ellen. Piers just stood in it, the water reaching his nose. Len looked up at Angie but couldn't see her through the downpour. He wondered why she would keep going, why she wouldn't see the danger everyone was in. He wondered where the grace was in all this.

So much new water came all at once that Len could not stay afloat. Holding his breath, he went under. He flailed in the rising water. He felt pushed around as if he'd lost control in an ocean wave. Finally the tumbling stopped, and he opened his eyes. He couldn't see the top. He thought he couldn't hold his breath much longer, and then he saw Angie. There she was standing in the water, arms outstretched, wings fully open. She smiled. She nodded at him to look around—and then he saw Welkeners all around him swimming, breathing, living in the flood. They were no more hurt than they were by the fire. Some were looping in somersaults. He saw Vida and Jacob do their sea turtle swim, and then Bennu swam over and pushed him playfully. Piers and Lizbeth coasted on their backs holding hands.

Then just as fast as it came, the water receded. Len watched it flow out down the trails to the south and the passageways to the east and west by the Ganderst Hall keyholes. The lake shrunk down, becoming a pond and then a pool, and then as Len struggled to keep his balance, the water drained out until only a few puddles could be seen. Angie pushed her wet hair off her face. Shaking her wings, she flew down to Piers.

Len stared in amazement at the unburned, undrowned Welkeners. He stooped next to a young girl beside him. She was the one whose face Sutton had seen as a husk. As she wrung out her clothes, she looked up at him. Her ravaged cheeks were smoother; her skin-shorn nose was not raw. The fire seemed to have burned away the rougher places, and then water brought new life. Len could see that her skin was not as it was before Morphane, but it was on the way. The same was true everywhere. For all the trauma of the fire and the flood, the wounded Welkeners looked healthier, invigorated.

Then Len noticed Terz.

Of course, he thought, Terz had been released from Ferodor as the others gained their freedom from Morphane.

Clearly, Terz hadn't fared as well. The wooden shaft of Mook's arrow had burned in the fire, right down to his skin. And unlike his neighbors, Terz coughed up water repeatedly. His cropped hair was gone, singed off, as were his eyebrows. Piers held him by the arm.

As Len started toward Terz, he saw Prester John and Ellen waving at him. He ran through the puddles and embraced them. Then Len hung his head. "I'm so glad you're OK. You know I regret—"

"Len, m'lad," said Prester John. "Don't worry yourself. All soldiers make mistakes."

"You're too generous, Prester John," said Len. "So what happened to Fatagar?"

"While in the firestorm," said Prester John, "I nearly snagged him from behind when I thought I heard Ellen call out, so I turned back to tend to her."

Ellen sat on a stone and rolled her eyes.

"Then as the water overtook us, I couldn't find him anywhere. I grabbed a spear and slashed all around at him. I must have held my breath for an hour."

"None of us needed to hold our breath at all, Your Eminence."

"Not so, Ellen Basala. I held mine because leaders must live by a higher standard. Anyway, I looked up through the water and saw the bottom of the carrier float away. I swam after it, but even my great speed could not catch it."

"I see," said Len. Then he felt a gust of wind against his back. He turned around and saw Bennu twirling a finger in his palm.

Piers stood next to him. "Good friends, The Welkening is not complete. It began with a burning and a washing. More remains: more undoing, more unveiling, more remaking."

Pressing into the wind, Len left Prester John and Ellen to better observe Bennu's turn.

Piers called out to Bennu. "Spread it wide. Be brave, falcon, be brave."

With his blobby gift in his left palm, Bennu sculpted the substance with his right hand. He poked at it, and Len felt the wind increase. Then Bennu stirred it. Len saw a tiny windstorm emerge, a whirling dervish like Bennu had described from the gate in Ganderst Hall. It grew. When it became the size of a large spinning top, Bennu launched it from the gift and sent it loose into the Welkeners. Then he created another and another. Len tried to keep his distance. Bennu spun out cyclones. And each one grew. The cyclones touched the ground, and the tops swirled upwards to twenty feet. When one pressed against another, it merged and gained strength.

A swirling cylinder came at Len. He spread his legs and leaned into the gale. His cheeks wobbled. He couldn't open his eyes to see what Bennu was doing. He couldn't shout out that he was about to blow away and that Bennu should stop. The cyclone inched closer to him. He worried he would get tossed high in the air or get sucked in like Terz did when they fought him. The cyclone blew him over and then swept him into the air. Fumbling in the nothingness, Len tumbled out of control. Then he bumped into someone.

He looked to his left and saw Vida smiling. She had her arms outstretched like a superhero, and her round body bobbed buoyantly in the tempest. She swooped under him and above him and then came close enough so he could hear her. "I've never been kittyhawked before, no sir."

Len laid himself out into the wind. He held his position horizontally then he banked down and recovered. He looked around and saw a regular flock of flying Welkeners. Like ice skaters in the air, Sutton and Zennor zipped along the rim of the cyclone. Piers soared by as if he'd been catching updrafts all his life. Even Lizbeth stayed aloft—and no one had a bigger smile. Len thought that here, in the eye of the hurricane, he felt a kind of swirling calm. Then he recalled Bennu's charge, "In the east, peace."

After two more revolutions, Len found Bennu at the very top, in falcon form. His screech could be heard in the whirlwind, and he dove through the center of it to the one lone figure not suspended in air. Terz sat on the gravel floor, alternately holding his ears and tugging his knees to his chest.

Gradually, the racing wind decreased. The flyers circled down, closer and closer to the ground. Len pushed himself into a vertical position and, like a parachutist, gently touched down. He saw Jacob land but keep his hand in flight, swooping it around in the breeze like kids do out a car window. With a ridiculous grin on his face, Piers folded his arms and leaned into the remaining wind until he was at a fory-five–degree angle.

Then the wind subsided. Len watched Bennu follow the cyclone out of Granite Flat, and he noticed that all the puddles were gone. As before, the convalescing Welkeners appeared more revived, their hair blown out of their washed faces, their eyes looking more full of life, as if the dust of Morphane's oppression had been blown away. Many wounds were well on their way to healing. Missing parts had been restored.

ༀ

Lizbeth looked at Terz. Though she had enjoyed coasting in the wind, her mood shifted as she saw the traitor push himself up on his knees. His skin, ravaged by the cyclone, shone a blistered red in the sun. He touched his raw arms delicately, as if they'd just been flogged. At first, Lizbeth wanted to comfort him in his pain; then she saw him as a miserable creature, the cause of so much suffering.

Mook interrupted her musing. He dropped his bow at her feet and held out the earth-moving box to her with both hands. "The fire, the water, the air, they won't bring back Alabaster. But we still have our tasks. Here. Your work needs to be done." He placed the carved box in her hand, his gray streaks shining brightly.

Piers nodded his approval. "Lizbeth, you will bring The Welkening to its end, and as you do, more will be undone than in the other three elements combined. It is by Soliton's wisdom, Lizbeth, that you have been told to wield your power well. Do what you must do, ox. But do not seek revenge."

Though she knew he was quoting the charge he gave her before her quest, Lizbeth also wondered how a statement could have better timing. She did not know what she would do to Terz if she let herself go.

She pulled up the lid and emptied the box. She scattered the soil around it as if it were seed. And it may well have been, for the ground beneath her started to grow. It shook and then trembled. Finding balance difficult, Lizbeth became an ox. In seconds, she found herself rising on a pillar of land. When it stopped, she peered over the edge. The pedestal did not begin an avalanche in imitation of Angie's fountain nor did it create a dust storm to rival Bennu's whirlwind. She stood nobly on the pillar, but she wanted something to happen. In her readiness, Lizbeth clomped a hoof down on the earthen pedestal. The pillar jolted down a notch. She clomped again, and the pillar shook and clunked down again. The faster Lizbeth pounded the surface, the faster the pillar descended, until it crashed back down, level with the ground.

Then all of Granite Flat shook.

It started rumbling out at her feet, and it grew in force. As the earth moved, so did everything upon it. The tremor growled and roared through the soil. Bebba the blind dropped to one knee. Prester John swayed back and forth till he fell on the ground. Lizbeth saw Zennor hold his staff for support, but then the staff gave way. Small rocks tumbled down from the walls, then boulders rolled, and both rock walls began to crumble.

Though she was not hurt from the fire or the water or the wind, Lizbeth found it difficult to relax and enjoy the shaking earth. Somehow she felt not only tossed around but sifted, as if the entire plain were settling out the good and the bad in her, threshing her soul into grain and chaff. In this trembling moment, Lizbeth felt as exposed as Granite Flat itself, without walls, without trees, without anything to hide behind. She saw every facade she'd ever erected come crashing down. All the masks, all the pretensions, broke before her.

If we must endure this, she thought, to be found true of voice, who will remain? What thing we've built will survive?

The shaking and the dividing, the sifting and exposing, continued. Rocks tumbled off until the walls were level. A few Deediers who'd been on top rode the boulders down, hanging on as best they could. Along the cliff face, Lizbeth saw the keyholes collapse, the walls crumbling until rubble covered the openings.

Lizbeth's pillar rose again, and she watched the ground below her reshape itself. The wider plain of two paths that led to the doors became narrower, the earth falling off the edges as a single path rose up. Scrambling to stay up on the path, Sutton, Zennor, and the others ran or crawled to the rising ground. Just before the path had become too tall to climb onto, Prester John leaped up and pulled Ellen Basala with him.

The path ascended until it became even with Lizbeth's pillar. The two places merged. To Lizbeth's amazement Piers, on the cliffside of the path, stood without wavering. While others held on for their lives, Piers flexed skillfully on the shifting surface, getting his sea legs on the dry but wavy ground. Lizbeth turned and saw Angie at the rear, also standing, using her wings for stability. Bennu soared above the tumult.

Piers bent his knees and then raised his hands. "Stand, Welkeners! This is the time to learn if you are true of voice. Now is The Welkening's shaking out, the unveiling. Rise!"

One by one, some quickly, some with assistance, the Welkeners stood. As Lizbeth lifted her ox head, she felt she was in fact aligning herself with Soliton and Piers and Welken's ways, even with this way of undoing, this earthquaking power beneath them.

Yet one did not stand.

Terz crawled on the moving ground, slipping one way and then the next, clutching Welkeners' legs and feet as his slid. When he wrapped himself around Lizbeth's front hoofs, she was torn between wanting to pull him to safety and wanting to toss him with her horn off the path and to his destruction below. She wished he hadn't turned his back on his guardian's calling.

Then the whole path seemed to take on a life of its own. It lifted up more dramatically and broke away from the cliff face. It roiled and trembled and shifted over to the east, away from Len and Lizbeth's covered doors. The standing Welkeners and Misfits held each other as they rode the path like the back of some giant lumbering horse. When the path moved out, Lizbeth relaxed. She let go and accepted her unveiling. Then pleasure came. Feeling safe on this colossal saddle, Lizbeth, the lover of stability, smiled through every dip or twist.

But Terz did not. He let go of Lizbeth's hoofs and belly crawled through the Welkeners and up to the front. He looked sick to his stomach. Then the path leaned, and he started to slide off the edge. Piers caught him by the collar. No matter what Terz did, he could not get any footing. To Lizbeth, the gravel underneath Terz acted alive, like it didn't seem to want to provide him support. No matter what Terz did—sit, stand, squat, or crawl—the ground under him moved out.

Then the rocks went on the offensive. Lizbeth did not issue a command or even have an intention, but small stones came at Terz from some unseen hand. He shielded his face, and Piers hung on. Stinging from the wind, coughing from the flood, aching from fire-burned skin and the arrow in his shoulder, Terz now received The Welkening's final battering.

As the rumbling slowed down, Lizbeth looked to her left. The two paths that came from the meadow had become one trail that followed the cliff face's abrupt turn to the right. It had built itself up toward a wall that faced east.

Bennu alighted next to Lizbeth and changed back into human shape. So did Lizbeth. Bennu said, "I don't get it. The path leads up to nothing, just another side of the mountain."

Then Piers stepped forth and, without anger, dragged Terz up to where the path met its dead end. He addressed the whole assembly. "Long ago, before the amulet was taken from the Tetragrammaton, a door existed here. When the theft occurred, the door closed up, and the path leading up to it dropped away. You see, the Welkening is a restoration—and one who transgressed is needed to make things right again." Piers set Terz down, leaning his head gently against the rock wall. Then Piers gathered the tiles from Len and put two on the ground on each side of the weakened Master. Lizbeth felt sad for him.

On their own, the tiles started to move. Like expert chisels they dug into the rock face, cutting their way in parallel lines up the sides till they arched overhead. When the four tiles met at the center, they reversed routes and chipped away down to the path once again. Slivers of granite fell on Terz. He became energized in an unnaturally animated way. He turned to face the wall, bowing his head to protect himself from the chips coming down. He reached out to grab the two tiles on the right side with one hand. At least he tried to. To Lizbeth he grasped at the tiles like he wanted to pry them off the mountain, like he wanted to possess the tiles again, to start over, to use the power he knew they had. He pulled, but the tiles kept moving. He could not get them loose. Then he stretched to the left to touch the other tiles.

Though the distance was too great for the diminutive Terz, he would not let go of the two tiles he touched with his right hand. He stretched and stretched to his left, and as he stretched, two things happened that shocked Lizbeth. First, Terz's arms elongated so that he could reach both sides. Second, his hand that touched the tiles on the right side merged with the stone, and his forearms turned gray and pebbly like granite, all the way up to his elbow. Lizbeth gasped. Terz clutched at the tiles as they finished their descent to the floor and hung on. Now both hands were one with the granite, and the tiles etched their way up the sides. Terz, perhaps too far gone to feel anything, did not cry out. He held on to the tiles even as they lifted him off the ground, even as they met at the center of the arch. He hung there for a second—and then Lizbeth shuddered as she saw the tiles pull him in. His arms merged into the top of the arch, then his head and shoulders. Before his chest entered also, his legs and feet took on the look of granite. Finally, all of Terz became part of the archway, as hard and cold, Lizbeth thought, as his own heart.

When the last of Terz got drawn in, the stone bumped up and grew. The substance of Terz traveled down from the center of the arch the way a mole pushes up soil. What was left of Terz glommed onto the outer edge of the archway, creating a raised, rounded border that ran all the way down the sides to the bottom. When his substance touched the path, the tiles pushed through to the other side, and the slab they'd cut out fell with a crash forward but missed Piers and the others nearby. The rounded edge framed the opening with short grooves that looked much like Terz's thick hair. Around the arch, chiseled words appeared: "How pale your flaws before the brightness of my folly."

"He said something like that to us," said Bennu. "Remember? When he captured us by the fire at night."

Without showing joy or remorse but with all the solemnity of loss, Piers stood under the arch. "These words will serve as a warning to all who think they are higher than others. It speaks to those who wish for more than they were meant to have."

Lizbeth stared at the empty space that Terz had occupied and saw the four tiles on the floor. She made her way to Piers. "I could accept Terz dying in a battle, or even getting smashed by the granite slab that just came down. But to know that the raised edge is Terz himself, I don't like it. It's morbid."

"I can see why you wouldn't want him to end up this way," said Piers, "but in Welken, 'the inner and the outer meet.' What we mean is that who you are on the inside will eventually come out; it will be laid bare. In fact, it becomes your legacy, and no matter what you've done, in Welken that legacy will somehow serve. As part of this archway Terz now serves to set this entrance apart and to caution those tempted to defile the Tetragrammaton for their own purposes. He wanted to remain close to the tiles, and so he shall, for you see," Piers paused as he stepped up onto the slab and under the arch, "the entrance leads directly into the Tetragrammaton. This door will remain open, and the power will be here for the taking, but we will be wise if we see that it is here for the protecting."

"It still seems harsh," said Lizbeth. "I'm sorry, that's just the way I feel."

Piers put his hand on her shoulder. "I do enjoy your tender heart, Lizbeth. Terz became what he was becoming. That's part of Welken's ways. Come, let us return the tiles to their rightful places."

CHAPTER THIRTY-NINE

THREE ENDINGS

Although I can lift my finger to point something out,
I cannot supply the vision. . . .

ST. AUGUSTINE, *ON CHRISTIAN DOCTRINE*

 Lizbeth waited for Angie to come from the back. As Piers stepped through the opening and waved the Misfits in, Lizbeth gently put her hand up to the raised edge around the archway. Cautiously, she touched it. She ran a fingernail into the carved lines. Everything felt like stone.

She was so intent, Angie's words surprised her. "Lizbeth, I'm mourning, too. In Chimney Cave, when we first met, he seemed so cute and helpful—but the sad truth is that he already knew about Morphane."

"Yeah, makes you want to go back and look for clues." She made a fist and pressed it lightly against the wall. "I dunno. I can't quite get used to how extreme things are here. One minute we're living out miracles of fire and water. The next minute a living being becomes part of a rock wall. Back home, Terz would have at least gotten a trial."

"You're right," said Angie. "But I've been thinking. Maybe in Welken everyone is on trial all the time, not in a bad way like we're being judged every second. I just get the sense that all our decisions matter, that what we do tells a story about our heart."

"Yeah, Piers said he became what he was becoming. It's kinda scary to think that that's true for all of us." Lizbeth walked through the archway. Just ten feet inside, she saw what she guessed was the back wall of the Tetragrammaton, a white marble surface that reflected light into the entryway. Its brightness reassured her.

Lizbeth held her tile up to the marble to see if the colors matched.

Angie said, "I don't remember being able to get around the Tetragrammaton from the other side, do you? Wasn't it a dead end, a closed room?"

Before Lizbeth could reply, Piers leaned toward them from farther up in the room. "Indeed, but the vistas have opened up. See for yourself."

Holding their tiles, all four Misfits joined Piers in the room of frescoes, the room they'd entered through the east door on their first day in Welken. It no longer had its extraordinary walls. Instead, the paintings gave way to a panorama of three-dimensional Welken realities. Lizbeth wondered if they could enter into it wherever they wished.

"One thing's for sure," she said. "Welken is never boring. Here we are inside a cave, and the countryside seems nearer than it does outside. I can even smell something coming from Primus Hook, lavender maybe." She felt in the air for the walls she remembered so well, but her hands met no resistance.

Piers also reached out into the openness of the room. "As I said, the vistas have opened up. Good friends, may the eyes of our hearts see into the distance as well. But first, before we go any farther, a different task calls our names. Come, let us return the tiles so that the Welkeners outside can come in and join our delight."

The four friends turned and faced the Tetragrammaton. While waiting for her next instruction, Lizbeth looked down at the tile in her hand. The ox on her tile moved. It ran around as if the tile were a tiny movie screen. The ox looked troubled then snorted and raced over to pull a boy out of a river. Then it stared back at Lizbeth as if to say, "Do you understand?" Then the ox froze back into its painted tile image.

By the time Lizbeth looked up to describe what had happened on her tile, the other Misfits were also glancing around with similar astonished expressions.

"My angel," Angie said, "my angel, she moved. She flew around right in my hand. She was inside the room where we were chained up, and she led each of you out of your cage. Cool, huh? I guess angels helped us in that room and we didn't even know it."

"Angie," said Bennu, "don't you get it? *You* were the angel in that prison guiding us to freedom. You've been so worried about letting Welken down in Mercy Bay that you've forgotten all your wisdom since then. And your story helps me know what my tile meant. The little falcon swooped down to attack something. The bird was fearless and skilled. I guess that was me fighting Terz. Doesn't sound like me, does it?"

Len elbowed Lizbeth. "Our friends back home probably wouldn't recognize us now—and not," he said quickly, beating the others to the obvious, "not because I look like I'm from *The Wizard of Oz* but, y'know, because we're different in other ways, too. The lion on my tile swept the back of his paw on the ground and bowed his head. It made me think of how much I could learn by listening. Me—listening—can you imagine?"

"Of course, we haven't needed to," said Lizbeth. "Why imagine when you have the real thing?" Then she recounted what the ox did on her tile. Lizbeth tried to tell what happened without embellishment. "I'm not bragging, you know. I'm just saying what I saw."

"You don't need to worry, Lizbeth," said Bennu. "I'll do the bragging. I think the little ox was telling you that you weren't a failure at the river."

Piers stepped into the middle of them. "Come, my friends. Return them. Return the tiles to their rightful places. It is time. In Welken."

"Of Welken," said the four.

Lizbeth set her tile in the opening reserved for it, and the others followed. The tiles glowed with gratitude—it seemed—and then Piers put the golden scarab in the middle. Two legs grasped the center, and each of the remaining four legs reached out to hold a tile. At long last, the Tetragrammaton was restored.

While reveling in the sight, Len wondered what would happen if he took the tiles out. If he were given the power to fulfill his vision, what desire would emerge? What, in fact, was he becoming? He thought he'd made a lot of good changes since coming to Welken. He was less brutally sarcastic. Maybe it meant he would turn the tiles into a nobleman. Yeah right, he thought, I'd make Prester John look like Abraham Lincoln.

Then Len stepped back and cleared his mind. "Just one question," he said.

"That I doubt," said Piers, smiling.

"OK, OK, you're right," said Len. "Here's *a* question: How did the amulet get in the museum? Oh, and here's another: Did you know that Morphane was made out of tiles? If so, why did you send us out to find them? And why—"

"There is a time for questions," said Piers, "and a time for answers. But now is the time to"—he paused here so he could shout the next word— "CELEBRATE!"

Like New Year's Eve partygoers hearing the clock strike midnight, the Welkeners roared their approval. Whooping and clapping, they streamed in past the Tetragrammaton, the healthy ones assisting those not fully recovered from their sojourn in Morphane's chaotic psyche.

Vida Bering Well supported a convalescing girl at her side. "Don't give me any excusifications. If the time comes to dance, we'll fredastaire with the rest of 'em."

Zennor came in carrying four children, and Mook had his arm around a Durrow woodsman who limped. More and more Welkeners filed in, smiling, shouting, laughing.

By the time the Misfits walked through the east door and into Ganderst Hall, the dim cavern had already been transformed into a glittering ballroom.

The guardians have been busy, thought Len. I'm not sure the Home and Garden Channel would approve, but they do have panache.

About ten feet up, yards of yellow fabric stretched from gold rings on one side to more rings across the room, creating a billowy false ceiling in places. Bouquets of flowers, Len could not imagine from where, stood tall in vases on every table in the room. Then Len overheard some guardians talking.

"White plates and blue tablecloths?" one said. "You mean that literally?"

"No," said the other, tossing a blue napkin on the floor, "I meant it litteringly. Honk!"

Len shook his head and wondered how this loony crew ever managed to get anything accomplished. Yet goblets stood at the ready, and punch (lime mint, Len discovered in a snitch) swirled inside a silver bowl. All the sconces shone brightly, but they hardly needed to, since Soliton's effervescence filled the hall from above. Len looked up at him. Ceaselessly, the orb spun out light and images ranging from rainbow showers to faces and dancers. Sometimes his essence took a shape meaningful to a particular Welkener. One image made Zennor laugh. Another teased Vida for her "verbifications." Len thought that nothing could be more contrary to Morphane, more his opposite. While Morphane absorbed and spit out death, Soliton shot forth life and empowered. Len felt larger for being in his presence.

With all the chairs and tables arranged against the walls, the vast center of the grand room begged to be filled. While Len watched, Welkeners formed a circle and waited. Then the music began. Guardians on drums and pipes, horns and strings, stepped out of side rooms and announced their glorious sounds. In concert with the melody, Solition sent out showering sparkles that drifted like leaves to the floor. When the sparkles hit anything, they twirled, and streamers went flying. Len guessed that Soliton must have spent some vacation time in the Window under the Mountain.

With open arms, the Welkeners invited the Misfits into the circle. Gladly grasping Vida's hand on one side and Ellen's on the other, Len prepared to be embarrassed by his inexperienced dance moves. The band played, and Len did his best. When his feet got tangled, Ellen and Vida held him up.

Then guardian chefs marched in with a feast so enticing that the dancing stopped at the first whiff of spice. There were roasts and meat pies, baked beans, currant scones, sweet potatoes, fresh peas, salads made up of exotic wild lettuces, and pies and cakes and tarts and cookies, most of which filled the air with cinnamon. Len realized he hadn't eaten for such a long time.

Just when full mouths quieted things down, a swarm of glimpses buzzed in. Soliton doused his lights. Into the shadows the glimpses flew in formation, creating brilliant designs with their light trails. Ten of them snagged ends of Piers's hair, stretching it out in full. With their tails glowing, the glimpses made him look to Len like an innovative thinker with a bunch of bright ideas.

"Too many riddles," called out one glimpse, laughing. "This is what comes from too many riddles!"

One glimpse landed on the edge of Len's cup and asked for a sip. Startled, Len spilled a drop, and the glimpses swarmed to lap it up before it hit the floor. Before long, Welkeners were patting their bellies, and Len was sure he wouldn't be hungry for at least another hour.

After a while Piers stood on a platform near the depleted buffet tables to address the crowd. "Good friends, we are honored to have with us Sarah Wace of Primus Hook; Lady Wace, the last one to have seen Bors." As the Welkeners applauded and sighed and whispered comments of admiration to each other, Sarah Wace walked to the platform. Her countenance shone with contentment and intelligence, adding depth to her extraordinary beauty. Her regal purple gown flowed with calm certainty.

Sarah Wace pressed her hands together. "I'd almost forgotten our gift for celebration." Whoops and cheers and clapping erupted. "After all that has happened on behalf of Welken, our gratefulness rises to the brim of our hearts, and we cannot contain the flow. Yet merely saying thank you feels like offering a single seed to a farmer. Even so our gratitude goes out. To the Welkeners who left their homes to band together against a foe more powerful than they imagined: Mook, Sutton, Zennor, Prester John, Ellen, Vida, Jacob, we thank you."

Amid the hoots and whistles, Prester John bowed and walked awkwardly over to Sarah while holding that posture. "Lady Wace of Primus Hook, those in the Highlands could not possibly accept all your praise, but I will try to bear it home honorably, for I know that I am . . . I am being kicked in the shin! Ellen Basala, please, a little more dignity, because as I was saying—"

Sarah blessed Prester John with a hand to his head and sent him off. "And for Piers, Lord of Primus Hook, we proclaim to all our neighbors your courage, your wisdom borne of study and faith, and your unspeakable suffering for our sakes. You have led and healed us, and you've carried us when we could not carry ourselves. And, yes, we recognize that you still carry the load of one who longs for liberation. You bear the weight of Bors within you, but one day soon, we will find a way to reunite his soul and body. Piers, accept our gratitude."

Loud applause exploded into Ganderst Hall. Many wiped tears away as Piers walked up to Sarah, kissed her hand, and waved back to the crowd. His own tears said all that needed to be said of his affection for the assembled Welkeners. As Piers stepped down, he embraced many. Len overheard him whisper words of thanks for service to Welken.

"And to our new friends," Sarah said, "they who call themselves the Misfits, Angie, Len, Lizbeth, Bennu, we call you misfitted no longer. You have been in Welken, and you have become of Welken. We will not forget to tell the story of your journey here and what that journey has meant to Welken. Morphane is gone! Terz is no more!"

In the raucous cheering, the four came up to Sarah Wace. To each one she bowed, held their hands, and kissed them. When they stepped off the platform, the hall nearly shook with shouts of joy. Len waved.

Sarah held up her hands to ask for silence. "The greatest sacrifice was made by the one not here. You know I'm talking about Alabaster Singing, she who sang her last verse in Welken's defense. More than we can say, we grieve her loss. We will miss what her silence said to us. And so now we thank Soliton for Welken's ways, for the promise of knowing her love once again someday, in the light behind the shadows. To honor her silence, let us be silent."

⌘

Lizbeth closed her eyes and mourned. Through her tears, as she was about to berate herself for not helping in time, Lizbeth saw in her mind a green hill, rich in the tall grass of late spring. A gentle breeze caressed the grass as a lover would his beloved's flowing tresses. And there, stepping out from behind the trunk of a cedar, stood Alabaster. She waved to Lizbeth and swayed in the flow of the breeze, as full of life and strength as anyone, her single white streak of hair shining in the sun. In one motion, she pulled at some tall grass and scattered the seeds. Then she faded from Lizbeth's view.

When Lizbeth opened her eyes, she looked around and saw her own feelings expressed on the faces around her. Somehow, she thought, everyone must have seen the same vision of Alabaster. It must have come from Soliton. She looked up at his whirling orb of shooting images and saw a sparkle fly down to her. When she clapped her hands at it, it disappeared, so she just kept clapping—and around her swelled a chorus of applause, everyone looking up, as happy as she was to accept the hope offered by Soliton.

When the clamor subsided, Sarah Wace relaxed her shoulders with a sigh. "So, Piers, what is next?"

Piers traded places with Sarah on the platform. "Good friends, we have accomplished much together, and we also have tasks that remain. We must find where Bors is hidden, search out what happened to Fatagar, and convene the council at Long House. If we remain true, we need not fear another Morphane. Now say your farewells to our four travelers, whose time it is to return."

As if they were in a wedding receiving line, the Misfits hugged each Welkener. Lizbeth cried and smiled till her cheeks ached. "I'm getting different kinds of hugs," she said to Angie. "Some seem final, but others seem casual, like they expect to see us again. Do you think we're coming back?"

"I think we'll always be connected to Welken." Angie kissed Jacob on the cheek and watched him blush. "And Welken is closer than we ever realized."

"That doesn't answer the question."

"You're right. My heart tells me that our time hasn't run out. I just don't have a clue what that means."

When everyone had said good-bye, Piers led the foursome through the east door. Fog rolled in from Goffer's Spit. Toward Alta Nez Falls they could see the Endel Inn's chimney smoke curve gracefully upward.

"Piers?" said Lizbeth softly.

"Yes?"

"I'm not sure I want to go home. I mean, I want to be with Mom and Dad and play softball in summer league, but I just don't feel like I belong there. Who would have thought I'd feel more at home in Welken than in Skinner?"

THE WELKENING: A THREE-DIMENSIONAL TALE

"Why not?" said Piers. "That there should be a place where we are at home is foretold in our longing for it. Our feet are meant to rest as well as walk."

"Then why shouldn't I feel at home back home?" She brushed away the thickening fog.

"You might yet. How old are you?"

"OK, OK," said Lizbeth. "I get the picture."

"The picture," said Piers, "is just now arriving."

As she looked out on the east room vistas, the fog thinned out, and the landscape began to change. Gradually, Welken faded into Skinner, the Nez River overlapping in places with the Lewis, the Great Alpine Reef to the north aligning with the McKenzie Butte, and foothills to the south drifting into green farmland. In the distance on the way to the Prester Highlands, downtown Skinner's buildings rose, and out west, though farther out, a thin glistening ribbon of ocean came into view. To the east, the Interstate highway roughly followed the contours of Welken's coastline, from Goffer's Spit to Mercy Bay.

Then Lizbeth remembered what Len had said about the museum and the Wasan Sagad changing places. She smiled at him, and he gave her a what-did-I-tell-you look.

And Lizbeth knew right where they were. They stood atop Wendell's Mountain, the highest point just south of town. She thought that this time they wouldn't need a glimpse to get back. They had a vista.

Bennu broke into the silence. "Do we just walk onto the mountain and into Skinner?"

"Do you know enough to take the next step?" asked Piers. "Then you know enough."

"I'm ready. The sky itself seems to be pulling me in."

Piers pointed to the trail off the mountain. "Lizbeth, Bennu, Angie, come over here. You know the path well."

⌇∾⋎∾⌇

Len couldn't imagine why Piers didn't mention his name. He felt hurt. "Maybe I shouldn't ask," said Len, "but what about me?"

"I was getting to that." Piers put his arm around him. "We must reckon with the fact that you have already spent time at home. More than we realize, time is a rope. It may grow slack enough so that worlds can loop together, but we must be careful. Time can hang us too. In this case we will need to wait for the loop."

"Meaning?"

"Meaning that you must stay with me for a short time while your friends make their way off Wendell's Mountain. You'll join up with them soon enough."

As disconcerting as it felt to Len to be left behind, he said nothing.

I'm the one who messed things up, he thought, so I'll just have to take what's coming to me.

Lizbeth hugged Piers, then stepped onto Wendell's Mountain, a small peak by Oregon's standards. Shielding her eyes from the sun, she waved back at Len and motioned for Bennu and Angie to join her. Angie walked to the edge of the path. She stopped, waited for Bennu, and then the two of them strolled onto the Oregon hilltop.

As the three hiked off the mountain, Piers and Len waved. Then Piers took Len back into Ganderst Hall, pulled two chairs into a quieter corner, and invited him to sit.

"Piers," Len said, not wasting any time, "I'd like to go back to the question about Morphane. Did you know . . . about the tiles, I mean?"

Piers took a deep breath. "All truths, in time, are good to tell, but not all hearers are ripe for the hearing."

Len wondered if he'd grown "fruity" enough. He smiled at his own joke.

"I sent you into danger," Piers said cautiously, "knowing less about Morphane than you might have guessed. I knew that you four seemed glazed into the very clay of the tiles, and that the tiles were gone. But Morphane? The door to Morphane's origin opened wider the more unhinged he became. I ventured this. For you to help Welken, you had to become of Welken. You had to be put in situations that tested you, that tested your affection for Welken's ways."

Len realized that just a few days ago, this kind of revelation would have infuriated him. Now he said, "I suppose I needed harder tests than the others."

Piers said nothing.

Len waited awhile, then decided to change the subject. "Will we see you again?"

"Don't you already know the answer?"

"I'm sure I should."

"Angie could tell you."

With this clue, Len's eyes lit up. "You mean . . . ? No, it's not possible. How could you be in Skinner?" Len sat with his head in his hands for some time. "You really expect me to believe that *you* are the ginger cat with the warm green eyes? And you're already there, in Skinner, waiting for us?"

Piers nodded.

"You, Piers, Lord of Primus Hook, you are a housecat in Skinner, Oregon? You are the cat I've petted in my lap and disciplined for scratching the couch?"

"Indeed. And you, Len, are a lion."

"Oh yeah, I guess so."

"And perhaps," said Piers, "there's something here to help us understand the amulet. I don't know how it got in your museum. But if *I* can get to Skinner, then maybe—"

"You think Terz took it there?"

"Or someone years before him? I don't know. I'm only a housecat, as you said."

Len and Piers sat in silence and watched the dancing in Ganderst Hall. Then Len felt that he had worked his way to another improbable conclusion. "But there's more going on than even this, right, Piers? When I was home, I read Mom's story about Percy and Bones, and that's where it became clear to me that somehow Ollie Ollie Otterson and Terz were connected."

"Perhaps more than connected."

"What do you mean?"

"Well, Otterson is chased by a cat named Percy, isn't he?"

"So?"

"Maybe the best way to tell you is to say that I'm in the story too."

"This is too much. How can you be *in* a story?" Len's mind heated up under the layers of revelation. "Stories are written. They're not real. They're just stories."

"They're not real? Len, if you've learned anything in Welken, I hope you've learned that there's no such thing as *just* a story. As you have experienced, many tales in our world are acted out in other places—and many events in the time and space of your world have spun their way into the stories of other worlds. Didn't parts of Welken remind you of things back home?"

"Well, yes, all the time." He thought a moment about the kings and queens in the mineshaft and so many crazy Deedyisms. "But all of this means that, um, what you're saying makes me think that, I mean . . . Percy and Bones really exist someplace."

Piers smiled. "So. Why should you be the only ones who are visited?"

After hours of conversation that felt to Len like minutes, Piers stood and led Len back through the east door. He saw that his entry point was closer to home than the top of Wendell's Mountain. As a tear made an unfamiliar trek down Len's cheek, Piers gave Len a hearty hug. Len took three strides into the sunshine and looked back. As Piers stopped waving, his hand fell forward into the sunlight that shone on the Oregon mountain. Only one finger caught the light for a second before his hand returned to his side—but Len saw it change. He saw fur.

Piers called out, "By the mews, you'll be home in two whips of a whippoorwill. All's well that the cooks don't spoil, my friend. Hurry home. Good-bye."

Just when he thought he couldn't be surprised any more, Len felt that Piers had taken off a mask to reveal his true self, only to take that mask off as well. As his heart settled back down, Len turned toward Skinner. Mossy evergreens stood definitively in the typical summer haze. Smoke from the lumber mill added to the fuzzy sky, and the Lewis River below him made him think of the Wilder, the Peterson homestead where everything began, and Percy, the "stray" cat who had adopted them. When he turned back around for one last wave, he couldn't see Piers.

Eventually, Len caught up to the others. He found the three of them sitting on the curb in front of the Nefertis' house.

I have so much to tell you, he thought, and this time you might be the ones struggling to believe.

But by the time he sat down next to them, they were ready to go off to their respective homes. He decided his stories could wait. For Bennu and Lizbeth, Len knew, the glories of Welken would soon be replaced by Sniffles, snappy slogans, and sappy greetings. He and Angie headed back to dentist jokes and their mom's manuscript.

As he stepped onto his front lawn, Len hoped to keep the mountain-high feeling as long as he could. Then the screen door slammed, and he sensed a sudden loss, like a pickpocket's ruse had worked, and he and Angie were stranded without enough resources. A note on the fridge made matters worse: "Len, call the museum. They have lots of questions for you. Angie, clean your room before you go anywhere."

"We're home," said Len.

Angie sighed. "Yeah."

Then the phone rang.

"Hello," said Len.

"Are you Len?"

"Yep."

"Well, this is Tommy, Odin's brother. Something's happened to him. If you had anything to do with it, let's just say, 'I wouldn't want to be you.'"

Then Len heard only the dial tone.

"Who was it?" asked Angie.

"Just an ol' Stinky Mink Boy acting tough. Too bad those guys don't know who they're dealing with." He made his hands look like he was extending his claws.

Then Percy bounded in from the hall and jumped up on the kitchen table.

"Hey, you furball," said Len, "you know better than that."

Len looked at Angie and raised his eyebrows. She raised hers higher in return. As Len smiled tenderly, Angie scooped up Percy with both hands and carried him into the living room. "I hope I'm not being too rough, Piers," she said. She and Len plopped on the blue corduroy couch and petted Percy, listening intently for a "So" or an "In Welken" to pop out. All they heard was "Meow."

Charlotte rushed into the living room. "There you two are, finally. The cat is hungry. Angie, it's your turn to feed him. But first," she winked and held up one finger, "first, you can tell me about the rest of my book."

When she read the scene in the English manor, Len and Angie nodded knowingly at the part about "Otterson" rolling off the tongue. Then Charlotte read about Ollie's attempted escape and his trouble with fire and the waterfall, his torn parachute, and getting stuck in the mud. "Now," Charlotte waved her hand like a magician, "here is the very last page in my book."

"OK, Mom," said Angie, "let's hear it."

"This comes after Percy and Bones have made the voyage home."

At last back in Virginia, Percy and Bones departed the ocean liner and made their way to Percy's waiting car. Bones's sea legs made him walk like a drunken gunfighter setting up for a duel. The spurs of the long passage left Bones aching for his own chair, his own bed, and his own vegetables to harvest. He sighed with relief when Percy pulled into his driveway.

Bones said good-bye, tightened his overalls, and strode directly toward the garden. When he saw weeds standing taller than the corn, he broke into a trot. He started to howl as he approached the raised beds. Then he saw shriveled carrot tops. "Oooo," he howled. Cutworms in broad daylight gnawing on the tomato vines. "Ooooooooo." Slug slime curling over half-eaten lettuce. "Ooooooooooooo." Bones fell to his knees. The weeds! The bugs! "Ooooooooooooooooo."

Honking his horn on his way out, Percy reveled in this latest victory over Ollie. He thought about how he and Bones were responsible for getting the little thief off the streets. Who knew where he'd strike next?

"Yes sir," Percy said aloud, "we nabbed that varmint just in time. Who did he think he was fooling in that *Jeeves* costume? As the brown book says, 'You can't tell a crook by his collar!'"

"Well," said Charlotte, "a good place to end?"

"As good as any," offered Angie, "though I feel sorry for poor Bones."

"I like it," said Len. "It's a good ending. And, Mom, I think you're getting better at character development."

"Thanks, Lenny. You're not doing so badly yourself."

"Mom!"

"I know. I know."

So. That's the story as far as it goes. A long journey, through sorrow and hope and joy. And though some bitter steps live in me yet, I can say that I kept walking and I arrived with the others on a mountain with grand vistas. At times, I have been of help. This is good. And though you might not know all, of course, now you know who I am.

WANT MORE SUSPENSE?

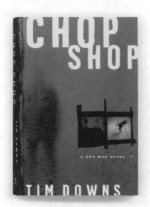

Intern forensic pathologist Dr. Riley McKay has noticed irregularities in autopsies at the Allegheny County Coroner's Lab. Suspecting foul play, she seeks help from forensic entomologist Dr. Nick Polchak, the Bug Man, renowned for his ability to solve murders by analyzing the insects on victim's bodies. Nick and Riley uncover a sinister link between the lab's director and PharmaGen, a start-up drug company specializing in genetic research. While Nick and Riley stay a step ahead of PharmaGen assassins, romantic attraction develops between them.
ISBN: 1-58229-401-1   www.bugmannovel.com

Forensic entomologist Nick Polchak (a.k.a. the Bug Man) is hired by thirty-year-old Kathryn Guilford (who is terrified of bugs) to solve her friend's death. When Polchak stumbles onto the mystery of how Kathryn's husband was killed years earlier, the action kicks into high gear, and Polchak finds himself on the run from someone who will do anything to keep it a secret.
ISBN: 1-58229-308-2   www.bugmannovel.com

WANT MORE ROMANCE?

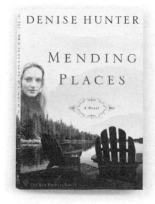

Hanna Landin's past holds her captive, but Micah Gallagher, the rugged mountain guide she hires to help the family's floundering mountain lodge, makes her wish she could move beyond it. Together Hanna and Micah face the past. But it's more horrifying than either of them feared, and Hanna faces the ultimate challenge.

ISBN:1-58229-358-9   www.denisehunterbooks.com

Welcome to Oak Plantation, an expansive rice plantation in the Old South. When the overseer's daughter, Camellia York, accidentally causes the death of the plantation owner, she is haunted by guilt. But when she finally tells the truth about what really happened in the cookhouse, she discovers a startling truth about her family's past.

ISBN: 1-58229-359-7

WANT MORE INTRIGUE?

After learning a horrific Gulf War secret, Meagan Juddman is consumed with guilt and bitterness—guilt over a shameful secret she harbors and bitterness over a suspected government cover-up. After escaping to her hometown of Twisp, Washington, she meets Tharon Marsh, a decorated officer in the Gulf War. Their friendship grows toward something deeper, until Meagan discovers that Tharon harbors a horrific secret that ties their pasts together.
ISBN: 1-58229-391-0

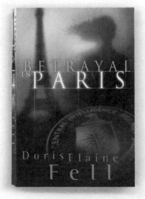

Amid the trauma of the September 11 Pentagon tragedy, twenty-seven-year-old Adrienne Winters fights to clear the names of her brother and father, who were victims of a double betrayal on foreign soil. As she pursues her quest, Adrienne discovers a gentle romance as she sorts out her family's history and her faith in God.
ISBN: 1-58229-314-7

HOWARD
Fiction

WANT MORE MYSTERY?

Fame has created a glimmering facade in Shanna O'Brian's world, but when the spotlight fades, even her success fails to penetrate the darkness of reality. With Shanna's ex-husband now in control of her record label, Shanna's life careens out of control. Shanna's need to reclaim possession of a life she's too often surrendered to others leads her down a path of self-discovery that is cruelly threatened by unseen forces.

ISBN: 1-58229-342-2

www.howardfiction.com

Christian Jr./Sr. High School
2100 Greenfield Dr
El Cajon, CA 92019